The cavekeeper's daughter

A novel of the great Bering migration

Nancy Boxer

PS press

Perfectly Scientific Press
www.perfscipress.com

Perfectly Scientific Press
3754 SE Knight St.
Portland, OR 97202

The cavekeeper's daughter was first published in 2008 by Nancy Boxer.

First Perfectly Scientific Press paperback edition: August 2010.
Perfectly Scientific Press paperback ISBN: 978-1-935638-03-2

Cover art by Julia Canright.

Visit our website at www.perfscipress.com

Printed in the United States of America.
9 8 7 6 5 4 3 2 1 0

This book was printed on 15% post-consumer waste paper.

Contents

Contents   i

Book 1: All that once was   **1**
Chapter 1: The cavekeeper's family   1
Chapter 2: Circle on the sand   6
Chapter 3: Like a stampede of bison   11

Book 2: Sad farewells   **23**
Chapter 1: A heaviness in the bones   23
Chapter 2: All there was to bury   32
Chapter 3: Let us leave this place of sorrow   36

Book 3: Exodus   **55**
Chapter 1: First steps forward   55
Chapter 2: Tide washed up   61
Chapter 3: Rites of passage   71
Chapter 4: Smoke and fire   81
Chapter 5: Combing through the tangles   95
Chapter 6: Staying on the shore   122
Chapter 7: Two logs afire   131
Chapter 8: Bleak night   141
Chapter 9: What kind of people shall we be?   148

Book 4: Into the cold   **157**
Chapter 1: Purging and cleansing   157
Chapter 2: The walrus people   177
Chapter 3: Next step   189
Chapter 4: Fish camp   195
Chapter 5: A sickly gray sky   212
Chapter 6: Bringing light into the dark   230
Chapter 7: Lift high the sun   254

Book 5: The crossing **267**

    Chapter 1:   Feet move forward again 267

    Chapter 2:   Inside walls of snow 285

    Chapter 3:   Watching the tides 297

    Chapter 4:   Water washes our feet 302

    Author's afterword 329

    Acknowledgements 334

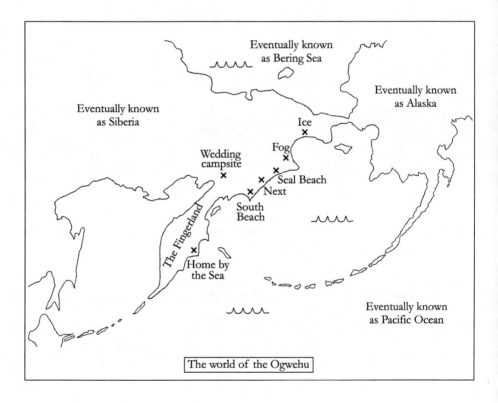

The world of the Ogwehu

Book 1: All that once was

Chapter 1: The cavekeeper's family

The voice. There it was, summoning her again.

At least it wasn't her usual harsh command. What more could she ask of Birdy, after all?

Don't be stupid, the girl told herself. Pretend you're too far away to hear.

The thought wormed its way in, and then was impossible to ignore. Surely by now she'd earned a break. Already today Birdy hauled the water and made meals for the family, watched the children, and kept them out of everybody's way. Picked whortleberries, crowberries, and raspberries, each from a different picking spot, rinsed them in the river, set them in rows on the stick-lattices to dry, and kept the birds from devouring them before they could be stored for the winter.

Some kids would be allowed to daydream while shooing away the flies and birds, but no, not her. She was given the baby's wrap to mend along with a pile of nuts to pound into meal. She tidied up after supper, rubbed salve on Great Uncle's aching back, told a story to her brother and sister. It was more than her older brother did; more than her friends were asked to do. *Wasn't that enough*, she brooded, weary to the bone.

All she wanted was a little time for herself after chores were done. A request her mother would refuse if Birdy was foolish enough to ask. So she didn't; she simply left the cave, sneaking off whenever she thought she could. If Mami was distracted and her fierce, jealous eye focused elsewhere, she might not even notice. Sometimes Birdy was lucky and got away with it. Please, she whispered, let tonight be that way.

"I'm going now, Mami," she called softly as she finished sweeping out the entrance. Hopefully her voice was too low to be heard. Maybe the baby would be crying. Hurriedly she set the evergreen-branch broom against the rock wall just inside the entryway. If she was quick she could get down to the beach and hide in time to hear the storytellers. The thought perked her up. "Don't worry, Mami," she said, making her voice even softer. "I'll be back before it gets too dark."

"Come here, Birdy," Mami warned, a harsh note from the interior of the cave. "You're not through yet. There's not enough firewood."

Impatient to leave, Birdy looked around. She might be far enough to get away with it. "I didn't hear you," she muttered, preparing arguments for later. "I already left. I was too far away."

The whole thing was completely unfair. Why was she always called to finish everybody else's work? Her younger sister was supposed to do the simpler tasks; her older brother was responsible for the firewood. If either of them was lazy, they should be punished, not her. Birdy was the good child; she always did as asked.

Well, almost always. Certainly she did today, desperate as she was to leave after the evening meal. It was days since she'd heard the apprentices practicing the tribal stories. And stories were what kept her going when she pounded hides at the river until her arms practically collapsed. Stories were what let her ignore the bruises, the on-going ache of the badly set arm from a beating last winter. It wasn't right, she muttered, indignation fueling her footsteps as she picked her way along the ledge to the path below.

She was a thin child. Tall for a girl eleven summers in age and strong—her muscles well developed from squeezing life out of this harsh land. Though her mother chided her for being plain-faced, a cheery quality emerged when she got away from home. Already her anger faded in the pleasure of the end to the summer's day, which, in this far northern region, lingered long.

Listening to the birdsong above, Birdy smiled as she scooted down the mountain, carefully skirting the bushes where her mother draped furs across the branches to dry. The last thing she needed was to make Mami angry, the clean furs falling in the dirt leaving no fresh ones for the visitors tomorrow.

Mami was regarded as a wonder outside of her family. Cavekeeper for the tribe, she enjoyed considerable status among the Ogwehu, the People who sheltered along the beach and up the ridges of this land that lay like a finger pointing into the sea. As Cavekeeper, Mami tended the hot springs bubbling from the depths of the mountain where the clan came to soak away their aches and ailments.

Her family had tended the hot springs cave for as long as anyone could remember. Mami welcomed the visitors, guiding them through the outer chamber where the family slept. Entering the middle chamber, she led people through the ancient words thanking the Spirit of the Cave for the sacred waters, asking relief from their pains. She escorted them inward, ducking their heads through the low entry passage. Took them down the slippery rocks, the flickering torches giving off just enough light to see as they eased into the roiling, steaming, sulfurous waters.

She showered affection on those needing her help. In turn they regarded her as that lovely healer who banished their aches and pains, if only for a day. Yet to her daughter she seemed more like a fierce owl ready to swoosh down and sink her claws in, always hungry and ready to hunt.

Though owls at least hunted only at night.

Birdy shrugged. Grown-ups could be awfully confusing. Kids were easier. Like her—all she wanted was to do her chores and be left alone to see her friends, hear the stories, and swim in the river with her cousins. Tonight Birdy intended to duck out of any further work. Tonight let Mami pounce on someone else.

She wasn't bad, she reminded herself. She worked as hard as any child of the tribe, probably more. Besides her other chores, Birdy had to keep the young ones away from the interior, especially when she heard the groans of a visitor who stayed for massage. Children could play nearby, could even sit alongside the bubbling springs while the grown-ups were soaking, but Mami would be furious if they ran through while she worked the muscles of an elder's body.

She should understand how hard it is to keep them away, Birdy often fumed. If she only saw the worried looks on their little faces when they heard their parents moan. When Mami was little, didn't she ever hear her mother make some horrible sound and go see what was wrong? Wouldn't she creep in to check if Grandmother was sick or hurt? Those kids were too young to understand that some kinds of pain are good, not bad.

No, Birdy concluded, Mami didn't worry about the little ones. Not her own, not other people's children either. Only the grown-ups were important to her. If a person was in pain, Mami often scolded, if they traveled to the cave for relief, if they paid a tribute to the cave and gave a present to the Cavekeeper—that's me, she'd remind Birdy, that's what feeds you, that's what brought that warm pair of moccasins you used last winter—those people didn't want their relief interrupted just to reassure their miserable little brats.

That's your job, she'd scowl, and if Birdy was close enough, she'd grab her ear and pull it hard.

Several days before Mami had Birdy carry some of the offerings—seal meat, ivory carvings—up the mountain to trade for venison and other favorite foods. Birdy reminded her they needed to gather more flowers, found in the other direction. Mami waved it off, and the next day they ran out.

That night she grabbed Birdy's arm and twisted it fiercely. No one else was around but Grandmother, sunk in her stupor, sitting silent near the fire.

"Everything was ugly today," Mami whispered harshly in Birdy's ear. "No petals to brighten the walk and make the cave nice. Do you think they'll visit if they have to trudge along a barren rock ledge all the way here?"

The hearth fire leapt crazily, sparking and crackling in loud, frightening pops. Smoke rose in the shadows and drifted, searing Birdy's mouth. Where was Great Uncle, or Aunt River? Mami would never hurt her if either of them were near.

But, strain as she might to hear a friendly footfall, no rescue came. Birdy was too frightened to do more than shake her head. If she argued when her mother was in such a mood, it only brought on something worse.

Though sometimes no answer infuriated her just as much. "Do you think they'll keep coming and bring the food that feeds us?" Mami repeated in a hoarse voice.

"P... p... p... probably," Birdy stuttered. And hated herself for showing any weakness.

Mami tightened her grip, jerking Birdy's arm higher. "Probably? I'd say not. And if your brothers and sisters go hungry this winter, will that teach you to keep my supplies handy? Will that remind you to keep the walkway nice?"

"Y... y... yes."

"Yes, what?" Her hands tightened again. Birdy let out a little yelp of pain.

"Yes, Mami. I'm sorry, Mami," she whimpered. Tears leaked out, but she didn't dare wipe them.

"And keep the little ones out of the way. We don't want any more embarrassments like we had last week."

Last week, when the baby squirmed out of Birdy's arms and left a pile of excrement in an unexpected location, just as two visitors left the cave.

Birdy was beaten for that one. Her legs still felt numb though she pretended, when anyone asked, that she bruised them gathering wood.

As the land flattened out, the mountain gave way to hilly forest. Here Birdy came to a fork in the trail and veered left, taking the path that led away from where most of the beach-dwellers lived.

Later that evening, she reminded herself, she should stop by Mogwen's hearth to say hello. She had to have a believable story if Mami or Great Uncle asked Birdy where she went. Mogwen was a friend, but also a convenient excuse, one her mother would easily accept. And that was important, because Birdy had to get down to the beach. Every night if she could manage, though unfortunately she couldn't, to hear the sacred stories.

It was in the evening that Falcon, the tribal shaman, gathered his apprentices to sit at the fire and practice telling the tales. Not the everyday stories that each family accumulates, but the tellings that mattered to the whole tribe. Not only did Birdy love the stories; she liked hearing the apprentices repeat them until they could retell entire tales without missing a word.

Birdy could recount most of them as well as any of the boys. Better, maybe. But no mere girl would be chosen as apprentice. Nor would she be allowed to perform them. Stories were part of the shaman's magic, a Father Sky power, not a Mother Earth power. If anyone discovered her hiding behind the bushes near their fire, she would be, well, she didn't even know. Maybe stoned to death, or floated off to be eaten by the killer whales. Falcon would close his eyes and descend into trance, riding the wave of the sacred drumming provided by the ring of apprentices behind him. He would pronounce her fate when he opened his eyes, stare her down across the flames. Whatever it was, it would be gruesome. So gruesome it was only whispered about when she asked Grandmother or Great Uncle about such things.

She had no desire to take up any of the shaman's other duties, just the storytelling. Why only the shaman and his boys could tell the stories never made sense to her. Something about the stories bringing a fresh breath of air into the People's lives, and air was the domain of Father Sky. Of course only men could practice His rites. Women were restricted to Mother Earth magic like childbearing and nursing the sick with plants. Birdy didn't pretend to understand it, but that was the way it was; that was the way it had been for so long that no one actually remembered why.

No one knew why, and nobody but Birdy would even question it. The one time she asked Mami, she only got slapped for her troubles. Still she loved to mull the stories over. She could practice them silently to lighten any long, tedious task. And when Mami railed at her or beat her until the defiant words left her mouth, she took comfort in her secret knowledge.

Chapter 2: Circle on the sand

They had finished chanting the blessings for the New Moon by the time Birdy arrived. The beach was empty except for the apprentices huddled around the fire. The shaman did not welcome an audience while his boys practiced tale-telling. Stories were a kind of magic, after all; best heard only when they were smooth.

Carefully she stepped across the sand to her usual hiding place. With the stealth of a wild creature she circled wide around the campfire, the darkening sky helping mask her steps.

"... the days were getting longer," the shaman was chanting, beating the drum rhythmically to accompany the tale. "And the nights shortened again. White still blanketed the Earth, and Bear slept on in his hidey hole. The winter food sacks were empty. Mothers were down to their last scraps of dried food. The People could feel their ribs, and the little ones cried with hunger in the night."

His words fell away though the drum beat softly, softly.

Hiding behind a small clump of bushes, Birdy carefully shifted on the sand. Summer nights were often chilly enough that she had to keep moving. Sitting cross-legged, a leg or foot would all too easily turn icy. The apprentices had that lovely driftwood fire to sit by, but there was no such comfort for her. She watched the circle, envious. Driftwood made a beautiful flame, sparking with bursts of blue and green against the night sky.

Unfortunately none of the heat reached Birdy this far away. But the stories were worth a little discomfort. She could shiver and listen, or wilt under the same old complaints in the cave every night. Which was no choice at all, as far as she was concerned.

Now the apprentices were asked to repeat the story. Three of them were from families she barely knew, living farther along the beach with the best families. The fourth was a frail boy named Antler, just a year older than her. He was from a mountain family; Birdy had seen him practicing spear throws with her brother and cousins. Antler was kind. He sometimes smiled a shy smile at her.

Another breath of wind arose, this one colder than before. The icy air found its way through an opening in her wrap. Tonight she wore a shirt over her shoulders, though she still shivered. She buried her feet deep in the sand hoping for some lingering warmth, but it got colder, damper as she dug down. Pulling the light summer hide around, she shifted against the wind, careful to stay silent.

Now it was a boy named Boulder's turn to recite a passage. People called him Boulder because he could be rock-like, sticking to arguments no matter how little sense they made. He was cruel to anyone younger or smaller than him, and only became stonier if confronted. If she were choosing apprentices, she often thought, she never would have picked him. "Shamans should be flexible and bend to the Spirits, shouldn't they?" she once asked her aunt.

"That's a good quality for shamans to have," River agreed. "They need endurance for the long ceremonies. And they should be stubborn, because people don't always want to do what a shaman tells them."

Boulder was having trouble recalling the next section. Falcon corrected him once, twice, a third time. On Boulder's fourth stumble Birdy began impatiently muttering the correct words. She caught herself just short of speaking aloud. *Grrrr!* She had to watch it; she couldn't risk getting caught. She shifted her feet, tucking them under her thighs to warm up. She shook her head when Boulder again got it wrong.

Across the distance she smelled an acrid scent. Boulder's afraid of what Falcon will do, she realized smugly. With a harsh reminder to listen carefully, Falcon motioned the next apprentice to take his turn.

With bad grace Boulder returned to his place in the circle. He did not offer the customary polite attention to the next boy. Boulder was muttering, shifting around, casting his eyes anywhere but at the speaker. This distracted the others, but Falcon chose to ignore him. He corrected a number of tiny aberrations in the story, and the rise and fall of the speaker's voice, rather than censure the bad manners agitating the apprentices.

Another heavy sigh from Boulder. "Stop it," the boy next to him hissed. Boulder gave him a long, hard stare. The other boy glared back, but he could not hold the look. Flushing, he glanced around the circle for support, but no one else responded. A change came over the boy's face. He'd either have to stand up for himself or let it go. He stilled for a moment, gritting his teeth. Finally he turned to Boulder, hissing, "Settle down and be quiet. You don't get to interrupt just because you're the oldest."

It was a small thing, but as long as Birdy had been eavesdropping, it was the first time any of them stood up to Boulder. There was a moment of silence while each boy looked around, waiting for someone else to react.

Antler caught the defiant boy's glance. He had little status in the group, being the newest of them. The boy to his right shuffled his feet, but offered nothing. Antler was the smallest and thinnest, the one most likely to be pummeled. Yet when no one else reacted, something in him seemed to come together. He hesitated, taking a deep breath, and pulled his shoulders straight. "He's right," he said. His voice quavered, but he gamely kept on. "We have to listen to each other; it's not fair otherwise."

"It's not fair, it's not fair," Boulder mimicked, turning a sneering face on him.

"Cease," Falcon warned, frowning at each in turn.

An owl hooted from the hillside above. The night sky was almost completely dark. With the darkness came colder air and another chill breeze. Falcon turned away from the fire to locate his fur robe.

In that moment Boulder reached across to grab Antler's arm and give the flesh a vicious pinch. "Don't talk that way to me, baby face, or I'll get you later when he can't see," he growled.

Antler tore himself out of Boulder's grasp. "Leave me alone," he said, his eyes flashing. "Falcon won't like you trying to take over."

Boulder seized the neck of Antler's robe and bunched it tight as if to choke him in his garments. Antler grabbed Boulder's fists and struggled to pull free.

Falcon turned back in time to see Antler gripping Boulder's hands. The boys were grappling too near the fire. The others, relieved for the moment of any danger of Boulder turning on them, were betting on the outcome in gleeful voices. Antler looked up to see Falcon scowl. "Boulder's trying to bully us!" he called out.

Good, Birdy thought to herself. Falcon will have to punish him now.

Falcon reached across the circle, causing the silent boy to rear out of his way. To everyone's surprise he grabbed not Boulder, but Antler by the arm. Boulder stepped aside, a smug grin on his face. Flicking back his robe so it wouldn't catch a spark, Falcon pushed Antler's fingers in the fire, a quick but effective warning. Antler bit his cheeks to keep from crying out. One brief, garbled sound escaped—in protest or pain, Birdy could not tell which.

"Be the Antler, not the Ant," the shaman admonished, his voice dark with warning.

The other boys watched, the quiet one smiling a sick smile, afraid that more punishment might be coming. From behind the bush Birdy was choking with anger. It should have been Boulder, not Antler, whose hand was thrust in the flame. Why did he burn Antler? All he did was stand up for his friend. It wasn't right, she fumed. Grown-ups were always doing things that made no sense. Her mother, making her do Thunder and Pout's work. Falcon, hurting Antler instead of Boulder. The shaman, making them hurt girls who just wanted to learn the stories. Grown-ups could be unbelievably stupid. She didn't want to be a grown-up when she grew up.

At least she didn't want to be like any of the grown-ups she knew.

It wasn't that she wanted to be a boy or anything. She liked being a girl. Liked playing with her friends, liked helping her aunt or grandmother when they asked for something. She didn't want to take her brother Thunder's place and have to hack away at the poor animals so the family had enough meat. There was just one reason she sometimes wished she was a boy. She could imagine learning the sacred stories and telling them at night. She could see herself grown up, the whole clan listening as she told the tales around the fire. She wouldn't keep people from coming to hear them, ever. She'd invite anyone who was interested. Men were so stupid sometimes; you'd think the bears would eat them all and leave the women in charge. Be the Antler, not the ant. What kind of teaching was that?

If he had to burn anyone's fingers it should have been that stupid bully who had to have everybody's attention. Boulder will never, ever grow up to be a good shaman, she fumed. No one could be, if they didn't care about anybody besides themselves. They should be able to listen, not just boast and brag and make people do what they say. They had to be willing to listen to the Spirits *and* to the people they served.

She looked up from her fists, clenched by her sides. Order restored, the boys were again reciting passages from the story. None of them got the part right where Falcon described the feast that ended the hunger after they killed the great whale. Birdy was growing restless. She knew that section better than any of them. Except for Falcon, of course.

To her it was the most interesting part of the story, where the women danced and were allowed to eat. Naturally the boys had trouble with that part. They weren't women; probably didn't care one bit about the lives of women. Men's lives were much more exciting.

Still, a shaman should remember every part of the story, just as he served the entire tribe. Shamans were supposed to teach and lead—men and women, grown-ups, children, and elders alike, not just their favorites. As the defiant boy neared that part of the story and hesitated, then picked up the subsequent section without remembering about the women, Falcon halted him with a shake of his head. "Who can say what's next?" he asked.

Antler offered a suggestion, too soft for Birdy to hear. Boulder blurted out something about the children playing games, but Falcon shook his head again. "Doesn't anyone know these verses?" he demanded.

Forgetting for the moment to keep silent, Birdy murmured, "I do..." then clapped her hand across her mouth. *Rats*, she cursed inwardly. *Ugly, sick rats, she could get caught! She could be killed!* Heart pounding, she ducked her head, hoping they didn't hear. Oh sweet Mother Spirit, Guardian of women and girl-children, protect me, she prayed silently. Let them think it was the wind.

Falcon cocked his head. "Did you hear something?" he asked. A stone was tossed in her direction, hit a branch and fell on the sand.

Don't answer, Birdy warned herself silently. Keep your breathing quiet. They didn't hear you, they didn't hear you. She kept saying it, as if the act of repeating the words could somehow make it true. Let them think it was nothing. I'll be good; I'll make an offering tomorrow.

Falcon nodded at Antler, who sprang up from the fire circle. Thrusting his skinny arms overhead, consciously deepening his voice to sound like a threat to intruders, the boy moved toward Birdy's hiding place. "Who's there," he demanded, his voice loud, though she thought she heard a quiver in the tone.

She burrowed deeper under her hide wrap. I'm a bump in the sand she thought, imagining herself melting into the earth, becoming brown and grainy, flat against the ground. There's no girl here, there's nothing of interest, just a pile of sand.

Closer he came, stabbing his walking stick downward, now only a few paces away. Walk right by me, she begged silently, in her mind's eye seeing him do just that. Envisioning was part of the camouflage training Great Uncle had given her and Thunder. If you imagine yourself blending right into a tree or the earth, you don't give off any fear for them to smell you with. I'm just part of the beach, she repeated to herself. A tide could rise and cover me; I'm only a grain in this great pile of sand.

Now he was only an arms-length away. Could he see her? His eyes slid by and then passed. She was painfully aware of every movement. Stay still, she reminded herself.

With his next movement the apprentice managed to provoke a reaction, though not from her. A tern nesting in the sand nearby, rose and skacawed, fluttering its wings and hopping clumsily away. Time to scoot, it seemed to decide. Leave the dangers of lunging sticks and noisy boys.

Thank you, Great Mother Earth, Birdy whispered. She trembled with relief as Antler ran back, waving his arms in triumph. He'd found the intruder and sent it scrambling. "Just a bird," he called with new-found confidence. "Just a dumb bird."

The boys hooted, jibing at his great warrior skills. The shaman let the chafing continue, and then settled the boys back to their task around the fire.

For the moment Birdy was safe, thanks to the Great Mother Spirit, thanks to Great Uncle's training. "Just a dumb bird!" she mocked silently, careful not to let another sound escape. "Ha, this particular Bird's smarter than all of them!"

She had to smile. If they only knew! Too bad she could never tell anyone.

Still she'd taken enough risks for one night. And so, once the boys were caught up in their instruction, she rose carefully. Hobbling on her stiff ankle, she backed away in silence, stopping for a quick visit with Mogwen and her family before sneaking back up the mountain toward the cave.

Chapter 3: Like a stampede of bison

In the early morning twilight, the sky slowly lightened from black to a deep, shadowy blue. Soon the eastern sky would glow and people would begin to stir. But for now there was a contemplative quality to the world.

Sometimes the younger hunters saw the end of the night after standing watch around the campfires. Nursing mothers might see the birth of the new day as their babies woke them. But often at the cave Birdy was the only one awake to enjoy it.

Birdsong roused her before the dawn, as it did most mornings. The air was just beginning to lose its chill. So much seemed possible this early. Perhaps Birdy would paint her sister's face purple with blueberry juice after breakfast. Maybe she'd be sent to gather mushrooms on the mountain, and cousin

Mindawen could join her. She rose, arms stretching wide, and let the coverings fall to the ground. This was her favorite part of the day, before the rest of the family rose. Before the demands began.

Outside, Birdy leaned against the ledge watching the wrens and jays dart back and forth. She was gazing, contented, into the treetops when Pout, the younger sister, stuck her head out of the cave. The girl shuffled over, rubbing her eyes sleepily.

She ducked under Birdy's arm, pulling it around her shoulders and snuggling against her. Birdy gave her sister an affectionate squeeze. "Hey, tidbit," she said, "you want to help me surprise everyone, getting the tea ready before they get up?"

Pout pouted as she often did, but after a moment agreed.

"Better get going," Birdy added, giving her a half-friendly shove on her backside. She ran to add kindling to the fire while Birdy collected waterskins from the storage area. Back outside, Pout skipped across the hump of the hill to the meadow where the river ran. The family went to the river for their cooking water. Drinking from the hot springs inside would make them sick.

As the water heated in the skin bag over the flame, she grabbed the sack of nuts and the leaf-wrapped scraps of ptarmigan bird left over from yesterday. She poured the nuts into a bowl and sent Pout out to crack them open, warning her not to return until they were all done—shells swept over the ledge, nut meats sorted into the bowl, and ready to eat. Grateful her sister hadn't started complaining, Birdy poked her head out for another appreciative glance at the morning sky. The sun peeked over the rim of the horizon, and a soft orange light began to warm the cave.

It was the nicest time of day, with the sun rising over the ocean to the east. But the light would soon wake the baby, and all this calm would end. Sure enough, within moments came the first wail. She heard Mami groan and put the babe to her breast. If she was lucky he would nurse himself back to bliss and they could relax a while longer.

But the wailing woke Great Uncle, who rose slowly from his sleeping space. Birdy sensed the creaking of joints as he painfully unfolded his worn, lean body. He ran fingers through his hair, the light reflecting on the sparkle of white that laced his dark locks, like the first sprinklings of snow on the soil.

Great Uncle was widowed young and never remarried. A few matches were suggested but he declined them, instead joining his sister's family. These days he could no longer keep up with the younger hunters. Yet he kept himself useful with snares and trapping, and he still crafted keen-edged knives and spear points. Maybe that's what he'd work on today, Birdy hoped. Her brother Oopsy, 4 summers old, loved to watch the knapping of stone tools. That would keep him out of mischief for the morning.

Birdy once asked Great Uncle how old he was. "I don't remember," he surprised her. "More than 40 summers. Someday you'll see, girl; it's hard to keep track of the years when the numbers get so high. Easier when the count still fits on your fingers and toes."

Numbers could be confusing when they got to be more than 20. But losing track of your own summer-count, Birdy could not imagine that at all. Every year seemed different, so full of events and changes. This summer there was the new baby. Last summer she started sitting in on the storytellings. The summer before, another People joined them to hunt the White Mammoth. Every year had its excitements and fears. The memories added up like berries picked and dried for the winter; lovely bites of sweet or tartness to keep them going through the dark times.

"I could use some tea, little Bird," Great Uncle croaked, not yet able to clear his throat. "Sure is nice of you girls to get it ready."

Birdy nodded earnestly. Praise was rare among members of the tribe. People expected everyone to do their best. But she was always glad to help her uncle, for who else ever noticed her hard work? Not Mami, who didn't let her take a breath as she finished one job before making her start another. Not her lazybones brother, hiding under his furs without even a nostril in the open air.

Not any of Mami's boyfriends, hanging around as they sometimes did, hoping Mami would disappear with them for a bit of conversation, or so mamma called it, in the innermost section of the cave. Grandmother, maybe, though she hardly said a word since her bout of fever last spring. Nowadays she spent most of her time looking off in the distance, rarely bothering to eat. Birdy worried that she was getting ready to join the ancestors, and she would never feel her warmth again

She filled a bowl for Great Uncle and brought it to him, careful not to spill a drop. His lined face lit up with pleasure. He took it gratefully, blowing on the surface before taking the first sip. "How about if you get one for yourself and keep an old man company while he drinks his morning tea?" he asked.

"Good idea," she agreed and ran to help herself. While she sat with Great Uncle no one would order her to jump up and do anything, out of respect for him. Otherwise Mami would soon be demanding she fetch her breakfast. Or send her off to gather nettles or some other hateful task. Birdy gratefully understood one thing: That Great Uncle invited her to sit with him as much for her sake as for his.

★   ★   ★

Midday, sun overhead, Birdy and Aunt River were picking blueberries at the far edge of the long-grass meadow. There were other picking places but none were as lush or safe. This close to the cave, the chance of encountering a bear was minimal. Bears and humans ate many of the same foods—salmon and trout, berries, cedar nuts, lilies. There was always danger that someone gathering food would bump into something bigger and worse-tempered than themselves. Bears usually avoided places where the People were fishing or gathering, but such encounters did happen from time to time.

But with River, Birdy always felt safe. Under her aunt's affectionate eye she could relax and be a child again. Birdy twirled in a circle, holding the half-filled bowl against her belly. Her head tilted towards the sun, hair swinging behind. A carefree smile lit her face. "Blueberries are fun," she bubbled happily. "There's no thorns to rip your arms up! No digging on your hands and knees! They're so ripe they fall right into your bowl. And they're yummy to eat, all warm from the sun!"

Her aunt glanced down, happy at the look of pure joy on Birdy's face. Usually the girl was frowning in concentration, the woman mused, or trying to suppress a wince. She was fun to be with when she wasn't being worked to the bone, poor thing. River smiled at her, delighted to share the pleasant afternoon. Her niece could use a lot more days like this. She reached over to brush the hair back from Birdy's face. "Doesn't this mess get in the way? Do you want me to braid it for you?"

Birdy smiled, pleased at the thought. Mami never would have offered. Braid *your* scraggly hair? she would have said. Why should I bother; you'll just get it caught on a thorn bush somewhere. If she even answered, instead of slapping Birdy for asking when at any moment one of the visitors might need her attention.

But this was River, who was entirely different. If there was anyone Birdy admired, it was River. Quiet Like the River, her full name, was absolutely perfect. So slow to anger and quick to forgive. Always ready to lend a hand, and uncomplaining as well.

River was tall with straight, proud shoulders, and watchful eyes. She had the prettiest face of anyone Birdy knew, with her neat, even features and a slight look of mystery about her. Reserve, Great Uncle called it; River didn't push herself on people. She didn't blurt things out or rush in with her opinions every chance she got. She held back, though if asked what she thought, she would offer it softly.

And she sewed such lovely clothing. Her dress this year was modest. It covered her breasts as well as her legs, for her aunt was not one to flaunt herself. She didn't need to; her fine features attracted enough smiles as they were. River had a quiet modesty, and a competence that shone. This dress, for instance, had a double band of stitching along the neck and another along the bottom. All that work, just for decoration! A simple thing, but nice to look at; she used thin strips dyed with berries and poked through the holes to contrast with the rest of it. River took care to fashion things that fit well and were pretty to look at, not only functional, not merely serving the purpose.

That's because River had all that time to herself, Mami often complained. Too old not to have her own mate, her own hearth and children, conveniently forgetting she wasn't married either at the same age. Eighteen summers already. Many girls were joined to a man at 14 or 15, soon after their first woman's bleeding. In most families, the father would make sure his daughters were mated by the time they reached River's age.

But just as there was no father pushing Cavekeeper to remarry, there was no one arranging things for River when she came of age. Great Uncle might have negotiated on her behalf, but he would never force a match on the family. Perhaps he figured she didn't want to marry. Mami wasn't eager to; maybe she followed her sister's path.

"Don't you want to get married, Aunty?" Birdy asked. "I would love to braid your hair with flowers for the ceremony. I could make you beautiful. More beautiful," she hurriedly corrected herself. "It would be fun to have some little cousins."

River smiled down at her niece. "Sorry, sweet one, not yet. I have enough to do, helping your mother with her family."

"Like Great Uncle does?"

River didn't answer right away. She looked up the mountainside, then back toward the cave. "Something like that," she finally agreed.

"Don't you want a family someday?"

"Someday, yes." Her face took on a wistful quality. "But not until I can start a family with the right man."

The right man. It never occurred to Birdy. Were there right men and wrong ones? Mami did not talk of such things. What was a wrong one anyway, someone who would die on you? Someone who didn't like the way you cooked the breakfast mush? She never thought about it before. "How do you know who's the right man?" she wondered. "What if the wrong one wants you?"

"Wrong ones already asked for me. Twice."

"And you said no?"

"That's right, child. I said no."

"Do you know who the right man is? Is he one of the People?" Suddenly Birdy was afraid she might lose her aunt. It didn't happen often, but sometimes a man or woman married outside the tribe. There was a woman who thought about following one of the Mammoth hunters, though eventually she changed her mind. If a woman married outside the People, she usually left to become part of her husband's clan. Birdy shuttered. She might never see her aunt again.

"Actually, Birdsilu, I might know who he is." A small smile played at the corners of River's mouth.

"Who? Tell me!" Birdy begged.

She hesitated. "No, I probably shouldn't say anything." Her hands rose, halting the flow of questions.

"Come on, who is it? I can keep a secret!" Birdy had plenty of practice keeping her own, though her aunt couldn't possibly know.

The smile on River's face slowly faded. "No, sweetie, sorry. There's someone I like, but I'm not sure he'll ever figure it out." A resigned sigh caused a shifting of the berries in River's bowl. She glanced down, then cast an appraising eye at her niece. "Birdsilu, do you realize you've been limping all morning? Let's take a look at that foot. Maybe you stepped on a thorn or something."

"It's my ankle," Birdy confessed. "I twisted it going down to the beach last night. I went to visit Mogwen." Mogwen. Right. The half-lie came easily to Birdy's lips. It was a good thing she practiced, or some day she might let slip the real reason she disappeared whenever she could. Better not to let anybody know her secret. Not River. Not Mindawen. Certainly not Thunder, nosy brother that he was. He couldn't keep a secret if his next meal depended on it.

River set her bowl down. She sat cross-legged and Birdy followed, placing her sore leg in River's lap. River took the girl's foot in one hand, supporting the rest of the leg with the other. She motioned for Birdy to swing her right leg around in order to compare them.

"That ankle's a bit swollen," she concluded. "You've done enough picking for now. Why don't you go back to the cave and have Grandmother wrap some strips of hide around it? Give it a rest for a few days. I'll keep gathering berries until they're full," she gestured at the bowl. "Don't worry, I'll bring yours back for you."

"Mami won't let me stay off my feet," Birdy argued, but she allowed her aunt to help her up. River was right; it was sore, sorer than it was that morning. At least she wouldn't have to carry the extra weight of the berries. Grateful for this small advantage, Birdy began hobbling across the long meadow towards the cave.

The ankle hurt a lot, she realized. She'd been ignoring it all day. With nothing else distracting her, every step sent pains spiking up her leg. If only she'd thought to bring a walking stick. But they set out knowing the bowls would be full on the way home, so of course they didn't carry anything extra.

Maybe River could help her find a walking stick. Birdy looked back but she was already too far away. She could no longer see her aunt by the bushes; she must have gone to the other side. She won't hear me shout, Birdy considered, not from this distance. Just to get help, she'd have to walk back and find her. She'd still have to walk home, and even with a walking stick it wouldn't be easy. Better keep going. She could do it. She'd done harder things than this.

Birdy brushed the hair off her face. She was working up a sweat. She should have let River braid it, at least then it wouldn't be all sticky like it was now. Both legs were aching now and she felt a twinge in her knee. *Arggh.* At least she was almost at the cave. Almost. Keep going, girl, it wasn't that much farther.

In fact she was close enough to hear shouting from the direction of home. There were at least two voices, or was it three? One of them was certainly her mother's. She couldn't make out the words, but someone sure sounded angry. Silence, followed by more shouting.

What was going on? Her mother hardly ever raised her voice with outsiders. And the visitors rarely got mad. It was almost sickening, but they fell all over themselves praising her. Sickening, because most people worked harder than Mami, and they could go for months without hearing anything nice said about them.

Now a man came striding across the grassy expanse. He was scowling, his brows furrowed, with a fierce look on his face. His torso was bare though the air was cool enough. Her eyes caught at his chest and stubbornly went no further. That chest, broadly muscled and tanned by the sun. A ragged scar ran diagonally across it, pale against his skin. The man was disturbing, no doubt about it. His very bareness seemed like showing off—flaunting his endurance, maybe, with that naked chest and the big scar. Which he probably got in some hunting accident, she grimaced. No amulet, either; wasn't anything sacred to him? Most people wore some kind of amulet, if only a simple shell with a puncture for the lacing to go through.

He was someone she avoided him whenever she could. People called him Kills His Enemy—a difficult name for a difficult man. There were whispers about him—that he slew his father, or his whole family, or maybe an entire den of wolves. Somehow he earned that awful name, and then nobody knew what to do with it. Some tried calling him Kills for a shorter name; others called him Enemy. As an everyday name, neither one stuck. Because nobody could work with someone called Kills or Enemy. How could you trust a man with a name like that? What did seem to work was shortening the name by dropping just enough to recognize what was left.

So it was K'enemy for short. One of the unmarried men of the mountain, he had taken to stopping in at the cave after the other visitors left. Often he brought little presents for Mami—a hare for the stewpot, an ivory carving—but he was rude to everyone else. He would walk right past Birdy or Thunder without saying a word; he almost tripped over Oopsy once and didn't even try to set things right.

As usual today, the man barely seemed to notice Birdy. He looked past her as he strode by, a tortured grimace distorting his bold features. He carried a stone hatchet and, though he held it carefully by the bone handle, sharp surface pointing toward the ground, Birdy gave him a wide berth as she passed.

Whatever the shouting was about, for Birdy to come across her mother so soon afterwards was risky. Mami would be in a foul temper after a fight with one of her men. Birdy should stay out of her way until she had a chance to calm down. Anyway, her ankle was throbbing now, worse than before. Tears leaked down her cheeks; she was so tired and sore. River said to stay off it, but of course she had to walk home. And now it felt like she walked on it for a whole day without stopping. Birdy sank into the meadow grass. Lay down on her back and stared at the sky.

Footsteps again. K'enemy going back to the cave, she figured, but didn't bother looking to see if she was right. Angry voices rose, but it was all so distant; what she noticed instead was the throb of her own blood pulsing in her neck and pounding through her ankle. What did she care if her mother was mad at her man friends? Let her get angry with every one of them, it wouldn't matter one bit to Birdy.

In a reverie of pain, she did not become immediately aware of the strangeness around her. There was a peculiar vibration in the air, and from every direction a fluttering of wings. Suddenly it felt so odd that she pushed herself upright, casting her eyes around the meadow. Normally you didn't hear much when a bird took flight unless you were close by. But at this moment birds rose from every side, and that in itself was bizarre.

All kinds of birds were circling, staying high in the sky. Not only hawk and eagle, not just the sea birds that soared for long afternoons seeking their next meal, but also the ptarmigans that normally kept to the ground.

She began to hear scurrying sounds, small animals running out from under cover. Oddly they ignored her as well the other animals emerging from dens, even those traditional enemies that usually made them bolt or hide. Rabbit brushed up against fox and both of them scampered away. Hawks ignored owls, though normally they might try to drive them off. Animals were running this way and stopping, then veering crazily in another direction. She'd never seen anything like it before.

Whatever it was, it scared her. Suddenly Birdy knew she had to get back to the cave. No matter how much her ankle hurt, no matter what mood her mother was in, she needed to find her. She had to get home.

Hobbling now with a sense of urgency, Birdy came over the rise. From there she could see the entrance to the cave. Almost home where she could rest her ankle. Just a few more steps. Yet something stopped her from moving closer. There was an uncomfortable pressure in her head. Her hair lifted up and down her arms and along the back of her neck.

Suddenly, a huge rumble. The noise came from all around, louder and deeper than a bolt of thunder. The earth began shifting and heaving underneath. Everything was lifted up—grasses, brush, trees. Suddenly she lost her balance and went sprawling, hands out in front. She felt the ground rising, jerking her along. Heaving and rolling like a giant fish might turn and twist to get away from the fisherman who caught it. Then another rolling heave, this one jerking harder.

With a series of cracks the cave in front of her collapsed. Horrified, she watched the mountain break into boulders large and small, falling and crashing against each other. Geysers of dust sprung up all around. It was shocking, unbelievable.

In the space of just a few moments, the place she called home, the comfortable rise in the mountain with its roomy caverns and the hot springs inside, the space she lived in all her life suddenly buckled and collapsed on itself. One moment it was there, just beyond where she was standing. The next moment it broke beneath her, sliding Birdy downhill till she came to a rest against a pile of rubble. For a long time she could not catch a clean breath in her throat. The air was thick with dust.

A wailing broke through, and then quieted. For a long and terrifying moment the world was empty of sound.

"Birdy, Birdy, oh thank the Spirits you're safe, what's happening? Is anyone trapped inside?" River was hurrying across the meadow, carrying the berries. Somehow with her usual grace she managed not to spill a single one. "Oh you poor thing...," and with that she bent, setting the bowls to the side, and traced her hand down her niece's scraped leg.

"Aunt River, the cave . . ." Birdy tried to say, but River shushed her and pulled her close. Hugging, patting her on the back, stroking her hair. Taking a deep breath, River finally pushed Birdy out at arms length. Gripping her firmly by the shoulders, she peered into her eyes. "I know, sweet one, I know. This is going to be tough. But we have to find out if anyone is in there. The family, Birdy! We're going to have to pull them out, anyone who's still alive. Are you with me, Birdy?"

Her throat was hot and dry, too choked to let anything through.

"Birdy, please. They're going to need our help! Can I count on you?"

Just beyond Birdy saw a tree, newly upended, its roots crazily pointing every which way. She turned back to River but she could not say a thing. Not a croak. Not a syllable. Not a sound.

"Look at me, Birdy," her aunt urged. "Some of the family might be trapped inside. Maybe there are visitors too, I don't know. We have to try and get them out. They could be hurt but they might be alive."

There was a sound, a shifting from the mound of boulders. They turned to watch, both of them. A man's hand found its way out of the heap and began pushing aside the rubble. River went to help, careful not to disturb the precariously shifting balance of sones.

Slowly K'enemy made his way out of the heap. He staggered to his feet, a dazed look on his face. He looked at Birdy, then at River, barely seeming to register their presence.

"K'enemy." River reached to touch his arm, but withdrew her hand when she saw him flinch away. "K'enemy. Are you hurt?"

He shook his head, as much to clear it, perhaps, as to answer her.

"Do you need ... " She stopped as K'enemy began to pull rocks from what had once been the entrance to the cave. Digging there would let them find anyone trapped inside, save them if possible, or retrieve whatever remained.

"Birdy," River urged her. "You have to go for help. K'enemy can't move all this himself. Your brother is down on the beach fishing with some of the other boys. Go find him. Can you hear me, Birdy? Bring him and anyone else available. We need help moving all these rocks so we can get them out. Birdy, BIRDY, do you hear me? You must get help!"

River shook her, seeking a response. Any response. "Can you hear me, Birdy?" she repeated.

Numb, Birdy finally remembered how to nod.

"Then go. Be quick! We have to try and save them."

"Will you be here," Birdy found herself asking pitifully.

"I'll be right here," River assured her, "doing whatever I can."

Sense returned, now that she knew what to do. Down the mountainside she ran, not even noticing her sore ankle in the urgency of the moment. She ran along the well-worn path, which she knew as well as she knew her right hand, crossing the small creek, ducking under the low hanging branches and down to the clearing where the slope turned gentle. There she stopped to take her bearings.

Which way would be fastest? Birdy looked at the beach below. A crowd of her tribesmen were dancing along the shore.

They didn't know. Could it be that they didn't hear the collapse above the sound of the sea? They were gleefully leaping about, gathering a huge school of fish that seemed to have washed up and now lay stranded on the wide, wet sands.

The tide seemed to have pulled way back. The water was further out than Birdy ever saw it, further than even the lowest tide of the moon cycle. So far out that even from this height Birdy could not see the blue-grey waves. Ocean had crept so far away that it disappeared from sight.

Then she heard another thunderous sound. Birdy ducked her head, but this was no cracking collapse of boulders; this one was a rolling sound that came from the direction of the sea. Someone was yelling, "Water! Look out, it's coming like a stampede of Bison!"

The people below went running, most of them, scrambling to get to high ground. Except for those still gathering fish, who seemed not to hear nor see anything but a great supply of food for the taking.

"Danger, danger!" people were screaming, and rushing every which way. From her perch Birdy was horrified to see a child fall underfoot.

Others were heading into danger, straight in the path of the wall of water hurtling toward them, trying to grab the young ones and pull them to safety. Birdy was too far to see faces, but she knew, she knew she had friends and cousins in the danger zone below.

Water came up and hit the beach with a roaring, pounding wall of sound. Masses of people were knocked off their feet, pushed by a tide higher than Birdy had ever seen. She stood there in shock, unable to move. The sheer amount of water coming at them was stunning, amazing. It would have been glorious to see except it was completely terrifying. The water overwhelmed all in its path with a power that swept everything away.

Waves crashed onto the land, tearing up the beach. In a heartbeat the water surged past the usual level on the sand. Now it was higher than the treetops. Now it was half way up to the cave, higher than Birdy had ever seen it reach. The foaming froth was pounding and fierce, sweeping away every person, every shelter, every pile of firewood in its path. The furious tide drowned out every other sound.

"River, River," Birdy cried. Turning from the horror she ran blindly back up the hill, back to the only safety that might remain.

Book 2: Sad farewells

Chapter 1: A heaviness in the bones

Oopsy lay asleep in Birdy's lap. She stroked his hair absently, staring into the campfire built hurriedly in the meadow. He was worn out, poor thing, and who could blame him after all that happened today: The cave collapsing on him, then being trapped alone for half the afternoon. His mother, his adored older brother, his sister and the baby all gone, leaving him behind. Grandmother, gone. Great Uncle, hurt. His home disappeared, and who knew where he'd wake up tomorrow?

Birdy felt just as lost. It was embarrassing, but she kept grabbing her aunt whenever River started off anywhere. She was afraid to let her out of sight. So many had disappeared today, she found herself following her aunt everywhere, even behind the bushes when she ducked around them for personal reasons.

Fortunately River didn't seem to mind, though she kept tripping over Birdy. Actually she seemed relieved to keep a close eye on what little family was left.

Throughout the afternoon, River put Birdy to work alongside her. They lifted stones as long as there was hope of saving someone or something from the cave. River's hide shelter was intact, so they stacked everything there they could salvage: Broken bowls, torn sleeping furs and the partial remains of tools and food pulled from the wreckage. When that became too gruesome to bear, they nursed the wounded being brought to the field.

Now River sat next to Birdy taking a much needed rest. A handful of others joined them around the fire, many staring wordless into the flames. What happened—it was too much to take in. They were like babies born in a world too wide to understand. Only where were the mothers to guide them? So many wandered aimless now that there were no more bodies to rescue, now that the screams of pain died away.

Birdy shivered and hugged her brother close. She felt a heaviness settling in her bones. It was more than ordinary weariness, though her exertions took a toll. It went beyond that; she felt a deep leaden weight settling in her belly, an absence of the life force as if she was wounded and most of her blood leaked away.

Others seemed to feel the same. They perched precariously on rocks and in the grass, becoming like stones wherever they came to rest. Some sat for hours without making a move. They could be there all day and night, might starve to death and possibly not even care. Fortunately a few instinctively began to go outside again. A small group of women came and went, bringing meat, water, and greens for the cooking pot, offering a soupy stew to whoever would take a bowl from their hands.

Yet for all their weariness many had trouble accepting food. Some took only a bite, and even this might be retched up. "How can I eat when my wife no longer can," one man sobbed.

Surprisingly, no one was embarrassed by his tears.

Everyone had lost someone, and most had lost many. Whole families were swept away, down by the roaring sea. Even in the mountains many were crushed by falling trees and boulders. This meadow under the open sky was the safest of all the places the Ogwehu lived. Here in this safe zone they gathered to see what remained.

A crowd collected, and yet it was pitifully smaller than just a few days before, on the night they gathered for the summer solstice. Smaller, for most of the ocean people were gone, and many of the mountain people taken too. The ones who could were leaving the meadow and returning with whatever possessions they still had. No one wanted to go back to the places that no longer seemed safe. Shelters were hastily erected here and there, dragged up from the soggy beach or down from the precarious wooded slopes.

"Women may weep, but Father Sky rejoices," a man murmured, placing his hand on River's shoulder. It was the traditional message of comfort. Father Sky rejoiced, of course, because their loved ones were joining Him in the Great Beyond. The saying was a nod toward a family's sadness. Yet it reminded them that there was a balance to life, and humans have but a small part in it. For most mourners the message at first fell on unwilling ears. Repeated enough on the day of bereavement, and through the months that followed, eventually it helped them travel a path toward acceptance.

Eventually, but not yet. On this day too many people said it to each other, and its comfort felt hollow.

"Father Sky has too much to rejoice at today," a woman named Falling Leaf muttered.

Her neighbor shushed her, glancing towards the heavens with a worried look on her face. "Stop it right now," she warned. "You keep talking like that, you'll bring thunder and lightning down upon us. We had enough trouble already today."

No one had much else to say, and a painful silence descended, followed by a restlessness, an anxious feeling that many shared. In the course of everyday life most of the People did a small number of predictable things. Cook, eat, gather firewood, hunt, prepare food for the winter. Anything else had always been directed by one of their customary leaders. If a major hunt was needed, the chief suggested it and asked one of the hunters to lead. If ceremonies were called for, their shaman oversaw the preparations.

Both those leaders were now gone. Each had served long enough that few recalled a time when they floundered about without them. Now who could take their place? This was no time to vie for leadership; it would have been unseemly to begin. Yet leadership was needed, today more than ever. People needed to be prodded out of their stupor or they would sit like stones until the snows froze them to the ground.

"Who is left of us?" asked a man called Two Stones. He was one of the men who came to River's aid that afternoon, working side by side with K'enemy and River's nephew Fire Bear. Two Stones, so named because when you asked him to bring you a stone, you could be sure he'd bring two. When asked to provide a few rabbits for a feast, he once brought a whole moose to stew.

Yet even Two Stones had not the power to bring back the dead. Though he and K'enemy did manage to dig Oopsy out of the boulders that threatened to crush the child. He revived Great Uncle who was unconscious when they found him, and now sat across the fire from Birdy with an angry swelling on his forehead and fingers secured with splints.

Two Stones began to take a tally of those who remained. It looked like there were several hand counts of people, perhaps 50 in number, where once there had been several times that. As the men started identifying their families, calling the names of those who remained, as the women tried to remember where they last saw their neighbors and friends, they could see that most of the Ogwehu had gone on to join the ancestors. Only a few stayed behind, still able to dance upon the earth.

It was a custom when someone died to toss a handful of savory leaves onto the fire. This sent a comforting scent into the heavens. Father Sky would be sure to direct the smoke, itself a prayer for safekeeping, toward the spirits of those who newly arrived. Now every time someone came to join the fire circle they threw savories onto the flames, but so many were added that the fragrance began to sicken in their nostrils.

Left Hand and Right Hand, Birdy's twin cousins, were chattering as they approached. Left's wrap was torn; Right had dirt smudged across her face. Otherwise they seemed untouched by the changes around them. They brought no leaves to add their respects. Shocked at this thoughtlessness, their mother frowned and sent them back, each blaming the other for forgetting.

"You were supposed to pick them," Left scolded Right.

"You said you were going to."

"I did not," Left whispered furiously.

"You always try to blame me. We passed those bushes at the same time. You could have picked some."

"You are *entirely* wrong. I needed my hands to hold my wrap together. Your hands were free."

Thankfully their voices began to fade away.

Now the twin's younger brother, Fire Bear, took the empty space next to Birdy. He was a lean boy two summers older than her. Bear's face was badly scraped, along with his chest and legs, but he was alive; that was what mattered most.

He reached to take the sleeping Oopsy from his cousin, cradling the child against his narrow chest. He'd been fishing on the beach, he murmured. Of all his friends, he was the only one who came back. He began telling Birdy about the great wave, at first speaking only to her, then to more as they leaned in to listen.

"It was so unexpected. We were wrestling on the sand, me and Thunder. The other boys were teasing us and jeering. Most of them were betting against me, so of course I wanted to show them I could win. I was going to beat him. I knew I could. I was just getting a good grip on him when it happened. I flipped myself on top of Thunder when there was this huge sound, a kind of loud roar. It sounded like a herd of animals thundering towards us, and then the water was all over and it pulled me away, right off him. I was riding this wave, face down, trying to keep my head above water. I didn't know where Thunder was; didn't know where any of the others were.

"I couldn't feel or see or smell anything but Ocean, couldn't hear anything but the roar of the wave. It was completely overwhelming. I'm shouting prayers to the spirit of the water, please let me live, have mercy on me; and, next thing I know, this wave's carrying me past bushes and trees, over the treetops, and, high above the ground. I'm still being carried by the water, and I'm reaching out to grab anything I can.

"I grab something, but it slips out of my hands. I grab again, and this time I get hold of a good-sized branch, and I hold on tight because I know if I don't, I'm going to die. Now I've got both hands on it, and the water's going past me, it's pulling me hard, but I'm still hanging on. Feels like my arms are about to be ripped off at the shoulder, but I don't let go. And my fingers! I can't even feel them any more! Finally the water goes away, and I'm dangling by my arms, high up in this tree, and all my clothing's gone. Even my amulet's been torn away. I'm naked like a newborn babe, but at least I'm alive."

Birdy glanced down at Bear's body, now clothed loosely in a wrap she did not recognize. Salvaged from someone else's belongings probably, she grimaced; someone who would no longer miss it.

People began questioning him. No, only a few survived. Most of the boys from the beach were gone; almost all the Higher Ones who lived there, and many of the mountain people also gone for good.

A woman broke in. She had been wailing most of the afternoon, for all her children were carried away. "My First Son, gone! First Daughter, tumbled from my arms! My husband was holding the baby, and both were washed away! Why should you live when they didn't?" She turned on Bear, arm raised to strike him.

Sensing the threat, Bear's mother hurried past the circle of women putting food together. Deftly she stepped in front of the distraught mother and grabbed her in a tight embrace. A neighbor led her away, murmuring a stream of reassuring noises, and directed her towards a shelter where she could cry herself to sleep.

Others rose, eager to describe what happened to them. One would barely finish when another rushed to speak. The fire circle grew larger as people kept crowding in. There was a surge of stories as unstoppable as the tide that hit them earlier that day. They had to give voice to their experiences. Had to, or grief would shatter them against the hard rock of despair. Instinctively they let their stories emerge, each leaking some terrible news. Every telling leached away some small measure of anguish or pain.

The one who lost a mother, and the one who lost his sister and two brothers.

The one who lost everyone, and the one who lost only one, but could not imagine life without that person.

The one who saw a friend smashed by the tide against a cliff, with no way to reach out and soften the blow.

The one who saw a parent and a husband crushed by the same tree, and barely escaped herself.

The one who lost no one in his immediate family, but was broken in the impossible attempt to lever a boulder off the legs and belly of a lifelong friend, who once saved his own life.

The one who broke an arm trying to free two loved ones, and had to hopelessly admit failure.

The ones still hoping to hear from family: Maybe they were hunting in the mountains and would return tomorrow? Maybe they were washed away, but might still swim back?

If there were fifty people in the meadow, there were just as many stories, and each needed repeating as that endless day became a never-ending night, a night whose darkness would go on as long as any of them still lived.

But any tide, no matter how strong, eventually recedes into an eddy. As Birdy began dozing off, River led her exhausted niece and nephew to the shelter where they could huddle together for whatever warmth and comfort the night might bring. Though even as they slept, there were those who lingered, repeating their stories to yet another cousin or neighbor. As if the repetition would make it better. As if slight variations in the telling might help them find some more bearable variation in the outcome, or, failing that, might find the courage to go onward nonetheless.

⋆ ⋆ ⋆

Someone was poking at her nose.

She hoped they'd stop. People shouldn't poke other people's noses, it wasn't very nice.

Birdy squirmed underneath her sleeping furs. She could tell by the first call of the warblers that daytime was almost upon them. Usually she was up by this time and glad of it, but today she yearned to burrow back insider her furs. There was something she should remember, but she did not want to. Not yet, anyway. She squirmed inside the furs seeking sanctuary, but the finger followed and poked her again.

A young voice complained, "Birdy, it's peepee time! Get up, I got to go peepee!"

"Go away, Oopsy," she grumbled. "Go ask Grandmother if you need help."

"I can't find Grandmother," he whined.

A moment passed. Birdy jolted upright. Of course he couldn't find Grandmother. Nobody could find Grandmother; she was completely covered by rocks in the fall-in. There wasn't even a body to bury today. That was what she didn't want to remember: All that was gone.

"Birdy, come on." Oopsy pulled at her hand. "It's up time, you have to get up!"

Up time, that's what Mami used to say when she was little. She'd cuddle her close for a few moments, and then say, "It's up time, little Birdsong. Time for the birdies to rise and catch some worms!" And Birdy would giggle with her. Mami would give her a playful push and they'd both get up, Mami to prod Thunder out of his coverings, Birdy to check on baby Pout. Oopsy was not even a bump in her mamma's belly yet.

That time was gone, she reminded herself. She blinked back a sudden prickling of tears. Throwing off the covers, adjusting her wrap, Birdy noticed the empty space on the other side of the shelter. "Where's Aunty River?" she asked Oopsy, an anxious lump rising in her throat.

"Outside," he yawned. "Aunty River goed outside."

Birdy lifted the bottom edge of the tent to peer out. Oh, thank you Spirits. There she was, bent over the hearth building up the fire. Birdy calmed herself with a long, shuddering breath. If her aunt was there, everything would be *haodisah*. In balance with the world. Sometimes they just said *hao*. Well, maybe it wouldn't be completely hao, but at least they would be safe. River would know what to do.

"All right, Oopsy," she conceded. "Let's take you to go peepee."

Oopsy reached up for her hand. The moment he was outside he bounded over to a bush by himself to get some relief. "Good boy," Birdy encouraged him, and he responded with a big grin. He had mastered all this last year, but today anything that worked as it should was something for which to be grateful.

River, shaking rock dust off a pile of furs, turned to watch them. The children would be her responsibility, she sighed. Poor kids. Their mother was gone; their grandmother was gone. She would have to raise them as hers, though surely her brother Rein, his wife Cookie, and Great Uncle would help. They would have to; she didn't know how they'd survive the winter otherwise. It was going to be tough for all the survivors, of course, not just her family. So much loss, it was almost unbearable to consider.

Though look at little Oopsy bounding around now, trying to catch grasshoppers. For the moment he forgot that everything's changed. That gleeful smile on his face—he's completely caught up in the hunt. As long as there's still dew sparkling on their wings, he can see them well enough to sneak up and pounce.

She suspected, however, that he would be wailing for his mamma by the time his belly started shrieking for food.

"Good morning Birdy," River called out. "Did you get any sleep?"

Birdy shrugged, the corners of her mouth dragging down. No surprise; it was unlikely to be a good morning as far as she was concerned.

River looked her over carefully. Birdy's hair was matted, and there was dried blood on her face. River shook her head, wiping dust from her hands. They would have to cope somehow. Work was the best way forward, and there was plenty of that. "We're all going to have to pitch in, Birdy. We will bury people and send them off as well as we can." Not as well as they should, of course, for who would direct their efforts now that the Chief and all the Higher Ones were gone? Who could lead the ceremonies when the shaman and his apprentices were carried away? "I see we never got around to binding your ankle, and you're still limping; let's take care of that now. You stay off it as much as possible today. That's an order, Birdy," she pointed an uncompromising finger at her niece, who seemed about to protest. "You can find ways to help that let you sit in one place."

So Birdy sat on a boulder near the fire while River went inside, emerging with strips of soft hide salvaged from the ruins of the cave. "This is what's left after binding Great Uncle's wounds, Bear's cuts, and Stork's bad foot. We're lucky there's anything left for you. We'll have to make more."

And with that, she frowned, for who would bring them hides or meat now that the cave and the hot springs were destroyed? They had no hunters, fathers, or husbands. Even Thunder was gone, not that he was yet a hunter, but he was beginning to be invited along by the other men. Great Uncle no longer went on the hunts. He didn't move fast enough to keep up with the others, and even if he did, he couldn't carry his share on a long trek back home. He did catch smaller animals with traps or snares, providing some meat for the stewpot, but the results were meager and it took too many of their pelts sewn together to make a decent sized blanket or robe.

As River tended Birdy's sore leg, others drifted over to share whatever mush or scraps of stew they found. They could have gone down to the beach to gather some of the fish washed up. It would have been easy, but no one volunteered. They were reluctant to face the wreckage. Maybe later. Just not yet.

Throughout the day there was a bustle of activity in the meadow, which Birdy watched from her perch by the central fire. River brought a pile of grasses to braid into cordage. Mindawen came over, and the girls shared an uncomfortable silence. "I'm sorry about your mother," Mindawen finally blurted out, reaching for Birdy's hand. "And your brother, too."

Dismayed, Birdy fixed a cold eye on her friend. She was not prepared for sympathy. More used to being on the move, to doing chores or plotting her next chance to sneak down to the beach, she was always the strong one. Her mother counted on her, and she helped her friends when they needed it, but she didn't like to think of herself as someone needing help. "That's not everybody. Don't you know anything?" she cried, anger sparking in her voice. "The whole cave came crashing down! My grandmother, my sister, the baby, plus there were some people from the beach; they all got crushed dead!

"Hey, what are you crying about," Birdy protested as she saw her friend's face crumble. The beginnings of tears gathered in the corners of her own eyes. "Don't you weep! It's my family that's gone, not yours."

"Oh, Birdy, you must be so sad."

"You're always crying. You're just a big crybaby. Don't be stupid," Birdy added, her voice rising anxiously though her words were harsh.

"I'm so sad for you." Her cousin looked away, surreptitiously wiping her eyes out with the back of her hand. "Aren't you sad? You must be sad."

"I guess." Birdy looked down at the coil of cordage she was working. She didn't know what to say. She didn't know how she felt except that she felt oddly empty. Her ankle hurt, and she seemed to be moving more slowly than usual.

Mindawen climbed the rock next to her. Birdy let her sit uneasily balanced on the ledge for a moment before moving over so they both had enough space. The two girls sat there, miserable, until Mindawen began to play with Birdy's hair, combing and braiding the strands, and Birdy allowed it, though usually she hated having people fuss over her.

Chapter 2: All there was to bury

Two Stones, along with Uncle Rein, was organizing the men. They would scour the beaches, the forests, and the mountainsides. They had to find the remains wherever they were, under rocks, snugged on branges, though sometimes all they found were sad little portions of a body for burial. A number of women followed, collecting whatever could be salvaged.

Though most of the beach shelters had been swept away, there were caches of food, tools that were only slightly cracked, and hides that were stiff with salt water but still could be rinsed and reworked. From the cave they retrieved a knife, another hide, and Birdy's cast-off, outgrown wrap. They'd saved it for Pout, but now some other girl would get it.

Yet of the bodies, they found only 17, and many of these were not complete. The rest of the missing lay in places unknown, in the water or cast upon far-distant shores. Maybe strangers will bury Thunder and keep his body safe from the animals, Birdy hoped. The thought made her choke, but she clenched her teeth and kept it to herself. She couldn't voice this to Oopsy, playing quietly at her feet.

Great Uncle busied himself directing preparations for the burials. With his injuries he couldn't lift or carry but he found other ways to do his share. He had once been a shaman's apprentice, he reminded the others. He knew how the burying ritual should go. Even if he never had the confidence of the Spirits, they would make do somehow. That was what they all could do, and no one could complain.

By late the next day, they were ready for the ceremony. It was important to bury the bodies as soon as possible. No one wanted wolves or other marauders sniffing them out; no one wanted a family member to become food for predators. Nor was it healthy to leave the corpses lying in the summer sun; it was too much of an invitation for some foul spirit if they left the dead untended.

Birdy almost did not recognize Great Uncle when she saw him again. He had daubed himself with charcoal and ochre paint, made by grinding two wet stones together and using the grit to trace the designs. The curving lines and symbols seemed foreboding, an alien presence on his face and torso. He no longer looked like their tenderhearted cave-mate. He had become the stern middleman between the People and the Spirits.

He stood in front of the line of trenches, which were interspersed with a series of shallow holes dug in the earth. Behind each trench a body was laid out: A cousin, an acquaintance. Birdy had some memory of almost every person. In front of each smaller depression was some token—a wooden bowl, an amulet, something representing those who were washed away without leaving a body to bury.

The men placed each body or token so that family members would be buried side by side. "So they can make the journey together," River explained to Oopsy.

"Why," he asked, tilting his head up at her, but she shushed him as the ceremony began.

Trapper slowly lifted his arms, and silence fell upon them. Now his arms were high, making a shape like the wings of an eagle soaring over the weeping crowd. Soaring eagle, wingtips aloft, their symbol for Father Sky. It was a reminder that He and the Sky Spirits looked out for them even when the winter winds blew cold, even when lightning cracked overhead and thunder woke them from their sleep. Then he reshaped his arms so each hand curved downward, a shape like the hillside, like Mother Earth beneath their feet. For She watched over them too, even as the tides were upon them or trees came crashing down; She sent nourishing food and water to drink, made sure they found places to shelter in as a good mother would.

He brought his arms wide, embracing all the People, and circled his arms, clasping his hands together. This was the third symbol, and everyone was included in this, the tying together of the Ogwehu, the People who met for ceremonies at their central fire circle. These were the signs most sacred to them, three symbols that together were tattooed on each man's left arm after his initiation hunt, symbols that were carved upon each woman's right arm after her first woman's blood. They were tattooed by cutting the area with a sharp blade. When the cuts healed, they left scars showing the sacred symbols. Father Sky, Mother Earth, and the Circle of the People that danced on the sands between the two Great Spirits, all that mattered most in the world.

Then Trapper turned his back on the people, facing toward the trenches. Opening his arms he recreated the same movements, this time including the dead before him. Then, motioning to the boy assisting him, he took the handful of savory leaves, set them aflame and waved the burning fronds over the remains, walking from the beginning of the line to the very end, weaving a pattern of smoke over them. He was chanting prayers that the shaman traditionally spoke for the dead, and Birdy was glad to notice he did not stumble.

Now it was time for the burials. Trapper motioned to Lost Four Teeth, an elder whose children and grandchildren were carried off by the overwhelming tide, who was alive himself only because he had lingered, gossiping with a friend on the hillside. The elder rose and together they placed the bodies from his family side by side in the first two graves, setting a special token of each of the missing in the narrow trenches next to them. After every body or token was interred, the mourner shared a few memories of each. Trapper waved smoke over them, and together they shoveled dirt into the trenches, placing three stones on top of the graves to mark them, one each for Father Sky, Mother Earth, and the People, and, more practically, to discourage animals from digging up the remains.

Then it was time for the next family, and the next. When whole families were missing, a cousin or friend added what tribute they could. This man, a good hunter who fed his family and helped mend the fishing nets, though he did not himself like the taste of fish. That one, a girl who showed promise in nursing the sick. This babe, whose smiles delighted his mother, while his papa was reminded of his father's face.

Now it was Birdy's family who was to be laid in their graves. Grandmother first, as befit the eldest. Since Great Uncle was performing the ceremony, and the only other male living with them was little Oopsy, River walked both children forward, and together they stumbled through the ceremony.

"My sweet mother," River said, humble in front of the crowd. "She was such a good woman. She taught me to sew and cook, and to respond with kindness even when someone is rude. When I was a girl she promised not to mate me to a man I could not bear, and, the Great Spirits' blessings upon her, she kept her promise. Ho," she concluded with the syllable they used to bring to a close all important tellings, the word which meant, variously, I am done, or I agree, or even, Amen.

As Trapper waved smoke over the grave, River reached down. Using her hand as a scoop, she pushed a load of dirt on top of Grandmother's blanket, all they had left of her to bury.

"Grandmother," Birdy took her turn. "She was always patient. She helped me watch the children, and when I was little I climbed on her lap for stories when Mami was busy." Birdy too scooped dirt into the grave.

Then it was Oopsy's turn, but he wiggled to one side, holding tight to Birdy's wrap. So Birdy grabbed his hand, loosened it from her clothing, and together they pushed more dirt inside.

Now, Mami's turn. Seeing into the pit for the first time, Oopsy noticed his mother's broken body. At first he was silent. Then, as River began to evoke memories of her sister, Oopsy let out a high wail that threatened on hysteria. Birdy grabbed her brother and held him close. She patted his back, rocking and crooning, swaying with the rhythms of her own heart. When River was through, she took the boy from Birdy's arms so that Birdy could take her turn.

"She was my mother," Birdy began. She had been going over what she could say all morning, but the words kept falling out of her mind and she had trouble lining them up in an orderly fashion. "Sometimes . . . sometimes she let me help at the hot springs. She liked it when I rubbed her neck and shoulders at the end of the day. When I had a fever she took care of me." She couldn't think of anything else to add. So she said, "Ho," and bent to sweep dirt over her mother's feet.

"Oopsy, do you want to say anything about Mami?" River asked.

"She was my Mami," the boy wailed, burying his face in her shoulder.

River nodded at Trapper to continue. Thunder was next in the line. But before he could begin the chant several people rose from the crowd asking to speak. Normally at burials people kept paying homage until everyone who wished had their turn. Today there were so many to remember that they were keeping each one short, limiting it to close family only. But there were many who were grateful to Cavekeeper Woman for easing their aches and pains. Sensing a great swell of emotion among them, Great Uncle inclined his head and allowed people to rise, one by one, and pay their last respects to his niece.

Finally it was Thunder's turn. River spoke about his speed in running, and about how brave he was. Birdy recalled looking up to him when she was small, how he loved to scare her but made sure she was never truly spooked. Oopsy by that time had fallen asleep, which was a relief to them all.

Before Trapper closed up Thunder's grave he paused in his role as shaman, taking a moment to be simply a member of the family. "This boy," he reminisced, "we have long called him Sounds Like Thunder. Sounds Like Thunder, for the noises of his belly." There were a few low chuckles, for Thunder was famous for his stomach gurgles. The men used to tease him, saying, "Don't take that boy on a hunt. His Thunder will announce he is coming, and all the animals will flee."

"Thunder hated his name, and for years he begged for a new one. I told him he would have to do something to deserve it. Just because you tell people to call you Eagle Feather or some other fine name, does not mean they'll start using it. But yesterday he earned himself a new name." At this, people sat up and leaned forward. Was this funeral also to be a naming ceremony?

Trapper signaled them to pay attention. "Yesterday this boy became Saves His Cousin, for two boys were wrestling, and either one could have been snatched by the waves."

Bear bolted up onto his feet. "He speaks true," the boy called out. "I was climbing on top of Thunder to get a better hold on him. He could have tried to save himself when the water was upon us. Instead he shoved me higher just as the waves crested overhead."

"Saves His Cousin," Trapper announced. "A fine member of our tribe. May his bravery bring honor to the ancestors. May his spirit shine out from the heavens. May he look down upon us, sending good fishing and hunting for many seasons to come." Fierce in his ceremonial paint, he directed his glance for a long moment up at the sky. Then he lowered his gaze to look down at the earth. He raised his head, regarding the crowd gathered on this solemn day. "Ho," he concluded.

And together they echoed, "Ho."

Chapter 3: Let us leave this place of sorrow

All through the evening, conversations swirled around the things that puzzled them—what made the giant wave and the heaving of the earth, and especially why all these terrible events happened to them. Such things were normally explained by the shaman, but he was gone, and the People were left to wonder on their own.

"Maybe Falcon did something terribly wrong," suggested one man. "Maybe Father Sky is punishing us for some bad thing he did."

"Or something we did," added another.

"Maybe Mother Earth is tired of giving us shelter in this place. She might be saying it's time to move elsewhere."

"Like when you stay with a cousin and eat up all their food, so they put your sleeping fur outside to let you know it is time to go?"

"Just like that."

Punishment, or weariness; how could they know? And if they could not figure it out, how would they find favor again with the Great Powers? No one among them had experience communicating with spirits. They were helpless in so many ways. They missed the leaders who organized the hunts, who decided which side was right when quarrels broke out. A child whimpered in the dark, and the emptiness pressed hard upon them.

Yet no gathering could stay silent for long. As parents reached over to comfort their children, men and women began murmuring again.

"Maybe we all did something wrong," someone finally said, and another painful silence descended, with only the popping and crackling of the fire to mark the passage of time. Each man, each woman, each child was busy examining their conscience. Did I do something to bring on such punishment? What did the ones who died do that was even worse?

It couldn't be her, Birdy assured herself. She was a good girl, even if she did sneak off to the beach whenever she could. That was wrong, she knew, but why would the Great Spirits punish her so harshly when they hadn't in two years of listening in? Oh, Mother Earth, Birdy suddenly realized; maybe all this was because of her. She promised to make an offering after she escaped undiscovered, but she never did. That was bad. That was so bad. Were all those people killed because of her?

Then her cousin Right spoke up, tears in her eyes. "I didn't pound the grass seed that morning. I told Mamma I did it because I didn't want to get into trouble. I meant to do it later, but I forgot."

"I was disrespectful to a whole group of elders," Left added.

"But you two didn't lose anybody in your immediate family," someone pointed out. "So that couldn't be it."

"We have to help everybody else in trouble," the distraught girl wailed. "That's punishment, isn't it? It's our fault, my sister's and mine; I know it. I feel awful."

"Shhh, it's not just you. Probably everyone here has done something wrong," a woman tried to comfort her. "I was short-tempered with my husband, and now I can't even tell him I'm sorry."

"I traded a knife with a crack in the handle to my neighbor for a perfectly good spear. I took advantage of his failing eyesight," a man confessed.

"I was supposed to help my father mend the nets but I was playing with my friends instead."

The confessions poured forth. Everyone was guilty of something. Bad behavior towards other people, disrespect towards the Spirits. And if this group of survivors did all these bad things, what did the others do who were not just injured, but dead? Someone started enumerating the sins of the deceased, but Great Uncle put up a warning hand and the crowd grew quiet.

He reached for the talking stick so that no one would interrupt him. The talking stick had long been a tribal tradition. It was too easy for people to interrupt one another. In the heat of discussion somebody would leap in the midst of other people's arguments, and fists might fly or resentments rise that took months to clear away.

Some time ago, a wise chief had picked up a stick and announced, "The only one talking is the one holding this in his hand." So the tradition arose that when one person finished what they had to say, they passed the stick to another who wanted a turn. The talking stick came to have a certain mystique, and people would bead it or attach feathers to give it a beauty befitting its status. And when a stick was lost or damaged, people vied for the privilege of making another.

"Let us not heap shame among those who cannot speak for themselves." Trapper paused to clear his throat. "Let us remember them with grace. If we hasten to speak of their troubles, perhaps we judge them too harshly. Who can say they did not make things right just before the calamity befell them? How do we know we do not wrong them when we insist we know what was in their hearts?" Signaling he was through, he murmured, "Ho."

Those who had been railing against the dead were shamed into silence. One child protested, "I know what my papa was doing right before he got crushed," but his mother clapped her hand over his mouth and whispered furiously that they would speak about it later in private. Not in front of all these others.

The evening grew cooler, and the summer dusk deepened.

"If we have lost Mother Earth's welcome here," Two Stones asked the question that nagged him all day, "if She no longer wishes us to dwell on our beach and mountain, then where should we go? That is what I have been wondering. Ho." He passed the talking stick on.

"Grandmothers and grandfathers, uncles and aunts," asked a nursing mother, "what's wrong with living here in this meadow in-between, right where we are now? Ho."

"There's not enough space," Rein answered. "If we are not welcome at the beach and we are not welcome in the mountains, we cannot huddle in this small meadow and gather enough food and fuel to get us through the winter. Ho."

"How do we know for sure that Mother Earth doesn't want us to stay," demanded K'enemy. He, who so rarely spoke, now burst forth with a torrent of words. "Why do you think She has turned against us? We are Her children. We may have done wrong, but surely we were punished enough. I say we go back to the beach and up the mountainside." He looked around, and, seeing some nod, continued. "We have lived here for many grandfather's lifetimes. We have made countless offerings to the Spirits, and surely they have not suddenly tired of us." He rose, shaking the kinks out of his legs. "I was not a man of the beach before, but I would like to make a change. I want to try living there, and I say, let's go now. Who will follow me?" Setting down the talking stick, he rose and strode across the meadow without looking back.

Two more stood and hurried after him, the grasses rustling in their wake.

Some spoke of returning to the mountain. Others wondered if the beaches farther beyond were devastated by the waves. One man began to chant a sad dirge reflecting the somber mood. Another brought out a drum to beat a simple accompaniment. The fire was dying down, so a boy crouched over it, adding sticks to the flames.

"Oh, looky, Birdy," Oopsy pointed upward. "It's night time. They should be sleeping." Sure enough, the sky was full of birds flying high and strange as they had the previous day. Just as before, there was a scurrying in the fields; a variety of animals began emerging from their dens. A growing horror began to dawn as a now-familiar rumbling started, followed by another heaving, rolling motion. Not as powerful as the day before, but frightening nevertheless.

Oopsy clutched at Birdy, who grabbed River's arm and held it close against her. Other women were holding their children tight, and men spread their arms to shelter loved ones within.

Finally the Earth beneath them stilled.

"I'd say the Great Mother has spoken," Great Uncle suggested. But apparently the shaking this time was a warning, not a punishment, though the warning was fearsome enough. As it became clear that no one in the meadow was hurt, people looked towards the beach where the three men disappeared. After all the recent deaths, it was alarming to consider the prospect of more.

Ah, there at last, a footfall. A sigh of relief went round the circle. K'enemy and his followers came stumbling back to collapse by the fire, shaken but unhurt.

Even with their safe return, people felt it was a warning. "As soon as we try going back to the beach, the rumbling begins again. We have been warned away. It's too dangerous to stay here," they agreed, and reluctantly they began to speak of other places the People might live. Perhaps they could still return to the mountain; maybe they could live there where they knew every berry bush, where they knew the bear dens and the salmon-spawning riverbeds, and only had to avoid the shore.

Was there anywhere else they could live on this long finger of land pointing into the ocean? Their hunting camp inland? Some spot further up the valley? Should they journey all the way west to the high mountains where the People had lived many generations before? What if they went south to the warmer lands, would that be better? Or north to find the cousins who split off, following the herds of reindeer that migrated every fall and spring? In each direction there were possibilities to consider, except to the east where recently there were people aplenty, but now only the fish, whales and walruses lived.

And so these things were discussed around the fire circle. Yes, everyone agreed, they should send scouts up the mountain tomorrow to see if the spirits welcomed their return. Though some wondered if living on the mountain would be enough, knowing they would miss having the fish, the seaweed that flavored so many meals, and the occasional feasts of crab or seal.

No, they concluded, there was not another good living space on all this finger of land, large though it was, several days journey across, a month's journey up its length. The ancestors were wise in choosing this spot. Everywhere else on this peninsula had some flaw making it unsuitable. There were other beaches, but they were too narrow or rocky to live on, or the tide was too swift to fish. Or there were no mountains behind them to offer a bigger variety of food, and wood or animal dung for the fires so the People could stay warm.

Throughout the long middle section there was space to spread out on. The People kept a shelter by the lake where hunting parties based their expeditions, but it flooded in the spring, and there were too many bears for the People to flourish. "Unless we want to become Bear's brothers and sisters," one man joked, but it was a bitter jest, unworthy of comment. Bears were surly, and as likely to maul or kill their own family as they might any creature they came across.

Though few of the women had traveled, most of the men had gone far afield. Scattered around this finger-land, a hunter reminded them, there were many dangers. There were boggy areas where the unwary could sink like a stone. Many of the mountains smoked with fires deep within, and some of these would vomit up bile that burnt a person's skin. There was a lake, blue and beautiful, but if you stepped in it, your feet burned as if they were on fire. There were places haunted by wild spirits where the earth bubbled like a cooking stew, where the ghosts felt vile, and spit burning water as the hunters crept by. No, the men agreed, if they could not stay on this very mountain, they should travel off this finger-land and look farther for a new central hearth. Ho.

Then people began speaking in smaller conversations about one thing or another. River nudged her sleepy niece, and the three of them dragged off to bed.

$$\star \qquad \star \qquad \star$$

"Help, come help!" someone was shouting. "There's a sea lion here in the meadow!" His message woke Birdy, and, judging by the commotion around the shelter, it woke many others in the camp.

Grabbing her wrap and fastening it quickly, not bothering to slide her feet into foot coverings, she grabbed Oopsy, who was hopping from one foot to the other, and ran outside toward the sound. Others were emerging from their shelters as well. Bear held his boyish spear, running towards the far end of the meadow. Rein, K'Enemy and others were gathering weapons with the mindfulness of hunters alerted to action.

For a sea lion to wander this far from the beach was unheard of. Sea lions never traveled beyond the sands. They were built for swimming. They had to waddle and inch awkwardly along like enormous caterpillars on dry land. He must have been thrown up here by the giant wave, the hunters decided, and they did not hesitate to take advantage. The bad fortune of one was a feast for another; that was how life was. They would enjoy this good fare today.

Led by Bison, only 17 summers in age but already accepted as one of the strongest leaders in the hunt, the men surrounded the disoriented creature and made a quick job of it. Several strong blows from every side, and it gave its life up to them, with only a few painful feints back.

Quickly the men began butchering the creature. River, watching from the edges, ran back to retrieve bowls for collecting the blood. Even with such a big catch nothing should be wasted. Waste today means hunger tomorrow—that was another old saying of the People. It came from one of their ancient stories, and people quoted it to justify all manner of things.

Still, it was more true than not. Whatever they did not eat right away could be saved, dried or smoked and stored for another day. The flesh of this animal could feed the meadow-dwellers for a week. Blood would add flavor to the stew. The fat could be rendered into oil, useful in medicines, good for lamplight. Sinew was used for sewing. Bones added flavor to soups, could be made into weapons or handles, sewing needles, or left for the dogs of the camp to chew on. Even the claws would be used as amulets.

The men arranged the carcass so that most of its blood drained into the bowls. That done, they struggled to turn the enormous animal on its side so they could slice down the soft belly, open it for skinning and cutting into manageable sized pieces. One organ was removed after the next. When they got to the heart, Two Stones cut it out and handed it to the boy who spotted the creature. "You get the first taste," he said.

The boy took his blade and cut a small piece of the bloody organ, placing it delicately on his tongue. To eat of a fresh heart was an honor, but he didn't feel it was entirely his to enjoy. He cut a piece and gave it to K'enemy who made the killing blow, and another to Bison. With a generosity that pleased them all, Bison cut the rest in pieces and gave some to each hunter who shared in the kill, even distributing tidbits to the boys who fiercely lobbed stones and thrust their blunt spears as best they could from the edge of the battle.

"Let us thank the spirit of this meadow," someone reminded them. They took a piece of the enormous liver and some of the intestines and buried them with prayers of thanks.

Then the men went off to regale each other with stories about the battle. The women took over butchering the carcass, for once the men were distracted and the urgency gone, who could count on them to finish the job?

It was a lengthy process, but as the sun moved across the sky, the women found they were enjoying themselves. Practical tasks were soothing after so much upheaval. Gradually a kind of ease set in, and they began to speak of more mundane concerns. Where they would live; whether they needed more hides for the winter; did they salvage enough for those who remained? Who might this girl marry, and what family would that person join?

Tentatively, little remembrances emerged, small opportunities to recall various quirks of the ones no longer among them, providing a chance to mourn. Remember how much Keterie hated sea lion meat; at least she won't have to wrinkle her nose at all this. Do you recall the time when Ungwaden grabbed a piece of sinew and somehow managed to tangle himself up with the moose he killed, and they had to slice carefully to free him without cutting him?

The women were laughing and crying at the same time, wiping away the blood and tears in equal measure when they felt another rumble of the earth begin. "Put down your knives!" River called out, and the women hurriedly braced themselves against the earth. Oopsy came running and took a flying leap into River's arms, burying his head deep in her side.

There was a long hush as people waited fearfully for whatever else the Spirits might send their way. Finally the earth grew still again. The birds returned to the trees, and normal sounds resumed.

"What happened," Cookie cried out, but no one had an answer until Bear came running across the meadow.

Looking back and forth between Cookie, Birdy and the others, Bear panted, "Some of us started up the mountain to see if we could live there, and now the rumbling's begun again."

"Is anyone hurt?" asked River.

"One of the trees fell on Otter, but he wiggled out from under it. We need help! I think he broke his leg!"

★   ★   ★

That night there was much to discuss. They could stay safely in the meadow for at least a handful of days, that was how they interpreted the gift of the sea lion. If Mother Earth sent such a feast, then they certainly could stay while they finished it off.

But it seemed they were no longer welcome on the mountain, just as they were unwelcome at the beach. It was a sign so clear, even they who were untutored in the readings of signs and portents could not mistake it. For each time their people returned to their old dwelling places, Mother Earth had rumbled and threatened them harm. No one was hurt the first time, but the second scouting expedition returned with a man maimed. If they ignored Her signals any further, who knew how harsh the next message would be?

Now no one urged them to stay on the meadow. "Let us leave this place of sorrow," pleaded the woman who lost her entire family, and no one contradicted her. They would stay long enough to gather strength for traveling somewhere safer. A place where the People could rebuild.

The young men were eager to go, for traveling spoke to them of adventure. But many of the women were reluctant. To them travel meant hardship and danger. Yet no matter which life the People chose, if they left this place they would have to travel some distance. They had to pass the many dangers of this fingerland before they could begin looking. And then what? In which direction should they turn?

A woman asked if they would become nomads like their reindeer-chasing cousins, like their own People were long ago.

Their People had not always lived in one place; they knew this from the ancient stories. Before they found this home by the sea, they wandered for many lifetimes, never calling any one campsite their home. From the stories they knew what it was like to trek, though now they were used to having a central hearth.

They wished Falcon was there to tell the old stories, for some of these related their earlier journey coming to this land. Though it was many generations before, the tales were passed down from shaman to shaman, telling about the places they traveled through.

Birdy had to clench her fists to keep from saying anything. She knew most of those stories, but she'd been warned for so long against this very thing. Falcon threatened pain and shame for her family. He was gone now, but his warning remained. Death or disgrace, either one dreadful. Her family had suffered enough; in no way could she risk adding burdens for Great Uncle or

River. She had to accept her fate; it was the way of the Ogwehu. Girls did not do such things; the consequences were dire.

After the first few times she listened in on the stories, she'd approached Falcon to ask if she could join the apprentice boys. She would never interrupt, of course not. She would bring firewood if he wanted, or clear the ashes afterward. He had flicked a contemptuous finger at her. "Go ask your mother to teach you all the little prayers for the hot springs," he sneered. "Ask Falling Leaf about herbs to smear over wounds. Mother Earth wisdom is for girls. Father Sky wisdom is for *men!*" She looked at him balefully, but he refused to soften.

As she turned to walk away, he cast another barb in her direction. "Girls who try to act like men are an abomination!" The very word sent a shudder coursing through her. Abominations, mostly misshapen babies, were taken into the forest and left to die alone. Or sent out to sea on a raft of driftwood.

Fortunately others around the fire recalled this or that part of the story, and though they did not know the tales well enough for a complete retelling, many impressions remained. The mountains to the west were many seasons' walk away, someone remembered. The Ogwehu left those mountains when the tribe grew large and there were too many crowding on the land. Fighting arose over who could hunt where, and the arguments got ugly. When some of the People began to hunt others among the People, hunting them down as if they were food for the winter, their own grandfathers' many times grandfathers decided to lead their families away. They preferred to leave their kinsmen forever than become a People who could mistake humans for elk or mammoth.

With that reminder, no one wanted to return there.

Someone else recommended turning toward the south where it was warmer, and would be easier on the elders and the young.

But another man reminded them that there were great sicknesses in the heat of the southlands and many of their kin were left beneath the surface of the Earth. Some still urged them to consider it for the ease of finding food in such places. But one woman cried out, "Grandmother, I am sorry to disagree, but are you so really so eager to join with the ones we left behind?"

Rein suggested going north. He wanted to find the cousins who followed the roving herds of reindeer. Occasionally the herd migrated back and this cousin People joined with them until the herd moved on again. The last time they visited, they took him with them to journey for a year. Rein remembered with fondness his time among these cousins. Plenty of food and warm furs,

he coaxed the others. Wouldn't it be nice to try a new way of living? They
had lost so many cousins, surely it would be a good thing to reunite.

Staunch, a friend of his, teased him. "Runs Like Reindeer wants to feast
on his namesakes," he suggested. This stirred a run of laughter around the
fire circle.

But Rein had more to say. "Grandfathers and Grandmothers, Aunts and
Uncles, we have a choice to make here. It's not just which direction do we
turn, it's where can we make a life that will be good for us. And not just
for us. When our grandfathers' many-times-grandfathers chose this place,"
his hand circled round, indicating the beach below and the mountain above,
"they were choosing not just for themselves, but for us who came after them.
So when we choose, we are choosing for our children as well as ourselves. We
are choosing for our children's children and so forth, like a river that flows
beyond what we see. Let us make our choice keeping them in mind, though
we do not yet know their faces or names."

"We know your face too well already, Uncle," muttered a man who was
tired of hearing arguments against his own position. But others shamed him
into silence, for it was rude to interrupt. Even if they were now living in the
ashes of their former lives, they could hold to their customary respect for each
other.

"I say, if we move to the south," Rein argued, "we move to the lands where
too many grow sick and die. Our old stories tell us this. I would not choose
that for my children's children; I want them to live and have children of their
own. If we follow the reindeer it will be a hard life, but a healthy one. I am
not frightened of a hard life; a hard life makes us strong. Strong and healthy,
that's how I want my children's children to grow up. So I choose for the north.
Not just for me, not just because I like the taste of reindeer meat." This last
statement brought on a few more chuckles. "But for all of us. For our children,
and their children thereafter. Ho."

This struck a deep chord around the circle. It was not so many years
before that a fever struck their People. Many sickened, but the worst hit were
the young, and many families lost a child or more. Since then the young had
come to be seen as especially precious. For if there were no children, who
would head up the hunters as they grew older? Whose chubby baby hands
would touch their weather-worn faces? Who would speak their names and tell
their stories when their bodies were laid to rest and their spirits gone to the
heavens?

Someone wondered if it was hard to follow a pack of animals. They would be living in their droppings; they would have to move at a pace set by creatures not themselves. They would never enjoy a fixed home site. And others mentioned how bitter the cold could be on the mainland north of their familiar finger of land. Danger lay in that northward direction, for even if there was less sickness, there were more accidents—falling through the ice, fires starting in crowded winter tents, and freezing to death if you were not careful and lucky.

The arguments roared back and forth, for the North and for the South, until it began to seem as if there would never be harmony again among the People, few though their numbers now were.

Other paths were suggested, but none had enough interest to lure anyone toward some third possible way.

By the end of the evening there was no consensus. Two hands-worth of people were convinced that they should turn to the south. Another hands-worth insisted that north was the better direction. The remaining people were not ready to choose. And so they decided on only one thing: That they needed more time to decide.

$$\star \qquad \star \qquad \star$$

River startled, hearing a scurrying sound in the brush. She'd been harvesting roots all morning, was even now carrying a load back to the shelter but the noise caught her attention and she took a step closer to investigate. They were keeping a careful watch, for even with so many people crowding the meadow some of the bolder scavengers—foxes, wolves—were tempted into camp. Darting in at just the right time they might carry away an entire afternoon's work. Or even a babe if the mother was careless.

She reached to push a branch away. In the dappled light a glint of sun reflected on a patch of tanned skin—a man she knew who lost his wife to the giant wave. The leaves overhead were swaying with the breeze. Another shaft of sun reflected off a bare buttocks, and a woman yelped, grabbing something to cover herself. Moments later the man was backtracking into the woods while the woman came towards River pulling her wrap to fasten it around her.

"What are you looking at," she complained to River.

"But . . . but . . . your husband?" River said indignantly, voice rising high at the end.

"Buried not two days ago, I know," the woman admitted. She looked around, grimacing. "You think I want it this way? Look here." She loosened the top edge, modestly covering her chest as well as the lower body. Now she reached in to expose her breasts, holding them up for River to see. "This is what I have to offer. And this," she waved one hand down her hips and legs, "that's what'll get a hunter to feed my children this winter. I've got four of them, you know."

"I'm sorry," River said hastily. "I didn't mean . . ."

"I don't have the luxury of waiting, unlike some." She looked meaningfully at River. "I have to stake a claim before everybody chooses up sides and leaves. If you're smart, you'll do the same." Tossing her head, she turned on her heel and hurried back to her children, who were playing nearby.

The smell of coupling lingered in the air. If I was smart, River thought, shaking her head. Maybe she was right. Even saddened as they all were by so much loss, there was a kind of wild energy running through camp. She felt it from time to time, a kind of thrill that they'd survived, even as they felt devastated that so many others did not. From time to time a fierce urge hit, some innate desire to build up their People, since so many had been taken away.

Of course River was elated that one particular young man had survived as well. Yet she could not imagine simply tapping him on the shoulder and nodding in the direction of the woods.

True enough, the one he loved was no longer in the way. But to pounce on him when he'd never yet given even a hint of interest in her? Smart or not, she decided after only a moment's thought, she couldn't. Certainly not like that. She would have to trust that things would work out.

$\star$ $\qquad$ $\star$ $\qquad$ $\star$

Though the sunlight sparkled off the river as it filtered through the trees, though she saw jays and rubythroats and thrushes darting from branch to branch, Birdy was not enjoying herself. Oopsy was playing with his cousins while she and her aunt took some hides to clean and scrape, preparing them to be sewn into clothing for the winter. Even though River promised one of the hides to Birdy for a new set of winter leggings, even though River said she would help her sew a beautiful design on them, the girl felt another dark mood taking over.

Helpless, that's what she felt.

Helpless to get her mother back, her home back, her—well—everything. People kept coming and going in the space that used to be theirs, messing up their beautiful meadow. Of course she wouldn't have to endure it much longer. They'd be going soon, though she didn't know where, or even who they'd live with. She was sure that she and Oopsy would stay together, but that's all she knew.

Working over the hides, her muscles were cramping. Her whole body was cold and tired. Still the work went on, as it always did. *Scrape, scrape, scrape, rinse.* Every bit of fat and muscle had to be removed, or the hide would rot and you couldn't use it for clothing. *Scrape, scrape, rinse.* Then, when it was finally clean, you had to work it back and forth. If you didn't work it enough, it dried too stiff to use. Work it too much and the hide would become fragile and easily torn. Too stiff or too fragile, either was a problem, and if you got careless, all that scraping was for naught.

Her mind drifted from subject to subject. It didn't much matter who she lived with, there would always be hides to scrape. The last time she had to scrape hides, she convinced her friend Mogwen to help. Mogwen was now gone. Birdy wiped the signs of grief from her eyes and nose. Her friend would never have to scrape hides again. She would never grow up and marry any of the boys they sometimes giggled over, and never have children of her own. Her brother Thunder would never have a family either. Oh, not Thunder, she was supposed to call him Saves His Cousin. Except he still seemed like Thunder to her.

With a sudden snort of laughter Birdy remembered a trick she once played on her brother, waiting for him until he lay down for the night. Everyone else was already asleep. Then, as he got under his coverings, Birdy made a rude thundering sound in the silence of the cave. He looked up, trying to find the source of the noise, and when he couldn't find it, lay his head down again. A second time she made the noise, which made him look around again. She was supposed to be sleeping so he didn't even glance in her direction until it happened once more. Then he pounced on her and the two of them wrestled, shrieking with laughter. Mami finally told them to hush or they'd wake the baby.

River asked what she was laughing about, so Birdy shared the story with her. "I did something just like that to your mother once," River confided. "I was younger than you are, and she was almost 16 summers in age."

"Did she laugh when you played the trick on her?"

"She didn't think it was funny, but your uncle Rein and I were rolling around. We had tears in our eyes, we thought it was so hilarious."

"Mami didn't think anything was funny, did she?"

"Your mother had many skills, but laughter was not one of them. It's kind of odd, because your grandmother used to laugh all the time."

Scrape, scrape, rinse. River, who'd been calm and dry-eyed for days, suddenly sniffed. She dropped her scraper on the bank. Hunching her shoulders, she brought her hands up, covering her face. "Oh, Great Mother, I miss her so much!"

Birdy looked up. Who did she mean?

"She was such a good mother. Oh, Birdy, you hardly knew her, she got so feeble over the last few years, but she used to be so merry. She was always saying things to make us laugh." River began to cry, tears falling into the stream.

Birdy kept scraping. She did not want to embarrass her aunt. Did not want to embarrass herself either by bursting into tears.

Finally River quieted, her breath ragged but easing. She splashed water on her face and sat up. "I'm sorry, Birdy, you must miss your mother too."

Birdy was silent, scraping harder against the fur.

"Don't you?"

"I don't know," she said reluctantly. "I guess so."

"Oh, Birdy, it's all so overwhelming. I know you must miss her; she's your mother! I'm sure you just don't feel it yet." River glanced uncertainly at her niece. "You will. I know she was tough on you, but you'll miss her. Her, and all the rest of them."

Maybe, Birdy thought. Maybe later. She'd think about it some other time. For now, it was *scrape, scrape, rinse.* Stop and pick the fur off the hide to make it smoother. *Scrape, scrape, scrape, rinse.* "What's going to happen to us, Auntie?" Birdy finally asked. "Everybody's talking about leaving. Where are we going?"

River sighed. "We'll have to follow Rein and his family. We don't have much choice."

"Why not?"

River put the hide down and wiped her hands on her wrap. "Birdy, it's going to be harder for us than life in the cave, no matter where we go. The cave never got as cold as most places get in the winter, so we'll need more fuel to keep warm. We're going to need more food and furs, and Great Uncle is too old to supply them all. Either I'll have to marry someone, and he will provide for us, or we'll join Rein's family. Either way, someone else will decide where we go."

"If we don't go with Uncle Rein, who will you marry?"

River looked at her hands, shriveled from so much time in the water. "No one, Birdy. No one has stepped forward and offered to support you and me and Oopsy and Great Uncle. That's a big burden, adding the four of us to any man's hearth. We're lucky Rein is willing to take us all in."

"I can work. I won't be a burden," Birdy protested. "And I can make Oopsy help out, I know I can."

River opened her mouth to respond, but stopped herself. Oopsy trying to help—he would get in the way more than ease the load. No matter what, they were looking at a rough time ahead. They should feel lucky to be alive, but it was hard to feel good just now, knowing how hard things were going to be. River sighed, looking away. "Thanks, Birdsilu. I know you'll do everything you can," she said, reaching down to pick up the hide. There was still a lot more work to be done, preparing for the winter cold.

⋆   ⋆   ⋆

Days passed in the flurry of preparations. The men spent an afternoon trawling the river for fish, and another day with the dogs flushing the meadow of hares and ptarmigan and other small creatures. This greatly added to the pile of food the women were preserving. Between tasks the men formed into huddles arguing over the choice of North or South. The women overheard many a heated discussion as they picked berries, roots and mushrooms in and around the forest. The groups kept breaking down and reforming anew. Plans were made and unmade again.

Finally one evening it was announced that everything had been decided. After the meal was over, Lost Four Teeth, the oldest among them, took the talking stick in hand.

"The time has come," Teeth said slowly. "Let every man who is going South now rise and bring his family to this side of the fire."

Most of the men rose. They reached out, some to family members who were clearly surprised. Soon a mass of people aligned themselves to the south, just over 30 in number. Enough that you needed two people's fingers and toes to make the whole count, or four people using only their fingers.

"Let every man who plans to go North take his family to that side of the fire."

The remaining families rose and moved the other way. Rein signaled River and the rest of them to join. They were the smaller group, just enough to need every finger and toe of one person counting, with 2 left over to start the count again.

"Let us see who will be our neighbors, and who we will miss as we go our separate ways," Teeth suggested. "Let us use this time to make sure that splitting apart is what we want to do." Family looked across the fire at family, neighbors seeing for the first time which of them stood across the divide.

"Let us ponder this for one more night and see if we come to any other decision."

"Ho," the People agreed, for it seemed wise, one more attempt to see if the divide could be bridged. It invited danger, breaking up into such small groups. To lose so many allies when they had already lost so much. Each side was aware that by their own choice, cousins would be divided from each other, friend separated from friend. They would all be lessened by the loss.

Yet with the extra day, not one mind was changed. No one was willing to say, although I do not like your path, I choose to stay instead of separating. And so, on the eighth sad day after the washing away of their loved ones, those going North rose early, gathered their bundles, and made themselves ready to leave.

The southward group would stay a few days longer, as they had some still needing to heal before they began a grueling trek.

As River lashed their bundles together, Birdy asked if she could say goodbye to Mindawen. Oopsy begged to follow, but River sent him instead to see if the rest were ready to depart.

Birdy hurried across the meadow, slowing down to duck inside Mindawen's shelter. The family was still resting in their sleeping places. Her friend's eyes were closed, but they fluttered open as she felt the wind through the open tent flap. Mindawen smiled and lifted the corner of her covering fur, inviting Birdy to share the warmth.

Birdy picked her way past Mindawen's sleepy father and sidled underneath. She looked into her friend's eyes, then lowered her gaze, feeling suddenly shy. "Goodbye, Mindawen. I will always think of you," she whispered.

"I will remember you too," Mindawen whispered. "Especially when I eat salmon." The two girls giggled, remembering a spitting contest they once had with the silvery bones of fish. What a messy day that was! Thunder had to flee, using his hands to protect his face from their aim.

"Here, I want you to have this." Birdy lifted her pendent, an ivory carving of a snowy owl that Great Uncle had made for her.

"Oh, Birdy, that's your special necklace, I can't take that," her friend cried. But Birdy insisted. She said it was for remembrance, and her cousin finally agreed.

Mindawen reached down at the feet of her covers, and brought out a small package. "I want you to have this," she insisted. "Open it when you get to your new home. Then you'll think of me, and I'll be thinking about you."

"And somewhere our thoughts will cross paths when we're both thinking about each other," Birdy said, excited. She raised her index finger and pointed it towards her friend. Mindawen raised the same finger and touched it to Birdy's, two fingers meeting across the space. For a long moment they looked solemnly at each other, both girls holding back tears.

River was calling, so Birdy tucked the little package into the pouch at her waist. The friends hugged for several heartbeats. Birdy rubbed her cheek against Mindawen's before she ran to join her family.

The sun was moving above the horizon now. The meadow grasses glistened with dew, and the birds were calling out their songs as they did each morning, as they would continue to do long after the People moved too far away to hear.

Laden with their belongings, the travelers trudged along, sadness lightened by excitement for the journey. As they walked through the meadow to the path that would take them beyond, Rein halted his new group, the group of those who would now be the People, and beckoned them to look one last time at the lands of their birth.

"Farewell," he intoned. "Farewell to this place which sheltered us so long." With these words, he tossed a handful of grass seed as a thanks-offering to the spirits. "Farewell to the sea that gave us so much food." He tossed another handful on the winds. "Farewell to those who have gone before us." Reaching inside the bag, he grabbed a third offering and tossed it aloft. "Farewell to our cousins; we wish them safe travels." He tossed a fourth offering, and with that, he turned to place his foot at the head of the path forward.

Birdy lingered, even as the others began moving ahead. "Farewell," she murmured, for she had her own goodbyes to make. She had been thinking about them for several days and now she was ready. In her mind she had phrased it formally, as she imagined it might be repeated in a story told to the People at some far distant time.

"Farewell to the cave. Farewell to my playmates, Mogwen and Thunder, to Pout and the tiny babe not even old enough to have his own name. Farewell to Mindawen and her family. And to all of our People who go South. For though they live, we will never hear their new stories, nor see their familiar faces again."

Book 3: Exodus

Chapter 1: First steps forward

This is the tally of the People walking north together:

Runs Like Reindeer, his wife Good Cooking Woman, his twin daughters Left Hand and Right Hand, and his son Fire Bear.

Trapper, his niece River, his great-niece Birdsinger, and his great-nephew Oopsy.

Two Stones, his wife Fierce as Wolves, his son Turtle (Tucks His Head In) who had 15 summers in age, his 8 summers' daughter called Little Mother, and his 5 summers' son named Lynx.

Staunch, his mother Falling Leaf, Keeper of the plant medicines, his daughter of 13 summers called Willow, and the babe they called Poor Thing since her mother was swept away by the tides.

K'enemy, who had no hearth to call his own, though he was cousin to Staunch and sometimes ate with him.

Bison, his mother Little Mouse, and his brother of 8 summers, Owl (Flies Silently).

This was the tally of the newly formed People. These were the ones who walked northward with hope for the future, though they feared they were few in number to survive the storms of winter. So as they walked, Trapper sang prayers to the Great Spirits that they might easily find their long-separated cousins, might make safe passage to some new central hearth.

⋆   ⋆   ⋆

As they began the journey, they spread out in a pattern so useful, they kept to it again and again. Two of the hunters would move to the front, spears ready if danger presented itself around the next bend. Another brought up the rear in case trouble came nipping at their heels. The remaining men and boys dispersed themselves throughout the line of the People, watching in case someone needed their extra strength.

The men shouldered lighter loads, as they needed to be ready to respond. All they carried was a spear, a knife tucked into their waist-thongs, a water-skin slung over a shoulder and a light pack, perhaps a sack of dried food wrapped in the sleeping fur hanging down their backs.

Women carried the heaviest loads. It did not please them to bear burdens better suited to the strength of men, but they were accustomed to it. They carried the youngest children, and sometimes the older ones too when they tired. They carried the bulk of the food stores, clothing and bowls, along with any furs their children might need for warmth or comfort, day or night.

They also carried tools tucked into their waist thongs: Knife, digging stick, and a sack for food or medicinal herbs they could forage along the way. And who would carry the hide shelters, if not them? If the men were asked, they would suggest sleeping under the stars; it is pleasant enough weather tonight, what do we need shelters for? Even if the night was late in the autumn, with the smell of snow in the air.

Older children carried their own furs, plus food and water for the day. An almost-grown child Birdy's age might carry a store of food or tools and some additional furs and skins. Fire Bear hauled a load too, for he was not expected to respond to danger with a full man's strength. Though if a wolf leaped out at Birdy or Oopsy, he carried a spear and knife, and would defend them to the death.

Walking, sometimes racing ahead, were an assortment of dogs that followed as they left the meadow. The older dogs stayed behind, along with those who recognized a friendly hand among the ones going South. Since Rein led the first group to leave, the dogs that followed were the more excitable ones, bristling with energy, eager to race ahead.

Among the Ogwehu, River was the only one who cultivated their company. With no hunter to provide, her food stores were never lavish. But she shared what she had: A tidbit for a hungry puppy, a fat morsel for any animal that made her laugh. She surprised everyone when she went so far as to give them names. "Come here, Stripes," she would say to her favorite, named for the bands of white fur on her legs. Stripes seemed to understand River, and so did her son called Guard.

On this day neither Stripes nor Guard ran ahead with the pack, nor darted off chasing small animals. They were weighed down by the bundles River tied on their backs. Although Stripes bent backwards nipping at her load, and Guard lay on the ground trying to wriggle it off, they were soon resigned, even proud, to carry their share.

"See the doggies." Oopsy pointed out to Birdy. "They have humps!" He was not the only one commenting. The men paid no notice; it was women's business and so no matter at all. But the women gawked, for who had ever heard of such a thing. Falling Leaf whispered furiously to Cookie. It had never been done before; would it make some spirit angry and bring wrath down on all of them? Did River want that dog stink all over the food? Was she carrying her share, or were the animals doing it all for her?

"What's the difference to you," Cookie defended her husband's sister. "A woman has to do whatever it takes. As long as no one gets hurt, who cares how she gets it done?"

"It just doesn't seem right," the older woman grumbled.

River couldn't worry what others might think. Her load was heavy even with the help of the dogs. Characteristically she carried it without complaint, and whenever they stopped to rest, she spent the break making sure everyone else's burdens were well balanced. Great Uncle, whose back was bent awfully close to the ground. Oopsy, who was carrying as much as River thought she could load him with. Birdy, though she could look after herself well enough; even Stripes and Guard.

They climbed higher, following the path around the mountain. The sky was clear and the sun pleasantly warmed their faces. Hawks soared overhead, drifting lazily before swooping down for their morning meal. The travelers could look back and see the sun shine on the blue-grey ocean behind them. Looking forward they saw a long vista ahead. Mountains wove together until they faded into the horizon: A wide river valley pointing northeast between two braided chains.

That was their general direction, word filtered down the line. They would follow the valley between the mountains seeking signs of their cousins. If they came across their cousins soon, all would rejoice, though they were probably north of this fingerland jutting into the sea, on the mainland with its wide swaths of grazing areas. If they had to, they would find a safe place to winter and continue in the spring. And if they met any other Peoples they would ask about their kin.

⋆ ⋆ ⋆

Oopsy lagged behind. He did all right at first, carrying his bag of dayfood and two small skins of water draped around his shoulders.

The fussing started later that morning. I'm tired. I'm hot. I'm thirsty, Birdy can you help me take a drink? This is too heavy, Cousin Bear, would you carry it for me? Can I have a ride now, pleeeeease?

With the first round of complaints Birdy looked at Bear. Bear rolled his eyes, and between them they agreed on one thing. They would ignore all of Oopsy's complaints or they'd end up carrying him most of the way, him and his water, him and his whining mouth.

Not only were they annoying; his complaints went against everything they were taught. Not complaining was a way of life. If you didn't like something, you changed it or you learned to endure. It was the manner of the People to ignore the discomforts no one could do anything about. Better to become stoic about the continual stream of small irritations.

This morning ignoring him worked for a while. As long as she walked with Bear, the two of them held fast. When Bear left to talk to his sisters, it was harder for Birdy to maintain her resolve. After another major bout of whining she finally gave in. He was so young, she told herself. He never had to walk this far before. She might be just as tired, but her legs carried her farther than his short ones did. Finally she let him climb on her back.

But her load was already heavy and she had little strength to spare. With his extra weight on her, it took a while to regain a steady pace. She had to slow; every step was an effort. Others passed her, and it was harder if they had to maneuver around.

She kept telling herself, just a bit farther to give him a break. She carried him until he grew so heavy she thought her back would forever hover near the ground. Surely he had enough rest by then. And if he hadn't, too bad. "Offsy, Oopsy," she finally said, forcing him to slide onto the ground. There he lay in a tangled heap, and made no movement to rise.

"Carry me some more, Birdy," he complained in a tone that would have been piteous if it weren't so obviously fake.

"No, Oopsy," she called over her shoulder. "Walk, or you'll get eaten by the bears."

"Come on, little guy," Bear said, coming up from behind. He smacked him lightly on the shoulder as he passed. As did the next person, Lynx, and then Little Mouse. Behind Little Mouse was K'enemy, who spat carelessly as he passed, not noticing that some of it hit Oopsy on the cheek. Wailing with indignation, the child lurched upright and scurried frantically to catch up.

"Carry me, Bear!" he demanded.

"Not me, I have my own burden, Oopsy Doops. Carry your own self."

"My feet hurt," he fussed.

Birdy didn't want to carry him, but she was ready to do anything to put an end to the whining. Making deals was sometimes the only way to keep the children content when she took care of them back at the cave. "Come on, Oopsy," she suggested. "You keep walking and I'll tell you a story, all right?"

His face brightened, and she congratulated herself. She could easily walk and talk at the same time. But which tale to tell? So many swirled through her head. Birdy preferred the stateliness of the ancient tribal tales, but those stories were simply not tellable. Not by her, a girl, and maybe not by anyone ever again. If the shaman was the only one allowed, then they apparently were lost for good.

But there were plenty of family stories to fall back on. It didn't matter who told those, nobody cared about them. With Oopsy trustingly holding her hand, she described a time that Great Uncle came back to one of his traps and, surprise! found not one but two animals caught in it. A mink and a sable, both coveted for their fur, though their rank-tasting meat was usually thrown to the dogs. Both animals had gone after the bait at the same time. In the fight to win the morsel, each got wedged in a trap made for only one.

Birdy described in great detail how they bit and scratched inside the tight space. When Great Uncle came to check on his catch, only one was still alive. And in the last moment as he opened the trap, the mink stuck his claw into the eye of the dead sable, a final surge of triumph before his own impending death.

"That's a good one," Bear complimented her as she concluded the story. "I know someone like that who feels they have to stick something in somebody else's eye, even after they're dead."

Birdy gave him a sour look. They both knew someone like that, but that person was now gone, and if Bear kept talking about her, he'd be sticking something in someone's dead eye too. "Shut up, you," she said, and he poked his tongue out at Birdy, but he did not say another word.

"More, Birdy, tell more," Oopsy pleaded.

So she started a story about Thunder. "Saves His Cousin," Bear reminded her. This time he gave her the pointed look.

"Saves His Cousin," she agreed blandly, going on to describe her brother's first hunt. Not his manhood hunt; he never had one. But the first time he was allowed to go with the hunters, to the high pastures of the curly horned sheep. As the story progressed, Birdy made her brother sound just a bit more heroic than he had been in life. It was he who spotted their target as she told the tale, thrilling the awestruck child. It was he who drew the first blood. And what did it matter if the truth got stretched, she asked herself? Oopsy needed someone to look up to, and there were few men left to admire.

Naturally he demanded another story. Birdy thought of sharing something about Mami, but she couldn't bring herself to do that. Not yet. Every time she thought about her mother, her stomach seized up and she was afraid she would have to stop in her tracks.

Finally she began talking about the games he and his sister used to play with Pout's little antler-carved doll. Oopsy listened for a while, his head cocked slightly, his face serious.

As the story came to an end, he interrupted his sister. "Why we leave Pout in the cave, Birdy? Why we don't bring her with us? She would like seeing the dogs like that." He pointed at River's companions, still nobly carrying their loads. Birdy did not answer right away. So Oopsy persisted, "She would too like it!"

Birdy looked at Bear, who raised an eyebrow but said nothing.

She did not know how to answer. She'd already explained about going to the ancestors and not being with the People anymore, but he didn't seem to understand. She could tell him to ask River or Uncle Rein. She could explain again about death, but why would he understand more this time? He was so young.

So instead she began another story, this one about a brave hunter much beloved by the People. And this particular hunter, guess what his name was? Why, he was called Oopsy!

"Like me!" the boy shouted.

"Like you," she agreed. And in the story the mighty hunter slew a ferocious sea lion and the whole clan feasted. The girl liberally borrowed details from the recent slaughter in the meadow. Only instead of a group of hunters, it was Oopsy whose bravery and skill brought down the creature.

Oopsy loved the story so much that he asked to hear it again. For the rest of the day he was content to walk next to his sister, occasionally asking about the mighty beast. How long his whiskers were. How big he was when he reared up. She made every particular aspect more enormous, just to keep the story exciting.

From time to time she heard him whisper under his breath, repeating phrases from the saga that he kept retelling. "Whoosh, the spear went in," he said, and something about the red blood drops flying, a phrase that he mangled creatively several times.

But there was one phrase that he got right, each and every word: "Then the mommies all said, 'Oopsy, you're so brave!'"

Chapter 2: Tide washed up

They made camp that night on a rise overlooking the river, close enough to draw water for cooking, high enough for safety if a sudden storm made the waters flood the banks.

The men caught a mess of salmon to spit-roast over the fire. The women were setting out sleeping furs. Children were tossing stones in the water to see who could make the biggest splash.

Suddenly the dogs alerted, and several of them rushed, yipping, back to the path they walked only a short time before. Guard posted himself in front of River where he stood alert, teeth bared and snarling.

"Someone's coming. I hear the footfalls," Bison warned. The crowd began murmuring. Was a bear following them? Maybe the southward group changed their minds and came to join? Bison grabbed his spear in case the newcomers were unfriendly. Bear leaped up, with Two Stones right behind.

Tension rose as they listened to the footfalls, and then the familiar greeting cry, "I come in peace!"

Bear was already grinning at a voice they thought they'd never hear again. "Hey, you rat-eaten piece of carrion!" he shouted. "We thought you were a buzzard's feast by now!" Gleeful, he ran forward to greet the bedraggled form emerging from the forest. A familiar face, though at first it was hard to tell whose, it was so discolored and bruised. Ah, it was Antler, the shaman's apprentice; they thought he was lost in the great sweep of the seas.

The boy carried a load across his shoulders which he now let drop. Bison stepped back to let everyone greet him. People were excited; nobody expected to see any of those familiar faces again. But was he really alive?

No one they knew had ever returned from the dead before. Some stepped forward, pinching his hands and arms to make sure he was flesh and blood and not some haunting spirit. Where they pinched, he flinched; that was a good sign. He seemed to be alive, but a few hung back just in case.

The questions went flying through the air like gnats to a fresh carcass. Where had he been all this time? Did he find their cousins in the meadow? Were any others with him?

There were too many questions to answer all at once. Ignoring them, Bear grabbed his friend's shoulders, and Antler grabbed him. They fell into a complicated ritual of fist on top of fist, first one way, then the other, followed by hand slapping hand in the air, then positioning themselves sideways, bumping hip to hip, hard enough that they both fell on the ground laughing with pleasure.

Owl came swooping in to repeat the ritual, and Antler allowed it though the boy was much younger and normally had little to do with him. Turtle, a few years older, got pulled into the exuberance. Others came up, starting with Falling Leaf who was a sister to his grandmother. She rubbed his shoulders affectionately before getting pushed aside by the crowd. Birdy gave him an enthusiastic hug which the boy accepted, though afterwards he cast a puzzled look in her direction. The rest took turns hugging or pounding him on the shoulder, each according to their preference.

His great aunt swept back, insisting he eat; they all should eat before pestering him for details. Of course this did not slow the questions, but Antler swallowed a few morsels offered with great ceremony before succumbing to their curiosity.

Yes, he got caught by the huge tide, which he hardly remembered. The last thing he knew was the roaring of water coming his way. He didn't know what happened to the other apprentices; they must have been carried Beyond. He himself was washed up on a beach somewhere south of their old homeland. Somehow he'd been bashed on the head and was delirious for days.

He thought he was dead. He was sure he was dead, but it turned out he wasn't. Though he had a taste of death, and the taste, it seemed, was like fish. No thanks, he didn't want any more of that trout to eat, he had had enough of fish for now. Maybe some of those roasted lily roots, they looked tasty.

The tide threw him up under a load of seaweed and rotting sea creatures. At least they gave him cover although it stank something fierce, not as much the first day or so when he was barely conscious, but more by the third day out. Still he couldn't complain, since the stench got him moving faster than he might have otherwise done.

"I'll bet," Rein chuckled. "A blanket of rotting fish would get me moving pretty quick."

"We should call him Sleeps with Fish," Staunch called out.

"Seaweed Hair," suggested Bison.

"Tide Washed Up," Two Stones said.

"Crab for Pants," Turtle snickered, using the word for loincloth.

"Enough already," Rein said. "Let's give the boy a chance to tell his story."

Unfortunately he recognized nothing around him. By then he was thinking clearly, though. There had to be other survivors, he just had to find them. And to find them he should move because no one was there answering his cries.

So he began walking south along the beach. He had to pick some direction; too bad he picked the wrong one. It was another day before he decided to turn around. He retraced his steps and kept going until he came upon a familiar place, though he hardly recognized it since everything looked different. How was it different? New boulders washed down the mountain. Wreckage was scattered everywhere, along with broken trees and brush upended by the tide.

No one was there, of course, but he found his family up in the meadow. Yes, they were thrilled to see him, and he, them. But when he heard how the tribe split up, he decided to join the north-choosing group. His mother tried to hold him back. How could he leave her again? Was he strong enough to travel? But he already felt better; the days of walking were days of healing. And the longer he waited, the harder it would be to catch up with them. "So, will you have me?" he said shyly.

A problem indeed. Usually a man-child Antler's age stayed with his mother's family until he was ready to fend for himself. Antler, however, had been living with the shaman for months by now. He already moved away once to make himself a new life.

"Why choose us instead of your mother's family?" Falling Leaf asked.

"I can't tell you why, Auntie." Shy, he looked down for a moment at his feet, then squinted up at the sky. "I just know this is where I need to go."

Rein looked at Staunch, who nodded acceptance. He glanced toward Two Stones, who shrugged and grinned. "We can use an extra fellow," Rein considered, turning back to Staunch. "He's one of your cousins, right?" Without waiting for an answer, he announced, "He'll live in Staunch's shelter."

"The home for lost children and unmatched leggings," Falling Leaf muttered. Already in the shelter with her and her widowed son were his motherless baby and his daughter Willow. In bad weather K'enemy joined them, who had no other family on the northward path. And now this nephew, brought by whatever odd wind blew them northward.

Some might cry. Others would rejoice. It was Falling Leaf's way to make comments that made people wince. But they knew her well enough to ignore her complaints. She would make the best of it and by the next day would be treating him as if he was her own. Still it was she who bore the burden of caring for him. It was thoughtless of Rein to presume his solution would be haodisah.

That evening someone called for singing and dancing, as they had much to celebrate. They were alive. They had made a new beginning. And another son returned to them from the Great Unknown.

Though it seemed that no drums had been brought to send their thanks Skyward. They'd pared down their belongings, and anything not essential was left back at the meadow. Every possession added to the weight they carried on their backs. Thus each had packed only the necessities. Apparently no one thought an instrument important enough to bring. A drum would not feed them for the winter; it wouldn't warm their bones, defend them, cook or mend their clothing. As they struggled with their packs that first morning, muscles shrieking with complaints, people kept stopping to set something else aside—a spare robe, yet another pot. A lighter load seemed worth the trouble of making one later, anew.

Yet if music-making was not essential, it would certainly add to the celebration. Turtle broke off two overhanging branches, stripped them of leaves and began clapping them together. Bison took a wooden spoon and beat an upturned bowl in time to the singing. People suggested favorite songs or chants that were sung with vigor or charm, and many rose to dance.

They danced with strong thumping steps and movements aimed at the Great Mother Spirit in the earth below. Alternating these with joyous dances whose graceful gestures aimed at the ancestors and the Father Spirit above. The music went on for hours. Rhythm and song had a way of wrapping people in a comforting blanket, protecting them for a while from their sadness and fear. As this person's beat mingled with that person's voice, as the dances followed the cadence, the people around the campfire began to feel they were bound together, a braiding of many tendrils into a chain stronger than any one of them could otherwise be.

It was the first time they let themselves laugh since the Day of So Much Dying. The sound of laughter felt like the beginning of a new season. Not yet the full flowering of the spring, but the first tiny buds, the palest poking of fresh shoots out of rocky soil. There was a sense of giddiness bubbling up around them. Some laughed louder than they should. Some of the playful shoving was just a bit too hard. That the playfulness was there at all, that was the miracle. The miracle of new life sprung from the seeds of the old.

Still the wintry mood did not entirely disappear. Though the dances and songs were heartfelt and joyous, the evening was threaded with ribbons of sadness. Often during the celebration someone left the circle and a muffled sobbing began. For in spite of their high spirits at the beauty of this river land, in spite of their relief at this first day's safe passage, they remembered too many who would never again dance with them under these bright and star-studded skies.

$$\star \qquad \star \qquad \star$$

Morning. They were packing up the campsite. Sleeping furs were rolled up, campfire coals buried under the ashes. People called to each other.

"Did you remember to pack the tinder?"

"Fill up your water skins; we might not find a stream along the trail."

Every time they started to leave, someone would call, "Stop!" and run to do one more thing.

Rein was about to signal them onward when Antler hurried over. "Wait! Don't we need to thank the Spirit of this place?" the boy asked.

Oh. Yes, yes of course.

River reached into her pouch and offered a handful of grass seed.

Thus began Antler's first public ceremony. A child would not normally be considered mature enough to officiate, but no one opened their mouth to complain. He took a deep breath, filling his skinny chest, and tentatively pronounced the words. "Thank you, Spirit of this beautiful resting place, for offering shelter here, where we were safe and well-fed." Blushing at the attention, he scattered the seed, and then they set out for the day's trek.

$$\star \qquad \star \qquad \star$$

The three of them walked together, Bear and Antler on either side of Birdy. "I dreamed that you came back to us," Fire Bear was telling Antler.

"When, last night? I was already with you by then!"

"No, you dolt," Bear laughed. "Maybe three nights ago."

Antler beamed back. "You dreamed me, and here I am."

"Yeah, I get all the credit for raising you from the dead. So you owe me lots and lots."

Antler snorted at this bit of foolishness.

Bear turned to Birdy. "Actually he came all this way so he could return the knife he borrowed last spring and kept forgetting to return."

"That worn-out piece of junk?" Antler was incredulous. "You should thank me it's at the bottom of the sea by now."

"You lost it? I made that knife with my own hands!"

"Yeah, when you were three years old."

"Which explains why it was a better knife than you ever made. In your whole life."

"Which makes it a better joke than you ever made. In your whole life."

"Guys, stop it!' Birdy protested. "You're friends. You don't need to poke at each other."

"Who's poking?" Bear asked. "We're just having a little fun."

"That's what boys do," Antler reassured her.

"Well." Birdy did not know what to say. It wasn't what girls did, but what did she know about boys? So she changed the subject; it was better than listening to them argue. "That was nice," she complimented Antler. "The little ceremony you did with the grass seed. Do you know all the prayers?"

He shook his head modestly. "I know but one grain of sand on the beach."

The saying was from one of their stories, a well-used reference, for the People valued humility almost as much as an uncomplaining attitude, courage, or strength.

"Somebody ought to know the prayers," Bear fretted. "Someone has to lead us. And it sure won't be my father!" The three of them laughed; Rein was notoriously forgetful when it came time for praying.

"It wouldn't be my uncle," Antler responded. No one could argue that either; Staunch was a good man in any hunt but he was more likely to joke than help people find comfort. Really, there was no one else suitable. Two Stones was more serious, but he was not one to step in and lead. Bison was a strong leader in the hunt but he was as eloquent as a seven summers' child. K'enemy spoke little, and Great Uncle was too frail for the outdoor ceremonies when it got cold.

"I could do the everyday prayers," Antler worried. "But I haven't been through a complete cycle of seasons, so there's much I never learned."

Bear asked the question beginning to form in the minds of every member of the tribe. "Do you think you can be our shaman?"

It wasn't just a matter of leading them to pray. The responsibilities went deeper. At this time of regrouping when so much of what they knew and were had been washed away, they were struggling to regain what leadership they could. They needed to make use of guidance in any form they found it. Even if it came with so little experience that it hardly counted. The clan was like the starving man who caught a fish the size of his toe. It was so small he'd normally throw it back, but in desperate times he had to eat it for whatever sustenance it could provide.

Birdy could see the worry in Antler's eyes. "It's what I was training for," he confessed. "It's what I always wanted to do. But I thought there would be more time before I stepped in. It's a big responsibility, being the Cushion between the People and the Spirits."

"If not you, then who?"

Cookie, walking behind, was quick to offer her opinion. "You'll have to do it, boy. No one else is going to take it on. Better to have someone doing part of it than nobody at all."

"I'm not sure I can do it, Auntie," Antler said in a sudden panic. "I don't have the shaman's sacred robe. There's no drum, no incense leaves or the special bark for the ceremonies. I don't think I know enough. I might say the wrong things. I'll do a bad job, and we'll all be punished for my mistakes."

"Nonsense," she reassured him. "You think Father Sky cares if you change the words around a bit? Surely He has bigger things on His mind than that."

She placed a comforting hand on his shoulder. "Of course I'm just a woman, so what would I know about Father Sky and his thinking," she hedged. "But I suspect He cares that we try to do our best. And that we are good to each other and to the world He created. That's probably all He wants from us—that we try to keep haodisah. Just do your best; nobody can ask any more of you."

Antler still looked uncertain.

"We're all trying to do our best," she added. "You think I'm fit for trekking all day long?" She opened her arms wide, displaying her stout body. "Well, I'm not. But I'm here, aren't I? Not giving up, just doing the best I can. You do the same." She reached out to squeeze his hand. "I was watching you with that prayer this morning. You have the right spirit for it. I think you'll do fine."

"You could talk to Great Uncle Trapper," Birdy added earnestly. "He used to be an apprentice a long time ago. Didn't work out, but he might remember some things. You didn't get to see it, but he led the burial ceremony before we left the meadow. Maybe he can help you practice the prayers or something."

"Do your best, and you'll do fine," Cookie said firmly. "You will; you'll see." She patted him on the back and, though he cast a doubtful look in her direction, his shoulders straightened and he began walking just a bit taller down the forward path.

*   *   *

That night around the campfire Rein told stories about his year with the Reindeer People. He described some of the cousins, how they tracked the reindeer when they got too far ahead, and lived through winters colder than they were used to on the fingerland. They could always feed themselves off the herd. No children had to suffer an empty belly while their fathers went searching for meat. "It's so easy," he said, getting enthused. "Whenever you need food, you just go out and harvest one." Harvest—the same word was used for gathering easy pickings like berries.

Staunch was skeptical. "Don't the animals fight back?"

"Of course they do. If you go out and grab a healthy male with a big rack of antlers, he'll argue with you here and here." He pointed to various vulnerable spots on his body. "You find one that's got gray in its fur and moves slowly. Sneak up behind it, staying downwind so it doesn't smell you and get skittish. Or a pregnant and clumsy one, lots of meat on that. Plus you get the tender fetus. Tasty and delicious." He smacked his lips. "Honest, boys, it's easy. Hardly any stalking needed."

Two Stones, who had taken part in mammoth hunts and bore the scars to prove it, asked, "It's not like taking a bison or a mammoth from the edge of their herds, eh?"

"Much easier. We hardly ever got gored. And you know how warm reindeer fur is, especially if you get them just before the snows when their fur is so thick."

"I guess we'll be following them everywhere once we join our cousins." Staunch rose and stretched, carelessly letting a fart escape. "Up and down mountains, across rivers. Every day we'll get to walk over their droppings. We'll be living on *top* of their droppings. You did it before, Rein, what's it like to live on top of reindeer droppings?"

"Better than living on top of your droppings," Bison interrupted, waving away at the smell.

"Better than living on top of your mother's droppings," Staunch shot back.

The women looked at each other and rolled their eyes. Little Mouse blushed.

Birdy, sitting next to Bear, whispered, "I don't understand. Why do guys always do that?"

"It's fun," he answered.

"That's fun?" she asked, incredulous. "It's like they're stabbing each other with their words."

"Yah, but they're stabbing each other with tiny little thorns. Everybody gets to show off that they don't mind; they're strong enough to shrug it off. Nobody gets hurt."

"Who wants to get stabbed at all?" She shook her head. "Why not avoid the thorns? If I'm picking berries I try to avoid the thorns. I don't like getting my arms all torn up."

"I dunno, little cousin. Guys just like stuff like that. Better to prick each other and make tiny little wounds than bash each other over the head and do some real damage."

★   ★   ★

K'enemy walked ahead of her today. River couldn't help but admire the muscular expanse of his shoulders and back. Most of the women didn't think he was handsome. His features were too sharp, his nose high and jutting, with a hungry look that put many people off. But River understood the misery that look covered up. He had been outcast for a long time, and who would not yearn for a soft welcome when it was denied for so long? She watched her sister pull him in and push him away enough times to develop a streak of sympathy for the man, though she kept quiet about it forever, it seemed. She knew what it felt like; her sister treated her much the same.

She was so happy he decided to come north. Here in this smaller group he didn't stick out oddly as he did before. He's quite a good hunter she mused, not for the first time. She could easily imagine a child riding high on those broad shoulders, calling, "Papi, Papi," and pointing out some amazing sight—an eagle diving for fish, the moon in the daytime sky. Stripes and Guard liked him; they always approached wagging madly away. Her mamma would have approved too, she felt sure of it. She didn't like him mooning around her older sister, but that was different.

Dreamily River saw herself sewing for him. The poor man had but one shirt to his name, and that had to do throughout the cold months. He could use a lighter one, and a better winter wrap as well. The one he wore last year looked pretty ragged by the time spring came around.

Poor fellow, with no one taking care of him for so long. She imagined him coming to her in the soft campfire light. Looking into her eyes and saying, "No one has ever made anything this beautiful for me. No one has ever been this thoughtful." Taking her hand and ... *oops!* So caught up in her thoughts, she failed to notice that she was about to bump into him in real life. Too late, she stepped on his heel and stumbled.

Ahhh! He smelled nice, she noticed, even as she tripped. Like man-sweat and berries; it was a heady combination. He whirled around and grabbed her arm to keep her from collapsing. In the confusion she barely missed getting her eye poked by the long spear he carried.

"Watch your step," he warned her briefly.

A secret jolt went through from the mere touch of his hand on her arm. It was so unexpected that it took her a moment to say what she should have said immediately. "I am so sorry, K'enemy."

He nodded briefly, and turned back to his usual silence.

She spent the remainder of the afternoon replaying that tiny bit of conversation. Trying to guess, was he annoyed? Or was he actually encouraging her?

With so few words it was impossible to tell.

Chapter 3: Rites of passage

Now that they reached the land between the mountains they would camp for a few days at the hunting shelter by the lake. Traveling took a toll on the food supplies and here they could build them up again. They would rest their feet, mend any tears in the footwear, wash the sweat away in the lake. And if the mosquitoes got too vigorous they would coat themselves with mud from the lake bottom to keep the pests from feasting off them.

The hunters ignored the beauty of the wide open vistas and snow-capped mountains, having seen it before, but the women stared, open-mouthed, all around. Reeds fringed the water, and ducks swam on its surface, folding their long necks underwater to fish. Reflections of the clouds and sky mirrored the surface with a vast blue beauty.

Overall, a good site for a rest. Bears frequented the area, but if they avoided them, all would be well. They would be busy even without having to defend themselves. The men needed time to sharpen their weapons and practice with stones and throwing sticks. The women planned to harvest grass seed and reeds. Turtle asked to have his manhood hunt. And Right began her first woman's bloodflow, so she needed a ceremony too.

Setting up camp went faster when they worked in teams. One woman held the poles in place and another stretched the hides over them. Fierce usually worked together with Little Mouse. River and Birdy partnered up, as did Cookie and Falling Leaf. The twins wandered around helping anyone who needed them.

Antler and Bear were gathering broken branches and tinder for the campfire. Oopsy, Lynx, and Owl waded through the reeds pretending to hunt. Little Mother followed, carrying Poor Thing on her shoulder, shielding her face from the stalks as they swung back in the wake of the young explorers ahead.

Once the fire was going, River began making porridge and chopping chunks of meat for the pot. Gathering pine needles for tea, she set them to steep and retrieved their bowls. She filled one for Great Uncle, sitting on the ground beside Birdy, another for Birdy, then one for herself. She began filling Oopsy's bowl as well, then looked around and saw he was not there. Just beyond, however, was another hungry face. K'enemy sat nearby, desultorily watching Turtle aim his throwing stick.

The first challenge of the manhood hunt was to bring back an animal entirely without help. By the time a boy was ready for his initiation, he'd already brought home many a rabbit, squirrel or fox. Because they'd done it so many times, this was the easy part of the test. Some hunters-to-be valued it so little that they simply took a sharpened stick, found a rodent hole in the ground, stuck the stick inside and skewered their victim, an animal large enough to feed a toddler, perhaps, though it would do little for an entire family.

Turtle treated this small test with more dignity. He stood just outside a copse of trees observing the movements of birds and other creatures. He quietly picked up his throwing stick, a piece of branch the length of his arm which he'd shaved smooth of bark. He had tapered the edges with careful shavings from his sharpest blade, which seemed somehow to help it fly further through the air.

Quietly he stood in the shadows blending into the forest. His target scampered from bough to bough. Focusing intently on his prey, the boy slowly took position. Letting his movement flow gradually, he was careful to make sure no twigs cracked underfoot to warn the creatures. Right foot angled back, arm behind his shoulder, he held the stick by the small end. Rapidly he flung it, snapping his wrist. The stick went winging with great force at his target.

It would have worked, for it hit the branch in the exact spot where the squirrel had been. However the squirrel was no longer there, having heard the rush of wind as the weapon came its way. The critter leaped just in time to the next branch, and Turtle's stick went clattering on the ground.

He should have waited for a small breeze to cover the sound. The young hunter looked around. Only K'enemy was watching, and Trapper, further away. K'enemy shrugged. Turtle waved an acknowledgment. So it would take a bit longer, he wasn't worried. He picked up his stick and headed deeper into the woods.

"No need to waste this good, hot food," River said out loud. She walked towards K'enemy holding the steaming bowl of porridge, signaling an invitation. A surprised look flitted across his face, but he followed her. They walked towards the fire, River's face pinker than usual, K'enemy silent as was his habit.

"That's Oopsy's portion," Birdy protested, pointing to the food in K'enemy's hand.

"There's plenty," her aunt responded.

"Oopsy won't like it that someone used his bowl."

River ignored the complaint. As well she should, Birdy thought morosely. Oopsy didn't need to know. And even if he found out, what did it matter? Hospitality was more important; being kind to the guests of your hearth. Though this wasn't their hearth, it was everyone's hearth. If it were anyone but K'enemy. Something about him made her uneasy. She hated sharing food with him, of all people.

She glared at him as he sat down. What was that around his neck? An amulet, it looked like, in a crudely sewn pouch that she never saw before. Funny, he didn't have an amulet the day she saw him stalking away from the cave; she could picture his bare chest in the sunlight. She peered closer, rising on her toes to see inside. It was white, whatever it was. An ivory carving of some kind. She could see only the little bit visible at the neck of the pouch.

It looked like the nickings men used for a fish's tail. Mami's amulet had the same shape, a little white fish carved for her by one of her admirers. Actually, Birdy thought, the charm had exactly the same shape, at least the part she could see. There, that extra nick at the top of the tail. Mami wore hers around her neck, but she took it off sometimes. Baby Pout chewed on it one day, and left that bite in the tail. Birdy remembered because Mami slapped her for letting Pout get at it.

"Could I see your amulet," Birdy asked, suddenly suspicious.

A muscle twitched at the corner of his mouth. Instinctively K'enemy reached up to block her view with his hand. He shook his head briefly, his expression unreadable. It was his right, of course, to keep it private. People often kept their personal objects hidden. They lost their special qualities if they were exposed carelessly.

Glancing over, River remarked, "That's nice, K'enemy. I've never seen that before." She hesitated. "It looks a little like the one my sister used to wear."

"It looks *exactly* like Mami's amulet," Birdy wondered.

Why wouldn't he let her take a look? Was he protecting it, or hiding something? When a hunter killed an animal, he sometimes kept a memento—a claw, a tooth, a stone from its belly. In ancient times, a man who fought another to become chief would take the amulet of the defeated for his own.

K'enemy disappeared back into the cave that day, arguing with Mami. And then was caught in the cave-in with her. They were fighting just before; she heard them. It wasn't just some little argument; it sounded worse than that. What happened to Mami's charm? She was killed by the falling rocks, wasn't she?

Wasn't she?

Suddenly Birdy felt sick to her stomach. Sitting nearby, breathing in his animal smell—she could not stand it a moment longer.

She couldn't walk away. That would be rude. It would be taken as an insult, walking away just as he sat down with them. If she left now, she'd get a stern talking to from Great Uncle. Maybe he'd even make her apologize. Ugh. She had to sit quietly and eat her food. But she didn't have to look at him; didn't have to see those pointy teeth chomping or hear his burp of satisfaction. Why didn't River invite Bear to join them if they had extra food; he would have been much better company. Anyone would have been better than K'enemy.

She turned her shoulders, facing away. If anyone asked, she would say she was watching for Oopsy.

Though it didn't stop her from overhearing K'enemy smack his lips with pleasure. Didn't keep her from noticing River smile, her head bent modestly low. She heard his thanks when he scraped the bowl clean, the slight gasp River made as she took the bowl and her fingers grazed his.

K'enemy strode off looking slightly dazed. The moment he was out of earshot Birdy leapt upon her aunt.

"Don't you do it, don't you dare do it!" she burst out.

"Do what, Birdy?"

"Don't you start ... liking him."

"I like everybody," River said. Her tone was innocent. A shade too innocent.

"Don't start *liking* him. You know, *liking* him."

"I don't know what you mean." River didn't look back. She was busy wrapping up the leftovers, gathering bowls and spoons to put away.

"Not him, River, please! You don't know him, I think he might be a ..." Birdy stopped. She did not know how to finish the thought.

"No, you don't know him, Birdy." River was firm. "Anyway, it's not any of your business." She walked away, leaving Birdy shaken and afraid.

⋆   ⋆   ⋆

In the freshness of the morning Willow and Birdy went to the lake to dig up a supply of reeds. They couldn't help but notice how amazing this place was. Amazing enough to make Birdy forget her worries. This huge expanse of fresh water, so blue; the snowy mountains, the fleecy clouds drifting overhead.

So still it was, and calm. With only an occasional ripple here and there: A fish breeching for a moment, an insect landing on the surface with its tiny, sprawling legs, a gull swooping down to capture a flipping mouthful of fish. A duck landing on the surface of the lake, belly-side down, wings still spread, feet shoved out before it. Wondrous, that's what it was. How lucky she felt to be alive. To enjoy having food in her belly and the sun on her face.

Off to their right they heard Oopsy and Lynx playing. Little Mother watched over them. In the distance two bear cubs played comically with each other. Willow pointed them out to Birdy and the girls shared a laugh.

"What are you two going on about?" One of the twins approached, her gathering bowl dangling from one hand.

"Here comes Left," Willow said quietly to Birdy. "She looks lost without her sister, doesn't she?"

"The right leg's going somewhere and the left's not ready," Birdy said lightly.

Willow smiled. "You got that right. Isn't that from one of Falcon's stories? You have such a good memory!"

Huh, Birdy thought; her friend gave her too much credit. It was just what everyone was saying back at camp. But she didn't mind a kind word. She did have a good memory. Learning all the stories, she never could have done it otherwise. Too bad she'd never get to show her just how good it was.

Left knelt in the reeds next to Willow.

"Where's Right?" Willow asked politely.

"Just somewhere," the girl mumbled.

"Where?"

Heavy sigh. "Getting her hair washed for the ceremony tonight. They're *entirely* fussing too much over her. It's so stupid. Just a boring old ceremony."

"Boring? You must be joking. It's her first woman's blood," Birdy pointed out. "They're tattooing her tonight, and there'll be stories around the fire circle. Actually I don't know if anyone will be telling the stories, Falcon would have done it but I don't know if Antler can. Anyway," she concluded, "there's nothing boring about it. There'll be lots of blood and excitement. And Turtle is becoming a man, that won't be boring either."

"What do you know? You're *much* too young to understand." Turning to Willow, she confided, "Isn't she *completely* too young?"

"I don't think so," Willow defended her new friend. "I like Birdy. I don't mind her being younger than me; she's smart and fun to be around."

"Well, she's *entirely* too young for me," Left sniffed. She stood, tossed her hair, and turned to stomp away.

Willow and Birdy looked at each other. Willow rolled her eyes. "*Entirely,*" Birdy agreed, and the two began to laugh.

⋆   ⋆   ⋆

Word spread round the camp, the men were returning with something big.

Turtle brought home a nice-sized partridge for his smaller test yesterday. This morning he led the hunters away before sunrise, and now they were coming back from the far side of the lake with a mature elk, already quartered. Each of the men carried a haunch or some other trophy back to camp. There would be a feast tonight and plenty left for later.

The women reached for their butchery blades, their scrapers and carrying bowls. But River's family had no hunter in the group, so there was no reason for her to join them. No hunter, so no share of the meat unless someone offered a gift out of kindness. That was hao, she sighed; that was the balance of things. They would eat fish today, unless Uncle caught a rabbit or something with his traps. It could be worse. At least they wouldn't go hungry.

Instead she bent over Trapper removing the splints on his fingers. He needed more movement than they allowed. Were they healed enough to stay loose? Would she have to splint them again after the ceremony? He flexed each finger, testing for stiffness. "Seems good," he reported. "It's about time. Those sticks keep getting in the way."

"I don't know," she brooded. "I think you should keep them protected. Do you need your fingers tonight?" Great Uncle and Antler would perform the

ceremonies together. Even if his hand was healed, Antler could do most of
the work.

"My young blood with his greater wisdom," Great Uncle teased Antler
yesterday.

"His great endurance with my enormous experience," Antler shot back.
There was a surge of laughter, but everyone agreed the combination was
fortunate. Or so they hoped.

River was glad to see him in good spirits. This new purpose perked him
up enormously. For years Great Uncle drifted at the edge of their family. Now
he was important again in his own right. She took a moment to brood on this.
It was not the only good thing to come out of all that tragedy.

She looked around to see Falling Leaf approach. The elder hadn't started
butchering her family's share of the meat, or there'd be more blood on her
hands. Instead she impatiently pushed her long white hair off her face. "I
should ask somebody to slice all this mess off with a hatchet," she muttered.

"I'll braid it for you," River offered.

"It's no matter," the woman answered. "That's not what I'm here for. My
son asked me to invite your family to share our portion from the hunt. And
you can have what's left after tonight. We have plenty of food stored already.
My son has been lucky," she concluded modestly.

"Your son is a skillful hunter," Great Uncle commented. "No need to be
humble."

"Oh, we do well enough," the woman admitted. "We do not go hungry in
our family. Though the children miss their mother." Their mother, who was
killed on the Day of Too Much Death. "Lots of people miss their families,"
she said, looking closely at River. "We have to pull together. Some people
need new wives. And some could use a husband."

Behind her, K'enemy was walking toward them. He too was carrying a
haunch, slung casually over his shoulder as if its weight was a mere twig on a
branch. He came closer before noticing Falling Leaf and her armload of meat.
Instead of greeting River, he blushed, turned on his heel and walked away.

"Wait," River called to him, but he didn't look back.

"What's that?" asked Falling Leaf. River could only shake her head. She
didn't know any more than Leaf.

"New families. Yes, Auntie, we need to make new families," she conceded,
accepting the invitation, for until new families were formed, her own would
need whatever food came their way.

★   ★   ★

"Daughter," Trapper began the ritual, and with that single word he donned the dignity of the shaman, representing Falcon and the earlier shamans back to the very beginning of the Ogwehu. "You who were a daughter of the Earth, you who were a child of the Sky, today you become a woman of the People." He rested one hand on her forehead, announcing formally, "This child becomes woman today."

He chanted the traditional prayers thanking Father Sky and Mother Earth for helping her reach past childhood to this day of great change. While he chanted, the women clapped their hands in a steady rhythm. The men were quietly intoning, "Heya, heya," with their own beat. And when Trapper brought the prayers to their conclusion, together they said, "Ho."

Now Antler set afire a bundle of savory leaves. Using the feather of an owl, he waved its sacred smoke around the girl. His hands circled the top of her head three times, then moved up and down all four sides of her body, sanctifying her from every direction. She had bathed beforehand and was anointed with fragrant oils; that was the cleansing of the body. This smoke cleansed her spirit to prepare for this bold change in life.

"Are you ready, Daughter?"

Right looked at Trapper. Today their family relationship was subsumed by this deep and ancient rite. She took a breath into her lungs. She squared her shoulders, looked at the sky, and then at her mother sitting with the women watching from a respectful distance. She did not glance at her sister at all.

"Yes, Great Father. I am ready."

Now for the ceremony of the tribal tattoo. Once in place, the tattoo would announce to any who saw it that she was one of the People. Cutting drained away the vestiges of childhood as the blood oozed out of the new-marked arm. As she endured the pain and began to heal, the ceremony marked the beginning of the life she would lead as a full-grown member of the clan.

Trapper chose a sharp blade. Antler took up a soft hide to wipe away the blood as he made the shamanic cuts. Right clamped her jaw to bite back the pain. She was determined not to embarrass her family or herself. She would not behave like a child fussing at every hurt that came her way.

Trapper made the first cut, an upward curving arc like the soaring eagle, wingtips aloft. The Father Sky line, the uppermost portion of the tattoo that each one proudly wore. Right blinked hard but did not cry; she bit down on her lips instead. Antler lifted a dipperful of water and let it flow down her arm. He washed the upwelling blood away, and blotted the skin around it.

Next Trapper cut the downward arc, the Mother Earth sign. Again Antler rinsed and blotted her arm so the shaman could see as he worked. Right bit her lips again, signaling her unflinching acceptance of the binding with the Spirits.

Now it was time for the hardest cut, for both the shaman and the girl. It took great skill to cut a neat circle in the flesh, and it was hard cutting into an area now tense and trembling with shock. Yet it made sense that the binding of a new adult to the circle of the People took longer and needed extra care. Surely it was a more complicated binding than the ties to Mother Earth who fed them each day, or Father Sky who brought the sun to shine and the rain to quench their thirst. The binding to the People was both the tightest and the weakest bond of all, the hardest to maintain without letting it strangle or fray.

Tears formed in Right's eyes, but she blinked them back. Antler daubed the wound and washed it with a pine resin wash. Pine resin—a gift of the sacred tree whose feet were in the earth but whose arms reached for sky. They used the pungent resin to wash most wounds. They'd found over time that a wound needed just this mixture of Earth and Sky spirits. Treated with the resin, a wound would heal in good time, and the flies would leave it alone; without this anointing, wounds would redden and grow angry. The anger might spread far enough to consume the entire body and carry it Beyond.

Now Antler took a bowl of resin and rinsed her arm with it. He did not bandage it with spider's silk as normal cuts might be, to stop the bleeding. Instead he left it open so the tribe could admire this symbol of her great change.

"Father Sky, I ask your blessing for this new woman, Swan," Trapper intoned, thereby giving credibility to the name she'd been begging them for years to call her. No longer Right, one of Rein and Cookie's twins, but Swan, that graceful creature who flew the sky and skimmed the waters on her own.

"Mother Earth, I ask your blessing for this new woman, Swan," he said, looking toward the ground, the lake and the mountains around them.

"Circle of the People, I ask your blessing for this new woman, Swan."

"We give it!" they shouted, and Rein let out a triumphant whoop. His little girl, now grown up.

Cookie ran up to her daughter. She searched her face, wiping the corners of her eyes, then used the same hand to wipe her own. She was grinning about as wide as a grin could stretch. "You didn't cry out! You were so brave, you made me proud," she murmured in her daughter's ear.

Swan unclenched her jaw at last, and leaned into her mother's arms. "I'm a woman now, Mami?" she asked in a small voice, and her mother glowed, nodding.

One by one the People came up to admire her arm. They congratulated her, as well as her mother, her father, and even her brother Bear. Only her twin stood off to one side, sullen instead of admiring.

Noting the ugly look on her face, Fierce grabbed the girl and shook her hard. "Get over there and tell your sister you're proud of her. Right now."

"No," Left said, deliberately omitting any term of respect for the older woman. "I won't. It's just a stupid ceremony. She doesn't need anything from me."

"She does and you will," Fierce insisted.

"This shouldn't happen," the girl wailed. "We're supposed to do everything together. She's not supposed to go ahead of me! This is entirely wrong!"

"It is right in every way except for you," Fierce admonished her. "You are spoiling it for her and everybody else. Stop this foolishness right now!" And she shoved the girl in the direction of her twin.

Reluctantly she did as told. But there was resentment in her eyes instead of love.

*　　　*　　　*

Turtle's tattooing astonished everybody, for he asked something completely new. Not content with the usual tattoo, he asked that an additional circle of scars be made all around. Antler added the extra punctures afterwards with a thorn he pulled off a nearby bush. And with each additional puncture endured, Turtle earned more admiration from the men.

"This day," Trapper announced, "no longer shall we call him Turtle (Tucks His Head In). This day he has earned the name of Sea Turtle."

The People hooted and cheered, for the sea turtle was respected for its tenacity and strength. And when Trapper asked their blessing, they enthusiastically cried, "Ho."

Chapter 4: Smoke and fire

In a moment of quiet around the campfire Cookie asked Rein how far they'd gone. "Are we almost there?"

Rein wasn't sure what she was asking.

"Will we find them in the next moon cycle? Our cousins! Catch up with the reindeer, get wherever it is we're going?"

Suddenly everyone was listening. They'd been traveling more than a month already, and she was not the only one wondering how much farther they had to go. Didn't they always say it was a month's travel to get off the fingerland?

But a month's travel for a hunting party was not a month's travel for a band with women and children carrying everything they owned on their backs.

"Well, that's hard to say now, isn't it? We still have a ways to go to the mainland. Maybe another half a moon cycle will get us there. We've done very well so far. You hear that – you've all done very well, every one of you," he emphasized, looking around the circle. "But we don't know where we'll find them, so I don't know if we're close or not. Ho," he added, hoping that would satisfy her.

Her puzzled look indicated it did not. "Then how will you know where to go, once we're on the mainland?"

"I don't," he admitted.

"You don't?" Falling Leaf broke in. "We thought you knew where our cousins went every year."

"I know where they went the year I was with them. Mostly the reindeer follow the same paths, but sometimes they switch. All we can do is look for their traces once we get there."

"But you don't know for sure where to go?"

"We'll be looking for signs. Tracking them like we track other animals. Musk ox. Elk. Mammoth. Steppe bison. We're good at tracking, aren't we, men?"

"Yep," Staunch said in a laconic manner.

"Done it since we were bitty little boys," Two Stones agreed.

"But what if we don't see any signs of them, Uncle? What if they went somewhere far away?" Little Mouse was frightened. Awkwardly pregnant by a husband who went Beyond on the Day of Too Much Dying, she was the first to tremble in any new crisis.

"If we don't find them, we look for another reindeer herd to follow. Or we find a new spot to live in. Or we set up winter camp and keep looking in the spring. How can I know what we'll do if something happens that hasn't happened yet? We'll decide then, that's what we'll do. Don't worry. We're getting close to the mainland, and there's still plenty of good traveling weather. We have a long time before we need to set up camp for the winter."

This was enough to satisfy the men. They knew this country from previous expeditions. They were used to an element of uncertainty, and many relished having to decide things on the spot as circumstances changed. So what if they didn't know where they'd be tomorrow? Their grandfathers' many times grandfathers had wandered for most of their lives; there were stories aplenty of that. They wandered on many an expedition themselves, and none of this frightened them.

But the women were murmuring anxiously. None of them ever did this before, moving through unfamiliar territory far from home. For the first time they were traveling instead of staying near the hearth and tending to their families. It was exciting, but also terrifying to them.

Cookie was not the only one who would feel a huge sense of relief when they settled somewhere. When they could organize the salmon harvest, gather firewood, set up sturdy lodgings against the winter cold. But the men were eager to push ahead. And it was the men whose thinking usually prevailed. Cookie had more questions, but she decided to hold them for another night. She needed to get used to the idea that no one knew where they were going. She wanted to mull over whether what they were doing was incredibly stupid, or if it was her own inexperience that made it seem so.

The silence was broken at last when Lynx popped his head up to ask, "Will there be a story tonight?" With that suggestion there was a brightening of eyes around the circle. If ever there was a night to mark with storytelling, this was such a time. Two big ceremonies today – surely they deserved to hear a rousing tale of some kind. Turtle began chanting, "Story, story!" and Owl joined the plea. Then Bison and, because she had been flirting with him, Swan followed. Soon everyone was chanting, "Story, story!" and looking expectantly at Trapper and Antler.

Trapper glanced at Antler before motioning for the talking stick. By the time it reached his hand, the din was so loud that he had to wave the stick to get their attention. Gradually the raucous calls subsided. "I must defer to young blood and younger memories," he apologized. "The stories I once knew have blown out of my grasp like autumn leaves off the trees."

He leaned across the circle and handed the stick to Antler. An anxious look flitted across Antler's face before the customary stoicism reestablished itself.

"Story, story," Turtle started chanting again.

Fierce hissed, "Shhh!" and the young hunter, who'd been basking in admiration since the tattooing that afternoon, was brought back to earth by his own mother. Supposedly he was a man but it seemed that more maturing was needed.

Antler looked from face to face seeking inspiration. Several moments passed, and yet he did not speak.

Lynx turned to the circle and complained, "Is there going to be a story tonight or not?"

"Maybe Antler doesn't know any stories." Turtle pretended to address the boy, but pitched his voice loud enough to be heard across the circle. He'd asked Antler to do a telling several times recently. Antler put these requests off with one reason or another: He was tired, he had to practice a ceremony with Trapper, he didn't feel well. There'd been enough excuses as far as Turtle was concerned.

Antler looked uneasy. Even if Turtle pretended to speak only to Lynx, he had to respond. He would lose face if he did not move to quash the doubt when anyone questioned him.

"Of course I know some stories. I know lots of stories," he insisted.

"Of course he knows some stories, Lynx," Turtle said, mimicking Antler's tone. "He knows lots of stories about why he won't tell us any stories."

Rein, the peacemaker, came to Antler's rescue. "How about if you tell just one story tonight," he suggested in the gentlest of voices. "Is there a story you can tell?"

Antler stayed silent, his lips compressed and tense. His eyes raced back and forth from Rein to Turtle and the others watching expectantly. Even without this confrontation, he often felt them wonder if he could perform as he should.

"Any story," Rein prompted.

"I ..." Antler hesitated. "It's not really proper. I can't tell the traditional stories without the sacred drum. And we don't have one anymore."

"I knew it!" Turtle said gleefully. "He can't do it. He doesn't know a single story."

"That's enough," Fierce glared at her son. For all the pride she felt in him, this outburst brought shame upon the family. "I don't see the talking stick in your hand. You wait your turn just like any other adult among us. Or we will treat you like the child you act as."

"Is a drum really necessary?" Rein asked Antler. "Surely Father Sky would look with favor at a telling on such a fine occasion, even without the sacred drum." Rein glanced at Cookie, who shrugged. Neither of them knew much about storytelling. They were Sagye, Mountain people, not Dehsda, the Higher Ones from the beach. They had little chance to hear the stories except at major celebrations.

"It's tradition," Antler insisted. He glanced at Trapper for confirmation. The older man nodded briefly. "We always used a drum with the stories. Without a drum, Falcon used to say the stories would be weak as mist, not strong like thunder and lightning storms. Sacred stories need the sacred rhythms; the rhythms are the bones. Without them they shrivel, and too much respect would be lost."

Ah, respect. Rein didn't have to hear any more; the mere mention of the need to maintain respect was enough. No leader could lead without it. No experienced leader would ask another to push ahead without whatever was needed to maintain that respect, so crucial to carrying people along with them.

"Hao then, son. But, some time before the winter, will you build a sacred drum? So we can have the stories for the winter solstice celebrations?"

Antler had to agree.

And when a skeptical look appeared on certain faces around the fire, Rein reminded them that the boy was as much shaman as they were going to get; they were lucky to have that much. Their southward cousins probably didn't even have that, and they should be grateful for what they had. "Give the lad time," he suggested, and murmurings fell silent.

*　　*　　*

The morning was full of birdsong, one of those warm summer days with crickets buzzing and the smell of greening in the air. Birdy was slicing roots for drying while trying to think how to warn her aunt about that horrible man, Kills His Enemy. For days she'd been trying to remember every little thing that happened on the Day of All the Dying. The more she thought about it, the more sure she was that he killed her mother. Hit her, maybe, or flung her against the wall just as the cave started to collapse. There was a lot of arguing, she remembered, and then those awful sounds. She didn't think about them at the time, but now she was certain it was the sound of flesh hitting flesh. Something she'd heard plenty of herself.

He might even have sliced her throat open with his knife or something, she thought. Like he would kill an animal; he was horrid enough to do that. None of the other Sagye even liked him, and the way he never looked them in the eye.

How else would he have gotten Mami's amulet, after all? If she died like everybody else in the cave-in and he found the pendant, he should have given it to Birdy. She was, after all, her daughter. She should have gotten it when Mami went Beyond.

That he didn't give it up, that he kept it like a powerful talisman around his neck, proved he did it. What else could explain the secrecy?

There were plenty of times she dreamed of raising her arm against her mother. Every time she beat her or said something demeaning, she imagined fighting back. Just because she never did it, didn't mean she never thought about it.

Mami must have done something even worse to K'enemy to make him actually do it.

Birdy hurriedly pushed this tendril of sympathy away. However it happened, it was a break in haodisah. If he could kill Mami, he might do the same to River. She had to warn her aunt. Had to. There she was, drying that nice haunch of meat given to them by Staunch and his mother, and what did she do, but go and ask K'enemy if he wanted her to smoke his share too. River expected Birdy to help, but she refused.

"You're tending our family's meat," River argued. "I've done the hard part, cutting it from the bone, trimming the pieces. All you have to do is keep it from catching fire and swat away the flies."

Birdy folded her arms fiercely across her chest. "I will do nothing for that man. Not the least little thing." She couldn't stand it. River was not only preparing food for him, she was beading their extra hide. She wanted to make him a storage pouch with the newly dried jerky inside. Birdy wanted that hide to make new leggings for Oopsy, but no, River was already stitching it for him.

"Then do it for me," River suggested, "if you won't do it for another member of the clan."

"No, no, no." Birdy set her face firm. Not for River either. And now she had to tell her. She hated having secrets from River; bad enough she pretended all those times to be clumsy when Mami hit her. But how could she tell her this awful thing? Everybody kept saying they had to work together. This was no time for arguing, Rein said just last night over the campfire. Old hurts should be forgotten so they could make a new life together. So they could survive. Not that he said that last part, but that was what he worried about.

"Why not?" River was incredulous.

"Because it's not for you, and you know it. It's for him. And I hate him."

"How can you hate him? What has he ever done to you?"

"It's not what he's done to *me*," Birdy muttered. "I just hate him."

"You can't possibly hate him. You barely know him."

"I know him enough to know I hate him. Don't want to know him any more than that."

River's voice took a soft, placating tone. "He's awkward with people, but he's a good man. You'll like him when you get to know him better."

"I don't think so."

"You will. Trust me on this, Birdy."

"I can't."

"Birdy, what has gotten into you? You get along with everybody. I've never seen you take against someone like this."

We have to be one People, Rein told them repeatedly. And if anyone has trouble with that, they should remember that survival for all was more important than any one person's feelings. If they had to choose between life and hurt feelings, they should choose life, it was simple as that.

Twice since they began traveling Rein had to stifle quarrels that threatened to become serious. Once when Two Stones and Staunch were arguing the best path around a certain mountain, and it became an insult match over how much game Staunch brought home, Staunch claiming more kills than Two Stones was willing to give him credit for. The other, when Fierce accused Little Mouse of taking the wrong sleeping fur. Both times Rein had to remind people they were all in this together. Which meant forgiving each other; biting their tongues if they had to, holding back the nasty talk. The Ogwehu were more important than just one person and her feelings; that's what Uncle Rein would say. So she couldn't tell River; she couldn't spread bad gossip about anybody. It went against everything Uncle Rein was doing to make them One.

"I just can't, that's all," she muttered stubbornly. "He can smoke his own stupid meat."

So, with an exasperated look on her face, River kept returning to the smoldering fire, interrupting her other work to turn the shreds of meat laid out on half the twig-woven lattice, though Birdy continued to tend the meat lying on the other side.

★   ★   ★

The women were asking for a sheep hunt. Mutton would make a nice change, and they wanted more fleece for bedding. When Turtle caught a glimpse of movement high on a peak ahead, Rein suggested they camp at its base. Some would harvest roots and seeds, some would fish, and some would hike the mountain and bring back whatever the Great Mother cared to give them that day.

Rein, Two Skins, Bison and K'enemy would go on the hunt. Cookie and River would follow to help butcher the meat and carry it back to camp.

Bison led them through an up-sloping grass meadow. The men moved rapidly ahead, exasperated at the women's slower pace. But River and Cookie would not be needed until after the men sighted their targets and brought them down. They may as well lag behind while the hunters moved on.

The women were gathering grass seed, chatting and humming as the sun moved across the sky. Their sacks were full, and they even had time to bathe themselves when suddenly there was a blast of sound, followed by a cloud of dark smoke boiling up from the top of the mountain. River looked at Cookie; Cookie looked back. "We better go!" Cookie said, as River yelled, "Run!" River grabbed the sack of seed and tucked it through the tie at her waist, keeping a hand along the bottom to support its weight. They headed downhill, Cookie in the lead.

"Should we wait for the men?" River asked.

"No time," Cookie called back, pushing aside a branch so it wouldn't snap in River's face. "I'm sure they'll catch up with us."

It wasn't long before the hunters came pounding along behind them. "Head to the right," Rein shouted. "There's a flow of lava coming down the mountain! We have to get out of the way!"

Cookie and River squeezed up against a tree to let the men pass, laden though they were with carcasses hanging around their shoulders.

The men had almost disappeared, but Rein looked back and shouted, "Hurry!" which sped them up somewhat, but not enough.

Rein and K'enemy hung back so they could each take a woman by the hand. Rein and Cookie were in the front. K'enemy looked over his shoulder. The smell of sulfur grew stronger, and the foul smoke clogged their nostrils.

"Can't you go faster?" K'enemy urged River. But speed was not River's strong point. She was a hard worker and capable, yet she moved with more grace than speed. Soon K'enemy tired of tugging her arm. Shrugging the carcass higher on his shoulders, he slid an arm under her knees, the other behind her back and picked her up. Even so burdened, they moved faster than before. "That's better," he panted.

"Much better," River dreamily agreed, and used her hand to push aside a hoof so she could rest her head against his heart.

K'enemy looked down at the woman he was holding. For the first time he seemed to notice her, her body warm against his, her face like a trusting child looking up at him. Finally he managed to get them far enough ahead that the plume of smoke no longer directly threatened them. Yet he felt a strange reluctance to set her down. He decided to carry her longer, making sure they were out of danger before setting her down.

"I can hear your heart," River murmured.

"Oh?" he said, curious. "What does it say?"

"It says, I'm strong. I'm strong. I'm strong."

He was not much good with words. But she smelled awfully pleasant. He took a deep, appreciative sniff. Spicy, earthy, a little flowery. Yes, she smelled great. Just like a woman should.

She wriggled closer into his chest. "This is nice," she teased. "You should carry me all the way home."

"Would you like that?"

"Mmmm." She reached up to brush her fingers against his cheek, where it was smeared red. "Are you hurt? Or is that sheep's blood?"

"Sheep's blood, probably. Don't think I got hurt."

"Oh. Good. I don't want you hurt."

Reluctantly he set her down. A shame, but by now it was necessary. He needed a good long drink of water, and to adjust the carcass that kept slipping off his shoulders. River sat on a boulder, patted the space next to her, inviting him near. Which he accepted once he set his burden down, found his water skin, took a long swig and then offered her some.

"You saved my life." Her tone was solemn.

"Did I?" She was looking at him, her eyes so wide. He felt lost; it was so confusing.

"I owe you my life," she whispered.

He felt a rush of feeling through his body. She seemed to expect a response, but he had no words at all.

Hesitant, he moved to touch her face. She did not duck away. So soft, the feel of her skin against his hand. The smell of her wafting into his nostrils. So fragrant and musky. So nice.

"My life is yours now."

Still he did not respond. How could he, he was overwhelmed by wonderful smells and feelings. Her face, so close to his. Her hair, her neck. Her breath, warming him. He could breathe the breath as it left her mouth.

His hand reached to stroke her cheek and she leaned into it, moaning softly. She was letting him touch her. His hand reached lower, touched her shoulder, brushed against a breast, a thigh. He shut his eyes, breathed deep, opened them again.

She adjusted her position on the rock so that her leg touched his. Her body leaned closer.

"I am yours," she repeated.

"You are mine," he responded, as much a question as agreement. When he took her hand in his, they each felt a shock. He looked at her. She looked back at him, eyes unblinking. His hand moved of its own volition, reaching the back of her head and drawing her into his embrace. Their lips came together, and they kissed. And lingered there, kissing, touching, noticing as if for the first time a thousand tiny details about each other, shapes and colors and textures of skin, and nothing of the world around them. Though if any of the boiling smoke came closer, they might have noticed. Might have.

Eventually they descended towards the camp, and somehow it was not so hard to talk with her anymore. She would cook the sheep in his favorite way, she promised. What do you mean I don't know your favorite way; you like it stuffed with roots and greens and roasted underneath the coals of the cookfire. What do you mean how did I know that, I heard you tell my sister once.

"You noticed me that long ago," he remarked, completely astonished.

"I have been watching you for a long time."

"You have?"

"Yes."

"How did I not know?"

She blushed. "I was biding my time."

He gave her a questioning look.

"Your attention was elsewhere."

"On your sister. Pah! If only I looked a little further."

"Well, now you have."

He fell back into silence. How embarrassing, that he withered away for so long waiting for that awful woman to give him another droplet of her affection. When all the time there was this beautiful young woman, so ripe and ready for him. And here she was telling him she was his. "You are mine?" he asked tentatively, not yet convinced she meant it.

"I am yours," she repeated, rubbing affectionately against his arm.

He felt a wave of feelings rush through, so huge that he could hardly contain them. Never before had he felt so blessed. They could have a life together. A real life. Not just a few reluctant moments snatched in the middle of someone else's pathway. This one he could have all to himself. She said so; she was his. Her, River, she would be his. His woman. His wife. He would no longer be the sad orphan, K'enemy, that outcast. At long last he could have a family of his own. A beautiful wife to love him and look after him, while he looked after her. He could see children laughing, running around, theirs.

He drew himself upright, a far look in his eye. "This skin," he pointed to the ewe still draped around his neck. "It shall be a sleeping fur for our first born child."

"Oh. I thought maybe Oopsy could have it. He needs a new sleeping fur, his is so worn."

That's right, he realized. He wouldn't get just her; he'd be getting an entire family. A good family. A family any man could feel proud to be a part of. "Of course," he agreed. "He can use it for now. By then I'll get him another."

It was fitting. This sheep had brought them together. It would feed them in a feast of celebration tonight. And its skin would cradle the first fruit of their togetherness. "Ho," he whispered.

She smiled to herself, and though she couldn't follow all his thoughts, still she agreed, "Ho."

⋆   ⋆   ⋆

The camp was deserted when they reached the lowlands. The shelters were all packed and gone. Rein wasn't worried. They must have heard the explosion, seen the smoke and the plume of molten rock snaking down the mountain. Even this far away they must have felt endangered, knew that if the hunters survived, they'd catch up somewhere safe ahead.

Certainly they would be easy to track. They made no effort to cover their trail. There were plenty of footprints, and in case they came back in pitch dark, someone set out a series of stones in the shape of a wedge, its cusp pointing the way.

A fast trot ahead, and they soon caught up. The Ogwehu were frightened, though less now that they were together again. Still the men conferred and decided to keep moving. They were eager to put distance between them and the Spirit of that mountain, so sick that it spat smoke and regurgitated bile, whose acrid smell followed them for most of another day.

That night they traveled long past sunset, eating from their stores and sleeping in the open, so great was the impulse to flee. Thus it wasn't until they set up camp the following evening that anyone noticed what they were missing. In the hurry to leave, no one thought to wrap an ember in a carrying bed with moss protecting it. They had no relay of coals to begin the next campfire. For the first time since they left their long-time home there was no spark from the old to start up the new.

They could start a new fire from scratch, of course, but it was a grueling process. Apart from the normal logistics of building the fire, much demanding work was needed to create the first spark. It took a lot of effort, and many blisters to make a spark and ensure it jumped from the fire starter onto the tinder where it would hopefully catch aflame.

As leader, Rein could sense a bleak spirit settling in. His People were hungry and weary. They'd been traveling for over a month and more, undoubtedly, was to come. Yesterday the volcano. Today they almost lost Staunch when he fell into a bog. And now this new discouragement, the loss reminding them of so much else gone. He had to do something before it weighed them down too deep. They needed a distraction to keep moving forward, or they might all sink into the muck.

So he pounced on his own son, who he knew was sturdy enough to bear the onus for them, at least for the night. The next day he would worry about tomorrow, if he had to.

"Fire Bear!"

The tone was enough to warn Bear to respond immediately. "Yes, sir."

"Where's the coal? Why didn't you pick up a coal? It's your job to carry it; how could you let us down?"

"Father, we were fleeing for our lives! I was helping mamma pack everything away! I was helping Fierce lash their things together! I was rounding up the little ones!"

"You forgot." Rein sent a stern look at his son. Followed by a method of redemption. "Go start a new coal. We need a fire tonight. And I don't want to hear of you forgetting anything else." He walked away, exaggeratedly shaking his head. "Children!" he called out to Two Stones. "This camp is full of them!"

"Don't worry, it's temporary," Two Stones called back. "Every single one of them'll grow out of it someday."

*　　*　　*

Birdy passed Fire Bear laboring over his coal. She was carrying water from the creek, but she set the water skins down to rest.

"Hey there, Birdy bird," her cousin called out.

"Hey there yourself."

"Looks like we're going to have ourselves a new uncle."

"Hmmph."

"Aunty River seems to have caught herself a nice sized fish."

"Shut up."

"This one doesn't seem eager to jump back into the stream."

"Shut up, Bear."

"You don't seem too happy, Birdy bird. Don't you want River to be happy? She's been singing all day. I think her face is about to crack in pieces, she's been smiling so much."

"I don't want to talk about it."

"What, you don't like him? Too bad. Pretty soon it's gonna be," here his voice got mockingly high, "Uncle K'enemy, please pass me the berries. Uncle K'enemy, can I get you more stew? Uncle K'enemy, help me untie this lashing; I can't reach it. You're so strong."

"I am leaving now." Birdy picked up the water skins and strode off, not even bothering to return the jibe. It was completely unlike her. Bear was puzzled. It was fun getting a rise out of Birdy, but he didn't actually mean to provoke her. What was she so sensitive about? K'enemy was odd, but he was a good hunter; he'd probably make a decent uncle.

Maybe it was some girl thing. The boy shrugged and returned to his labors.

⋆   ⋆   ⋆

"Tell me a story, Birdy," Oopsy begged. "Can you tell the one about the boy who got to wear fur?" It was well after supper, and the long dusk was beginning to deepen to black. Around the camp some were singing; others were quietly gossiping or mending things for their families. Oopsy was beginning to droop, but he liked a story at the end of the day.

"The one about how we came to wear clothing?"

He climbed up onto her lap and rested his head against her. "That one," he agreed. "Pout likes that one too."

"I know, sweet guy." He looked wistful in the flickering light. "Do you miss your sister?"

The boy nodded, thumb stuck in his mouth.

"Me too, Oopsilu. I think about her a lot, her and Grandmother and Thunder."

"T'under," he lisped, "he goed under the ground."

"That's right, we buried him under the ground, him and all those other people."

Oopsy looked like he might burst into tears, so Birdy quickly began to tell how the People long ago began to wear animal hides to help them withstand the cold. It was one of the shaman's stories, so she chose her words carefully. Not carefully in the sense of making sure every word was perfect. She could not tell a story perfectly; that might reveal her secret to anyone who might overhear.

She could have told a safe family story but Birdy and Oopsy both loved this particular tale. She had told it to him several times in the traditional manner, but she knew she shouldn't tell the full version again. He was getting old enough to repeat it to Lynx, and pretty soon everyone would be asking about it. Someone might guess she could recite the whole thing.

Instead she decided to tell a shorter version. If she used easier words and dropped some of the detail, she could still tell it to her brother. And if anyone overheard, she could say she remembered some of it from last winter's telling; too bad Falcon wasn't there to tell the true version.

The story begun, Oopsy nestled on her lap, his sadness already forgotten. There was a granddaddy much like Great Uncle, and his faithful daughter who looked a lot like Birdy grown up, and her little boy, very much like Oopsy himself. The People were wandering through mountainous lands, and they suffered from chills on their naked bodies, especially at night.

One morning as winter came upon them, the boy almost couldn't rise at daybreak, he was so frozen and stiff. He was freezing, though his Birdy-mamma had made him a good sleeping space near the fire. His granddaddy worried about the boy. So he tried one thing and another, each of which Birdy described at length, until at last he figured out how to make furs like the animals had. And the boy grew up to be a great hunter like Bison and Sea Turtle; that part was not in the story, but Oopsy insisted it was true.

When it was over, the sleepy boy begged for just one more.

Birdy was still thinking about the story. That granddaddy went a great distance to work out a new idea for his grandson's sake. And when they discovered how warm these wraps were, it helped not only that child, but the whole clan. If he hadn't discovered how to prepare furs, they could not have moved into the colder lands where there was more room for the People and the hunting was better.

Figuring something out had to be good for the tribe. It wouldn't have done them any good if he kept it secret. More people would have died of the cold.

Her thoughts moved to her aunt, who she always imagined when she heard about the loving mother in this story. Just as Oopsy thought of Birdy, for she had been more mamma to him than Mami ever was, so Birdy thought of River.

River, who now wanted her own family. And with K'enemy! She couldn't imagine her graceful aunt going to that brutish...brute! The idea made Birdy so angry she felt her jaws clench and the blood shouting in her veins. She'd rather see River become Staunch's second wife. Or be married out of the tribe and never see her again. Just not be mated to that wolf of a man who surely killed her mother. How could she choose him of all people?

Oh. Of course. River actually didn't know that K'enemy killed Mami. She forgot for a moment that she never told her. Nobody knew, because Birdy kept it to herself. It seemed like a bad thing to tell, because Rein said they all had to pull together.

But he was a bad man, K'enemy was, bad like a piece of rotten meat. Nobody else seemed to realize it, but Birdy figured it out. She was the only one who could see how rotten he was. Just like the Grandfather in the story who figured something out that nobody else knew, and he had to share it for the good of the People.

She had to tell River. She'd never marry K'enemy if she knew what kind of a person he really was.

That was it; she would tell River about K'enemy. This wasn't just bad gossip. Knowing things was always better than not knowing. Like in the story; knowing the new thing you could do with the hides kept people from freezing to death. Knowing things was good, so telling her aunt must be the right thing to do. They wouldn't be safe living with K'enemy; he might turn on River or Oopsy or her and kill them too.

She had to do it to keep them safe; that had to be more important than worrying about hurting people's dignity and the tribe sticking together and all that. Telling would restore haodisah; that was important for their survival too.

Quickly she stood up, sliding her brother off her lap. "Sorry, Oopsy, it's sleepy time for you. I have to go talk to Aunt River."

Chapter 5: Combing through the tangles

The sight of the two of them strolling through camp, K'enemy's arm thrown casually over River's shoulder, sent Birdy fleeing to Aunt Cookie. She could speak to River, but not in front of *him*. Cookie didn't ask any questions, just let her curl up next to Swan for the night. Not that she actually slept. She was mad at River; madder still at herself. River spent so much time with him, she would probably have to pull her away in order to tell her about it. In fact it wasn't until midday the next day that she forced herself to approach, clenching her fists so hard the nails dug into the palms of her hands. Even so, seeing River tucked between K'enemy's outstretched legs and mending his moccasins (*mending his moccasins! Like they were already mated!*), Birdy could choke, she was so distraught.

His face looks so cruel, she thought miserably. The face of a predator, always on the hunt. She shuddered, remembering the awful look he had on that terrible day. Keeping K'enemy so far to the side of her vision that she wouldn't have to let him into even the corner of her eye, Birdy stepped over Bison's legs and approached her aunt.

"River, I have to tell you something," the girl whispered.

"The sun shines brightly on your face today, Birdy," her aunt smiled. "What is it?"

"Not here," she hissed. "Alone."

"It's all right, Birdy. I don't have any secrets." She sent an affectionate glance in K'enemy's direction. "Not anymore I don't."

K'enemy placed his arms around River, pulling her protectively against him.

"Well I do," Birdy insisted. "Come on." She reached for River's hand to yank her onto her feet. "Come on!"

River let Birdy pull her just out of earshot. Birdy positioned herself facing away from *him*.

"I have to tell you something, River," she repeated.

"Tell away," her aunt said cheerily.

"You're not going to like it. It's ..." Somehow none of her carefully prepared words seemed right. "You just can't marry him, that's all. You can't."

"Of course I can, Birdsilu. He's not married to anyone else. I'm not married to anyone else. Rein gave us his blessing. I know you don't like him, but there's nothing to stop us from getting married."

"Yes, there is! You don't understand. He is a madman!" The word she used meant, literally, *wild storm person*. In the effort to persuade her aunt,

Birdy grabbed one of River's hands between her own and was pumping her arm up and down in the air.

River glanced down at her arm. The only wild storm in the area came from Birdy herself.

Birdy caught the quizzical glance and dropped River's hand, flushing a deep red. But a little embarrassment was not enough to stop her. "He killed Mami, River. I'm sure of it. He killed your sister, so you can't possibly marry him!"

"Birdy, what are you talking about?"

Now that the horrible truth had been spoken, the words came tumbling out. "He killed Mami on the Day of Too Much Death! I was there. Everybody thought she died in the cave-in, but she must have been dead before it all started. They were arguing, and I heard some awful noise. He must have killed her, and you can't marry him; he might kill all of us!"

River cocked her head quizzically. "Slow down, girl. You better tell me exactly what happened."

Birdy closed her eyes and took a deep breath. They were picking berries together that day, remember? And River noticed her limping and sent her back to the cave. But it was hard to walk. Her ankle was hurting and she sank into the tall grass to rest, was dozing, maybe, but then she heard people arguing. It was Mami and K'enemy, she was pretty sure. For a while she thought maybe there was another voice too, but she was kind of groggy, and anyway the voices stopped, and K'enemy came through the meadow. He had an axe in his hand; he looked so mean and *ugly*. He went back to the cave and there was more yelling, and then it got quiet.

"And now he has Mami's amulet," she fumed. "You saw it yourself. Don't you see, he must have killed her, and he let everybody think she died in the cave-in. But he killed her, Aunty, why else would he be wearing her amulet around his neck? He might kill you too, and I couldn't stand it." Her voice cracked. "Mami's dead, and Grandmother and Thunder, and you'll be dead, and I'll be all alone!" She burst into tears.

"Shhh, child, you won't be alone. All of us here are your People; you will never be alone." River took the girl in her arms and rocked her, smoothing her hair until the cries began to lessen. "Now tell me again what happened."

Birdy repeated the story. This time there were no tears, just a growing indignation in her voice and eyes.

"So you didn't actually see K'enemy strike your mamma with his axe," River probed. "Or with his hands or anything else."

"No. but I know he did it. He must have! That's why he has the amulet, like a trophy, to remember."

"Birdy, your mamma was crushed by the cave-in," River corrected her. "I pulled the rocks off her myself. There were no knife or axe cuts." She shook her head. "You don't even want to know that stuff. She was crushed, that's what killed her; nobody murdered her. There were no axe marks; her head was crushed by the falling stone."

"No," Birdy insisted. "Mami was dead *before* the earth started moving. They were fighting. I heard them. He must have beat her to death or something."

It didn't sound believable, even to her. How could she make River see? Nobody else believed that sweet Cavekeeper Woman beat Birdy, either. But she did, it was true.

"You said yourself you didn't see it. You must have confused things. It happened so quickly. There was so much destruction that day; I think it got mixed up inside."

"He killed her, River! You have to believe me! He is a madman."

"Birdy, I've known K'enemy since before you were born. He is not like that. When he gets angry, which is rare, he is like a stone axe himself. Solid and purposeful. Not wild at all."

Like a stone axe. To Birdy that somehow seemed even worse. They might get chopped to pieces by him in their sleep instead of being strangled or flung against the rocks. "River, you can't marry him; it's too dangerous!" Frantic with worry, she grabbed River's arm again.

River pulled away. "Birdy, calm down. Terrible things happened that day. The Earth was wild. The Ocean was wild. The animals were completely mad. But I do not for a moment believe K'enemy went wild and killed your mother. He is solid in a crisis; he does not get like that. He is a very gentle man behind that tough face. Someday you'll get over these unreasonable feelings and be able to see for yourself."

Birdy fumed. Why couldn't River see what was so obvious to her? If only she came sooner that day she would have seen it herself. Unfortunately the only other person who knew was K'enemy, but he would never confirm it. Tell on himself? Hah. Though when you asked people who did bad things, sometimes you could tell they were hiding something, even if you didn't know exactly what.

Like the time she asked Oopsy and Pout about the bag of spilled nuts, and they tried to act innocent, but their eyes moved all funny, and they squirmed away. Maybe, like them, K'enemy would squirm if River asked about it. Then she'd know Birdy was right, and she'd push him away, and they'd all be safe. Maybe he'd even leave the People, and they'd never see him again.

"Just ask him, Aunt River," she urged. "Ask him about that day. Ask if he went to see Mami at the cave, and make him tell you what happened." She tried to make River promise, but River refused. Birdy could only hope she would ask him anyway.

And if not, she thought miserably as she watched her aunt return, heard her say to K'enemy, "Oh, just a little something to work out between Birdy and me," if she couldn't save River from that dangerous man, then she would take Oopsy and move into Rein's shelter. Or if Cookie said it was too crowded, Great Uncle might set up something for the three of them, Great Uncle, Oopsy, and her.

⋆ ⋆ ⋆

Birdy kept watching, on and off all the next day. So when River put down her sewing, took K'enemy by the hand and led him into the woods, Birdy dropped her work to follow. She was desperate to hear what they said. Would River push it hard? Would she notice if he wiggled with his words? Or would she believe him, no matter what he said? More than anything Birdy needed to hear his answer. If she could find some hiding place close by, that would be best. She wanted to see his face and judge for herself.

But Cookie saw her leave the chopping with a pile of roots half cut up. And when she saw who Birdy was following, Cookie put a hand out to stop her. "Don't go there, girl," she warned. "Give them some privacy. They're a courting couple. They need time alone."

Blushing deeply, Birdy came to a halt. "It's not that, Aunt Cookie," she protested, eyes begging her to understand. "I wouldn't care if they were kissing, but that's not what they're going to do. They're talking about something, and I need to hear what they say."

"All the more reason to stay back, child! Whatever it is, let them work it out in peace. It takes a lot of working through to make a good marriage. The more they do ahead of time, the better it'll be for them."

"I'm not going to interfere," Birdy insisted. "I just have to hear what he says."

"No you don't," Cookie warned. "Whatever it is, it is none of your business. Let them be." And she sent her back to finish the chopping, and after that, to pick nuts from a patch of trees in the opposite direction from where River and K'enemy went.

Those chores hurriedly completed, she was finally free. Braiding rope, that was a task she could set up anywhere. Then she could innocently be working as she tried to listen in. She'd already picked grass for braiding; all she had to do now was retrieve it.

Then, *thunk!* A throwing stick went awry from its target and hit her square on her back. Birdy went sprawling, the armload of grasses flying in every direction. The men laughed, but Bear came running up, apologizing profusely. "Are you hurt, Birdy? Let me help you up." He was brushing dirt off her hands and knees, trying to gather the loose stalks and generally getting in her way.

"Leave me alone, it doesn't matter, I'll get it later," she cried in frustration. It was taking far too long. She might still catch a bit of their talk if Bear would only leave her alone! She scrabbled to her feet and pushed past him. But he kept bunching stalks together and thrusting them at her. *Grrrrr.* She could see it on his face—he wanted her to tell him she was just fine, but she was too impatient.

"Thanks," she said, harshly shoving him aside.

"I was just trying to help," Bear protested. She knew he felt bad, but she was so intent on getting away that she didn't care.

"Please let them still be there," she muttered, hurrying toward the flat stone marking the place where they entered the grove. It would make a good seat. She could set the grasses for braiding to one side and let the rope coil the other way as it left her hands. That is, if she could hear enough from there to make it worth settling in. And if they didn't spot her.

Another *thunk!* A softer one this time, at the back of her head. Followed by raucous laughter, mostly from Turtle, though she also heard a giggle from the twins. Apparently they switched from throwing sticks to tossing animal bladders; they'd filled one up with water that burst apart when it hit. Now she was soaking wet—hair, body, her wrap clinging with a cold sogginess that was quite unpleasant. She turned to glare at the offenders, which only made them laugh harder.

She was beginning to get the sense that she wasn't supposed to overhear this particular conversation.

She could get something to blot herself dry. She could find something to change into. Or she could sit on the rock, wet and miserable, and listen for any conversation that might still be happening. If there even were any conversation, after all this.

She chose to sit.

Having finally reached her destination, she set the grasses in an orderly fashion, stalks neatly lined up, fat ends pointing behind her, narrow tops pointing ahead. She squinted up at the sky to see how long before it got too dark to see.

All the while straining to decide on the time, was that River's voice she heard? Seemed like it. What was she saying? "How did you" or "How will you" and something about blood. She could hear the tone more than the actual words; it was River's higher pitch, and she sounded angry. Birdy caught some of it, but she kept missing words, enough that it didn't do much good to sit, shivering and trying to make out what they had to say. Maybe she should gather her things and inch closer, though she wasn't sure she could get closer without alerting them.

Oh, Great Mother, Antler was walking toward her now, what could he possibly want? K'enemy was talking now but she couldn't make it out, not with Antler plopping himself on the rock where she was about to coil the rope. If she ever actually made any; if any of her plans went right, the way things were going today.

"Antler," she sighed. "What do you need from me?"

"I wanted to see if you were all right, Birdy," he said. "You got hit with Bear's throwing stick, and he's afraid to ask. He said you kept giving him ugly looks, so I said I'd come and see."

She waved her hand dismissively.

"Oh. Good. Also," he hurried on, not noticing her impatience, "I've been wanting to ask. Oopsy told Lynx the story about how we came to wear clothing, only he didn't seem to know it was one of our sacred tales. He said you had lots of good ones about whales and things that you like to tell. It's just that I need to know the stories better. I have to practice, so I thought, maybe," he looked up, blushing, "we could, you know," and there he stopped.

"What," she prodded, not caring how rude it sounded. If he finished quickly, maybe she could still catch whatever River and K'enemy were talking about. "Come on, Antler, what do you want from me?"

"To swap." He gulped. "I could tell a story and you could tell me if I did it right. At least, for as much as you know," he apologized. "You probably don't know much, but you can at least tell me if I sound good." His voice was hopeful. "When everybody's walking, we could walk together and I could practice without anyone hearing us, or maybe we should practice in the evenings if you'd rather do it then. The parts you know, you can tell them to me, and then I can try them on you. And you can prompt me if I miss anything. That way you get to hear the stories; you'd like that, right? What do you think?" He was flushed. Breathless. On edge.

She had been looking at Antler, but now she heard a noise from the forest behind them. Turning away, still straining to figure out what was going on between River and K'enemy, she did not immediately answer.

He took a look at her frowning face, and cocked an eyebrow at her. "Or do you know more than you pretend?" he asked, grabbing her shoulder. "Was that you, that night on the beach, when I scared off that bird? I thought it might be you, so I never told anybody. I didn't want you to get in trouble. Were you listening when we practiced our storytelling? Do you actually *know* the sacred tales?"

Just then River emerged from the forest. Her aunt was scowling, her head held high, lips pressed in a tight line. K'enemy followed, but branched off in another direction. His shoulders were hunched and he looked unhappy. *Good*, Birdy thought to herself. Maybe she didn't have to worry about any wild storms coming into the family. All of a sudden she felt light as air. Another throwing stick could hit her and she probably wouldn't notice. Five more sticks could hit her. Ten.

Brightening, she turned to the boy anxiously waiting next to her. Hope and worry shadowed his face in equal measure. The stories were the weakest part of his training as a shaman, she mused. He was getting good with the prayers and ceremonies. When they approached a new campsite, for instance, he quietly set about asking the spirit of the grove or glen for its blessings, and they got it; not once since the beginning of their journey had any overnight spot harmed them with an avalanche, flood, or falling trees.

He was becoming a fine shaman; Aunt Cookie and Uncle Trapper both said so, even if he was still, like her, a kid. Even though not everybody gave him credit for it. Turtle gave him a hard time about the stories. And some of the grown-ups still saw him as a child, not as the man he was learning to be.

His face, she suddenly noticed, was no longer round as a child's; it was becoming angular and hinted at strength. They were the same height when they began the trek, but he was taller now. Ropy muscle was developing down his arms and legs, and she saw him suddenly, not as just her cousin's buddy, but something new, unfamiliar, alien. Exciting and a bit scary at the same time.

The kind smile was still there, but now it was balanced with thoughtfulness. Often he had an other-worldly gaze when his attention left the immediate surroundings and traveled elsewhere. Willow thought he would be handsome some day, and Birdy was beginning to see she might be right. But handsome was not as important as thoughtful or kind. Those were the qualities that she liked most about him.

She felt a new appreciation dawn inside her; respect and an unexpected formality. How could she continue to joke casually with the person who spoke to the Spirits every day and kept the whole tribe safe? That he could do such a thing, that he could regularly transcend the petty pushings and sparrings to converse with the great powers and especially with Father Sky—it was an awesome and amazing thing when she thought about it.

Never before did this occur to her, not with Falcon, and not until now with Antler either. Falcon was such a forbidding presence; she didn't like to think about him at all. But this was her familiar friend Antler, and he could do all these wondrous, transcendent things. She ought to be nicer to him, she decided. She should help him any way she could.

And if practice was what he needed, she could do that.

They would both enjoy going over the stories. She could help so that he could tell the stories in the old, sacred way. They wouldn't be lost to the People after all. And she would get a chance to tell the tales with expression and meaning, just as they ought to be told. Even if it was only to an audience of one. To Antler, her friend. Oopsy would hear the stories both ways, the proper way at the fire circle, and her own shorter, livelier versions. He would forget she sometimes used to tell the whole thing, and her family would be safe.

"Of course, Antler." She flashed a bright smile at him. "I'll be happy to do that; it sounds like fun. When do you want to begin?"

⋆   ⋆   ⋆

Among the People there was little thought of sin, evil, or punishment. What they thought of instead was a sense of wholeness, *haodisah*. A kind of easy harmony connecting them to the green world around them, and to those who sat with them every day around the fire circle. When they thanked the Great Mother or blessed Father Sky, it was their way of showing they appreciated the blessings provided them. A day when they found food, or shelter from storms, returned uninjured from a hunt, any of these days might have been significantly worse, so they were grateful, sending thanks and hope that such blessings continued. And when the wholeness was marred in some way, torn or broken, they felt bewildered that such a thing could happen and a need to heal it up again.

For River the wholeness had been ripped apart with a wound so deep it was hard to know if it ever could heal. She entrusted her heart to this man, poured all her dreams and longings into his bowl. But now the bowl seemed to have a crack in the bottom.

For so long she was certain he was the one for her. During the months he spent sighing after her sister, through the days when she prayed that he'd choose the North just as her family did, never did it feel like there might be anyone else. Even now she couldn't imagine setting him aside like a fish gone rotten, that made you ill if you tried to make a meal of it. She couldn't imagine taking another in the arms that fit his so well. But how could she trust him when he did such a thing? Though part of her understood clearly how he could.

She had long seen the ugliness that lay within her sister. She sheltered her nieces and nephews from it, hoped it would heal into something more whole. When she was small, her mother protected her from the worst of the ugliness, and she did her best to protect her sister's children in turn. So she could see, in part, why K'enemy felt he had to do what he did. Remove the danger to the children. Stay her sister's right arm in order to protect Birdy. Who was again planning to beat Birdy blue, this time simply because she was embarrassed when a visitor asked where her daughter was sneaking off on all those nights.

That ugliness was like a hole in her sister's spirit, festering with rot. No matter how many blessings came to Cavekeeper, they were never enough to let her heal and grow whole. The terrible truth was that the ugliness, the rot, the laziness, and the temper had been there a long time. River hadn't seen the beatings, but she saw plenty of ways her sister was ugly to her children. So, though she was shocked to hear what her sister was going to do, she was not entirely surprised. No, not actually surprised at all.

River was the youngest surviving child of her family. But there was once a younger sister called Cheeks for her wide, beaming face, born two summers after River. From her first days the two played with more harmony than most sisters. Sometimes they followed Rein, but more often they tagged along after *her.* Nosy, the name their older sister had as a child, shortened from Nose in the Air. Nosy was smart. Tough and aloof, which made her more fascinating than ever.

One day Nosy took a fishing net and walked in the direction of the creek. She wasn't supposed to go anywhere by herself; no one was supposed to go anywhere alone and especially not girls. But Nosy often went her own way, which was one of the things that made her a figure of awe for the younger ones.

That day their mother told her to take her sisters along, or not go out at all. So all three girls set out for the pools where the fish liked to linger in the depths. There Nosy cast her net, daydreaming, while the younger girls played under the flickering canopy of the trees.

They were on their way home when they heard a rustling in the brush nearby.

A wolf was tracking them, its long, gray silhouette almost invisible behind the trees except for the gleam of its tawny yellow eyes. Those eyes, black-rimmed and slanting, could laugh and be playful, or just as easily intend to kill. All this River noticed in a moment, and had to wrench herself to break the hold of his stony glance. She screamed, freeing them to run. River and Cheeks each grabbed one of Nosy's hands and held tight, though their sister did not grip their hands in return.

The first thing to drop was the net, and then the fish Nosy caught, two good-sized trout. They could sense him pausing to decide between two possible feasts. The fish, a mere snack, and yet so easy? Or follow the flesh still dashing ahead, to be his only after a fight that might wound him?

Nosy used the time to bring them round a bend in the mountainside. There the rock face was steep and fractured. Luckily they found a small fissure to squeeze in. It was no cave; only a crack in the rock, but it gave some protection on two sides.

Cheeks whimpered. River tried to hold her quiet, sliding a comforting arm around her shoulders. The wolf came prowling, sniffing the air for clues. It didn't take long to catch a hint of them. He sauntered up, paws padding against the dirt, tail swinging with a casual confidence that made Cheeks whimper more.

Nose was reaching for a stick, a branch, anything to keep him away. Her hand touched a dried clump of bush. She pulled at it, yanking the woody plant loose from its roots, and started beating at the beast. He drew back, biding his time, tongue hanging out. The girls watched fearfully, praying he would leave. And he did slink a few steps back into the woods, but this was merely a feint. He ambled from behind a tree, this time toward Cheeks.

Nose stepped forward, yelling and jabbing at him. She got him once on top of his head; another scratched him in the eye. He whimpered slightly and moved off into the trees. The girl took that moment to pivot and run towards home, not looking behind to see if her sisters followed.

River tried getting Cheeks to open her eyes and stand. "Come on," she kept urging. "We have to run!" But the younger girl kept her eyes scrunched shut, arms tucked in, too fearful to move. River grabbed Cheeks by the hand and managed to drag her away from the side of the hill, her legs skittering uselessly behind.

She was a limp weight at first. River tried pulling and murmuring encouragements. Her legs began to unfold as they dragged on the ground. This made her harder to move, but finally she stumbled to her feet and began running.

By then the wolf was following again.

"Wait, Nosy! Help us!" River called, but their sister was far ahead and did not stop.

Nor did the wolf, moving closer still. He snapped at the girls' legs, and then at the stick River used to fend him off. Finally he ducked his head lower, coming in from the side. From that angle he managed to clamp his jaws around the smaller girl's knee.

Cheeks screamed and tried to pummel him with her fists. River grabbed a rock and beat him with one hand, bashing it like a hammer stone against his skull. Her other hand still held tight to her sister. He growled as she drew blood, but he clamped his jaw tight and pulled. Her sister was howling in pain and fear.

River used the stick to lever his teeth apart. When that didn't work she tried pulling her sister with both hands. It was no contest. The wolf had more weight behind his grip. No six-summer's girl could match his strength.

He yanked the child backwards out of River's grasp. Cheeks held her arms out, calling for River, for their mother. Tears running down her face, River chased them, calling across the widening gap. The wolf ran, the child's leg clenched between his teeth. Dragged across the ground, Cheeks tried to grab onto a tree root, a bush, but the beast pulled her onward. River was falling behind. When he was far ahead he dropped her, then picked her up by the neck and gave her a violent shake.

The silence was unbearably loud.

Never again did River follow her big sister. For Nosy was one who took care of herself, and she would throw another to the wolves if she felt she had to, so she could stay ahead.

There were days when River still felt the pull of her sister's little hands in hers. And, though it was too late to save her, for her sake she tried to look out for others and keep them safe.

And if no one needed saving, what was almost as satisfying was to make something of beauty—a pretty necklace, a nicely sewn shirt. There was ugliness enough around, and sometimes all it took was a bit more attention to create something with a sense of harmony and wholeness. Something that not only was useful, but gave the eye pleasure and the spirit a sense of ease. This was her way of keeping haodisah.

For all his manly skills, K'enemy was, to her, another poor creature who needed saving. He'd been shunned and made unwelcome at almost every family's hearth longer than any person should be. Yet he, like her, looked to save others. And if she needed saving, she and their children, he would do that even at the risk of his own life. He would not run from the wolves and leave the weak ones behind.

She and he—it seemed so right. Until yesterday, when she finally listened to Birdy, and then made K'enemy tell her what happened back at the cave.

She spent a long night tossing and turning, trying to take it in. Yes, he killed her sister, but he did it to save Birdy's life.

She didn't die in the cave-in after all. She died just before, and her death was at his hand.

She was killed to save Birdy's life, for Cavekeeper kept trying to end it. Not end it, as in sending her Beyond. But ending all the goodness of it, which is what K'enemy had felt when his own father did much the same. Whenever he tried to intimidate, to overcome them, and enforce his way. To revenge himself for petty slights, making the family cower or cringe.

He didn't notice, until that very day, how much like his bullying father she was. They argued about it that day in the cave, the visitor leaving after K'enemy overheard his busy-body questions. Cavekeeper must have been thinking out loud; K'enemy overheard that too.

It would take time for River to get a grip on it. In fact the whole thing took her breath away.

Why would her sister do that, and to sweet little Birdy who did so much for her? It just didn't make sense. Not that people always made sense. River knew about the occasional slap, and the belittlements. But beating her bloody, a precious child; wrenching her arm so regularly? It made no sense. And yet she believed K'enemy. Terrible though it was, she knew her sister. And could see her doing such things, if she could keep it hidden.

River thought she protected the children, and now it looked like she missed too much. She felt sick thinking about it. Poor Birdy, who bore the brunt of it. Poor little thing.

Then there was K'enemy. That was an even tougher piece of meat to chew. River did not flinch from the idea that sometimes killing was necessary. K'enemy's bullying father died similarly, and few mourned his passing. But it wasn't just the killing that was so hard to take in. What made it harder was this thing about trust. K'enemy had let her kiss him, sew his moccasins, make him a shirt. He pledged himself to her, and let everyone see them together. And never once told her about this.

She felt like kicking him. How could he let things go this far and not say anything? When she asked, he could hardly look her in the eye. He said, his voice almost too soft to be heard, that he thought she knew and already forgave him. Because Birdy saw him there, and River said Birdy told her everything, which she now saw was far from true.

He must have hoped it was true. Maybe he was afraid to make sure it was. Because if she didn't already know, he risked losing her when he told her what happened that day.

She loved him, she realized; she did, still. But if he could be so careless about something as big as this, how could she ever be sure he wasn't hiding more? Not just in the past, but in their lives to come?

Could she ever trust him again?

Her hands reached down to cradle her belly. She felt a deep abscess right through the middle of her being. Oh, she missed her mother; if only she were here! She would have held River, crying, in her arms, patted her on the back, and stroked her hair. Let the familiar comforts heal her, at least enough that she could think again. "Mamma," River prayed, sending her thoughts Skyward. "What should I do? How can I know if he is the man I thought I knew?" Her next thought might have been heaven-sent. *Rein.* Ah yes, she could talk it over with him.

⋆　　⋆　　⋆

The thing about your knives, Rein often thought, was that you had to keep them sharp. Otherwise you'd go off to butcher some carcass and find yourself scraping the meat instead of cutting through. Whether it was the women chopping it or the men killing it, having a sharp blade made all the difference. It meant having a fresh haunch in the stewpot instead of watching the creature escape while your family made do with berries and roots. Certainly it made the difference between having your wife finish her work with enough energy left to give you a nice little thank you that night under the furs, and having her curse you for laziness and her own achy arms and blisters for the next several days. No doubt about it, a sharp edge saved a lot of trouble. So periodically he gathered Cookie's knives and choppers, along with his own weaponry. Sat apart and proceeded to chip away the blunt edges so they'd be pleasingly sharp to use.

Today he gathered all the stone blades and went off to do this satisfying chore. He was half-kneeling, one leg before him and blades arrayed, the already-honed ones set to the left, the still-blunt ones on the right, when River came seeking his advice.

"Watch out," he warned her. "There's sharp chips all around." He indicated a spot at a distance. "You'll be safer over there." He aimed a piece of antler just so at the blade, a small hammer stone tapping the top of the antler to give it enough force to knock off the blunt edge. *Tap, tap, tap.* He stopped to look at what he accomplished. *Tap, tap. Tap, tap.*

"Father Sky rejoices," River offered politely.

"That He does. And the same to you."

"How fare you today?"

"Me? Fine." *Tap, tap.* "Cookie, fine. Right, Left, Bear, fine, fine, fine. What is it you need?"

"It's about K'enemy," she wavered.

Tap, tap. Rein squinted at the flint before him, then resumed knapping a particularly stubborn surface. Maybe he should try working from more of an angle. "What about K'enemy?" he asked warily. It was bad enough having to step between two arguing people. One of his least favorite things about having leadership foisted on him. He was even more reluctant to intercede in a lover's quarrel.

"Oh, Rein." River twisted her hands in anguish. "I'm not sure I should marry him."

Tap, tap, tap. "After all that mooning around? I have seen you two together; you can't let go of each other. What's changed?"

"What's changed?" She gave a forlorn sigh. "Everything. Birdy came to me yesterday. She accused him of killing our sister just before the cave-in. Cavekeeper did not die from the rockslide; she was already dead by then."

"What?"

"It's true. I asked K'enemy, and he admitted it. He killed her. Said he did it to protect Birdy. Our sister," her voice turned sarcastic, "our lovely sister used to beat her bloody and, oh, Rein! I never even saw it! Birdy always pretended everything was hao. You know how she winces sometimes if you bump her arm? That's from a beating a year ago. Remember how she limped all last winter?"

Rein lifted an eyebrow, questioning.

The corners of her mouth turned down in disgust. "On the day of the great tide, Nose was getting ready to beat her something furious. K'enemy heard her talking about it and decided he had to stop her."

"Did he have to beat her to death to stop her?"

"Probably not. But to stop her for good? Maybe. Anyway, the cave-in started around then; maybe that made it worse."

"Hmmm." *Tap, tap, tap.* "People hit their kids all the time. What's the problem? I know I've hit Bear a few times. Sometimes the twins are almost asking for it."

"Not hitting. Beating. Breaking bones sometimes. When Birdy broke her arm she told me she was careless and tripped, gathering wood. Well she wasn't; that was Nosy. And the split lip she had just before Solstice? Nosy again. Did you ever notice how she flinches when you come up on her suddenly? What do you think that's about?"

"Her mother," Rein said heavily.

"I think so."

Rein shook his head to clear it. Suddenly he looked up at her, tossing down the blade in his hand. "River, do you believe this story?"

"Actually, I do."

He wiped his forehead with the back of his arm. "A mother, hurting her child like that?"

"Well, it was Cavekeeper, not Cookie or anyone normal we're talking about."

"Yeah, but even her ..."

"You know she was always odd that way."

"She certainly was not the best of mothers, but beating the kids like that? I assume it wasn't just Birdy and that she did it to the others too."

"Birdy got most of it. Thunder was big enough to stand up for himself. She was a harsh woman," River sighed. "She used those kids like tools most of the time. Yes, she could be fun and sweet, especially toward the little ones. But most of the time she was not that way at all. I guess I only knew a small part of it. I tried to cushion them. Mamma tried too. But there was obviously a lot we didn't protect them from."

"I should have been watching more myself," Rein brooded.

"You had your own family to look after," she offered.

"True. But still ..."

Still. He should have known.

Though nobody else seemed to notice or do anything either. The chief. The shaman. Any visitor to the cave might have seen how she used Birdy, belittled her, neglected her when she didn't need something. Lots of people might have stepped in, or said something at least.

But Rein was family. Of all people, he should have been watching out. He knew what his sister was like; he probably should have done something about it long ago. Instead he and Cookie moved up the mountain to raise their family away from the cave. They had their reasons. But he could have paid more attention.

There were many times in the first years with Cookie that his sister came into their shelter to borrow one of Cookie's scrapers, an awl, a piece of hide. And if she even bothered to return it, there was always something wrong—the edge was blunted, the hide torn. Or the thing returned was just different enough, Cookie was sure she switched it with another not as good. It was why they finally moved away, not just to be closer to Cookie's favorite picking spots, but to make it hard for his sister to raid his wife's stores whenever she felt like it.

As a child, Nose sometimes took his weapons unasked and used them to bait and skewer small animals. She didn't cook them for meat and just left them to rot, breaking hao. She didn't bother returning his blades, another break in hao. Yes, that was her, a person outside haodisah. A woman who did not notice or care if she destroyed the harmony among all things.

Even if Cavekeeper did not intend to destroy her daughter, such casual violence was a kind of death, an ugliness with no redemptive purpose that should not be borne. This new thing; it was not so different from when she skewered hares or lemmings and left them to rot. Finally he saw what K'enemy saw more readily, what he grew up with and for too long overlooked: That she who enjoyed setting pain in motion was someone who should be stopped. If only he had paid more attention.

Though he probably would have told himself that having Great Uncle, their mother, and River nearby was enough to contain it.

River watched from underneath lowered eyes. In the past she might have grown impatient. She'd be poking him, "Come on, what do you think?" But as chief he deserved more respect. He had to think not only for her and the family, but how these things might affect them all.

Still it was hard to wait, especially after a night full of doubts. Finally she broke in. "K'enemy killed her, Rein. He admitted it. And I don't know what to do next."

Rein lay down his tools. "Why did Birdy keep this to herself?"

"She didn't. She tried to tell me as soon as she realized. But I was in love and didn't want to hear anything bad about him."

Rein nodded slowly. There was no need to blame either Birdy or River for this.

"Yesterday she told me the whole thing. Twice; I made her tell it a second time."

He placed a cautionary hand on her shoulder. "Do you want to lay the rest of your life next to the man who killed your sister?"

River sighed. "You know, I really miss our mamma. I miss Pout and the baby and Thunder. But I do not, even a little bit, miss our sister. Everybody loved her except for us. She was a fire we always had to tend, or it might burn out of control. Do you know how many afternoons I spent looking after her family? When I could have been laughing with my friends, or chasing after guys? Every girl has to take care of her nieces and nephews sometimes, but not all the time, worrying like that. And did she even thank me? Ever? Do something nice in return? Exactly once since she began having children. She offered me an ivory necklace, something one of her man friends gave her, someone that she didn't like anymore. She said I could have it if I wanted it. Of course it was broken; several of the beads were cracked."

"You're angry at her," Rein guessed.

"I was outraged! But I didn't do this for her. I did it for the kids. I hated seeing them neglected. Insulted. Physically hurt. I stepped in where I could." She sighed, embarrassed to be so bitter. "I couldn't stand to live with her in the cave. But I couldn't stand to live far away, either."

Silence fell upon them. Each was furiously sorting through a tangle of misgivings. Finally Rein looked up to ask, "You still want to marry him?"

"Would it seem stupid if I say yes?"

He smiled. "It's only stupid if you don't love him. Or trust him. I guess it's pretty much the same thing."

"That's it exactly." River pointed a finger at him. "Do I love him? I suppose I do. I mean, what is love, anyway? I feel this bond with him. Like we're tied together with a rope that nobody can see. Every time he goes away I feel the tug. I'm always aware of where he is. It feels like a cold wind when he's somewhere else and warm and comforting when he's back. I never felt that way with anybody else. Even now I feel it as we sit here and I try to figure out how angry I am." She snorted impatiently. "If any other woman came and made flirty eyes at him, I'd probably kick her teeth in."

"Hmm," he said, beginning to smile. "Or pull her hair out."

"Go for the eyes."

"Punch her till she drops."

"Tickle her, at least. Till she screams for mercy." River suddenly grinned. "Thanks, big brother. I guess I must still want him. But can I trust him?"

"Can you?"

"He didn't say anything until Birdy told me herself."

His eyebrows shot up. "Not a thing?"

"Not one word. How could he hide something as big as that from me? I thought I knew everything about him."

He paused, considering. "And now you're wondering, is this the only thing he's hiding? The only bad surprise he'll ever spring on you? Or could there be more, and you'll always be ducking them?"

"Exactly. How do I know?"

Rein gave his head a good scratch while he thought about it. "You never totally know. You think you know someone, maybe you grew up with them, know the family and what they ate for breakfast yesterday. Know what everybody got into trouble for when they were young. You knew them yesterday, you know them today, but you don't actually know them tomorrow. You can't. You can guess what they'll do if something happens to them, but you can't really know for sure. Now take Staunch, let's say you decide to accept him after all." For the past month Staunch had been asking if River would become his mate, but Rein held off giving him an answer.

At this, River made a face at him.

"You marry Staunch, you know a little more of what you get. Because he already had a wife and children, and you know they did okay. Willow's a good kid, and Poor Thing will probably turn out fine too."

"I *don't* want to marry Staunch."

"I know that. But K'enemy's a little harder to guess at. He's pretty much had to scrounge. I don't know what to tell you. Just this." He picked up his tools, addressing the stone. "Can you picture him killing anyone else?"

"Yes," she said firmly. "He's not a wild person, but if it has to happen, I can see him doing it again. There's been times someone had to die, and the chief would ask one of the men to make sure it happened."

"Is that hard for you to live with?"

"No, not really," she admitted. "But K'enemy didn't wait to be asked. He went ahead and did it on his own."

"True, but this was a lot like what happened with his father. Nobody noticed the harm going on, and nobody was saying stop, children are getting hurt."

"It's not exactly the same as with his father."

Rein shook his head. "It's not all that much different, either."

"So maybe he thought, no use asking the Chief, it didn't do any good the last time. He better just go ahead and act for the sake of the children."

"That's my guess too. Did you ask him why he didn't say anything before all this?"

"He said he thought I knew. He assumed Birdy told me, because she was right there. He figured I already forgave him or something."

"Hmm. I'm guessing he didn't want to think about it too hard. Probably hoped it would all work out fine."

"I think you shot that one right through the heart," she agreed.

"Men can be stupid that way sometimes. Did I ever tell you the time when. . . "

"Yes," she interrupted. She knew exactly that story he was going to tell, and she didn't need to hear it again. Old news between him and Cookie. Cookie of course had her own side of the story, which differed wildly from Rein's. Though they managed to move past it, and only rarely brought it up.

"There you have it. So the real question is, can you forgive him for this bit of stupidity that came about because he wanted you so much? He was afraid he might lose you, if he misjudged your mercy and understanding, and you couldn't actually bring yourself to forgive. Can you forgive him for that?"

River stared at him. Misjudged her mercy and understanding? How could anyone think she didn't have enough mercy and understanding? Her, of all people. "Probably," she answered reluctantly. A moment went by. "Yes, I can forgive that part of it. But only if he tells me everything, from now on. *Everything.*"

"Well then." *Tap, tap, tap. Tap, tap.* He looked back at his sister, considering. "Are you going to tell Birdy, or do I have to?"

"About her mamma?" River was horrified. "We can't tell her that."

"You don't expect to keep it a secret, do you?"

"You can't tell a girl her Mami was heartless enough to want to beat her almost to death! Can't we just tell her she got crushed by an early avalanche of rocks, K'enemy saw it happen, and he took her amulet because he loved her?"

Tap, tap. Working gave Rein time to consider the proposal. "She would never believe that, River. She was there and she heard the noise."

"We'll have to think of something else then."

"You can't just make something up! What'll you tell her when everybody starts talking about what K'enemy has to do to make things whole again?"

"What do you mean, what he has to do?"

"Come on. You and I might agree that our sister deserved what she got. But you can't have people running around killing others just because they think it's a good idea. You do that and you get people killing each other every time they want somebody's wife or their food cache. We have to call everybody together and talk this through. He has to do something so that he can still be part of the community."

River stared at him, aghast. "Then everybody will talk about it, and she'll hear how her mother was ready to throw her life away. We have to protect her, she's just a child!"

"River, that makes no sense."

"You're chief now; you can decide anything you want. That's what chiefs do. Make K'enemy do something simple so that we can all get over it. That way we can keep this to ourselves!"

"I'm not the chief," Rein protested.

"Well, if you aren't, who is?"

He opened his mouth but closed it again, knowing there was no one but him. He never asked to be chief. Didn't want the responsibility. This was just one incident. If he took it on, there would be a never-ending series of them. He didn't feel wise enough to figure out every little problem presented to him. All he wanted was to join their cousins in the North, and now he was suddenly chief? He wasn't ambitious. Never dreamt of toppling the old chief like some did, not even when he was young. All he wanted was his wife and his family. Oh, and a nice big pot of reindeer stew bubbling away on the hearth.

"We don't have anyone to comb out the tangles," River reminded him. Combing out the tangles, their expression for refereeing between arguing sides. "We don't have anybody telling us, let's weave a big fishing net for everybody, let's make sure nobody gets left out of the hunts. We only have you. I say this is up to you. You decide what K'enemy has to do to make things whole. Make him do it and make him promise never to do anything like that again. We can tell Birdy it was all an accident or something, I go ahead and marry K'enemy, and everything will be fine."

Rein shook his head. "No. It's not right. This affects everyone, so everyone should help decide."

"Maybe my way's not right but it's not right to do it your way either," she argued. "Sometimes there's no right way, but you still have to do something. You're always saying, choose for the sake of the children. This is for the sake of the children. One child, anyway. Your niece, Birdy."

"For the sake of the children, there should never be secret decisions like this one," he argued back. "They should be shared. Because I'm not always gonna know the right thing to do. I don't know if I can figure out the right thing this time, and the next time might be worse."

"Then set something up for next time. Tell somebody else they have to do the deciding. Or let everybody talk it over around the fire circle. Starting right after we get married, K'enemy and me. It's just a few days away. Meanwhile there's nobody but you, and you're going to have to figure out what to do. So do this now, this once. And set up something better for next time."

She had to work to contain her exasperation. "Come on, Rein, you owe it to her. You said so yourself, you should have done more to protect her from Cavekeeper. So do it now. Protect her from the last bit of ugliness our sister brought about. Why should Birdy's heart get broken when it doesn't need to be that way?"

He closed his eyes. What a tangle; it made his head hurt. He sat for a moment cursing his fate. When that didn't make it all go away, he picked up one of Cookies' choppers and flung it, hard as he could into the trees. "I hate it! Hate this ugly, secret, behind-people's-backs kind of thing!"

"Just do it once, Rein. Then set things up so you don't ever have to do it again."

Slowly he nodded. Maybe she was right, but he didn't like it. Still he could see how it could be done. Once and only once, he decided firmly, and not at all after that. After the wedding he'd get everyone to talk about how to decide this kind of thing. Not that he'd tell them all about it, but he could say *if* something came up he shouldn't have to decide all alone; let's figure out what to do instead. All right. They could set it up so it wouldn't have to happen again. Reluctantly he nodded.

But first he had to talk to K'enemy.

River went off to fetch him. At first the young hunter had trouble meeting Rein's eyes. Even sitting at eye level in front of him, on the hastily swept ground where Rein was chipping blades. It could be that he was even sitting on a few sharp shards. That's good, Rein thought with a petty but pleasing sense of glee. Give the man a few extra reasons to squirm.

Finally K'enemy broke the silence. "Sir?"

Ah, Rein thought to himself, a good sign. Sir. The term literally meant Great Father. It was used sometimes to address the Chief or the Shaman, but more often by children who were being called to task. "So, you ready to take on whatever I suggest?"

"Yes, sir," K'enemy said quietly. "None of this is River's fault, you know."

"I know that. Though I suppose you could say some of it was mine."

At this, K'enemy looked up sharply. But he was expecting censure, not the note of sympathy that someone else might have heard in Rein's voice, and so he did not respond. His head bent again, like a dog expecting to be hit. Only without any complaining, keeping a dignified set to his shoulders. Rein could appreciate that. The man could take pain without a whimper.

"K'enemy, look at me."

K'enemy looked up.

"I always thought that if someone killed somebody else, accidentally or on-purpose, they should take over all the responsibilities the other person had. That's the only way to even come close to making things whole again. Make sure nobody else is all that much worse off than before. And they should do it cheerfully. You understand me?"

K'enemy nodded warily, his eyes locked on Rein's.

"Cavekeeper was responsible for her children and her mother. Her uncle too, though he can forage for himself. And for her sister, if she needed anything. All this is now on you. For the rest of your life, if any of them need a thing, you be ready to provide it. If Trapper falls ill, you see he's taken care of. If Birdy never marries, she stays at your hearth. River—you keep her well fed and clothed. Oopsy—let him follow you, learn from you, teach him to hunt. For the rest of your life. Do you agree?"

K'enemy's jaw was open. "But ..."

"No buts. No exceptions. Until the day you die."

"But I would have done it anyway," he managed to get in.

Rein chose to deliberately misunderstand. "You will have to do it, no matter what. This is how you make up for it. Do you accept?"

K'enemy nodded. "Gladly. Sir."

"Starting right now."

"Thank you, sir."

There was a moment of silence. K'enemy couldn't leave without receiving a sign that Rein was finished giving him a hard time. And Rein needed a moment to decide if he was done giving the fellow a hard time. Seemed like there should be more. Oh yes, of course.

"K'enemy."

"Sir?"

"You have killed twice. Both times, perhaps, for good reason. Maybe; I can't really say. But I cannot let you do it again. Not on your own, anyway. Not just whenever you wake up and decide the People would be better off if some particular person was sent Beyond." K'enemy started to protest, but Rein stopped him. "Now maybe there will come a time when we all decide the People would be better off without somebody or another. Maybe then we'll ask you to kill again. And if we do, we won't make you take on all their responsibilities. Or if someone attacks us, I'd feel better knowing you'll be ready to do it again. Until then, can you promise you won't kill anybody else? Because I want to be able to sleep at night without worrying if you're skulking around somewhere."

K'enemy opened his arms to show he was hiding nothing. No weapons, no ugly thoughts or plans. "I promise to do as you ask. Sir."

"No violent acts unless the clan asks you for it?"

"No violent acts unless you ask for it."

Rein looked for a long moment at him. There was no guile in the man's face. He nodded to River, and then to K'enemy. One never knew for sure about anybody, he reminded himself, but for now this would do.

"Oh, and, K'enemy?"

"Yes, sir?"

"No more sirs. I'm just a man like you. I don't call you sir; you don't call me sir. You might save my life some time for all I know. In the meantime, go away. You have people to take care of."

He backed away, still thanking him, still calling him sir. Would the man never leave? Wasn't it enough that Rein gave him a way out with dignity; did he have to bombard him with sappy promises and those raw, grateful eyes?

Wait. There was one more thing. "River," Rein called after her. "The two of you work out what to tell Birdy. I don't want to have to tell her some story or another. I'll back you up in whatever you say but I don't want to lie. Just let me know what you said, so I don't get it wrong."

"I'll talk to Uncle too," River promised. "But no one else has to know. No one else *should* know."

"No one. Not even Cookie," he agreed with relief. Because he knew he wouldn't be able to lie to her. If she asked, he'd have to shrug. He could do that much without giving it away. Probably.

*   *   *

Was the wedding off or not? River avoided K'enemy for a day, raising Birdy's hopes. She wouldn't tell anyone, though Birdy pestered her about it. Nor did Cookie know whether she should keep separating out the finest grass seed to scatter ritually at the end of the wedding ceremony.

Falling Leaf kept reminding Cookie, "She still could marry Staunch if she wants to."

Birdy, overhearing, nodded vigorously. Staunch with River? She and Willow would be sisters, and K'enemy could disappear somewhere; she didn't care where. But to Birdy's dismay, within a few days the wedding seemed to be on again.

"Birdy, you will be safe, I promise you that," River said. And then, "It's complicated, but it's really his story to tell. Why don't you go ask K'enemy about it?"

As if she would.

And when Birdy kept tagging after her and insisting she had to know, River shook her off. She would only smile sadly and say, "Your mother's death was brought down on her by the Spirits themselves. K'enemy is not to be blamed; that's all you need to know."

*   *   *

In the middle of the next day's walk Antler accidentally bumped into Bison, and they got into a small scuffle, half joking, half real. Bison bumped Antler back, who came close to losing his balance. In turn he put his foot out and Bison jumped over it, nicking Antler's ankle. Antler play-punched Bison, but with each jostle the encounters grew more raucous. The contest became verbal when Bison called out, loud enough that everyone nearby could hear. "Hey, Antler. You know what your name means?"

"What?"

"They usually come in twos. Antlers," emphasizing the last part of the word. "Not antler. I guess you only carry half a rack."

Overhearing this, Turtle gave a hoot. "Half a rack? You only have half a rack? Hey, everybody, Antler only has half a rack!"

Owl chortled and called to Lynx, though he was too young to understand the slur. "Half a rack! He said Antler's only got half a rack!"

Antler flushed, his face turning a deep red.

K'enemy, walking behind, started laughing with the younger boys. "Half a rack, Antler, that's all you got?"

His remark infuriated Birdy, though she'd been smiling uncomfortably until then. The younger guys' teasing was bad enough. But a man his age ought to know better than to pick on a boy so much younger than him. Maybe she couldn't stop River from marrying him, but she didn't have to like him. Certainly she didn't have to pretend she respected him. Especially not when he acted like a kid and insulted her friend in the process. Knowing it was none of her business, still she leapt to Antler's defense. "Half a rack is better than no rack at all, K'enemy," she said with disdain.

Turtle called out, "Oooh, K'enemy, she really got you there!"

Antler placed a restraining hand on Birdy's shoulder. "Thanks, Birdy, but I have to do this myself."

Birdy frowned, worried that he could not.

"Be the Antler, not the Ant. That's what Falcon taught me. He may be dead, but I'm still learning from him."

Turning back to K'enemy, Antler said in an exaggeratedly casual tone, "Half a rack here," he gestured towards himself, "is better than a full rack with some of you slippery maggots." He paused, letting the jibe sink in. His eye lit on Turtle. "Antler is an ancient and honorable name. Antler was our earliest tool; our first knives were made of it. Or don't you listen to the stories when we tell them every year? At least if it's made of Antler," he puffed his chest out proudly, "you know it will be hard enough to do some real damage."

Bear told him later that, for a first effort, it was not too bad. In any case, K'enemy snorted; Turtle turned away and ignored him for the rest of the day. Almost everybody else laughed. This time not at him; they were actually starting accept him at last.

Turtle dropped back in line to keep an eye on his mother and sister. Bison moved ahead to confer with Rein. With the two of them gone, Birdy turned to ask her friend, "What did Falcon mean, be the Antler, not the Ant?"

Antler gave her a sideways glance. "It means to be strong. To be ready to defend myself if I have to. To stab when attacked if that's what is needed."

"It means to wear pretty, frilly thingies on his head that the girl reindeers might like," Bear suggested helpfully.

"It means smacking your friend when he needs some smacking," Antler retorted, and landed a solid backhand on Bear's rear end. To which Bear responded with a playful punch, and Antler poked him back. Birdy finally intervened, placing herself between them as they continued on the forward path.

Up front Rein was urging people to go faster. Returning to the middle part of the line Bison repeated the summons. "Let's keep it moving, folks. We got a distance to cover today."

And for many more days they did just that. Kept it moving, covered the distance.

Chapter 6: Staying on the shore

Since they left their home by the sea, the New Moon had passed, and a Full Moon, then another New Moon. Trapper performed the moon ceremonies with Antler's help, but, at the last New Moon, Antler conducted them while Trapper stood back. It was a passage—Antler growing into new responsibilities—though no one remarked on the change.

Though surely they noticed. There was an embarrassing pause when the People were supposed to address him formally during the ritual. The shaman was always called Great Father. But Antler still looked like a boy, and it was hard for them to call him that. Finally Rein pronounced it, Great Father, and the ceremony went forward.

Now they were almost upon the next Full Moon. They traveled most of the finger land that was the world they knew, moving northeast to where it joined the mainland. Ahead would be wider country—mountains and marsh, forest and meadow. Soon they hoped to spot signs of their Reindeer Cousins. "They," Rein reminded everyone, "who will soon be Us."

Once on the mainland they would set up camp. They would celebrate the Full Moon. River and K'enemy would wed, and all would mark the next step forward.

★   ★   ★

"It's gonna happen. Admit it, Birdy, it'll happen whether you like it or not."

Birdy turned her back on Bear. She was reluctant to admit to admit any such thing.

"What's gonna happen, Bear?" Willow asked. "What are you two arguing about?" The four friends were walking near the rear of the line, but Willow and Antler had completely missed the beginning of the conversation between the two cousins.

Bear threw up his hands in frustration. "Just because she hates K'enemy, she refuses to talk about the wedding. And she has to talk about it because I need her to do something that night."

"Why don't you wait until it's over and ask her to do you the favor then?"

"It's not a favor for me; it's for her. And it's not just something to do whenever she feels like; it has to happen all through the wedding, from beginning to end."

"I know what it's about," Antler told the girl. "It's something from one of his dreams."

"His dreams?" Willow gave him a blank look.

"You don't know about Bear's dreams?"

She shook her head, no.

"They have a habit of coming true. He really should be a shaman. You'd make a good one, Bear."

"Not me, I'm too fidgety. I'd probably stick the smoking leaves up somebody's nose."

"He'd be good with visions," Antler told Willow.

"Visions," Willow mused. "Have you ever had a vision, Antler?"

"No, not yet. Falcon said I was still too young. Too skinny, maybe. You have to fast for several days first, you know. But Bear's dreams are a lot like visions."

"Not every dream," Bear demurred.

"Not every one, that's true. Last spring he had a dream about a sea lion wandering around the meadow by the hot springs cave." Antler chortled. "A sea lion up in the meadow, can you imagine?"

The other three turned to look at him. "There was a sea lion in the meadow, Antler," Birdy informed him. "Didn't you hear about it?"

Antler stared at each in turn.

"I forgot I had that dream," Bear mused.

Birdy told Antler about the poor, lost creature. "Made good eating, though," she concluded.

WIllow turned to Bear. "Are all your dreams some kind of vision?"

"No. Most of them are dreams like everybody has, which is good. Otherwise my head would be crammed with too much stuff."

"When you're dreaming, can you tell if it's a real vision?"

"Sometimes. The ones that come true usually seem different. There's a kind of intense feeling. Like someone's telling me, hey, pay attention, this is important."

"Did you have other dreams that turned out to be visions?"

"The one before this one about the wedding? It was about Antler walking with me and Birdy on the trail going north. I dreamed it a few days before he caught up with us. Everybody thought he was dead but I wasn't so sure, because of that dream."

"Yeah, Birdy told me about that." Willow slowed to adjust her pack. "So you can usually tell which dreams are important?"

"If I think about it. Though there's one that I just can't decide about."

Bear cast a shy glance in her direction. She seemed to be fascinated. He preened a little at the attention. It felt kind of nice to show off. Immediately he thought of the camp dogs, wagging their tails at anyone who tossed them a bone. The image made him squirm. "There's this one dream I keep having. It feels like one of the vision dreams, but I've been having it since I was small."

"And it hasn't come about in all that time?"

"Not yet."

"Well?" She signaled him to continue.

"There's this cute little baby bear. It's crawling around inside some kind of big shelter. He keeps getting into the sacks of food or tangled up in the bedcovers; it's kind of funny. But then he backs up into the hearth by accident and his fur catches fire along his back and shoulders. He's howling, trying to swipe at his fur, and I grab him and haul him out of the tent. Throw him into the snow and roll him around until the snow puts out the fire."

"That's how Bear got the name Fire Bear, because of the dream," Antler pointed out.

Willow nodded thoughtfully. Interesting, what the person's name said about them, once you knew the story. "Tell us the dream you had about the wedding. Is it one of the pay-attention dreams?"

Bear nodded. "But Birdy won't listen."

"Maybe I can make her listen."

Bear sighed gratefully. Maybe Willow would have more influence. "It's just that she has to stay with me or she won't be safe. The whole time," he emphasized.

"That's the dream?"

"No, that's what I know she has to do. In the dream I see us camped out; River and K'enemy are at the fire circle with Antler and Great Uncle conducting the ceremony. That's how I know it's their wedding. There are these men." He paused a moment to think.

"What men?"

"I don't know. I can't see which men. There's just this sense of danger when Birdy goes anywhere near them. I'm not one of them, so I know if I keep her with me, she'll be all right. If she goes off without me, it feels like something bad will happen."

"That's the whole dream?"

"That's it."

"Can't you tell who they are? Or when, exactly?"

"It's not like something that already happened," Bear said, exasperated. "Not like a real memory where you go over it and remember more detail. I only know the feeling I have, that she has to stay with me or she'll be in trouble." He raised his voice, directing it at his cousin. "You have to stay with me, Birdy. All through the celebration, you hear?"

Birdy snorted, but she did not refuse.

"She hears you," Willow insisted. "I'll make sure of it."

★   ★   ★

How nice it seemed to be working out, Great Uncle thought. They finally set foot on the mainland, a day before the Full Moon. Early enough to set up camp at this good site inland, giving the women an afternoon and a day to prepare the wedding feast. They could hold the Full Moon ceremonies at the same time, and relax for a day before setting out again.

He was absorbed, sorting through his small horde of possessions. Wasn't there a spare piece of hide to cut up for the special lashings? Ah, there, not a large piece but long enough for the purpose. Antler would pick a fresh supply of savory leaves. He was a good lad. Hopefully there would be enough time to teach him everything he needed to know. Some day soon the Great Father would take him home. He could feel that Sky breath rattling his bones. Yes, it would probably be soon. Soon enough that every new sunrise seemed like a precious gift.

At least his family would be taken care of. River, married. Birdy and Oopsy could live with River or with Rein. Rein would be a good leader. He tried to be too nice. It might be hard if he ever had to make any tough decisions, Trapper imagined, hurt anyone's feelings, or sacrificed someone for the good of the tribe. But he was doing fine so far. He talked about doing things for the sake of the children's children. That was wisdom; a very good sign.

He may as well see if he could catch a little something to contribute to the feast. River was his niece, after all. He spotted some promising tracks near the river as they came over the rise. He took several traps of different sizes with him and set out looking for trails to set them on. Over there's one, but it was narrow, hardly worth the effort if all he caught was a mouse or a vole. Yonder trail was wider; he'd set one there.

As he worked, his mind drifted back as it did so often these days. Back beyond the recent years of small loves and disappointments, the animals that eluded his snares, the wife who died trying to birth their daughter. Back to the days of his youth, to the bright summer when he was one of the chosen ones.

Days they spent learning the chants and the rituals. Nighttimes, listening to the stories. Practicing to be the Cushion, whose head was in the clouds, though his feet were firmly planted. He recalled the sonorous voice leading and instructing them. The longed-for arm draped approvingly around his shoulders, his own face flushing with unexpected attention. Not often enough though, not nearly often enough.

It took him many years to realize that it should have been a lot more often.

Young as he was, he could have made a fine shaman. Was he not doing well these days, in this unexpected second chance? What a comfort your ceremonies are, people kept saying. How eloquent, and we never even realized. All the prayers he made for good traveling weather, and they had it, they had it; hardly any rain to slow them down, and this pleasant warmth holding unexpectedly as they headed into the northern lands.

Yet in his foolishness he let himself be convinced to let it all drop away. There was many a time when he recited the prayers without mistake, but the shaman who was shaman before Falcon—Like a Cold Wind he was called—his eye barely registered all the good that Trapper did. His eye lingered elsewhere, and it took these many seasons for Trapper to realize it was through no fault of his own.

Grimly he recalled the way Wind conducted the ceremonies at the New Moon. As each one approached, the apprentice boys would see a special sparkle appear in Cold Wind's eyes. His color rose, and his gaze would linger on one of his favorites. This favoritism was one root of the problem, Trapper concluded long ago. If you were not one of his favorites, you were nothing. Worse, you were an impediment in the master's eyes.

A cold shiver ran through him. The New Moon ceremony, a minor event but for the hidden ceremonies that followed.

At the conclusion of the ceremony, as the People drifted away, Wind would signal his acolytes to take up their torches. In absolute silence they followed him down the beach, his hand lightly gripping his current favorite. The procession followed a little-used passage, down a rarely traveled ravine and up to a cave hidden in the farther mountain. There in the crevasse the apprentices would build a fire and the secret ceremonies began. Someone would pick up the drum. Someone else would bring forth the special concoction and hold it to their lips. Wind made sure each sipped at it. How many swallows to take, that was something he would instruct each boy separately.

The furs and robes would drop away. The boys would leap and dance, their naked bodies gleaming in the firelight. The drum beat a hypnotic pulse; the drink passed around again, and the smile widened on Wind's face until all you could see was his smile. His anticipation. Only the boys who had once been his favorites knew that there was a third ceremony to be performed later that night. As for the boys who had not been so favored, they could only guess what might take place in that most private rite.

Three moons in a row, he who had been Trapper's beloved friend was the one chosen. Now for a fourth time Wind crooked his finger, the same as before. Trapper, passed over again, watched his friend rise, solemn with the attention, and disappear into the cavern, not to return until daylight.

Without the master the music continued. With no one to frown or forbid it, the boys drained the remainder of the special brew. The music and dancing grew wild and eventually died out as the boys succumbed to sleep, slumping against each other amid the discarded bowls and furs. And in the gray light of dawn Trapper watched his friend emerge. An ugly, awkward grin marred his beautiful face.

No one talked about that innermost ceremony. Not the current favorite, nor any of the previous ones. Not when Trapper appealed to his dearest friend, promising silence, offering a fine obsidian blade that the friend had long envied. Instead of learning more of the innermost rituals, Trapper watched his friend retreat from the boys, responding only to that firm hand on his shoulder. As the moons waxed and waned, it became too painful to have only silence meet his imploring questions, to feel a cold rock wall instead of laughter and kinship. To know in his heart he'd never be chosen, and the choice that was made had lost him too much.

The next time he visited his family, after his brother teasingly invited him to join when they set out to hunt the Mammoth, he surprised everyone, including himself, by accepting. And for the next several summers he did not return to that fire circle by the sea.

Better to be trained this way. One on one, as he and Antler were doing. Openly, with no favorites and no hidden purpose that had little to do with Father Sky and much to do with Cold Wind himself.

Still he found himself dreaming of those days, waking with that long-lost friend's name on his lips.

Eyas. What a tender little fledgling he was. Actually, he thought, they both were.

Enough, he scolded. There was no need to wallow in this sourness. Let the past lie in the past. Let the today's sun shine on your leathery skin. Enjoy the warmth, for it is fleeting and it may be gone tomorrow.

He looked up, noting the position of the sun. Yes, there was time left in the day. He could set several traps and get a little fishing in as well. He was testing the first trap when he heard footfalls. The birds stopped chattering; the small animal rustlings ceased.

Birdy came running up, her hair all tangled, dirt in smudges across her face. "Great Uncle," she gasped, working to catch her breath. "I've been looking all over for you!"

"And here you found me," he smiled. He brushed the dust off his hands and sat on the ground, motioning her to join him.

"You're the only one left. You have to help!"

"Help with what, child?"

"Help me stop Aunt River! She cannot marry that man; he is full of ugliness!"

Ugliness, or rotten, the closest words they had for evil.

"I told her plenty of times, but she won't listen," Birdy continued pleading. "You have to make her stop. Uncle Rein won't; I already asked. Or, I know! Just tell her you can't marry them, and don't perform the rites."

"River won't listen?" he repeated, patiently.

"No." Her face fell. "She's planning to marry him, no matter what I say."

River had already spoken to him. But, like Rein, he hoped he'd never have to discuss something that was only partly true. Too easy to get tangled in that kind of spider's web. So instead he responded sideways. "Now tell me, child, why should she listen when you tell her not to do what she wants to do?"

"Nobody understands how rotten he is! She won't be safe. He might kill her in her bed!"

Great Uncle looked at the sky, moody and overcast above them. River wouldn't listen, just as her willful sister didn't listen when people suggested she change her ways. Nor did Eyas listen when he begged him to beware of another cold wind. People usually needed to work things out themselves.

At least she cared; it said a lot for the girl. She was loyal to the ones she loved and didn't ignore them until she needed them. He looked back with an affectionate regard. "So, Birdy, what do you do when someone won't listen, but you're sure they're in danger?"

"What do you mean?" She squinted up at him.

"Let's say Oopsy is playing somewhere, and he's about to fall in deep water. What do you do?"

"Grab him and take him somewhere safe."

"And if you can't grab him in time?"

"Tell him, 'Stop! Watch out!'"

"And if he doesn't pay attention?"

"He falls in, and you see if he needs help getting back up the bank."

"And if he needs help getting out?"

"You jump in after him."

"There you go, then. You think River's going to fall in deep water, and you're yelling at her to stop. She's ignoring you. Either she doesn't think it's too deep, or she's sure she can keep her footing. Or maybe she thinks she's not as close to the edge as you think."

"But she's wrong," Birdy insisted.

"Maybe. Though just maybe you're the one who's wrong." He withstood her frustrated glare. "Unlikely, of course," he said tactfully. "Either way she's not listening when you yell at her, is she?"

"No," Birdy admitted.

"So, you're yelling, and she's ignoring you. What do you do?"

She mumbled something he could not hear.

"What would you do if it was Oopsy?"

"I said, watch to see if he needed help," she conceded. "But Great Uncle, please don't marry them. It will be much easier that way."

"Easier for you, maybe. Will it be easier for River?"

"Of course."

"Will it?"

Birdy hesitated.

"Do you like it when people tell you what to do all the time? Wouldn't you rather they let you work it out?"

He could see her wrestling with it.

"Was it good doing all that work with your mamma telling you, do it this way, stupid child, do it that way, and yelling when you did it wrong? Don't you like it better when people leave you to do things the best you can?"

"I guess."

"Darn right. Other people are the same. If you're right and you make River stop, she'll resent you later. If you're right but you let her work it out herself, she won't be mad afterwards. You don't want her to feel about you like you felt about your mamma, do you?"

"No!" The very thought was horrifying.

"So, stay on shore and keep watching out for her. You won't be the only one there, I promise."

Birdy looked down at her feet. "You aren't just saying that, Great Uncle? You aren't just saying that because you're scared to step in?"

It could have hurt. He had been quiet for too many years, letting Birdy's mother have her way even when he could see how harsh she was. Especially with Birdy. Perhaps he should have stepped in more. At the time he told himself it wasn't his place to interfere; he was living with them after all, in her cave. She was Cavekeeper Woman, and he, a worn-out husk. He had to exist within a small niche in the walls of her hearth, or leave if it was too tight a squeeze.

But mostly, he felt he did what he could. He forgave himself for his shortcomings, just as he tried to forgive others for theirs. Just as he forgave Birdy this small stab at his dignity.

"*Pffff*," he finally responded. "An old man like me? I don't have anything to lose, Birdy. If I'm not scared of dying, then I'm sure not scared of living."

And since he had nothing more to say, she left him looking after his snares. She might be unhappy with the result, he figured, but at least she didn't feel quite so alone.

Chapter 7: Two logs afire

Today the clan would remember how she got her name, Cookie mused with a great deal of satisfaction: Good Cooking Woman and well deserved the name was. Her family ate quite happily, thank you. Somebody was always dropping by their hearth at suppertime to ask about something, and, oh sure, Rein, I'll stay to have a bowlful! Yes, Cookie, seconds would be much appreciated.

Most people were happy with good food in their bellies every day. And why shouldn't they enjoy the good things given by the Great Mother? There were dangers enough around; they should savor the blessings as well.

So what if she walked slowly, seeking those elusive herbs to flavor the stews? Yes, her carrying sack was heavier with that stash of salt crystals, and bulky with mushrooms from the woods. But it was worth it for the savoring, the grateful smiles Rein gave her, the affectionate squeezes on the shoulder or rear. She patted her ample belly contentedly. Life seemed very good indeed.

Her eyes lit up anticipating the pleasures of the ceremony to come. She welcomed this break from walking and hauling such a heavy load. A few days of cooking, eating, laughter and song—it was her favorite kind of day. Already she had two different stews bubbling away. One with mutton and lily roots, onions and mushrooms, the other with the ptarmigan Uncle Trapper brought, to which she'd add greens. There were blueberries simmering with nuts and honey; they would make a lovely treat. And in the pit dug underneath the fire she was roasting swans caught by Bison and Turtle.

Other women were cooking too. It was always good when people pitched in. Falling Leaf, for example. The woman wanted River to marry her son and complained about it often. "Took that haunch we gave her and then promised herself to K'enemy!"

To which Cookie tartly responded, "Did you tell her it was an engagement gift?"

"No."

"So you were generous when her family was hungry. Very kind of you. So what's wrong?"

Nothing the woman could think to say. So eventually Falling Leaf decided to be gracious. They had to live together, after all. She had to set up cooking fires with River every day, butcher cuts of meat with Cookie, walk into unknown territory where K'enemy might save her from harm. When in doubt, being generous made more sense than saying something snooty that could come back and nip at her later.

Little Mouse was grinding lily roots into flour, to be mixed with berries and honey, ladled onto a hot, flat stone and seared as flap-cakes. Fierce sent Little Mother and Lynx to pick greens and maybe cedar nuts; they were starting to come in. Yes, it would be quite a feast. A fine beginning for their marriage. A wedding with an ample supply of food augured an ample and tasty life together. That's how it was for her and Rein. That's what she wished for River and her chosen one.

Off in the distance the men were bantering. "Tonight's the night you'll be tied together," Rein reminded K'enemy.

"All night and all day, with only three hands between you," Two Stones added.

This was their tradition at a wedding. The new couple was tied at the wrist, his left to her right. Until the next sunset they remained bound together negotiating food, bedding and all the necessities of life. The custom made it real, two people who had to begin working as one to build a family. Cookie smiled. She remembered her own tying. How scared she was, yet pleased at the same time. The shy grin Rein flashed her as the shaman fastened the wedding thong. The clumsy fumbling with their clothing, the giggles, the excitement. The tenderness and several embarrassing bruises that resulted. That barely-slept night, half-waking every time either one needed to turn.

Turtle, that bumbling man-child, was needling the groom. "You'll have to help her pee! Ha! You might even have to wipe her bottom!"

K'enemy had withstood the ribbing till then, but this evoked a threatening growl. Good, Cookie thought with great satisfaction. He'll defend her from stupid little slights. If a man defends his woman on the small things, it's a good bet he'll be there for the big ones.

Down at the creek, her daughters were helping River bathe. Too bad Birdy-girl resisted joining them. She was missing all the fun, silly child. Swan and Left were gathering flowers, some to braid in River's hair, some to daub their aroma on her skin. Swan invited Birdy along, but she turned her down. Said she'd rather help Cookie and so she had, though she disappeared a while back and was nowhere to be found. Not that she was needed still, but it would be easier if she were around to stir or change the hot rocks as they cooled down.

Whatever had happened between Birdy and River, it was too bad. River did her best to reconcile them. Cookie grimaced. She was embarrassed for River; the whole thing seemed pathetic. "Please be with me for my wedding day, Birdsilu," she pleaded. "Won't you set aside your grudge to celebrate?"

The stony look Birdy gave her sent chills up Cookie's arms. After Birdy finished digging the fire pit, Cookie suggested she go wash off in the creek. "While you're there, why not relax with the girls? They sound like they're having fun getting ready for tonight."

Instead Birdy marched upstream from the others, and nobody had seen her since.

It was too bad when families couldn't get along.

Suddenly a noise caught her attention. Actually it wasn't a noise but a silence, peculiar with any group of people. A sudden alertness swept through the camp. People stopped talking and set their tools down. Now she saw from the direction of the sea, three hunters coming into sight. They were carrying a fresh-slain walrus between them.

There was something different about them. They walked with a bouncing gait. They were stockier than any of the People. Their word-sounds, carried on the wind, were full of sharp noises, not soft with the breathy sounds familiar to her. From some other tribe, she decided. Let's hope they were friendly.

There were three of them, so three of the Ogwehu stepped forward to meet. Rein, Bison and Staunch grabbed their spears, though they held them upright. Upright, as walking sticks, so they would not provoke a fight. Yet with blades poised to tilt forward in case a fight was offered.

Seeing this, the strangers set down the carcass and retreated behind it. They put their heads together, gabbing all the while. The middle one looked straight ahead toward the camp. Glancing around, he picked out Rein as the one to address. He shouted but no one understood the sounds.

Rein shouted back, "Who are you? Do you come in peace?" though his words were just as meaningless to them.

Ostentatiously the man laid down his weapons and stepped forward. Rein too set down his spear and walked toward them. The two approached, stopping a few paces apart.

Rein was good with words, Cookie reminded herself. If anyone could make sense of their garbledy talk, he could. He knew the speech of the Reindeer People—similar to theirs except they had more words for reindeer and for different ways to herd or capture them. Rein was slowly teaching these, but she found them hard to remember. Rein had easily picked up the language of the Mammoth hunters who visited a few summers back, not enough to gossip, but enough with hand signals to have a halting conversation.

Even now he was trying the foreign talk he knew. With some success it looked like, for the newcomers seemed to recognize some words.

For quite a while Rein spoke. Their leader conferred with his men, then turned back to reply. Rein gave them a puzzled look, then his face lit up and he'd try something else. They went back and forth using words and hands, and Cookie got dizzy trying to follow it.

Their leader pointed beyond the creek, then up at the sky, then elsewhere in the heavens, finally moving his fingers like a person's legs walking.

"I think these people live that way," Rein shouted back. "Northwest, maybe half a day's walk. They hunt for seal or walrus sometimes, and bring it back for food."

He spoke again to the strangers, hands dancing in the air, and they nodded, seeming to understand.

Their leader now pointed at Rein's upper arm. Rein's voice rose, great with excitement. The two of them had a fast exchange, and Rein turned back to report. "He recognizes our tattoos! He's seen them before!"

The man pointed at his left shoulder and then at Rein's, each laughing with a kind of delighted recognition. "He says they saw people with these tattoos several summers before. Or maybe he saw them several times, I'm not sure. They're off that way!" Rein pointed northeast, then turned back to confer. "There's a big herd of reindeer, and the tattoo people followed. It has to be our cousins he's talking about!"

Another flurry of questioning and partial comprehension. Cookie could see by the number of times they gave Rein a puzzled look that some things were understood and others not. But something got through. Their cousins were northeast, so the People would go there too. Which was nice, because they hadn't found fresh reindeer tracks, just a few old trails that might no longer be good.

Rein returned to camp, the newcomers following. "I invited them to celebrate with us. They offer slabs of walrus for the feast." Rein motioned towards the edge of the camp. They could set up there. He pointed a finger at the carcass, and then at Cookie.

Cookie understood what that meant. It was her task to prepare their contribution. Naturally. The more guests, the more merriment. The more people, the more mouths to feed. And here she thought she could finally sit down for a bit and relax.

She sighed, but it was laced with forgiveness. Outsiders, plus their first real news of the cousins. It would surely be a memorable wedding. Cookie adjusted her wrap to keep it from getting bloody while she hacked away at the carcass. She brushed her hair back and put a welcoming smile on her face. Already she was planning what she needed to prepare this offering. Where was that Birdy girl, anyway? Now she could really use another pair of hands.

★   ★   ★

It was a good sign for the wedding when Father Sky blew the rainclouds away. The night would be clear for the ceremony. No one would get rained on; the ritual fire would not sputter out. It would blaze bright and bold, especially the wood set on the hearth by bride and groom, two ceremonial logs afire, and if the embers lasted long, that would be auspicious too.

But first the Full Moon ceremony, with Antler chanting prayers. Trapper distributed pieces of lily root sliced cross-wise into circles, pale as the moon in the night sky. They were to eat them, taking the night-sky light inside to guide their dream-journeying. Though instead of eating his, Lynx held it high and danced in circles until he got dizzy. "I'm holding the moon in my hand!" he shouted, and Oopsy followed his lead.

Everyone else arranged themselves around the fire circle, Staunch's family to the left, as befit the relations of the groom, Rein's family on the right where the bride's people should be. The rest sat in the middle, opening up to welcome the outsiders in.

Trapper clapped his hands together, and the murmurs died away. "Who comes from the men to be joined today?" he intoned.

K'enemy was thrust forth from his family's enclave. He stumbled, propelled by pinches, pokes, and an arm punch from Staunch. Both bride and groom were traditionally pushed forward with many small punishments, leaving their families in pain. Thus the joining began with bride and groom feeling immediate relief from pain. Let the marriage commence with them knowing that their lives would get better than before.

"Who comes from the women to be joined today?"

Rein gave River a joyous shove, Cookie, a playful slap. Swan and Left each poked her. Oopsy kicked his leg out, but missed her altogether.

Birdy wasn't planning any punishment. She hated the very idea of hurting River, who had hugged away so much of her own pain. Her stomach roiled. She was so afraid this marriage would be bad; how could she add more hurt to that? Great Uncle said River had to find her footing in the water. She wouldn't listen to Birdy and stay safe on the banks. She should, but she wouldn't.

There was a family story, Birdy suddenly recalled, from her grandmother's time. A man was wooing two sisters, and until the bride was thrust forward, no one was sure who would be married that day. A teasing image flitted through her mind. They could push Left forward instead of River. But she doubted that Swan would agree to it. She enjoyed strutting around with Bison and Turtle, even catching Staunch's eye.

No, it would never work.

"I will protect you," K'enemy was now pledging to River. He laid a new-made blade on the ground at her feet.

"I will make you fine, warm clothing," River responded, pointing at the new shirt he proudly wore.

"I will feed you, and our children," he said and set a pile of fresh-caught fish in front of her, one of them still flipping its tail.

"I will bear your children and care for them," she replied, cradling her womb.

Taking her hand, he laid it against his chest. "I bind you to me, and no other."

Laying his hand between her breasts, she echoed, "I bind you to me, and no other."

"As long as there is breath on my lips," and with a delicate touch he brushed his hand along the side of her face.

"As long as there is breath in my mouth." Touching her lips, she caught his hand and held it tight.

Trapper gently pushed their heads together, face to face, letting their breath mingle and become one. In the silence that followed, many wiped away tears.

Now Trapper called on the Great Spirits to bless the bride and groom. According to tradition, he asked for four blessings, one from each of the directions: Good hunting, strength, a steady arm, and a patient temper for the groom. For the bride he called for strength, healthy children, good medicine, and a forgiving heart. When he finished, Antler smudged them both with savory incense. On this day he used a pure white feather to wave the smoke around them. Then Trapper called for blessings from the groom's family, and the bride's, and then from all the People. Amid hooting and cheering, the blessings were given.

He took K'enemy's left wrist and held it to River's right one. Antler handed him a ceremonial blade. Quickly he slashed a small cut in each and rubbed the cuts together. "Their blood is joined," he announced. "Now these two are one."

"Now these two are one," the clan echoed.

Antler handed him a bowl of pine resin wash for the wounds, Father Sky and Mother Earth blessings mixed in the body of the tree. Trapper took up a leather thong, wrapping it three times around their wrists and knotting it, then held their bound hands high so all could see. "Let this marriage be a shining like the Moon above," he pronounced, pointing their arms toward the bright circle in the sky.

"Ho," the People agreed.

And so it was that they were wed. Quiet as the River and Kills His Enemy, joined for all their days.

$$\star \qquad \star \qquad \star$$

"The wedding story," Little Mouse called out. "Can we tell the wedding story?"

"Let's hear the wedding story," Fierce agreed. "Do you know that one, Antler?"

No he did not. Several were married just before he began apprenticing, but none in the months after. Nor did Trapper remember enough to tell it. But between all of them maybe the tale could get told.

It was a story which Birdy had never heard at the shaman's circle. This gave her a great sense of ease. She could recall bits and pieces just like the others, free to take part in the telling without worrying she would give too much away.

The Wedding Story, they called it. Though it was not about a wedding; it was a romantic tale of courting against great odds. They told it for luck to any newly wedded couple, for it spoke of love that lasted, creating a family that carried down through many generations. And hopefully the newly wedded couple would do the same.

The story began with a girl so beautiful and sweet in disposition that four men of the tribe vied for her. One of the men was enamored with her long, silky hair, and he brought wooing gifts of ornaments that he placed in her smooth locks himself. Another loved her soft, husky voice, and he offered special gifts of honey. The third loved her for her comeliness; he draped her with rabbit furs and ermine. The fourth brought few gifts, for his hunting already had to support his widowed mother and her children; thus he had little to spare. Yet with his meager offerings he brought a promise to cherish her and their future offspring no matter what ill fortune came their way.

The father favored the fur-bearing suitor. He was a fine hunter, brave and strong, and what better could a man ask for his daughter? Though the honey-bearing man was a great woodsman, and helped slay a bear that threatened a child of the tribe. The mother of the maiden preferred the man who carved beautiful wood and ivory ornaments for she felt that a man who could cherish her daughter's beauty would go to great lengths to protect her.

Still she found it hard to turn away the last man, for she knew that bad things can befall even the most beautiful of women, and a husband whose heart was loyal would be a husband who could help her daughter flourish, and their children.

The parents argued, as did the grandparents and the elders, but no decision could stop the arguments roaring across their hearth. Finally the mother convinced her husband to let the wooers keep wooing through the winter and the spring. Their daughter would marry whoever they agreed upon at sunset on the longest summer day. In the meantime they would see what happened.

At this point the flow of the story faltered. No one remembered much about the calamities that befell the poor girl. Some fever maybe that made her hair fall out? And the ornament-bearing suitor drifted off to marry another. Additional disasters left the girl frail and ailing, and one by one the men found other maidens, all but the loyal one who kept coming to pay his respects.

The outcome, Fierce as Wolves recalled with a satisfied wagging of her finger: They were married at the solstice, and when they emerged from their night and day of isolation, the new wife was fully restored to her former beauty and strength.

Birdy told the last part, where the newly-joined husband and wife spoke tenderly together and offered their hearts to each other. And the People in the circle were moved as they rarely were, hearing such a tale. Because she spoke with as much passion as a child who has never known passion could speak, and yet the child may long for it, and recognize it when she saw it. And as she spoke the words, she realized that this same passion danced between her aunt and her new husband, a dance she recognized and had to honor. Though she regretted it, she was glad such a thing could exist, for it told her that someday she might feel the same.

And the men cleared their throats and pulled their loved ones closer. The women wiped their eyes gratefully. The children rested their heads in comfort against their parents. And Antler, seeing the beauty of what Birdy contributed, caught her eye and held it, nodding in recognition.

$$\star \qquad \star \qquad \star$$

As with most gatherings, at first the men and women mingled, only to separate apart. So it surprised no one after most of the food was gone to see the women crowding around River, leaving the men to themselves. Without their mitigating presence, the men began giving K'enemy a good verbal scraping and all seemed to enjoy it, including the victim himself. Even the outsiders who understood none of the language, although Rein tried to interpret. Though how could you translate "dead moose farts" or "balls the size of mammoths' ears"? Still there were plenty of grins and backslaps, and a feeling of camaraderie settled in.

The strangers could add nothing to the taunts and boasts, but they reached into their pile of belongings. The smaller one brought an animal bladder over to the gathering of men. They'd filled it with some unknown beverage, knotting it at the neck to hold the liquid in. Making a great many unintelligible explanations, he unknotted the sac, put it to his mouth, tipped his head back and took a deep draught. He offered it to his leader, who took a swallow and passed it to Rein.

Rein held the bladder to his mouth and took a good swig. It was not water, nor tea. Not crushed berry juice, nor anything else he ever tasted. It was sour with an odd sensation of thickness. Disturbingly it burned his throat, though the liquid itself was cool to the touch.

"Pah!" Rein spat out the residue and wiped his lips, then reached for a long drink of scalding tea to rid him of the taste. He pointed to the offending liquid. "What is that?" he asked.

The strangers were poking each other and snorting with laughter. The next one picked up the container and drank with evident pleasure.

After a series of guffaws their leader attempted an answer. He made a brief guttural response that told them nothing. So he began to act out the process of picking cloudberries, gathering them in a pile, crushing and mashing the fruit. He put his hands in a circle, holding them high towards the heavens, repeating the process twice.

"The juice of crushed cloudberries? Three moons, 3 months?" Two Stones guessed.

"They let the berry juice sit for 3 months? No wonder it's gone bad," growled Rein. "And to think I drank that bear piss."

His friends shivered in sympathy.

The bladder was still circling around. The strangers seemed to enjoy it. Staunch took a polite taste, grimaced, and quickly passed it on. Bison passed it over to Turtle without even raising it to his lips.

Turtle looked around, and came to a decision. "I'm going for it," he told his father. "Those guys love it so much, one of us ought to be man enough to give it a real try."

Two Stones raised an eyebrow, then shrugged. His son was a hunter now and could make his own decisions. "Try it if you want," he said.

Turtle raised the sack to his lips. He took a tentative swallow and his face went into immediate contortions. Tears came to his eyes but he blinked them back, and took turns whenever the bladder came around again. Subsequent sips were not as hard to keep down. When he looked up, the strangers grinned and gave a nod of approval.

Chapter 8: Bleak night

Oopsy was still running around with Lynx, the two of them leaping with the dancers and running back to the cooking pots, helping themselves to sticky fingers full of blueberries cooked with honey. Somehow this turned into a complicated game of tag, hiding and finding each other in the dark, occasionally careening into the stewpots and discarded piles of bowls.

After the overtired boys went sprawling in a heap against Great Uncle, Fierce grabbed Lynx, Birdy took Oopsy and made them sit until they calmed down. The boys struggled, for their energy was still high, but Fierce insisted.

"Can we at least have a story, Birdy?" Oopsy begged, eyes bright with hope.

"No story tonight, Oopsy," she frowned. "The music is so loud I can hardly think."

He nestled against her, flinging his legs across Bear's lap as well. After a while Fierce rose and took Lynx to sit with his father. The three cousins remained, watching the dancers. Oopsy's eyelids began to droop, but he wasn't ready to sleep, not with so much excitement in the air. His lids would lower, then pop open. "Is K'enemy gonna be the daddy of us now?" he asked sleepily.

"Never," Birdy said, folding her arms emphatically. "He's only River's mate." She deliberately used the word that indicated a pairing for temporary tasks like gathering food instead of the term they used for husband, member of the family.

"Then who's gonna be the daddy of us?"

She made a face. "No one, Oopsy. You're not going to have a daddy. Mami's gone Beyond; there's never going to be another daddy for you and me."

"A daddy has to be married to your momma, Oopsy," Bear explained. "You'll have to settle for my dad and me. Don't worry, little guy. We'll look after you."

"I want a daddy of my own," he whined. Lynx has a daddy. Owl has a daddy. Why can't I have one?"

"Because," Birdy said bitterly, "it's too late to get one."

"But I want one. Please? You could get me a daddy, couldn't you Birdy?"

"Nope. I'm still a kid so I'm not marrying anybody, and even if I did, he wouldn't be your daddy."

"But why?" he persisted.

Birdy squirmed. All these questions left a bitter taste in her mouth. "Look, Oopsy, you just aren't gonna get one, so shut up about it. Please. Just shut up."

He looked at her with wounded eyes. Birdy was immediately ashamed. She never yelled at him like that. It wasn't his fault River was marrying the wrong person. Birdy felt helpless. She wouldn't mind having a daddy either. Someone to look out for them. Protect them. Laugh in the big, comforting way that lots of fathers had. Yes, they had Uncle Rein; he would never let them starve. They had taken to pitching their shelter by his so that he could listen for any danger that came in the night. But he had his own family to be the daddy of, in addition to taking the Chief's role; he had enough responsibilities already. And Great Uncle, she loved him, but he could barely protect himself let alone anyone else. K'enemy was the only other man standing at the edge of their fire circle. Even so, Birdy was not about to welcome him in.

Bear stood up and stretched. "I'm still hungry. Come with me, Birdy?"

"No, I don't want anything else."

"You have to come with me, Birdy," he argued.

"Go on by yourself. I'll be fine. Oopsy will keep me safe, won't you, Oopsy-doops?"

"You gonna keep her safe, Oops?"

"I'm strong," Oopsy sleepily agreed.

"You should still come with me, Birds. Bring him with you."

"Go, go!" Her hands urged him away. "I am perfectly capable of sitting here without getting into trouble."

He snorted. "Yeah, you're perfectly capable of something, all right."

Birdy rolled her eyes. "Go on, you dolt. Bring back some extra food in case Oopsy gets hungry."

"Oh, here comes Turtle, and Willow's right behind. Maybe they'll sit with you until I get back. Turtle," he called out. "Stay here, will you? Just while I'm getting food." Catching Willow's eye, he indicated Birdy. She nodded, sitting next to her friend while Turtle collapsed to the ground in an exaggeratedly comical fashion.

"I will be right back, Birdy. Don't go anywhere without me." Without bothering to wait for an answer, Bear hurried away.

Birdy waved him off. He'd been hovering all night, leaving only when Willow came to give him a break. Go ahead and good riddance. She was sick of everybody chirping at her. Nag, nag, nag. They all said the same thing. She should stop fussing and accept K'enemy. River and he would have a good life together. Be careful because Bear's having dreams again. *Grrrr.* She just wanted everybody to leave her alone. Let her have some peace so she could think her own thoughts and not worry about everyone else.

She greeted Willow with a reluctant smile, then glanced over at Turtle. Something about him looked off, but who cared; she didn't need either one babysitting her. She scanned him with a critical eye. He didn't seem feverish, and there were no obvious wounds. Still he looked queasy or something. He was sweating, though it wasn't warm tonight. He moaned, his mouth opening like a dying fish. Without any warning he suddenly lurched upright, clutching at his belly. His legs propelled him forward and he took several ungainly steps before falling down and retching. Fortunately he was far enough away to miss them.

"You are disgusting, Turtle," Birdy said, drawing away from the mess.

Willow shook her head. "He's sick, Birdy. People don't retch unless they're sick."

"He wasn't sick before."

"I should help him. But I can't leave you; Bear still hasn't come back. I'll take him down to my mother," Willow decided, looking over at the dancers. "She'll give him the attention he needs. Don't go away," she warned.

Just what she needed; even her friend was bossing her around tonight. "I have to get Oopsy to bed," Birdy reminded her.

Willow considered. Rein's shelter was nearby. Surely nothing could happen in the short time that she'd be gone. Probably Bear was overreacting anyway. She had dreams all the time and if she acted on every one of them, she'd be in a lot of trouble. She nodded to Birdy, then went to Turtle and pulled him upright, using both hands and all her weight behind them. Draped his arm around her shoulder and began steering him away.

Birdy gave a sigh of relief. She could almost taste the silence. Maybe not silence, there'd be singing and dancing for a long time tonight, but at least she might get a break from her friends telling her what to do. She still had to get Oopsy to bed. Peace and quiet—it was hers as soon as he went to sleep. To be alone for a while before she had to crowd into Uncle Rein's shelter, where she and Oopsy would be staying from now on. River could invite them to her hearth all she wanted; there was no way Birdy would accept.

"It's late, Oopsy-doops. What do we need to get you ready for bed?"

"I need some water. Can you gimme?"

"You sit right there." She positioned his unresisting body against a pile of furs. "I'll find some water for you."

She shook the nearest water skin, but it was drained dry. The next one she found was kicked over and trampled during the festivities. There were dusty footprints all over it, and no water inside. She'd have to fill it and bring it to the shelter or someone was bound to get thirsty during the night, most likely her. Bear would be mad but honestly, if she could look after Oopsy, she was certainly old enough to look after herself. "Oopsy, don't move, not even a squinch," she warned. "I'm going down to the river. I will be right back."

★   ★   ★

There were two ways down to the creek. She set off for the farther path; the closer one was steep and she didn't feel like scrambling tonight. No sense risking her footing in the darkness. Though it wasn't so dark under the light of the full moon. Anyway she'd rather avoid all the noise and commotion. She had enough pretending that everything was going to be hao. It wasn't. There was nothing to smile about as far as she was concerned.

She skirted past the rocky outcrop and the scrubby area beyond to where the land dipped down to the creek.

Half-way down the slope she could no longer hear the sounds of singing from above, though the sharp, rhythmic slaps of Bison's spoon on the wooden bowl carried even that far. Bison and Antler both, she reminded herself. They made good music together. Even with just two sticks, Antler carried a steady beat. A solid pulse that would be good for storytelling too. Bison made some kind of counter-rhythm that danced around the main beat. The combination was so lively, even Great Uncle got up to dance.

The further she got from camp, the more the sound faded. There were other sounds she heard better down here. Crickets with their late-summer chirpings. Owl, returned from a successful foray, with his contented "Prrrrek-prek-prek." The sound of a fish breeching the surface, though most of his friends were long asleep. The ... moaning? Was that someone moaning? Was someone down there sick or hurt?

Another like Turtle? If two people were sick, they'd all be getting sick soon. All Birdy's senses came alert. Which direction did the sound come from? Ah, there it was again. She was almost at the creek. Turn now and pick a path over the rocks; careful not to slip on that wet moss. Around the bend—there it was again; who was it?

At first all she saw were forms and shadows. She barely made out three different shapes. Amid the shadows, moonlight reflected on a cheek here, a naked arm there. Approaching cautiously, she saw two of the strangers but who was that between them, the third man? No, the silhouette was too slight; it looked more like a woman. A girl, she thought. Her cousin, Left. She's wounded? Are they trying to help her up? No. She's struggling against them. They're not trying to help her; they're trying to hold her down.

Birdy crouched, fingers moving through the rock-strewn soil. She picked a stone with a solid heft to it. "Leave her alone! What's wrong with you?" she called out. "Let her go!"

There was a sudden upsurge and the next thing she saw, Left was on her feet. The two girls locked eyes for a moment, and then Left turned and fled the other way.

The men cursed incomprehensibly. The smaller man started following Left. The large one grabbed him and pulled him back, muttering a string of harsh commands. The two began moving forward. Towards Birdy. They were now a few steps away and coming closer, fists bunched. Birdy turned, but she lost her balance and stumbled. The surface was sharp and a jagged stone cut into her leg. She tried to rise but they were upon her now, four burly arms and a torso pinning her down.

Two of those arms pressed her shoulders hard against the stony ground. A third one gave a quick tug and ripped her wrap away.

Birdy was trying to shove him off of her but her buckling and heaving did not push him away. Instead his weight fell upon her with a thud that knocked her breath away. Heedless, he was forcing her legs apart. Falling on her and growling with an animalness that shocked her.

He pushed himself on her, prying her open. The smaller man held her hands above her head, locking her wrists in a numbing grasp. His other hand pressed her head down so she couldn't use it to butt the first one and break his nose or teeth.

He, on top, slammed the weight of his body against her. Again her breath was forced out, and she couldn't seem to catch it. She choked, gasping, and the man pinched her silent. His wrap was off and the center of his body exposed, a fevered, fleshy stick poking into her, ripping her open. Her insides were tearing; she could feel it in sharp, hot little tugs. She was being torn apart in a place she barely even knew she had.

Her legs where they joined her body—it felt like they were about to snap apart under the strain of his weight. She hurt with every move he made. She wiggled, trying to free herself but he thrust her back against the rocks. Sharp, jagged stone dug into her back. Dug into the muscle. Pressed painfully against her spine.

Any more pounding and she was sure she would break in two. Like a pheasant, cracked along the backbone for easier eating.

He panted, grunting, and a drop of his sweat fell on her face. Nasty, disgusting sweat, but in a way it was a relief. A small insult to focus on, instead of crying out with every thrust of his. She struggled against him but he was so much bigger, it was overwhelming. Thrashing and heaving to fling him off did her no good. Worse; it seemed to excite him the more she tried to resist.

A great weariness washed through her, and she sank inward. Her legs stopped kicking. Her fingers stopped reaching for things to scratch or yank.

"Help me, Great Mother," she began to pray. And then, simply, "Mother, Mother," like a heartbeat. Letting it grow loud enough in her mind to drown out everything else.

There was a gush of something warm inside her. Was he peeing? Bleeding? Was that her own blood she felt?

Her hands still locked overhead; she could not reach down to find out. Maybe she would never know. Maybe he would kill her. Skin her and roast her. Eat her like an animal.

An endless moment passed, and finally the thrusting man rolled off.

With his weight gone, trembling set in. Could she move an arm? A leg? She tried to shift a hand, a foot, but nothing would respond.

Then the second stranger came forward. He looked down at her body and grunted at his friend. Spat, rubbed his hands, then slapped her in the face. The blow was so hard that she saw bursts of light behind the eyelid on one side.

Mother. Mother.

Mother.

She was only intermittently conscious. Between little spurts of pain she heard him shed his wrap and lower himself on top of her. Another weight on her legs. Another forcing, widening, ripping. Pounding. Wrenching. He bit her neck. Squeezed her chest on each side. Where the breasts would be, if she were old enough. He too pounded against her. Ripped at her until the bloody warmth gushed through her again.

mother

moth

mo

The weight lifted at last. A few sounds drifted in—someone clearing their throat and spitting, a stone skittering along as the men walked away. There was a space of time and nothingness, nothingness and time. She heard no sounds, thought no further thoughts, except to notice in occasional fits that the air grew chilly and the uncomfortable moistness on her legs and belly felt worse with the breeze.

She was drifting in blankness, a fallen feather on the surface of a cold sea.

The next thing she knew, Bear was stroking her shoulder and Willow, wiping her face and belly. She was sore. She ached through and through. There were sharp rip-pains between her legs and dull, aching pains down her head and back.

The moon was higher than she remembered.

At least the awful men were gone.

Birdy tried to sit up, but couldn't. Tried to lift her head. Could not move it off the stone, she felt so dizzy.

"We were looking all over for you," Bear worried. "I told you, don't go anywhere! What are you doing down here anyway? Why didn't you listen to me?"

"Shush, Bear, she's hurt." Willow's voice was soft with concern. "Did you fall, Birdy? How did you hurt yourself?"

Birdy looked from one to the other. Opened her mouth, but couldn't answer.

"Let's help her back to camp," Willow decided. "Look, her wrap is all torn. She needs something hot to drink. And a poultice; look at the back of her head."

"I was just gone for a moment! She was supposed to stay with you and Turtle! I told her not to go anywhere. I knew something bad was gonna happen."

"You did your best, Bear," Willow patted him on the arm. "Turtle got sick, and I thought that was the bigger danger. It's a good thing Oopsy came to ask where she went. She would have been laying here a long time if we didn't come looking for her."

One arm was flung over Bear's shoulder, the other went around Willow. They brought Birdy back to camp, half stumbling on her feet. They started to set her by the fire, but Birdy made a shooing-away motion with her hand, so they set her in the quietest place in camp, right in front of River's shelter. Where she sat, legs folded under, rocking back and forth all night long, refusing food and comfort except for the warm presence of Stripes and Guard on either side, accepting only a bowl of hot cedar tea, and then, only from Willow's hand.

Chapter 9: What kind of people shall we be?

Rocking, rocking, forward and back. Moving kept her warm. Even under the hide Bear draped over her she was shivering. Goosebumps ran up her arms whenever another searing image of those ugly faces flashed through; their horrid breath making her gag at the mere memory. The bite of teeth sinking into her neck. That tight grip on her wrists, her hands tingling, her body going numb. If only the numbness came sooner. If only it never went away.

Willow's soft voice helping her. She didn't want to remember that, as it only made her cry again. Any more kindness—she didn't think she could stand it. Think instead of the rock beneath her back, cold and solid, full of sharp edges. Think about the rock she held in her hand and used to bash him until the other one grabbed it from her. He almost broke her fingers taking it away. She felt a fierce urge to pick up another rock and bash him again. She could see it in her mind's eye. A stone. A boulder, even. A boulder dropped on his head by a bird, a giant bird, a rock big enough to crush him. She didn't mind if it crushed her too, as long as he was crushed flat. Both of the outsiders squashed like bugs, just what they deserved.

She could imagine the evening differently. If it were a family story she could change some parts of it a little bit. Crush them, like Mami got crushed in the cave-in. She could throw rocks at them from a distance. No, she might have hit Left instead of the men. Too bad she didn't have a spear to hurl at them. Too bad she didn't have Bear and Antler at her side, both armed with spears and throwing sticks. And all the rest of the clan aiming at those stinking strangers; they'd be killed in a moment with the weapons of the People leveled at their throats.

She might have gone the other way to the creek and never seen them. Left would have gotten hurt, but Birdy would be safe. If only Oopsy didn't ask for water. If only he asked for it earlier. If they stayed a day longer back at the meadow. One day more, that would have done it, or one day less, either way. Then they'd never come across these awful men and she and Left would both be safe.

Those swollen red *things* they shoved up her, then rubbed violently back and forth like they were trying to start a fire. Stupid penises. It was not that she'd never seen one before, with all the little boys running around naked. But she never saw one on someone more than seven or eight summers in age. Never saw one that huge and ugly. Swollen, like it was infected with deadly poison. She shuddered. Was that how women got swollen up carrying babies, did they get infected from the man's swelling?

Precious Mother, was that what men did with women when they could? Is that what K'enemy was doing to poor River this very night? Is that what Mami did with the men who came to visit her? She didn't have to; nobody made her. Why did she let it happen to her, she who was afraid of nothing?

Would this horrid thing happen to Birdy again some day? It never should have happened. She didn't even have her woman ceremony yet. Was there some way she could stop growing up? Because for sure she didn't want to marry and live through such an awful thing again. The ripping. The tearing. The hurting in that very tender place. Would it ever heal and feel normal again? You couldn't put a poultice on it; how would it ever stay on?

A moan escaped, then a continuous stream of low sounds, a mournful murmuring. Willow came again to check on her, and Bear kept a fitful watch from a distance.

Hours passed. The sky began to lighten, and after a time others shook themselves awake. First a jay opened its beak to twitter at her, then a ground squirrel poked its head out to consider the situation. Poor Thing began crying, and there were rustling sounds as Falling Leaf rose to attend to the baby.

Now River stumbled, half crouching through the flap of her shelter, dragging K'enemy after her by his thong-tied wrist. "Birdy, what in the name of the Mother are you doing here?" she asked. "Wait, you can tell me in a bit," and the two of them shambled behind some scrub to perform the first task of any morning.

"Now," River said at last, striving mightily to adjust her wrap with one hand. K'enemy stood behind, his eyes only half-open. "Let's sit with Birdy," River told him, and she sat facing her niece, forcing him to follow suit.

Rocking, rocking. River was here now but Birdy's lips were glued shut, though at least the moaning died away. Her whole body felt stuck, frozen like a solid block of ice. Maybe River could chip away at her with a hammer stone and an awl, and things would splinter off, one at a time. Maybe K'enemy would use his axe; that would probably work better. There would be a pile of Birdy chips. River could melt them at the fire and drink them and then she'd know everything from the inside out. Little Birdy stories would come bubbling out of her mouth. Bubble, bubble. They'd float up in the air and go pop. The thought made Birdy snort, and that was a start.

"What's the matter, Birdsilu," River asked again.

Of course her aunt was worried. Everybody was supposed to leave them alone until sunset. Birdy of all people should have left them alone, would have yesterday for sure, but that was yesterday, or was it last year, it felt like forever ago. She did not feel like the same Birdy she was yesterday. Today she was a broken Birdy girl, not a sturdy Birdy anymore. The endearment, Birdsilu, broke her control. Tears leaking out, she fell into River's arms, River's and

K'enemy's since his were dragged along. Birdy had to accept his hovering if she wanted any comfort from River.

"I hurt so bad," she sobbed, and when River started peering under her eyelids and into her mouth, Birdy pointed at the most painful areas, the back of her head, the area between her legs. In fits and starts the story emerged: The two men attacking, Left grabbing the chance to escape but she didn't send anyone to rescue Birdy. The empty water skin that started the whole thing. The attack and her attempts to fight back. By this time River had given up any attempt to probe her wounds. She was simply stroking Birdy's hair and holding her, crooning and rocking. K'enemy sat upright shaking his head, shifting his weight occasionally to correct the balance so none of them would go sprawling in the dirt.

Now they were conferring. River wanted to break the lashing so K'enemy could round up the men and chase down the outsiders. K'enemy felt much the same. Most likely the strangers weren't too far ahead. They'd been drinking and carousing for much of the night; they might have left only a short while before.

K'enemy pulled the knife from the thong around his waist and made short work of the binding. River took it as a keepsake, and the three of them walked over to Rein's shelter.

By now the camp was beginning to stir, so it was easy enough to wake him. River did the talking. Birdy was going numb again, not responding to questions unless they came from her aunt, and only then if River looked directly into her eyes. The rest of the time River kept an arm around the girl. When there was a lull in the questioning she took Birdy to Falling Leaf for balm and bandaging.

"It's not the kind of thing I should decide alone," Rein mused aloud, looking sideways at K'enemy. How odd, he reminded himself. Just a few days before he wanted an opportunity to get everybody involved in deciding things, and here it was already. River asked him to wait till after the wedding. Well, it was after the wedding, though just barely.

He sent K'enemy one way to rouse the camp, while he went the other. People began gathering at the fire circle. Soon everyone was there except for Birdy and Willow who was swabbing her wounds, Little Mother taking care of the young ones, and Left who kept burrowing under the furs and refused to leave her bed.

Rein told them all that befell Birdy the night before. "So we have two tasks before us as I see it. We have to decide what to do." His statement was greeted with fists slamming into hands. "But first I think we have to decide how to decide."

Cookie raised an eyebrow at her husband. "What do you mean, how we decide? Go ahead and tell us what to do! You're our leader, you've been deciding things since we left home."

"I have not," he disagreed. "All I decided was, I wanted us to go north." His eye caught River's, who looked away. He'd decided one other big thing at his sister's urging, but they weren't going to mention that now. "You all decided to come north as well, and so we did." He looked around the circle, making contact with every person there.

"We agreed on that, and I knew more about the way so I've been pointing out how to get there. But this is a new thing and I shouldn't decide it alone. One of our children has been attacked. Do we attack back? Do we aim to kill them? Do we walk away? It's too much for me to think about alone because too much is at risk. Our honor and our lives, both. All of us need to help figure this out."

"Dayeogwen used to decide things when he was the chief," Two Stones pointed out.

"I am not Dayeogwen. I do not wish to be like Dayeogwen. I have spent a lot of time thinking about when he was chief and I don't think he always did right for us. He was not wise enough to decide everything by himself. I'm not wise enough to decide everything myself. Everyone here is smarter than me in some way."

This was so unexpected that no one knew what to say.

"Bison is only 17 summers in age, but he is wiser than me about the hunts," Rein pointed out.

Bison looked up, startled at the compliment.

"Two Stones knows more than me about getting things done. Staunch is wiser about conserving his energy until it is needed."

"That's because he's lazy," Falling Leaf remarked.

"Falling Leaf has her medicine wisdom. Trapper and Antler have talking-to-the-Spirits wisdom. My wife is wise about anything to do with food."

Cookie nodded, pleased to be acknowledged.

"My son has his wisdom ..."

"Fire-coal wisdom," Bear muttered, rolling his eyes. He was still smarting from the reprimand after they fled the lava flow. Needling his father was one way of coming back into balance.

"We all have something important to add. The point is, all these different kinds of knowing should be stirred into any decision we make."

Though he looked in no shape to travel, and stared blearily around the circle, Turtle had no patience for debate. "Uncle," he croaked. "Somebody should chase them down, or they'll get too far and all our plans will be for nothing."

"That's wisdom too," Rein pointed out. "Though I think it's best to decide what to do *before* we begin doing it."

"I say we find them and kill them." Fierce set her hands emphatically on her hips. "Anyone who attacks a child should be put to death. Slowly or swiftly, I don't care; they're not fit to live."

"Life is a gift of the Great Spirits," Trapper reminded them mildly. "Do we wish to spit in Their faces by destroying that gift? Even if we are deeply provoked, shouldn't we take more time to consider?"

"There's no time," Turtle protested. "Somebody has to go right now. Grab them and bring them back. Then take all the time we need to decide."

Rein took the talking stick back from Turtle. "This is just as I said. We all have wisdom; we all should help decide."

"Everyone seems to have a different opinion," Two Stones pointed out. "Fierce says kill them. Trapper says life is sacred. Turtle says to rustle them up and figure out what to do later. There's probably ten more opinions around the circle here. How do we decide which one's right?"

"I say, we're already doing it," Rein concluded. "I say, let us all decide together. Let us be a People who talk in the fire circle until something makes sense to us all. Let's not be a People who give all that power to any one person; let us share it instead. Let us accept wisdom from every stone and boulder, from every man and woman, from the young and old. Let us say ..."

Heads were beginning to nod. There was wisdom in this new idea. But before Rein could get carried away by the power of his own words, which everyone knew he was capable of doing, Two Stones stepped in to conclude his speech for him. "Ho," he said firmly. It was simple, yet effective.

For a long moment no one signaled for the talking stick.

There was a feeling that something major had happened, and the silence was profound. But finally a hand reached out to nab the stick, and a tentative voice asked. "So, what do we do now?" One suggestion after another was flung across the circle. Kill them? Trapper's admonishment hung heavy, and no one still argued for that. Ignore the attack and keep going forward?

"Who are we if we do not stand behind our children?" someone asked. A strong consensus developed to go after the men and punish them in some fashion or another. Teach them a lesson, they agreed. No, they would not kill the offenders. But make them pay; that was a different matter.

"We don't want you men to risk your lives," Little Mouse worried. "Where will we be with all the hunters gone? If they fight, and you never come back?"

"What will we be if we let others hurt our children whenever they feel like it?" Rein echoed one of the arguments from before. "Do we want to be a People unwilling protect our future? Do you want our children to say we didn't care enough to keep them safe? What kind of People do not respond when their children are threatened or hurt?"

"Cowards," Two Stones responded. "We must strike back."

"If we die, we do it for our children and for the children's children to come," Bison suggested. There was a moment of respectful silence, for his words especially moved them, coming from one who had not even one child as yet.

Rein nodded. "I cannot think of a better thing to risk our lives for."

And no one argued differently.

Still left to decide was how far the punishment should go.

"Cut their pricks off," Fierce growled. But Falling Leaf pointed out that they'd bleed to death if their manhood was removed, and they already decided not to kill them, wicked though they were.

"Cut off their foreskins," K'enemy said, the first words he offered in council that day. His idea began to take hold. It seemed fitting—not too little a punishment, not too much. Give back the pain they gave Birdy. Let them remember this for the rest of their lives. Every time they used those offending organs to piss away their wretched drink, every time they tried to unite with a woman they would remember what payment they got when they took something not theirs to take.

"Can we get going? We should leave right away!" Turtle urged.

Now the only talk was of who and how. Rein, K'enemy, Two Stones, Bison and Staunch would take their weapons and follow their tracks. Yes, they had a head start, but they were heavily laden with walrus meat. Surely the hunters would catch them before it was too late. Before they reached their families, who could help counterattack.

Turtle would stay behind. Though he spoke fiercely, he looked too pale. He was wretched and puking for much of the night. The spoiled berry juice they poisoned him with had clearly taken its toll. Perhaps the strangers intended to poison them all? Could this all have been a plan to kill them and steal everything? And when only Turtle joined them, they took a vengeful swipe at Birdy, and left before anyone discovered her?

In any case, he would help pack up the camp and flee eastward. Later they would head north again. The boys would obliterate their trail. Fire Bear and Antler could use branches of pine to sweep the dirt clear of tracks. Owl would make sure no stone was kicked loose, no leaves or branches bent with a fresh underside showing palely to catch the eye of an observant tracker. No sense making it easy for the strangers to follow if they came seeking revenge.

"Won't they know we're traveling northeast?" Little Mouse asked fearfully. "They told us about the reindeer people off that way."

"They think we're heading north because I told them we came from the south," Rein decided. "Maybe they'll think of northeast also since that's where they said our cousins went. We can't know exactly what they're thinking, but if we head East at first and they can't find our tracks, they will soon give up, we hope. The best we can do is make it hard for them. Don't light a fire tonight," he warned Bear. "We don't want them to spot the smoke."

"How will you find us?" Little Mouse fretted.

"We know where to look. We'll catch up, don't worry."

So the travelers split, with one group of hunters heading off to stalk their prey, the other moving away from danger. And each group worried about the other until the following night when the hunters safely rejoined them, when K'enemy put a small, leaf-bound package into Birdy's hand and told her they'd made the men pay, and to keep this payment tucked away as long as she liked, until she was ready to open it.

Which would probably not be for a long, long time.

Book 4: Into the cold

Chapter 1: Purging and cleansing

Pulling. Tearing. It hurt whenever Birdy walked. And she was always walking somewhere: On a trek, fetching water or food. Her thighs rubbed painfully together. The torn places pulled, and it hurt.

It hurt even to remember, so she tried not to. But how could she forget when every woman looked at her with pitying eyes. When men passed her by, their glances skittered off her face like mice caught nibbling at their food. As if when they saw her, they remembered what happened and were ashamed at the bad things men could do, but at the same time they kind of, guiltily, liked it.

Sick of it all, she sought out her cousin, who might have understood. After all, both of them were attacked, not just Birdy. She wanted her to know she wasn't angry like everyone said she should be. But Left kept ducking away whenever she came near; one more scar from those awful men.

How did women live with the pain men caused them? Mami never looked hurt. She was solid, Birdy mused with an unexpected sense of admiration. She did what she needed, took what she wanted. And men admired her for it. Mami was like the walls of the cave, like stone, and if she was in a man's path, he was the one to move.

She should be more like her: Cold as rock and impervious to pain. Being nice, Birdy decided, was what got her hurt. She'd been too nice, doing anything people asked. Too nice a daughter and all that got her was more work. Too nice a sister, and it brought her those awful men. Too nice a cousin saved Left, but now she wouldn't even talk to her. Too nice was like River, who married a murderer. K'enemy wasn't nice at all and he snagged River, the best woman around.

Just then Oopsy came looking for her, his face puckered up with pleading. "Help me gather tinder, Birdy? Aunty Cookie needs it to light the fire."

"Of course, sweetie," she answered without even thinking. Suddenly she stopped. That's exactly what she did, every single day. Help everybody but herself. Well, no more. She would do her share, of course. But she didn't have to do everyone else's. Let them do their own work. She pulled herself upright, glaring at her brother without a shred of remorse. "Do it yourself," she said brusquely. "I've helped you gather tinder plenty of times. You know how. You don't need me anymore."

★   ★   ★

The dogs barked wildly that morning and woke everyone up before dawn. They went tearing away after a flurry of grouse and the camp quieted down, but the damage was done. Poor Thing was screaming, and everybody else was cranky too. The previous day they hardly managed to travel any distance. A thick, billowing fog covered the area, and they had to wait until the sun was high before it burned away enough mist to see. To do otherwise was foolish; they might walk in circles or head blindly toward a crevasse.

So this morning Rein was doubly eager to get moving. But instead of packing up, Cookie emerged from their shelter and sat emphatically on a log. Her shoulders ached something fierce. Her joints twinged. "I'm not moving," she announced. Looking at her husband's anxious face, she softened slightly. "I don't actually think I can.

"Surely we are not still in danger. Do we have to go on? It's already getting cold enough to see your breath at night. For days I've been saying we should set down somewhere and prepare for winter. We can't keep going on like this."

Rein looked carefully at his wife, considering. She didn't just look tired; she looked bone weary, and he knew she was hurting. A persistent crick had developed in her back, and all his rubbing at night failed to make it go away.

He glanced around to see who else was ready to inflict their opinions on him. The men were going about their business, but the women stopped clearing things away. Falling Leaf was openly watching; Fierce was pretending to rummage through her food sack, but he could feel her attention on him even if her eyes were, wisely, elsewhere. Little Mouse set down her bundle. Poor woman, pregnant by a husband now gone.

Willow stood with Birdy and just beyond, River was nodding at Cookie's suggestion.

He sighed. He wanted to find their cousins before settling in. If they could spend the winter together it would be easier on everyone. His cousins knew this land better than he did. He thought for sure they'd find signs of them by now. Could he get his people through the dark months without their help? Ever since they left their old home he hoped he would not have to.

"We still have time," he suggested to Cookie. "Let's keep moving until the leaves fall. We can look for a better campsite for the winter. Maybe, the Spirits willing, we'll find our cousins too."

An exasperated sigh went round the ring of women.

"Should we talk about it around the fire circle?" he temporized. But they were shaking their heads no. "Not even worth debating?" They were forming a line, every blessed one of them with arms folded against him. "All right, we'll stay here a few days. Send the men scouting. If we find our cousins like I hope, we'll go with them. If we don't," everyone was nodding, because no one but he believed they still might find them before the winter set in, "then at least we can find the best winter campsite around."

"Hoo hooo!" Turtle shouted.

Bear and Antler did that complicated hand-slap, hip-bump thing they did when they were excited. The women smiled. And Cookie murmured, "Maybe your bed will be warm tonight after all."

★   ★   ★

Left was gathering grass seed in the field above. The wind blew in quick gusts, sending chills down her arms. But today she didn't mind; in fact she was glad of it. Glad that mamma sent her off, alone. They were all being mean to her ever since River's wedding. Ever since those strangers grabbed her. They did not succeed in forcing themselves on her, but, she shuddered, she got hurt that night. Badly. Bruises on her arm where one of them grabbed her, bruises on her neck where he bit her. Like she was a piece of meat or something.

Not that anyone cared. No, it was all, poor Birdy this and poor Birdy that. What about poor Left? Or better yet, poor Eider? They couldn't even get her new name straight. Everything was wrong. It was entirely unfair.

Birdy, Birdy, Birdy. She could spit, she was so mad. Wasn't she just as much a victim as her? Or, she would have been except that she got away. If she could get away, Birdy could too. Though she didn't, so it was her own fault, wasn't it? But everybody kept saying Left should have done this or that. Gone for help, screamed at the men, stayed and punched them. Why didn't she? She was scared, that's why. Scared and hurt. She spent the night shivering in her bed. Not dancing and flirting all night like her stupid sister.

Which was the other thing that was entirely awful this summer. All of a sudden everybody loved Right and they hated Left. They were twins. They should have been tattooed at the same time, but no, Right started bleeding first, she always had to be first, and now all the guys liked her.

By the time Left began her woman's bleeding, everybody already hated her by then thanks to that stupid Birdy. They couldn't forget it for even one day, which spoiled her whole becoming-woman ceremony. People hardly even smiled during the ritual. Instead they nodded like they were doing her a favor to watch.

She asked Great Uncle to do a naming since it worked so well for Right. That dried-up stick of a man warned her it might not work. He said people have to want to change their habits; they probably wouldn't change just because you asked them. She didn't want to hear that. It worked for her sister, so it should work for her, shouldn't it?

But it wasn't working. They still called her Left, only now it was mocking, or it was from Turtle at least, which hurt. She didn't want to be Left, not even for one more day. She wanted to be Eider, for the beautiful ducks with their soft down and their graceful movements on the water.

Tears formed in her eyes. She missed her grandmother. It wouldn't matter so much when people treated her mean if Grandmother was still alive.

Grrrr, she couldn't stand it any longer. Her bowl was full, but she hated to return to camp where she'd wither under her mother's snort of disapproval every time Eider asked for anything. Her father barely seemed to have time for her these days. Aunty Fierce gazed past her like she was a stone in the path. Willow, who should have been a friend, kept looking at her with pity. Who wanted that? Then there was Turtle. She had to ignore him because he kept making comments that were *entirely mean.* Worse, she kept seeing her sister shove Bison around and him shoving back, each of them laughing. She wanted Bison to shove her, not Swan. She wanted him to tease her and smile. Not at Swan. At Eider.

She had to find another reason to stay away. Other people got to leave camp. Her father sent men scouting in different directions. She could scout too. Not alone; she wasn't stupid. She would take Bear with her. He could bring his spear for safety. Maybe they'd be the first to find their cousins. They'd be proud if she and Bear found the Reindeer People. She would finally be known as Eider, and he could be called Reindeer Finder. Or, Finds His Cousins. Finds His People, that's a good one. Soon they'd both be known by better names and everyone would like her again. All she had to do was find him and get on their way.

⋆   ⋆   ⋆

"Sure, why not," Bear agreed. There wasn't much reason to stay in camp. Papi only sent the men scouting; but why couldn't the two of them go? It would be a hoot. Like the play expeditions he and his friends used to have, pretending to scout for woolly mammoth or whatever. Only this time they might come back with something real. A great new winter campsite. Rabbits for stewing. Something good; he didn't care what.

Bear rooted around gathering essentials. A knife, which he stuck in his waist thong. His water skin, which needed to be filled before they left. Sleeping fur, yep. *Rope*, came a tiny voice inside. No, no need for rope, he wasn't going to climb trees or entangle moose by their antlers. Small sack of seeds to munch on, yep, got that. *Rope*. Nah, too heavy. *Wind it around your waist; you won't feel the weight.* All right, he'd bring some rope. He picked up a good sized length.

Longer. Longer? Longer would be too heavy, he argued with himself. *Longer.* Sighing, he tied another length to the end. *Longer still.* All right, another length. Surely that'd be enough.

Left was tapping her foot impatiently. "Aren't you ready yet? Come on!"

They went due east, or as close as they could, given the hills in their path. East because the ocean had been east for as long as they could remember, yet now they lost sight of it and they missed the briny smell. As they walked, picking their way around the mud before them, occasionally flinging clods at each other for the fun of it, Left began doing imitations. First of their father, then their mother, then almost every other person in camp. They were laughing so hard that tears came. Left wiped her nose with the back of her hand. She looked disgusting even to his uncritical eye.

"Thanks for coming with me, little brother," she finally said. They were somewhat restored, having used leaves to scrape much of the muck off. She spit on her hands to clean them, then reached for his sack of seeds. Took a handful and began to nibble delicately, one seed at a time. Unasked, Bear noticed, but he didn't protest. She would just ignore him if he did.

Leaning on one elbow, head tilted back, Left confessed, "That's the most fun I've had in a long time. This whole summer has been awful."

"Mmmph," he agreed, stuffing seeds in his mouth.

"But here's the plan. We find something really great and everything changes. We bring whatever it is we find, and everyone loves me again. Swan and I get close, the boys start liking me, and ..." Bear lost track of what she said as he drifted into a daydream of his own. Only to be swatted awake as she concluded with a final, "and you get whatever it is you want. What is it you want, anyway?"

"More food," he sighed, reaching for the sack only to find she had finished off his provisions, having brought none of her own. Typical, he thought. "But since there's none here, we should go."

"Oh, are you still hungry?" she asked brightly. "We can pick some of those rosehips over there." She pointed to a bramble nearby. The petals were gone, but the bases were good for a snack.

"You pick them. I already provided my share of the food."

Hurriedly she gathered a handful and ran to catch up. Keeping only a few for herself, she handed him the rest. "Sorry," she conceded. "I'll pick more if you like."

"That's all right," he said magnanimously. "You can go grubbing when we get hungry later, which I'm sure we will be." He plunked his foot down hard in the next puddle, deliberately splashing her.

She flashed him a grin. She was relieved to be so easily forgiven. Nobody else was forgiving her these days.

Still he couldn't resist the opportunity to rub it in. "I can't believe you left on an expedition without bringing even a morsel of food!" He was panting now; they had been walking uphill for a while. It was starting to level off, with just a small upward slope to the crest. Bear hoped they would soon have a glimpse of the sea.

"I can't believe you left on an expedition without bringing more food for your big sister!" She gave him a playful shove.

Her timing was unfortunate. Though he'd been picking his way around the muddiest places, the stretch in front was deceptive. The ground looked solid but it was slippery, and there were no stones to offer traction as his body went skidding across. Flailing for balance, he lurched, skidding to the top of the hill. Sheer momentum carried him past the muddy shelf of rock.

"Bear!" she gasped, peering over to see her brother slide down the hillside. Sliding fast enough to be funny, until she saw he was not slowing down. Then she started getting scared.

Bear had no time to be afraid. "Stay there," he shouted. The last thing he needed was to have her try and rescue him, which would probably end in disaster.

Normally he might already be slowing down enough to halt himself with the clever use of feet and elbows. But not today, not as mud-daubed-slick as he was.

He tried stabbing downward with his spear but he was going too fast and couldn't thrust it deep enough. The spear caught, only to twist out of his hands. He grabbed at the tall grass but the stalks uprooted, and then got caught underneath him, making it more slippery. He stuck a leg out, but it got bent, almost twisting him around enough to aim downhill, head first and moving fast.

Bringing his arms close to his body, he felt a lump around his middle. *Rope.* Oh yeah. *Find the end and unwind a length.* Not all of it, he told himself; leave some wrapped around. *Fling the rest and snag it on something.* Good thing he had such a nice long length, it should be able to catch somewhere. On something big enough to hold his weight. Not there, that's too small to hold anything. There's a bush coming up, try that. Steady, ready, toss it!

The rope tangled in the branches. He slid farther, but the tangles slowed him, and thankfully the rope held.

All his weight hung off one arm. He twisted around to set his knees and legs underneath. He'd have an odd set of bruises tomorrow no doubt, and a juicy selection of scrapes to impress Oopsy with. But for now he was safe. No broken bones, no busted head. What else mattered?

His sister, of course. He looked up the hill. Left was crab-walking down toward him, avoiding the battered path he'd made. Zigzagging to pick up his spear and water skin. Concern creased her face. Should he let her worry? He could probably get a good scare out of her; that would teach her not to be so careless.

Never mind; he'd be nice. She'd been having a hard time, and he felt a sneaking sense of sympathy. She wasn't so bad, for a sister. She didn't really mean to almost kill him. Probably. Not this time, at least.

"I'm fine," he eventually called to her.

She nodded but did not say a word.

He expected something—more teasing, a sigh of relief. Instead, silence. Her worried frown did not fade.

"What's wrong?" he asked, alerted to her mood.

"Look for yourself," she hissed. "Smoke," and she nodded ahead. "There's a campfire over there, and it's not one of ours."

⋆   ⋆   ⋆

The four directions, Rein smiled to himself. You send scouts in four directions and they come back with four different possibilities. If there were ten directions to send them, they'd probably come back with ten possibilities.

Bison and Staunch returned from the west reporting about Mammoth, which meant a goodly cache of meat and hides for winter shelters.

Two Stones and Turtle came back from the north having found a good wintering site, with a river for trout and salmon, and few wolves or bear nearby. Very promising, they concluded.

The south was where they came from, so there was no need to send anyone that way. And to the east, Bear and Left found a settlement near the coast.

"What do they look like?" Bear responded when asked. "They look like people!"

But Left noticed more than her brother did. They were shorter than the People and heavier in build. Rounder faces with eyes more aslant. They had three big shelters, with feathers and bits of shells strung over the entrance flaps. The children ran naked, chilly though it was, and the woman wore wraps that fitted each arm and hung straight to their knees. She wanted one like that for herself.

Now people were looking at Rein with a *What do we do next* look on their faces. He shook his head. "What are you all looking at me for? We should decide this together, not just me. I know but one grain of sand on the beach."

Ancient wisdom or not, Staunch could not let it pass unremarked. "One grain? I wouldn't say one grain, exactly," he drawled, looking at his fingernails. "Two or three grains, maybe. You're being modest, Rein."

Cookie turned playfully toward Staunch. "Come on, old friend. My husband knows many grains. Give him credit for at least five or six."

"Maybe even ten," Bear added helpfully. "But that's it. Any more and we'll be counting grains with our toes."

"Nobody wants that to happen," Staunch retorted. "We'd get all that sand in our toes. All right, Rein. You know more than you're ready to admit. Not one grain, you modest old fart. Ten grains of sand and not a single grain more."

Rein shook his head mournfully. "And you think you need me to lead?"

They were smiling, but still waiting for instructions. Well, at least it was obvious what to do. If it weren't for Bear's report, he'd have them move to the new winter site. When the temporary shelters were up, he'd send the hunters off for Mammoth or whatever they could find. But people nearby changed everything. They might be dangerous. Or they might be friends.

"We better not move camp until we see what they're like," he nodded his head toward the east. "Who volunteers to come with me?"

Every hunter stepped forward.

"Staunch. Bison. Bear, you'll show us the way. The rest of you stay here with the women and kids. Be ready to pack up quickly and get out of here. If we're not back in three days, Two Stones, you take charge and keep everybody safe."

"Take that fresh haunch of meat with you, Rein," Cookie suggested. "Visitors are always more welcome when they bring food."

"Good idea. Any other suggestions?"

Two Stones looked worried. "What do we do if you don't come back?"

"You'll have to decide that yourselves." Two Stones was a good man to get any job done once you told him what the job was. "If I don't come back, you're in charge." He still looked nervous, so Rein decided to elaborate. "It's a lot like being Papi, only the family's bigger. And you're doing a fine job of that," he nodded at Turtle, Little Mother, and Lynx.

Two Stones looked at him for a long moment before nodding. He might not want it, Rein reflected, but he'd do what was necessary. Hopefully it wouldn't be needed. "Give us a going away blessing, Great Father," he asked Antler.

Blushing with the attention, Antler turned away to select savories and a feather from his bundle. He waved smoke around the four travelers, saying prayers for safety. The smell lingered on their clothing, holding some sense of protection around them. Or so they hoped.

⋆   ⋆   ⋆

By now Birdy was often able to forget. Yesterday the whole morning went by, and she'd been almost entirely free of it. She and Antler were practicing stories, and helping him completely occupied her mind. And when Oopsy asked for a tale last night, that was another period of blessed relief.

But this morning she woke up trembling and a helpless feeling overwhelmed her. She'd been dreaming about that night again. His weight, crushing her so she could hardly breathe. The other one holding her arms so no matter how much she thrashed or twisted, there was no escape.

Almost every night she dreamed of some piece of it. She tried staying up all night once, sharing the watch with Bison. He was thoughtful enough not to ask about it, but the effort to avoid speaking was itself a trial. Until they started telling each other hunting stories, Bison telling tales from personal experience while Birdy retold what she heard from others.

After their throats grew raw they fell silent, staring into the fire. In the deep and starry blackness the camp lay still. Finally, from within the comfort of the silence, Birdy found herself confiding in Bison. Voicing out loud for the first time her secret wish. Not that she actually knew the stories, no, she didn't let down her guard that far. But that she longed to tell them, not like chanted prayers but like the stories they were, full of folks with their struggles, good or bad. She wanted to spread the sacred stories around the campfire like a comforting blanket for the People to shelter under.

Bison actually said he'd like to hear them told that way. And others might feel the same—his mother, the young ones, actually almost everyone grew restless during the long intoning at Winter Solstice. If stories were told in a pleasing way, that would make it more of a celebration. Even though it might seem funny to have a girl tell the tales instead of the shaman.

For Birdy, that magical phrase *Why not?* left a tiny crack in the hard rock wall of *No, absolutely not.* A tiny crack, which might in time let who-knew-what seep in.

The following night she went to bed, exhausted from two days with almost no sleep. Since then she often stayed up late to exhaust herself and avoid dreaming altogether. Sometimes she kept the men company at night around the campfire. Other nights she worked late with Antler on his storytelling.

At least now Antler could tell many of the tales reasonably well. Though he faltered if a day went by without practice. Storytelling did not come naturally to him. Even if he had the words right, he couldn't relax with it, didn't know how to let the story be part of him so it flowed on every breath.

Some people were natural healers and they had a touch that comforted the sick; some were natural hunters and they knew the exact spot to thrust the spear. Some had an ease with cooking, with children, with making tools or skinning beasts. And there were more who had to work hard at these things in order to get them right. Which was how it was with Antler and his storytelling.

He could do it—he had to do it—but she could see it would never come easily. People would get restless, and it would be painful to watch him strain when it should be sweet and smooth, like taking a breath.

A powerful struggle for him. Though not as wrenching as the one she was struggling with—she would finally say it—the attack. Great Uncle was once attacked by a wolf, and got all bitten up with his leg broken. He had nightmares too but in a few moon cycles he was healed again. She would be also, he assured her, though the nightmares might still come occasionally.

There were times when she felt he was right. She could put on her Mami face, cold as stone, and could feel underneath, the bones begining to heal. Not that she had any bones broken, but she felt broken like that sometimes. Her spirit. Her courage. That place between her legs. Often it felt broken, with jagged edges that would always be painful no matter how much healing was done. She hoped Great Uncle was right. Often she feared he was wrong.

Aunt Cookie kept patting her hand and saying it would get better. That nobody would hold it against her. Some day there would be a man who would love her. All a man wanted was a cheerful demeanor, she assured her, as well as some good cooking and a nice warm bed. River said she would find a good husband to protect and love her, and she would love him back. Meanwhile she had family to take care of her and the rest could go sink in a bog.

They were all trying to help. And maybe they did, but she was getting sick of the whole thing. Sick of feeling weak and helpless. She wished she could forget it ever happened. Go back to the way things were before. Or go forward to some time when so much had happened since that it seemed like nothing, like some scrape on the knee that she had when she was as little and innocent as Oopsy.

Surprisingly, one of the easiest people to be with was K'enemy. The best thing was that he didn't talk. He didn't fill up the spaces with babble. He did what he could to help. Went after those men, gave her that tidy little package that was shoved for now at the bottom of her sack. And then he let it rest.

It was odd, because before the attack she was afraid of him. But River said he was not to blame, and she trusted River. The things Birdy worried about before the attack seemed small to her now.

She found herself often trailing after him. Sitting next to him to eat. Joining him and River and Oopsy in the shelter at night. Sometimes it even felt safe enough there for her to fall asleep.

Today when he said he was going fishing, she offered to come along. He would catch them, and she would clean them and bring a bowl for the roe; fish bellies were swollen this time of year.

She stretched, feeling the breeze toss her hair around. She hadn't bothered tying it back and now it tickled as the wind blew it about. The wind blew some of the scales around too as she separated fish skin from flesh, and the scraps sparkled as they caught the light. Though not for long. Guard and a few other camp dogs followed and were snapping up every stray bit of fish as fast as she could discard it. The dogs seemed to like meat better than fish, but they didn't always get meat. They didn't always get food of any kind, back in the camp.

Having caught a mess of fish, K'enemy stretched his back and unkinked his legs and arms. He set Great Uncle's traps to dry on a mossy root, glancing at her from a couple of paces away.

There were mallards floating on the surface of the water, and they watched them dive. A dove was cooing softly. The insects were buzzing, and the dogs lay down to nap. A bug landed on the water and a small fish breached the surface to swallow it whole. They watched the ripples spread outward, the rings widening until they reached the opposite bank.

Unexpectedly K'enemy began to speak. "I didn't kill her, you know."

Interesting how he didn't even have to say it; she knew exactly who he meant. At least it was a different misery than the one she was dwelling on. "I guess you'd say that even if you did," she muttered.

"Well I didn't. You can believe me or not." He shifted uncomfortably, his eyes moving away. "I never wanted to hurt her. I loved her, you know. I asked her to marry me several times, but she always just," embarrassed pause, "laughed."

Laughed. Birdy could imagine it, her mother enjoying his discomfort, a sly smile creeping over her face. "Why did you keep hanging around, then?"

"She kept inviting me back," he said simply. "I used to think she missed me. Kept hoping I could convince her to marry me and we would always be together. I wouldn't have to keep peeking into the cave to see if she was too busy at the hot springs, or with her kids—with you," he nodded.

"Not with me," Birdy sniffed. "I was the one watching the kids most of the time, not her."

"Yes." He was oblivious to her tone. "I was happy when I saw you taking care of everybody. It meant she might have time for me. But she hardly ever did. Unless she had a hankering for salmon or needed firewood toted. Then it was, Oh, K'enemy, you are the sweetest man! We'll have a lovely time together. *After* you get back with the fish you promised."

"And you still wanted to marry her?" Birdy could not imagine K'enemy fitting into life in the cave. She could see him as one of her mother's play toys—there was really no other way to describe it. Her mother used to play with people like some girls played with dolls: As something to be picked up and toyed with from time to time but didn't really have any needs of its own.

Which was just how she treated me, Birdy realized. She'd pick me up occasionally to pet and fuss over, but mostly I was someone to take care of things for her. Someone to make her to look wonderful to everybody else.

She never understood before why she was so angry at her mother. Mami didn't pay attention except to tell her what to do next. Birdy simply didn't matter to Mami. She cared about the visitors; she always cared about the newest baby, but the rest of the family were like the stone underfoot. Useful, but nothing to spend an afternoon fretting over. If anything went wrong, *whack!* Then she could ignore Birdy again. Birdy would have been miserable if it weren't for Grandmother, Great Uncle, and River. They cared about her. They cared about her a lot. Who did K'enemy have to care what happened to him? Poor K'enemy, she suddenly thought. All he wanted was to matter to someone.

Both of them were looking off in the distance. K'enemy was trying his best to think how to answer her, but it was hard for him to respond since everything had changed so much by now. Why did he want to marry the woman anyway, he wondered. She was selfish and cold, and she didn't care if he suffered. Looking back it seemed that what pulled him to her was not the woman herself but the cave, the family, the sense that he was needed and there was space for him. He longed to share a hearth. He'd missed that a long time. What did Birdy ask? Did he really want to marry her mother? It was hard to remember; he felt so different now. "I did want to marry her," he finally said, "but I probably would have come to my senses soon enough. There were others, you know. I was not the only one chasing her."

Hearing this made Birdy feel stupid. She was there all along; she probably should have noticed. But every single day there were visitors, and she was always getting sent out to do chores. She never tried to distinguish who came for the hot springs and who came especially to visit her mother. She had to ask if she wanted to know.

Though she was not sure she really wanted to know. It didn't make her happy hearing this kind of stuff. But if other people knew embarrassing things about her family, she should probably know them too. "Who else?" she finally asked.

"There was someone secret," K'enemy recalled. "She wouldn't say who because he was married and she was still toying with him. I tried to make her drop him so she wouldn't hurt some other family but instead of promising, she threatened to drop me. So I shut up about it, though I almost let her go ahead and drop me. Now I think I should have. Maybe I would have noticed River sooner." He sighed, shaking his head sadly. "She did say it was over with him, but it could be she said that so I wouldn't think badly of her. Then there was Dolphin, he was her newest one, and before him there was Tortoise, but she said she didn't want any old men sniffing after her, told him right to his face when he brought a present she didn't like."

Birdy remembered Tortoise fondly. He wasn't old at all, she thought, angry at her mother for being so disrespectful to him. Birdy never knew he was more than a visitor seeking balm for a pulled muscle when he came to the cave. Just another visitor, but one who sometimes stopped to ask how she was doing, who actually took the time to notice how good she was with the children.

K'enemy inclined his head, his expression dry and grim. "We had an argument that day. I don't remember exactly what about. I went away mad, then decided to soak myself in the hot springs in spite of her being there. She glared at me when I came back inside. There may have been someone else with her, standing in the shadows. I was just coming out when the earth rumbled. I tried to get her out alive but it was too late. All I got was her amulet."

"Oh, that's how you got it. I wondered." She flushed, looking down at her feet which were vigorously kicking holes in the riverbank. "I even thought maybe you killed her and took it to remember."

"I loved your mother, Birdy," K'enemy said reproachfully. He clenched his fists tightly. "Now if someone else killed her, and I'm not saying anyone did, River said you probably got it mixed up and she was crushed in the cave-in. But if someone was hiding and killed her after I left, I can't believe it was Tortoise. He was paying attention to old Clamshucker's widow by then."

"Good for him." She was disgusted with the whole subject. Every new thing she learned about her mamma only made her feel worse.

"Which still means Dolphin could have done it, though nothing's for sure. If she was telling the truth about that married man. You know, it could fit. He was used to getting anything he wanted. Had a quick temper when things didn't go well for him."

"Who was he? I don't remember anyone named Dolphin."

"He was about my age, old enough to settle down. I always thought he was entirely too good looking for his own sake." Birdy nodded, beginning to remember someone who maybe fit that description. "His father was the old chief. He let his son run a little wild. The old man was too busy keeping the peace between other families. I guess he didn't have time to keep his eye on his own. Girls were always making flirty eyes at him, offering him little tidbits of food. Whatever he wanted, he was used to getting somehow."

"You're jealous!" Birdy exclaimed, smiling for the first time in days. "Don't deny it now."

"Maybe I was. Not anymore, of course. I'm the one who is still alive, not him."

"If he had all those girls after him, what did he want with Mami?"

He was quiet for a moment. Finally he spoke, in a tone tinged with regret. "She was a beautiful woman, Birdy. Maybe you never saw that, but she was."

Birdy shot him a skeptical look.

"Could be he liked the challenge. Everybody else was always falling all over themselves to do things for him, but she was something different. Your mother, well, she'd show you she was interested, and then she'd play hard-to-get. It's like dangling food in front of a hungry dog, then yanking it away. Makes him lunge for it even if there's other scraps laying around."

"With all those other girls after him, why was he hungry, like you said?"

"Your mother knew how to make a man long for her, little one. She knew how to feed a man just enough to make him hunger for more."

There was a dark undertone in his voice. She watched him for a moment. "You think he killed her?"

He rubbed his hands one against the other, as if he had dirt or blood to clean off. "That kind of thing could drive some men to violence," he mused. "I left in a huff that morning, too angry to pay much attention. I was going to go back up the mountain, go stalk some big animal and take my mad out on it, but then I changed my mind. I never saw who was coming next. Might have been him or anybody. We'll never know. Couldn't tell for sure who was in the cave when we were digging them out."

"Maybe she was trying to get rid of you because she knew he was coming," Birdy said in a rush of excitement. She could see it all now. Probably her mother sent K'enemy off so she could see her other boyfriend. She already sent Birdy off with River to pick berries. Thunder was away with his friends. Grandmother and Great Uncle were in one of the inner chambers, so she could have left the little ones in their care. K'enemy unexpectedly returned and she had to get rid of him before Dolphin showed up. So she sent K'enemy away mad. But then he came back. And Dolphin probably saw K'enemy and got jealous, grabbed her, and shook her hard as she tried to escape. It was just like one of the women's stories about love and jealousy, and she got smashed into the rocks and died.

"Then you took her amulet so you could remember her always?" Birdy asked, excited. And failed to notice that he paused before giving a curt nod.

A tragic love story. She could tell this story, she just knew it. Maybe not right away, but some day. It wouldn't be a sacred story, more like the wedding story that anyone could tell. Already the beginning was forming in her head.

She looked up and was surprised to see K'enemy watching. She had been so intent working things out that she forgot he was waiting for her reaction. Well she didn't have a reaction. She didn't know how to feel about her mother. It was too weird with all that about her men friends and everything. It was too much to take in.

She knew how to feel about the story though; that was something she could work on. Stories were good. Stories were life. Stories were as much of life as she could handle sometimes.

Actually they could be better than life, because sometimes you could make them come out the way you wanted. And the ones that you weren't supposed to change, you could shape the way people heard them, which was almost as good.

"How did you get your name," she suddenly wondered.

"Oh, you don't want to know about that," he said, backing away.

"Of course I do, silly. That's why I asked."

"I don't think so. It's not a story for children."

"I am not a child," she protested.

"You're, what, only 11 summers in age? That's still a child by my reckoning."

"I may be a girl of 11 summers, but I am not a child. Not after *this* summer I'm not."

He looked at her, considering. "Maybe you're right, but it's not a nice story."

"Please? Tell me anyway!"

He guessed that he owed her. If he'd been more forgiving, she would have had her mother still. Though surely she was better off with River looking after her. As was he.

So maybe he didn't owe her much, except of course he promised River and Rein that he would take care of her needs. Still, that was different. He had to protect her and make sure she was fed, but he had no obligation to bare his painful past.

Yet stories were a comfort to the girl, anyone could see that. And if he could help her forget some of her misery by sharing his, at least some good would come out of that old ugliness. So he told her the twisted tale of his father. Who was charming except when some foul spirit entered him and he'd speak in that awful, enraged voice. At such times he turned on his wife, K'enemy's mother, and screamed a barrage of foulness at her.

There were times when he beat her senseless. And sometimes K'enemy and his sisters felt the force of his fist, which was almost unheard of, in a People who cherished the young for the future they would someday bring. K'enemy tried to get the shaman to drive away the ugliness. The man came to see his father once, but the rotten spirit stayed hidden that day. Father persuaded Flies Like Falcon that his son was lying. There was no ugly spirit in him. Falcon didn't notice the son's limping, or the wife's extensive bruises; he went back instead to his shelter at the beach.

That day K'enemy's father said his son was no son of his any longer, bringing shame on the family like that. He was no son; he was his enemy, and no longer could he live with them. From then on K'enemy had to make his own sleeping space, tend his own fire, and find his own food. He slept under the stars until he was able to slay and skin enough animals, skin them and complete a shelter of his own. Even so, K'enemy tried to keep an eye on his mother and sisters and intervene when the ugliness returned.

Until the day when his father beat his poor mother to death. K'enemy was sick with a fever and didn't even hear her screams. Afraid for the lives of his sisters, he waited until he regained his strength, crept into his father's shelter late one night and slit his throat in his sleep.

"I used to be called First Born," he told Birdy. "I was the first child, first grandchild, and everyone loved me. Now people shudder when I come near. K'enemy's not a name I like," he confessed. "But it's the truest name I could have."

"It's kind of a gruesome thing to call you, isn't it?"

He nodded, considering. "You have to understand, Birdy, I'm not ashamed. I did what I had to do in order to keep my family safe. When people first started calling me Kills His Enemy, it was painful to hear. But that's who I am. It's not pretty, but it's true. No one else would do it. They wouldn't believe me. Not the chief, not the shaman, and not my father's own brothers. There were others on the mountain who watched him in his rages and didn't move a stone to protect my momma. You think anyone ever tried to stop him besides me?" He snorted. "I'm the one who will kill his enemy if it has to be done. No one else has earned that name. Besides," he added, "it's as much about other folks as it is about me."

"What do you mean?"

"Some people use my name to remind themselves of their own failures. That they didn't put a stop to the ugliness, so I had to."

"Then it's a good name," Birdy concluded, deciding right then to like him. Yes, he was awkward around the fire circle. But River was right: He was a good man.

⋆   ⋆   ⋆

Since he was a boy, K'enemy often found himself leaving the company of people to find solace in the forest. If his father was raving or a girl responded to him with a sniff or a glare, whenever some unfairness slapped him in the face, he left the shelters for the company of trees.

He would wander until he found some large grandfather tree that called to him. Walked around it, chose the most comfortable spot and sat. Leaned against the trunk, legs resting on roots, head tilting skyward. There his heart could settle. His pulse slowed until it seemed to blend with the slow pulsing of sap flowing up the tall column behind him. He sensed his breath mingling with the breath of the tree, the breathing of every creature in the forest and beyond that, the breath of all life.

This slow thinning of his boundaries, stretching until he felt them no more, let him feel, blessedly, part of all creation. This was what made him whole again. Haodisah. It salved his hurts and loneliness so that when he rose to wander among people again, he could take his place among men.

Today the very act of lying sent him fleeing treeward. Because a lie was a break in the wholeness. It went against haodisah, and for him to be the one lying made it harder to bear. A lie was like a deliberate breaking of a branch, when you knew the sap would flow out of the wound. Instead of nourishing the tree so that new fruits could grow, so that new limbs could stretch out and support another bird's nest, instead the sap would run on the ground and the break point become an opening for some ugly spirit to enter, fester, and lead to the tree's decline.

Sprawling now against a large pine, allowing his mind to empty out, letting the necessary ugliness of his own words drip away, the peace could finally seep back. At first, noticing only the calls of the birds overhead, the buzz of insects. The flashes of light and shadow as sunlight filtered through. Then the smells: Greenness, dry leaves, acrid animal scents and the familiar odor that was his very own.

Thoughts began to creep back in. The talk he had with Birdy went reasonably well, for all its tensions. He was sorry to hurt the reputation of Dolphin, a not-so-bad man. Not that he'd mind, being dead these past few months. Anyway it was for a good reason. And it allowed the man to do a good deed for the People, he who had mostly lived for his own pleasures. Now he could help set a girl's heart at ease. Birdy should never learn the truth. At least not for a long while, he and River agreed. River had forgiven him already. For her own sake, and for the rest of the family, which would forgive him too if they ever found out. But, she insisted, there was no need for them to hear of it. Especially not Birdy.

He didn't regret killing the woman. All he regretted was having to lie.

He sighed. He would have to live with it. Unlike most lies that broke *hao* out of greed or thoughtlessness, this was more like a scar that formed over a break already in the skin. It was needed to protect the delicate wound so it could heal underneath. And when it grew stronger, the scab might fall away and the ugliness disappear, having become part of the new strength.

Someday he would tell Birdy the full story, he decided. He would tell her when she joined with some man as husband and wife. By then she'd be ready to know the truth.

No, he wouldn't even wait that long. He'd tell her after her first blood ceremony. She deserved to know what really happened. Yes, it might reopen the wound but it was better that way. You couldn't make things right, living in a spider's web of lies. A makeshift home that might suddenly break apart and drop you from up high. Like when his father lied to the shaman and the shaman let him be. And then his mother died of it, cruelly, which probably would never have happened if only the truth were known.

He needn't keep the secret a day longer than that. River wanted to protect Birdy, but the best way to protect the girl was to help her grow up strong and true, let her know the truth as soon as she was old enough to take it in. Then she wouldn't have to rely on them to protect her because she could do most of it herself.

For now River insisted that he not tell her the truth. Especially not after all she'd been through. And River was incapable of lying; she would never manage to do a credible job of it. So if a lie had to be told, they agreed he would have to do it. And he knew from personal experience that if you had to do something distasteful, you did it thoroughly the first time or you'd end up redoing it again and again, and never get free of the horrible thing.

Most of what he told her was true. The teasing her mother did, the men she had waiting on her. He did love her once, awful as she was. It took him a long time to see what she was instead of what she pretended to be. That she was more like his own rotten father than his sad, loving mother. Well, everybody made foolish mistakes when they were young; he didn't feel bad

about making his share of them. He was lucky that it didn't work out the
way he longed for, back then.

He would make whatever further reparations the People wanted if the
truth came out. He had no regrets for killing that woman. She had an ugliness
in her, not quite as violent as his father's, but ugly just the same. While she
lived, everything she touched was scarred, and nothing around her could ever
be whole. Would Birdy be better off knowing more about that awful woman?
He honestly did not think so.

No. The foulest of spirits were not to be borne. Once seen for what they
were—like sharp, uncaring blades half-hidden in a bed where only softness
ought to be—they needed to be seized and broken before more unwary victims
were pierced.

Sometimes he thought of that moment, just the two of them inside the
cave. Could it be he misunderstood her? Could it be the same wild spirits
that made the animals run amok that day had entered her too? Entered him
as well so that he let loose an anger that should never have been?

But every time he put his hand back on the rope tying that moment to
the next, he circled back to the same place. What she planned to do—it
would not have been the first time she beat her daughter bloody. She even
bragged about it to him. And no matter what he said, no matter that, among
the People, it was wise to cherish the children and thus to protect their own
future, she didn't feel bad about it. Not one stinking bit.

From that very moment he knew she was an enemy, not just to him, but
to all the People. Even if they didn't know it yet.

And they did not name him K'enemy for nothing.

Chapter 2: The walrus people

Four of them set out at dawn the next day. Bear led the way, guiding them
past various landmarks—a gnarled pine thick with cones, a boggy lowland,
the place he and Left churned up the mud flinging it at each other. Carefully
he steered them around the slick spot near the overlook, choosing a dry place
nearby to observe.

Three large shelters nestled in the last set of hills before the water's edge.
These people had chosen their location well, Rein decided. The hills protected
them from gusting winds. Yet they were near enough to hunt seal or walrus,

pick crabs off the beach, or turn inland for salmon or trout, deer or elk, berries or greens when their interest lay that way.

There was something familiar about it. The shape of the dwellings? The line of the beach? "I think I know these people," he murmured, a smile growing on his face. "Follow me, men!" Quickly he began descending the slope.

"Who are they, Papi?" Bear asked.

"They're the Walrus People," Rein called back. "We visited when I lived with our cousins."

Staunch looked at Bison, who looked at Bear. "Shouldn't we approach with caution?" Bison asked. "What if they're not as friendly as he remembers?"

Staunch shrugged. "Let's hope he knows what he's doing."

The mountainside facing the ocean was covered with low-lying shrubs and grass leaving them visible for most of the approach. "Good thing he's not worried about sneaking up on them," Bison said. "There's no cover at all."

"No need," Rein called back. Getting closer, he began calling, "*AiAiAi,*" holding his hands up, palms facing toward the settlement. It could have been a cry of attack but it wasn't; it sounded more like a greeting for old friends.

Below, the people turned to see what was coming. Several emerged from their dwellings; others came up from the beach. After a moment one man raised his hands and echoed Rein's cry.

Reaching the settlement, Rein set down his spear and slapped the man's palms three times with his. There was a flurry of enthusiasm in two different languages.

As Bison, Bear and Staunch neared, Rein waved them forward to be introduced. "Do what I did," he warned in an undertone. "Slap his palms three times. That's their way of saying welcome." He pushed Bison forward. "Don't forget the *AiAiAi.*"

So Bison followed his example, and Rein announced the young man's name along with his parents' names, his parents' parents' names, and what sounded, in these other People's words, like praise for his virility and skill as a hunter. To Bison he said, "This is Takoonde, son of Gaalute, son of Deeq, a great killer of whales and walrus. He is my friend."

"No, no, not Takoonde. That for young boy." The man indicated a spot in the air at approximately chest height. "Now I name Takeet."

"Ah, Takeet," Rein complimented him. "A great name for a hunter."

"What's it mean, Papi?" Bear whispered.

"Er, walrus testicles, I think," Rein said under his breath.

"Dad," Bear scowled. "You must be joking."

Rein shook his head.

"What was his name before that?"

"Bladder. Like a seal's bladder, they blow it up and the children play a game with it."

"Walrus testicles? That's an improvement?"

"Bear," his father warned. "You need to be silent unless you can say something nice. We don't want to offend these people; they could be good friends. Anyway, have you ever really looked at a pair of walrus testicles? They're pretty impressive."

Turning to Takeet, Rein smiled and slapped him on the shoulder. "Takeet. A fine, strong name for a leader of men."

Then he pulled Bear forward, draping his arm around him. "This is Bear, son of Runs Like Reindeer, son of Thunder in the Sky. He is a good boy, with the strength of his mother and my own great beauty."

At which, Takeet snorted merrily.

"Dad!" Bear squirmed uncomfortably. "Why don't you say I'm the one that found them?" His father said such nice things about Bison when he introduced him. Why did his own introduction have to be a big joke?

Takeet had a big grin on his face. It was the only thing he was wearing. Nor were most of the people clothed, Bear noticed. Though it didn't seem to matter to them. Nobody tried to cover themselves up. Nobody was shivering either, though Bear knew he'd be cold if it weren't for the wrap he wore. A child stood, half-hiding behind his mother's legs. He turned away and let loose a stream of pee, and nobody seemed to care how close it was to the shelter.

In the meantime Takeet was grabbing Bear by the arm to feel his muscles. The boy had to make an effort not to flinch at the strength of his grip. "Strong boy," the man said with approval. "He make fine hunter. Many walrus he get."

"That's my boy," Rein agreed, and then introduced Staunch with another string of compliments.

When the introductions were complete, Bison set the haunch of meat at Takeet's feet. "This is for you. For your people," he explained.

The leader looked them over. "Who kill, you?" he asked Bison. "Not you." He poked Rein in the middle. "You too fat."

Both men laughed. Rein poked him back. "You're one to talk! You were a scrawny little lad when I last saw you. What happened?"

Takeet motioned at the woman standing directly behind him. "She keep feeding. If no eat, she throw me out of bed. Take skinny new husband to fatten up."

His wife smiled shyly as their eyes turned toward her.

Now the rest of his people moved forward to be introduced. There were perhaps 30 or 40 of them, and Rein gallantly resolved to remember each name.

Takeet motioned for food and tea. Everybody looked for places to sit, choosing boulders or pieces of driftwood, or cleared spaces on the ground. There was no fire circle to sit around so the people sat haphazardly, facing every which way.

Takeet was telling Rein that he led this village now. The leader before him froze to death in an ice storm. "How long ago?" Rein asked, but the man simply shrugged.

"They don't really know how to count," he explained quietly to Bear and the others. "You listen, you won't hear them saying more than one or two. That's all the numbers they know. One, two. Anything more than that, they just say 'many'. Or 'many many' if it's really a lot."

"Why does he speak our language, Papi?"

"They trade sometimes with our cousins. Reindeer meat for walrus, antlers for tusks, that kind of thing. So he speaks a little of our language. And I learned some of theirs."

Now Rein began telling Takeet why they were traveling. When he knew a word in Takeet's language he used it. To show respect for his People and to get them to laugh, which they did, repeating his rusty pronunciations. It sounded odd to hear their sad story punctuated with laughter, but it helped establish a pleasant bond.

"And so we were wondering," he concluded, "have you seen our cousins the reindeer-followers recently? Because we have come far, hoping to join them."

Takeet shook his head. "Not since we boys, they no here since then. Maybe you?" he asked another man sitting nearby. "You see Reindeer People?" He repeated the question in their language.

The man, Dagoote, nodded. "We see cousin people."

"You saw them? When? This year? Last year?"

The man scowled. "Two summers? No, sorry, no," he corrected himself, "many."

"How many many?" Bear broke in.

"Many."

"That could mean 3 or it could mean 10," Rein reminded him. "He won't be able to say any better than that."

"Maybe next village know," Dagoote offered.

"There's another village?"

Takeet said yes, there were many settlements of their people. His, they called South, or sometimes Walrus Beach. Dagoote's was called Sad, because they lost many people in an accident the previous winter. Then there was Seal Beach, where many, many seals liked to bask. Next was Fog and beyond that, Ice. Because there was ice all year round on the shady side of mountains, and pieces of ice floated in the sea.

"That's five," Bear announced eagerly. He held up his hand and waggled all five digits at the man. "They have five settlements."

"Many," Takeet allowed, and he invited them to stay. "Winter coming," he explained, "no good for travel."

There was another flurry of words between Takeet and Dagoote.

"Dagoote say you come with him for winter, many walrus, they show you make good home."

Rein nodded, and responded directly to the man in his own language. Turned to his own people and reported back, "I thanked him for his kind offer. We don't have to accept. We can confer and decide later."

Just then there was another rush of conversation. One of the Walrus People stepped forward and said something to Dagoote, who argued back. Staunch looked quizzically at Rein, who shook his head. It went by too fast for him to understand. Both men stood with hands on their hips, looking each other over. One of them quickly slapped the other on his face. The other punched him back, and they proceeded to paw and punch each other, none of it hard. This went on until one of the men let himself fall to the ground in a comical way, his arms flying high, his legs flopping exaggeratedly about. The other fell down too, looking just as silly, and the Walrus People burst out in gales of laughter, joking and slapping each other.

"You catch any of that?" Staunch murmured to Rein.

"They're sure having a good time," he demurred. "Wish I understood the joke."

Takeet turned to Rein. Pointing at the closer one, "He say we ask you, stay us. We find you; we deserve honor. He say," he indicated Dagoote, "you no like walrus bladder stink of South village. He think you have better," he took a moment to find the right word, "better likes than that. Then he say," pointing to the other man, "if you like smell fish fart breath, you like live at his village, go ahead. Then he slap and he slap back and they fall on ground. All very funny."

"Very funny," Staunch said, quiet enough so only Rein could hear. "Like children, they are."

"It's not all that different from the banter that passes for conversation between us."

"True enough," Staunch agreed. "I guess that means we'll fit right in."

Later after food, tea, and more silliness, some of which they even understood, Staunch sought out Rein. "I'm tired. You think we can get a good night's sleep somewhere?"

"Oh. Well, maybe, maybe not. They're pretty good hosts, but sleep might not be so easy. Don't be surprised if they are unusually generous with their hospitality."

"What do you mean?"

"They can be very, er, giving. At least they used to be. You'll see."

Several women came to lead the hunters away for the night. They were separated and offered spaces among the blankets and bedding in the three large shelters where the Walrus People slept, piled together in relative harmony. That night there was a fair amount of giggling in the dark.

The next day both Staunch and Bison looked unusually tired. Yet they were exceedingly cheerful, kept breaking out in grins, and neither one complained.

⋆   ⋆   ⋆

"We have several choices as I see it." Rein had the talking stick.

He waited for the murmuring to die down. "One," he said, holding up the first finger. "We set up camp for the winter with Takeet's people. They help us make three big shelters like theirs, and we live next to them. In the spring we say goodbye and start looking for our cousins again.

"Two." He held up the next finger. "We go with Dagoote and stay the winter with his people. They need us, we need them. They lost a lot of folks last year, and it's safer getting through the dark times when there's more to huddle up with. We'll build a hut or two like theirs, and the rest can fit into their extra spaces.

"Three." Another finger joined the first two. "We move camp to the site that Two Stones and Turtle found. Maybe we visit and trade with the Walrus People but we live apart.

"Four. We keep going and see if we find a better wintering place. Or maybe we find our cousins. We can always come back to the camp Two Stones found. Or to one of the Walrus People's settlements, if that's what we decide."

The chorus of groans quickly quashed the notion of traveling farther.

Cookie asked for the talking stick. She wanted to know more about Dagoote's people. Who lived there, how many men, how many women, how old the children were.

"You don't know these people," Rein tried to explain. "They're not smart like us. They're kind, they're excellent hosts ... "

"They certainly are," Staunch grinned appreciatively.

"... they know how to live in the cold, but they're not so smart as us."

"Not so clean, either," Bear muttered, but was quelled by a glance from his father.

"You ask how many. They don't count, and we didn't go see. I asked them to describe who was there. Best I can tell, there's maybe 15, 16 people, something like that. Four or five hunters, several women, and a pack of half-orphaned kids. And way more space in their shelters than they're used to. Dagoote was in Takeet's village trying to recruit some of them to move up there."

"Are they interested?"

"They're going to wait and see if we fill up the spaces."

Little Mother asked for the stick. "Their kids don't have any mammas or pappas?"

"We don't know for sure. Probably some don't, and some have one or two."

It was unusual for a child to speak out in the council circle, but not unheard of. Though she meekly ducked her head, the girl persisted. "I think we should help them."

Two Stones took the stick from her. "My daughter has a good point. Where we're needed, we'll be welcome. If we stay in the first village, even if we begin as friends, we may not stay friends, two different Peoples rubbing up against each other for so many moons."

"Like two sticks of wood rubbing against each other," Fierce added.

Rein nodded. Tempers might smolder. Sparks could fly. It was tough enough being isolated when a bad run of winter storms kept family trapped together. If they threw their lot in with another People, they'd have to get along until the spring no matter what provocations arose.

Little Mouse rubbed her growing belly protectively. "What do we know of these others? You only met one of them. What if they turn on us once we're there?" She glanced worriedly at Birdy. "The last strangers we met seemed pleasant enough, but then they weren't."

Rein scratched his head. "I suppose that's a possibility. But there's more of us than them. What do you think," he asked Bison and Staunch. "You met everyone I did."

"Either village is fine with me," Staunch declared. "They were very friendly to us. I don't relish going it alone all winter in a new area. We don't have time to find the best hunting and gathering spots."

Bison responded more cautiously. "These Walrus People are very nice. But they're different from us. We don't know how different because we just met them. For one thing, they're all greasy and dirty, it's enough to make you sick! Sure, they were nice, but I don't know if we want to live with them every day. I say we go our own way. Be friendly, trade with them, and ask their advice, but we should keep a separate hearth."

"I'm sure the Walrus tribe has their ways." Left felt protective of their new friends. She and Bear had found them. In her mind that made them hers. "I agree with Staunch. I bet living with them will be fun."

"It'll be safer to live with people who know this land," Cookie volunteered. "This seems like a harsher place than we have ever lived in before."

She pulled her wrap close. "The sun seems weaker here. The trees are smaller, and the berries too. The foxes Great Uncle has been trapping—their fur is thicker than we saw back at home. I'm guessing this winter will be tougher than we ever faced. We should make use of these People's experience; they know how to survive here. And, like Two Stones said, if we're needed, they'll be grateful for our help. So even if it doesn't work out perfectly, we should part as friends. We don't want anyone hunting us with their spears by the end of winter."

No one seemed afraid of living near the ocean in this new place; that was one worry Rein could forget. And no one seemed shy about speaking out to help decide things. That took care of another. They were talking right and left, all around the council fire. Even some of the children were expressing their opinions.

When all the talk was done, they agreed to accept the invitation to Sad. But they decided not to call it Sad. Instead they would call it Next Step on the Path. Or maybe just Next.

★ ★ ★

They met Dagoote at South Village, where they camped overnight before heading north. In their days of travel they passed several areas worth coming back to—good fishing spots, large tracts of pine and cedar with their ripening nuts. Rein was happy to see fresh signs of reindeer. "I can see you slavering for your favorite stew," Cookie teased him. He smiled back, but she knew he would have been happier had they seen any people-tracks mixed in.

Still, any sign of reindeer was good. They would need hides for clothing, bedding and warm winter footwear, and the meat would be a boon. The People enjoyed an occasional meal of seal or walrus meat. But to depend on such like the Walrus People did for the entire winter? There were some that would rather eat sand. They were mountain people, not beach people, more accustomed to meat than sea creatures. They would have to do some hunting on their own.

Dagoote ran ahead to let his people know they were coming. So when the People reached their new winter camp there was a cheerful gathering and offering of food. But first the greetings, the introductions, the getting-to-know-our-new-friends time.

Those who'd done it before went first so the rest could follow. With his small cache of words in their language Rein helped by introducing them. Names, lineage, strengths and skills. The hand slapping, the nods and grins, the elaborate compliments went over with a great deal of glee.

Then Dagoote brought his People forward for their turn. First, a grizzled hunter with only a few teeth left in his mouth. An elder, Rein reminded them, so be respectful. As if they would forget. His name was Unqileer, and he nodded in a friendly way. Then Gaagatade, taller than the others, though smaller than their own hunters. Next, a man bold of face called Imaleen. Tusk, Rein interpreted.

Four children were introduced, all boys, and then the introductions seemed to be over.

"What about the girls," Birdy wondered aloud, standing next to Willow. "Don't they have names?"

"They must," Willow said, uncertain.

Birdy sidled up to Rein. "Uncle," she whispered. "What about the girls, can we meet them?"

"Right," he agreed, and repeated her question to Dagoote.

Dagoote pointed at his wife. "Vedeelon." He pointed out another woman, saying the same thing. Again and again, until he'd indicated all five, and then stopped.

Rein pointed to the girls of varying ages.

"Gedeelon," Dagoote said dismissively. "Gedeelon, Gedeelon, Gedeelon."

"That didn't help," Birdy complained. "They can't all have the same name."

Comprehension dawned on Rein's face. "I think Gedeelon means girl. And when one of them becomes a wife, she's called Vedeelon."

"They don't get their own names?"

"I guess not." He blinked. "I never noticed that before."

"How do they tell them apart?"

"Well, they must know they're different people. They just don't get different names."

"But if they want that particular woman over there, how do they call her so she comes and nobody else?"

"I don't know, Birdy," he frowned. "But I'm sure we'll find out soon enough."

She scowled right back. To have no name, how could anyone know who you were? Because among the Ogwehu, names recalled the stories that told people something essential about you.

"They're different than us, Birdy, but you'll get used to it. Remember, they're going to help us survive this winter. We have to get along. Can I count on you?"

She grimaced. But of course, what choice was there? She nodded slowly, conceding the point. They had to get along this winter. Survive and look for a better place later. Their cousins hopefully would be more like them.

★ ★ ★

The Full Moon passed, and a New Moon as well. The women worked hard getting ready for winter, stopping only when the twilight deepened and they couldn't tell if they were about to stab a finger with their bone needles or the piece of hide they were stitching. Then a few chunks of walrus or fish skewered and cooked quickly over the fire, a mug of tea, and finally they fell into bed. Which was, at first, in their worn hide tents, but now some slept in the new shelter their hosts helped them build.

It was a huge dome made with hides stretched across several whale ribs which they scavenged from an old skeleton beached nearby. They sank the ribs into the dirt, anchored by whale vertebrae at the base and brought together at the top leaving a small hole where smoke from the hearth could escape. Where the poking pole would be pushed through, in case snow settled on top and blocked up the hole. They would die if that happened. The smoke would curl around inside the shelter, their eyes would tear up and they'd gasp for breath. The smoke had to travel skyward because smoke belonged to Father Sky. And if people tried to hold a Father Sky thing on the Earth, they sickened. Things had to go where they belonged in order to keep everything in balance.

Inside, the shelter was divided in two by a curtain of hides sewn together and hung from the ceiling supports. The front area was for storage. In the rear, there was a rock circle hearth with bedding laid around it. It was warm and cozy with many sleeping there. It would be warmer still if they had time to add a second layer of hides.

Not everyone fit in the shelter at once. It easily held ten without too much crowding. More could squeeze in if they didn't mind tight conditions. For now, River's and Rein's families stayed in the old shelters. Staunch, Bison, Turtle and Owl offered to stay with the Walrus People. Antler and Bear slept a few nights under the stars until the night they woke up with frost in their hair. The next day they set up Staunch's old shelter and slept there, and sometimes Lynx and Oopsy crawled in. When the second shelter was completed, things would be easier.

None of the women or girls wanted to stay with the Walrus People. The Walrus women were different than what they were used to. They tried speaking across the language divide but they didn't get far, and it was frustrating to try. Birdy would smile and say something like, "Pretty hair," and point to one of the other girl's braids. The girl would smile shyly and look down, but she wouldn't offer anything back.

They were kind enough. They showed with their hands the best way to get a needle through the thick walrus hides, how to make it rain- or snow-proof by coating it with seal oil over the stitching, things like that, but their eyes would skitter away. They didn't talk much among themselves either, which meant only the men and the children were learning their language, and only they were making friends.

Why the women looked down so much became clear within a few days. One of the older girls was carrying a load of meat to the permafrost cache dug in the north-facing side of the hill. Birdy was walking behind carrying additional food for storage. The girl looked up when one of their hunters, Imaleen, came down the hill. The man flushed when he saw them and barked something at her in a harsh tone. The girl cowered, making herself look small. Her tremulous response brought another string of menacing words from him. He picked up a dead branch and advanced on her. Birdy cried out and tried to get between them. The man pushed Birdy away and proceeded to whack the girl four times before walking off.

Several of her tribesmen looked away, impassive, minding their own business. None of them said anything to him or her. Birdy hurriedly stored her load of provisions and went back to offer help. Surprisingly the girl pushed Birdy's outstretched hand away. She stood up on tottering legs, brushed herself off and began picking up the spilled packages of meat. When Birdy bent down to help, the girl grabbed a bundle out of her hands. She muttered something which meant nothing to Birdy. Her meaning was clear though, between the tone and the worried looks she cast around her. "Go away," she seemed to say. "Thanks but you're just making it worse. Staying might get me in bigger trouble. Please, just leave!"

Nor was it the only time any of them observed some act of cruelty with no apparent cause. Always aimed at a woman or girl, never at another man or boy. Man to man, what they saw was humor and jokes. Man to woman, it was cruelty or indifference at best.

"You're probably lucky he didn't hit you too," River said when they tried to puzzle it out. "K'enemy says the men expect the women to do all the hard work, everything but the hunting. He and Bison saw a man drive a stake through some poor woman's hand one day."

"A stake?" Birdy was incredulous.

"He took a sharpened stick and hammered it in with a hammer stone."

"Great Mother, why would anyone do such a thing?"

"They weren't sure why. She must have done something the man didn't like. They said she lay there for quite some time staked to the floor until he finally relented and let her loose."

"Can she still use her hand?" Whole families could starve to death if a vital part was maimed.

"Probably not so well as before. She lives over there," River indicated the farthest shelter. "I haven't seen her since."

"The Walrus People seemed so nice and jolly at first."

"They are nice and jolly. The men have fun with each other. But I don't envy their women at all. We seem to be safe because we're guests, but I don't want to test their patience."

"I'm being as good as I know how," Birdy worriedly assured her.

"I know you are, Birdsilu. Keep in mind it's only for the winter."

Chapter 3: Next step

Cookie hoped they had enough food set aside for the winter. They'd had one good salmon harvest, now smoked and put away, and they were waiting for the next heavy rain to return for more. Meanwhile they gathered sacks of pine and cedar nuts, moss for soft bedding and medicinal plants for teas to carry them through the cold season. The men were still hoping for another hunt. None of the Ogwehu wanted to rely on the walrus and seal stored in the hillside. They gathered firewood, animal dung, moss, and lichens for burning; they had hides to keep the women busy stitching hoods and parkas, hand coverings and footwear like the ones the Walrus People used.

Great Uncle and Antler kept trapping fox and wolverine. Wolverine made the best edging for the parkas, kept a person's breath from icing up the parka and melting when they came inside, making their clothing too damp to dry. Which was bad because no one could stay warm if they went out with wet clothing. They could freeze to death; some ill spirit might enter their mouths when they shivered, and they'd get sick and maybe die.

Except the Walrus People didn't understand about catching some ill spirit. They said the Great Spirit punished them for bad thoughts, for cursing against the cold maybe, and that's what made them sicken. They cursed a lot, those Walrus People. They got mad and yelled, "I wish a toothache on you!" or "You be blinded with pain!" Or, "Your testicles should freeze and fall off at your feet!" If they were frustrated, they might mutter, "Seal's blood!" under their breath, or sometimes "*Guurd!*" which, apparently meant bear or mammoth dung. Their worst insult, apparently, was to tell another hunter, "You smeared with the woman's blood." They'd screw up their eyes and say, "Your face all smeared," and the men would leer at the humiliated one.

The hunters didn't mind the curses but they argued with their hosts about other things. The Walrus People didn't believe in the Mother Earth Spirit, just in one Great Spirit. The Spirit sounded a lot like Father Sky to Cookie, but they insisted he was different. Staunch asked them, how could they not believe in the Great Mother when they could feel Her underneath their feet? Unqileer shrugged. "Who have power, man or woman? Man. So must be man spirit make us all."

Cookie didn't think it mattered if you believed in one Great Spirit whose breath ran through everything, or two Great Spirits and a lot of little ones like her People were taught. What mattered was that you were respectful of the powers around you, and didn't take your next meal or the health of your children for granted. But some of the men got huffy until Rein stepped in and reminded them to be respectful of the Walrus People's Great Spirit along with their own. Cookie told Rein how surprised she was that Staunch of all people, the most lackadaisical of them all, got upset and argued about it. Rein threw his hands up, saying you never could tell what sliver would get stuck in someone's foot.

But the men were excited about the new weapon they were learning to use. The Walrus People called it *atlaatal*, and it was pretty complicated. After watching them hunt, Two Stones and Bison raved about its power. Walrus was harder to kill than almost any other target. Shooting them in the body did little damage because they were so fat. They'd glide under the water and eventually the spear floated up with the tide. Hunters had to pierce them between their tusks, or get right inside the hole in the back of their skulls. To get those small targets with a spear, they had to get close. Which was hard without the walruses noticing and sliding into the sea.

But the atlaatal gave them power from a distance. Which made hunting safer—walrus, bear, moose, mammoth, it didn't matter what they targeted.

"You don't have to get right up next to the animal," Bison explained. "Saves you getting ripped apart by some big old buck!"

"You aim from a distance and it goes right through," Two Stones agreed. "Not like a spear or a club. You can be pretty far and still hit your target."

The men borrowed one and set about trying to duplicate it. Each atlaatal consisted of several parts: A handle, a bone tip attached to it and a small spear with a blade at the far end. Most of the hunters made several spears to use with each handle so they could aim one after another.

You took all those pieces, Rein instructed Cookie, stalking your prey. When you were ready, you hooked the spear part into the handle, holding them with the blade on top. You took your stance. (This he carefully demonstrated, as if she would ever try it herself. What he really wanted was for her to admire him, so of course she did. Several times, in case he missed the first two or three effusive compliments.)

You stepped forward to aim, snapped your wrist and let the thing go. The daart would fly off. ("That's what they call the spear part, a daart," Rein told her. Though it was easier to say 'dart' and when the men got excited, that's how they pronounced it.)

It took several days to make these new weapons. Every step had complications to look out for. "You said these people weren't smart, Papi," Bear pointed out as he fumbled, attaching a stone blade to its shaft.

"Guess I wasn't so smart leaping on that conclusion, was I, Bearsilu?"

"You said to make friends with them. And you always say, praise your friend's strong arm and don't stomp too hard on his weak toe. That's what you say friendship's all about. But you must have forgot."

"Right you are, boysilu. Guess I stomped too hard on their weak toes and didn't wait to see how strong their arms were."

"Even you get to learn new things, right, Papi?"

"Even me. Learning's not just for young pups like yourself. There's always more for all of us to learn."

⋆   ⋆   ⋆

More and more, the women stayed indoors to work. Even though the light was dim inside, the cold made it necessary. Sewing outdoors with gloves on was awkward. And without gloves, fingers quickly got too cold to function.

River and Little Mouse were sitting in the relative quiet of River's shelter. Little Mouse cast her eye over the other woman. "River. Are you . . . sheltering?" Their term for carrying a baby until it was ready to emerge into the world.

"I'm not sure." Her eyes misted. "I don't really know. Its times like this I really miss my mother. She'd know for sure."

"You have the signs of it. Your eyes look different. How does your belly feel? That's usually how I know."

"It feels tender. Complains when I eat anything. Do you think everyone knows?"

Little Mouse shook her head. "Come, let me take a look."

River put down her sewing. Little Mouse slipped her hand down the front of River's wrap. "Your breasts feel hot. That's how mine always felt." Reaching further, "Your belly feels hard and full. Did you say you can't eat anything in the morning?"

River shook her head. "Whatever I swallow comes back up. Even tea."

"Try just a few seeds at a time. Go do some chore, come back and nibble a few more. That always worked for me. Ask Falling Leaf for some of her herbs. She'll have something to strengthen you. It's a lot of work, you know! They get heavier as they get ready to come out." She patted her own bulge with satisfaction. "No matter what else goes wrong, at least this is solid."

What else goes wrong? River looked at the woman with sympathy. Sheltering a child with no father was no easy thing in normal times; it must be worse while they traveled. "Do you miss him?"

Little Mouse impatiently pushed her lank hair off her face. "No. Sometimes. I don't know."

River laughed uneasily. "Which is it?"

"I miss the him I loved as a young woman. We had such a rightness to us, you know? But it frayed away with a lot of stupid little squabbles. Now I miss the comfort of him being there." She made a rueful face. "Every noise makes me nervous. I miss having him tell me everything will be fine. He always felt that things would work out."

River tried to remember the last time she saw Little Mouse laugh. Maybe it was as far back as last winter's celebrations.

"All those stupid arguments! I wish I could have one more day with him. Hug him and fix his footwear, cook his favorite stew. And love him 'til we both fall asleep. Then if he went Beyond, at least we would have one day that was like it should have been. Then I wouldn't feel so bad."

"What are you so afraid of, Little Mouse?"

She picked up her sewing again. "It's better, I guess, staying in one place. I don't have to watch Bison take the lead and wonder if he's going to surprise some bear or have an avalanche fall on him, something like that. And Owl, the way he prances around, there were times I was sure we'd be scraping his dead body off a cliff. Sometimes I'd tell this little one," she indicated her belly, "I hope you enjoyed that kick, it might be your last."

"When?"

"Are you kidding? Every time we were in danger!"

"Like when?"

"When we almost lost Staunch in the bogs. When the lava poured down the mountain towards us. At your wedding when we invited those awful men in and look what happened to your niece. Now with these new Walrus People, who knows how that will turn out?"

"Maybe I'm a fool, but that choice didn't seem so dangerous to me."

Little Mouse shook her head. "Go ask Birdy if she's scared. She probably feels more like me than you. Every time my son goes hunting, there's danger. Doesn't it frighten you when K'enemy goes off with the men? Musk ox, mammoth, bear, elk—any of them could turn around and kill."

"I hardly think about the danger when K'enemy goes hunting," River confessed. "He's strong, and I know he'll come back safe."

"I used to think that way too. But now I think, I would throw myself in front of my sons if I could, and let the beasts gore me instead." She looked at River and shrugged. "Why not? I've lived my life; they still have much to live for. The thing that frightens me most is, what if I don't see the danger in time? What if I'm watching out for Owl, and something hits Bison instead? I don't think I could stand it if either one went Beyond before me." Her voice was low and fervent. "When I could offer myself, and maybe the Spirit would be kind enough to take me in his place."

River stared at her. "But ... if Father Sky decides it's someone's time to go, it's their time. Surely nothing you do can stop it. Falcon used to say ... "

"I know what Falcon used to say, but I don't believe it. He didn't know everything. You've heard the men with their hunting stories. How many times did they aim at a faun and the doe came in front offering herself instead? Or a bird pretended to be easy prey and led them away from her nestlings? If the deer and the birds can do it, so can I. You'll see when you have your own child. Even when they grow up you still hope they're safe. You'd throw yourself in front of danger if you could so long as they could escape."

"You can't live that way, Little Mouse. You can't live in fear all the time. Bison is strong and swift. You have to remember that."

Little Mouse did not answer directly. It was clear to her that she could never think like River thought she should. Reminding herself they'd probably be fine would do nothing to stop her worries. Neither did she want to argue the futility of it. "I'm out of sinew," she said instead. "Do you have any extra?"

"Of course. Take this piece. Little Mouse, tell me, were you always this frightened before?" Before this past summer. Before all the dying.

"No. But I am now. And I don't know how to get back to how it used to be." She sighed. "I feel like there's more death coming but I don't know who." She made an apologetic face. "I don't want to frighten you. Maybe it'll be one of the Walpeople."

"The what?"

She gave a mirthless laugh. "That's what Falling Leaf calls the Walrus People. Walpeople. Bison and Staunch thought it was funny and neither one can keep anything to himself. So now all the guys are calling them that. Of course they have their own names for us."

"Like what? K'enemy doesn't gossip enough. I always have to go somewhere else for the juicy stuff."

"Bison says they call us the Walkers. Or the Sore Foot People, because we walked from so far away. Imaleen calls us Disasters. He said it's because we survived all those disasters, but Staunch thinks he calls us that to keep their women away. Apparently some of them want to join us. I don't think they like being nailed to the floor, can you imagine?"

River snorted.

"Anyway, Imaleen combined the two names and called us the Walking Disasters. The Walpeople thought that was pretty funny."

"That fellow Imaleen, he's kind of mean, isn't he?"

"Just to women."

"I stumbled into him yesterday. I don't know why; I just seemed to lose my balance."

"I'm always a little clumsy when I'm sheltering a babe."

"Maybe that's it," River mused. "Anyway I stumbled and fell right on him. I was apologizing, looked him right in the eye and said I was sorry, but he kept glaring at me, the more I said how sorry I was."

"That was probably your mistake."

"What, apologizing?"

"No, looking him in the eye. He probably thought you were being insolent. You haven't noticed how the Walwomen keep their eyes on the ground? Apparently only men can look other Walmen in the eye."

"You think he didn't even hear me?"

"Probably he was too mad thinking how you insulted him, looking at him eye to eye."

"Oh." River flashed a wry grin. "Well, if I have to insult someone, I'd rather it be him, and not someone I like."

Little Mouse smiled. No further comment seemed necessary.

Chapter 4: Fish camp

The driving rain kept them indoors grumbling, but it promised another big run of salmon. They waited three days for the worst to pass. Spats broke out, though the Walrus men deftly turned most of them into pratfalls and shoving-jokefests, which kept the tension down.

Finally a day dawned, misty but dry. They were more than ready to go somewhere, anywhere, leave the shelters and stand under the open sky. Unqileer went through camp asking who wanted to fish for probably the last time before winter. Within moments people were gathering outside, they were that eager to spend time away from the camp.

He led them through the hills to a branch of the great river where the salmon were swimming over each other's backs in their determination to move upstream and spawn. These fish were more fierce and muscular than those back on the fingerland. They paid little attention to the predators along the way, human or bear, though usually the bears were wary and hid in the shadows.

Once the men chose the site, the women set up camp along with the smoking fires and lattices for preserving salmon. The men began catching many many, just as promised by Dagoote, using bowls, spears or even their hands. They stunned the new-caught fish, holding each by the tail and jerking it sharply against a rock. The older boys slit them lengthwise, removing the guts and turning them into collecting bowls. Children took turns running the flesh to the women tending the fires.

★   ★   ★

The argument started with a simple remark Bison made as they were resting, midday.

"It would sure be nice to hear some stories tonight," he said wistfully.

"Yeah, it *would* be nice having stories around the campfire tonight," Turtle echoed, looking around for Antler.

"'Thtorieth," Oopsy agreed. "I like 'thtorieth." He had lost two baby teeth and his pronunciation was terrible, but in a charming sort of way.

"Could we?" Little Mother enquired. "All us kids would like it. Even them." She nodded toward the ragtag group of Walchildren who followed her everywhere, and slept crowded around her at night like a brood of new puppies. "They'll understand most of it." Which was true; it was the children who could speak each other's languages best, and often they were grabbed from their games or chores to translate since they spoke both tongues better than any except for Rein.

Turtle raised his voice. "It *sure* would be *nice* hearing *stories* around the fire tonight."

Antler responded in a mild tone. "We still don't have a sacred drum, Turtle."

"Did Falcon always use a drum when he told stories?" Cookie squinted in the effort to recall. "He usually used it, but it seems like once or twice he did a telling without one."

Staunch lazily added, "Wasn't it ..."

"At Fish Camp!" Bison grinned. "It was at Fish Camp!"

"Feesh caamp," Dagoote was happy to participate even if he didn't fully understand.

"I don't remember Falcon coming to Fish Camp," Falling Leaf objected. "He liked to stay back with the older folks."

Staunch gave her a heavy-lidded look. "He came at least once, a few summers ago."

"The year we had that really big salmon roast," Bear reminded her.

"Oh, right. I twisted my ankle that year so I didn't go."

"Which is why you don't remember."

"We all begged for stories. He finally told a few one night, and he didn't have a drum with him," Turtle remembered.

"Feesh caamp!"

Staunch slapped Dagoote good-naturedly on the shoulder. "That's right. Fish Camp!"

Oopsy sidled up to Antler. "'thtorieth tonight? Pleath can we have 'thtorieth?"

On the far side of Antler, Rein spoke in an undertone. "I thought you couldn't tell stories without the drum."

Antler scowled. "That's what Falcon taught us. The stories need the drum to carry them to the ancestors and the Great Spirits."

"But they're right. Falcon told stories that night and he didn't have a drum with him; he just told them plain."

"I don't remember that. He taught us to always use the drum. The drum beats take it higher and deeper, so the stories and rhythms travel to the Earth and the Sky. They're not just for us, you know. They're our highest offerings to the Great Ones, that's what makes them sacred. If you don't tell a story that way, it's like any old family story. You could be telling about how Oopsy lost his tooth or something."

Turtle's voice rang out. "If Falcon could tell stories without a drum, Antler, why can't you?"

Sensing a challenge, the other voices stilled.

"He was a better shaman than you. He did it, and no lightning bolt struck him down."

"The tide washed him away," Bison reminded his friend.

"Yes, but that was three years later! If Falcon could do it, Antler should be able to!"

Everyone looked at Turtle, who looked down, but then continued, louder than before. "What's wrong, Antler, are you afraid? Scared that you'll make a mistake and that the Earth will swallow you up for being a bad little shaman? Frightened that a tree will fall and crush you like it did your cousin Three Skins?"

This brought a shocked silence. Turtle had gone too far. How could he be so disrespectful of their shaman, even if he wasn't yet fully a shaman? How could he mention Three Skins so callously, who died in agony on the Day of Too Much Death?

They looked at each other. Fierce was about to scold him, but she hesitated. This would be a huge embarrassment to her son, being admonished like a child. But really he'd gone too far. Challenging Antler who was only doing his best, taking on such an important role while not yet even a man.

Rein was urgently asking if a few stories told casually, not the most important ones, but a few simple ones, almost just for children, could be told.

Antler was trying to think.

All the questions people asked of him, and he really didn't know. If only Falcon were there to ask! Because sometimes Trapper didn't remember the answers, and Antler sometimes thought he knew but wasn't sure. Like Cookie said, he could only do his best. But he often worried, was his best enough?

There was so much for which he wasn't ready. He and Birdy were working on the stories for the solstice. They hadn't covered anything else. Everyone was working so hard to prepare for winter that there wasn't time, and they were exhausted by the end of the day. Especially her. The very stories Rein was suggesting, maybe the chief was right that they weren't as disrespectful to tell. But those were the ones he didn't know well. He hadn't practiced them since before they left their old home.

He wasn't that skilled with the stories yet but surely he'd improve, people always did if they worked hard enough at anything. It didn't matter if it was hunting or flint knapping, skinning animals or chanting the stories, things got easier and smoother with experience. He was counting on that.

But even with the stories he knew best, he stumbled here and there. Still had to be reminded, or he'd forget bits and pieces. It was the most discouraging part of becoming a shaman.

Maybe he'd never be ready. Storytelling didn't come easily to him, of that he was increasingly aware. Frustrating, because it seemed so easy when Birdy did it. Maybe he'd never get good, and then what? He couldn't stop telling stories, couldn't let them die among the People or they'd be like animals with no sense of who they were and who their ancestors were. But he couldn't tell them badly, that would dishonor the grandmothers and grandfathers whose stories they were, as well as the Great Spirits whose blessings the stories celebrated. And he would lose the People's respect.

How could he be the Cushion if he didn't have the confidence of those he was cushioning? Surely he would lose that if he told the stories badly. But they believed less in him every time Turtle questioned him fiercely and he didn't have a good response.

He clenched his fists, considering. He could go ahead, and if he made mistakes when he was being pushed into it, wouldn't people dismiss those mistakes? Wouldn't the Spirits look past those fumbles, as they might not some more solemn occasion?

Yet if he gave in to Turtle, was that another sign of weakness? Wasn't it a bad thing, giving in to the demands of an ordinary hunter? As the shaman, he had to be firm about what he knew was right. He had to do things as perfectly as he could, and this would be far from perfect.

But if Falcon sometimes told stories casually instead of solemnly, how could he insist it couldn't be done?

The tension was broken by the Walhunters, masters at turning tension into silliness. Dagoote and Imaleen were clapping rhythmically and chanting, "Feesh Caamp! Feesh Caamp! Feesh Caamp!" Quietly at first, but as they got more enthusiastic, others started clapping with them, which inspired Unqileer to take Gaagatade's hands and pull him onto his feet, bumping each other hip to hip with every repetition of the word "Caamp." So it was, "Feesh *(clap)* Caamp! *(bump)* Feesh *(clap)* Caamp! *(bump)*."

This became a kind of dance, moving forward and jostling each other with comical zeal. Then Gaagatade pulled Left out of the crowd and got her to bump hips with him. Unqileer protested in a mock-vehement tone, why not him, to which the younger man exclaimed, "You no pretty, old man!"

This brought a great cheer from the crowd. Unqileer pretended to be hurt. Ostentatiously he turned his back on Gaagatade and reached for Little Mouse. He almost could not pull her up, ungainly as she was with her vast belly, but Bison helped push his mother upwards, hands bracing her from behind and they managed to get her, laughing and blushing, to join the dance. Soon everyone was stomping, clapping, or gleefully banging hips together, repeating "Feesh Caamp!" in the accent of the Walrus People.

Except for Turtle, who resisted, and Rein, holding him apart from Antler and negotiating to end the hostilities. Each of them had to give a little. The outcome being that Turtle would stop jibing at Antler, and Antler would "practice" a few stories without the drum. Like a boy tagging along on a hunt with the men before making his first manhood hunt, Rein suggested. These, to be told on the last night of Fish Camp.

*   *   *

That night after the men declared themselves done for the day, the women were preparing porridge for supper. Everyone nibbled on fish all day so hunger was not a problem; they just wanted a simple meal to fill in the crevices.

Holding a bowl of mush in his hands, Antler sat down beside Birdy. "Father Sky rejoices," he said formally, though he'd seen her many times in passing.

"Yes, I'm sure He does," she answered. "He gave us a good day for fishing. The salmon are amazing here."

"They are. We received many blessings today."

"Many many," she agreed, the phrase making them both smile. "We have so much fish, I'm sure we can get through the biggest, coldest, horriblest, absolutely worstest winter there ever could be!"

"With Her help and His, we certainly should." They each nodded solemnly at the reference to the Spirits. "Listen, Birdy," he rushed to add. "After prayers, will you work with me more on the stories? You heard what Rein asked."

Oh, right, Birdy thought, deeply disappointed. She should have realized he needed her help again. Especially after that argument with Turtle. Here she thought he was coming to visit, two tired friends at the end of the day. *Pflrrgh!* Ever since she agreed to help him practice, it seemed that was all they did together. No more easy times of walking and chatting. No more swimming in the river, racing to see who'd cross first. She missed the early days of the trek. Sure they were hard, but also fun. His friendship was one of the things that made it so.

Before, there were jokes and teasing. Showing each other some unusual stone or vista, pointing out how Oopsy carried his pack or Poor Thing made faces, helping each other with their loads. But now between her and him there was only, "Birdy, how does the part go where the People came over that mountain?" or "Did I get the cadence right for the story?" or "I need you to tell me that ending again, Birdy." It wasn't as nice as she thought it would be, working on the stories together. Anyway she was exhausted; all she could think about was crawling into bed.

"Can we skip tonight, Antler? We had a long walk getting here, and this afternoon I was tending the fire; my throat's all dry."

But Antler promised Rein he'd be ready by the last night of Fish Camp. That gave him only three or four nights to practice, depending on how long this rise of fish lasted. He'd been pushed into it, but still he was determined to make it perfect, which meant working with her every night until then. "I just need to practice three stories, Birdy. Just three, that's all. The rest can wait until we're back."

She shook her head. "Sorry Antler. I'm exhausted."

"Three stories, Birdy. These are ones we haven't worked on, and I need to get them right."

"Antler," she frowned. "I feel completely stupid, that's how tired I am; I can hardly think. Listen to me, I'm slurring my words, I'm that tired."

"Three stories, that's all," he urged. "The one about the clothing. The one about learning to fish by watching the bears, that's a natural story for Fish Camp. And the one about learning how to swim from the dolphins; people always ask for that if someone falls in the river and ends up swimming downstream."

She folded her arms impatiently. "I can't, Antler. I'm hoarse from all the smoke and I can barely keep my eyes open."

"How about just two stories? We can skip the fishing one tonight; I know it better than the others."

She narrowed her eyes and didn't even bother to respond.

"One story. Come on, Birdy. The dolphin one, that's what I need the most help on. It's not even very long. Please! Then you can go to sleep."

She closed her eyes and swayed, demonstrating how spent she already was.

"Birdy, I need your help," he insisted. He could see her exhaustion, but his anxiety ran deep. It was vital that he do it, and do it right. Or his fumbles would mar more than just one evening; it might be months or years before they thought of him again with respect.

"I am the Cushion between the Spirits and the People," he reminded her. "I ask you again for your help." His voice, made stern and commanding.

"No," she croaked. She started to cough and, once started, had trouble stopping. He offered his bowl of tea, frowning impatiently but determined to be polite. When she regained her voice she continued, though she was still hoarse. "Not tonight, Antler. I can't."

"Do I need to command you in the name of the Great Spirits?" He pulled himself taller, but his face, confusingly, alternated between wildly different feelings—incredulous that she refused his request, she who was always willing to help, and the beginnings of an indomitability that he would develop as he grew into his role as shaman.

"What, are you going to curse me?" Birdy glared in disbelief. He was her friend, her companion. She could not believe it was coming to this. "For wanting to wait until tomorrow, when I will probably be happy to help?" The image of her mother with her cold face refusing some demand flashed through her mind. Stone-Mami, she remembered. Put on the Stone-Mami face. He's going to push me; fine, I'll turn to stone. Try pushing against that.

"*Pflttt!*" She waved her hand dismissively. She turned and walked deliberately towards the river where she rinsed her bowl, then stalked past him again, noticing but refusing to respond to his shocked and anxious face as she ducked into River's shelter and flung herself onto the furs.

She tossed and turned for quite some time, exhausted though she was, before falling into a troubled sleep.

★　　★　　★

In the sparkling morning sun Antler stood in the river flipping salmon onto the banks. It was easy working this level stretch where the waters were calm except for the frenzy of fish. Their ceaseless pressure—he could feel them bumping against his legs but the urgency itself he felt in his chest and belly, a kind of thrumming. He felt it like he could feel a thunderstorm blasting in, or a great tide from the sea. A force of nature, powerful and awesome; something that made a person grateful for the very breath that moved in and out of his body, the same breath that moved through each deer's nostrils, rattled the branches in the trees, and swept in over the foaming waves.

The strength of that force made him aware of everything around him: The chattering of children and the sun warming his shoulders even as the water chilled his feet. He enjoyed an awareness of every muscle in his body, the power in his hands as he clamped fingers around a fish, and the smooth curves his arms traced tossing them on the banks where others picked them up as fast as he flung them. Taking from life in order to give life, a cycle they were all part of, and some day when he came to the end of his many seasons dancing on the belly of the Great Mother, his bones would be buried in the soil underneath a favorite tree, and give life back to Her other creatures.

But not for many years yet. He knew that as well as he knew his name. Knew it because he saw it in his mind's eye, his own face, familiar through the reflections he saw in rivers and lakes, though grizzled in this fleeting vision from weather and age. There were others in the image too, but the only ones whose faces were clear were Birdy and Bear, still comfortably linked. There was not much else he knew about the future; he was no dreamer like his friend, but that was one thing he trusted and knew.

And for him it was enough.

For quite some time he let his mind dwell on that small, satisfying vision. It gave comfort, which he needed today for he worried about the task before him. Somehow telling stories made him more nervous than performing any of the ceremonies. Ceremonies had a rhythm of their own, and Trapper would help if he needed prompting. But the stories were different. They were more complicated, for one thing. Everyone watched and listened, eyes and ears on him alone. If he faltered, there was no hiding. He'd probably blush and people might laugh. If he made a lot of mistakes they'd snicker for months, or not even bother to tease him if it was that bad.

But the mind is a tricky thing, wiggling like an otter sliding down the banks, like a small boy who cannot sit in place too long. The repetitive task— bending, catching, flipping, bending, catching and flipping—was monotonous, soothing, and lent itself to wandering thoughts. The drum he should start making but didn't want to. The last ceremony he held and how it touched some but left others unmoved. He reviewed the story about the dolphins but his thoughts kept slipping off to the conversation last night, how Birdy looked for a moment like she might cry. Then she looked so severe; it made him wither in his bones.

He didn't mean to hurt her. She was always so reliable and generous. Steadying Trapper when he wobbled, helping River or Cookie when they needed a hand. Oopsy, with his incessant demands. Willow and Falling Leaf as they gathered plants. He felt terrible about pushing when she was so weak. But there was no one else to ask for help. He shut his eyes, hands continuing their task. And while his eyes closed to the world around him, a vision appeared from somewhere: The image of Birdy, terribly thirsty, stopping to take a drink.

That's it, he realized; that's what she's doing. She is learning to stop when she's thirsty and take a drink. Helping everyone drains her dry, and she's finally learning to take what she needs to sustain her. She wasn't trying to be difficult; she just needed to restore herself. That's a good thing, he decided. And was filled with a kind of pride for his friend, even as he wondered if her new learning would make it harder for him.

He was one of the reasons she felt so drained. His need for help had its part in wearing her down. He thought that story practice would be good for both of them. She needed something to keep from dwelling on her sorrows. The attack on her, but also the sadness for those in her family who died. He knew that sadness kept coming back from the way she spoke of her sister Pout, the baby, Thunder, and her grandmother. Antler lost people too but he chose his loss, which made it easier. No one in his immediate family died; he simply left them to come with the northward walking people, all on the strength of that vision of himself with Birdy and Bear.

And now Birdy was worn and thirsty, like a ... a ... the image that came was of a berry bush picked clean by birds and people. Where no one had thought to give thanks to the bush or make offerings to refresh its spirit. A bush like that was in danger of drying up and dying, without anyone caring enough to restore its strength.

All beings were the Great Mother's children together on the Earth. Each needed to give as well as receive; it was part of the balance of things. This knowledge was taught by the shaman and was something that every good mother told her children and every wise hunter instructed his sons.

The pine that gave of its life's blood for resin, for example, and offered pine nuts to eat, soft boughs to place under the bedding to cushion a sleeper from the hard, cold ground, that was a tree whose favors should be matched with gifts in return. The spirit of a bush that offered good fruit, that was a generous spirit for whom they were grateful. A bush which fruited abundantly, which gave luscious berries so round and ripe they almost popped off their stems into the pickers' bowls, whose sweetness stained their lips and tongues until they were laughably reddish-blue, that was a bush the women and children regularly thanked. Most often through gifts of the body, watering it or nourishing its roots as the bush had nourished them.

The spirit of a bush that pricked them and gave few fruits, and of those, only sour ones, that was a spirit to be avoided unless someone decided to propitiate it with offerings for the following year. Because quite possibly the bush soured when some witless person only thought to take, and never give anything back, which might be fine for a while if the spirit was patient, but no being could survive such treatment forever. Its bounty would dry up and it would turn dry or sour, though it might be coaxed back with enough patience and care.

Clearly Antler needed to give Birdy something back, just as the bush that fed him needed more than the fleeting pleasure of his company. Working together on the stories was draining her. He needed to restore the balance and help her thrive again. He'd offered to do a cleansing, but she refused that already. So maybe some sort of gift instead. Not something merely useful. Something beautiful. Something amazing to lift her spirit, restore a sense of wonder and joy. Haodisah.

He would ask for help. Make a prayer for the right thing to come to him. He had always been lucky that way. When he made a request for help needed by someone else, it never took long before it came.

It was why he was destined to be shaman. For what else did the Cushion do, really, except ask for help—for health and healing, good hunting, good lives and marriages—for the sake of others in the tribe. And thank the Universe afterwards for the blessings provided.

He felt a great sense of relief. Now that he knew what was needed, he would ask and his eyes would be open for just the right thing. Something wonderful to lift her spirit and assuage the pain in her heart.

And when it came to him later, in the belly of a fish he was cleaning, a beautifully smooth, gold-shaded nugget stone, he recognized it immediately though he'd never seen anything like it before. It was the color of the rising sun, the rich color of duck's eggs, shiny. He held the stone in the palm of his hand turning it this way and that. It seemed to grow warm in his hand instead of staying cold as other stones did. There must be a warm spirit within, he decided. How right for Birdy; it will warm her heart.

It had an odd shape that seemed perfect. Slightly lumpy with an unusual hole in the middle. Almost a circle, with no beginning and no end, just went round forever. Like a good story well told, and then it lingered in the mind and called to be retold again. A stone that spoke of the stories told between them as they practiced and smoothed and perfected the stories.

He washed the stone clean of its fishy residue. With his next break he picked a fistful of grassy stems, cleared them of leaves and seed heads, braided them together and poked the braid through the hole in the stone. When he knotted it into a necklace and watched it dangle, glittering and beautiful in the sun, he knew he'd found just the right thing. And when he saw her standing over the fire, he put the loop over her head, lifting her hair so it lay smooth from the nape of her neck. She held the gift up to admire the color and could not stop rubbing its smooth surface. She closed her eyes and smiled a sweet, shy smile at him, and he whispered a prayer of thanks. The balance was coming back, and things felt more right than they had been for some time.

★   ★   ★

"Long ago, long ago, long ago."

Antler opened the telling with the traditional summons to the circle. Three repetitions of the phrase warned them to settle in by the hearth, to quiet down, and listen. Each "long ago" was a separate invitation—the first customarily addressed to the ears, the second to the heart, and the final one to the spirit. The storytellers knew that only when all three of these joined were their listeners truly able to hear.

This would be their last night at Fish Camp. People were tired, satisfied with the harvest. Expectant and looking forward to hearing stories after months without. Worrying, would the children sit still so the grown-ups could enjoy themselves? How would the Walpeople respond? Which tales would Antler tell, and how well would he tell them?

"As well as a mammoth trying to fly," Falling Leaf predicted glumly.

"As well as you, midwifing a baby," Cookie chided her. "He's your kin. You should hope for the best."

"What's the best, that only half the stories are lost?" Falling Leaf said ruefully. "If we lost half our knowledge of medicine plants, think how bad things would be."

"If half the stories are still with us, that means a lot was saved," Cookie insisted. "We should be grateful that anything is left. We could all be dead, you know. I thought about going down to the beach that day to gather seaweed. I could have been swept away with everyone else."

Falling Leaf grimaced, but she settled back quietly.

He began with the ancient story of how man learned to fish by watching Bear. He started slowly, deliberately, each word flowing like water over smooth stone. He described the ancient times when their People ate berries and seeds, and slept in the trees. But when the rains grew rare and the forests dried up, when the trees began to topple, they fled to the grasslands for safety. At long last they came to another forest where they first met Bear. Who, of all the beasts, was the most ferocious and wily. They hid in the shadows to learn from him so they could feed the children and live.

So far he's doing fine, Birdy thought, relaxing just a bit. She touched her amulet, that almost perfect circle, signaling to Antler: Great, keep going!

Antler continued describing how they followed Bear, hiding behind trees and boulders, watching from the hills above. Thus they discovered many places to find water. And ...Birdy, watching closely, saw his momentary hesitation. Casually she lifted her arms overhead as if to stretch, letting the fingertips of each hand meet above her. *Shelter. Cave.*

The story continued, men stalking Bear to find where he slept. Discovering the den and deciding to seek their own rock shelter and soon they found their first cave home.

Here again Antler came to a stop. Across the circle Birdy placed her palms together and wiggled them slightly, side to side. *Fish. It was time to speak of fish.*

Sitting next to Birdy was an orphan girl Little Mother had named Rabbit, for her upper lip was cleft almost to the nose like a hare in the fields. Rabbit glanced sideways, seeing Birdy move. She put her hands together and made the same motion. Little Mother, sitting further down the circle, placed her hand on top of Rabbit's, frowning slightly. They had to be respectful of the stories, she'd warned, preparing them for this night.

Antler was describing how the men watched Bear. If he upended a decaying log to feast on slugs or termites, there might be something left when he wandered away. If he piled up a mess of fish on the banks of the river, the men stole one or two from the pile when he went back to catch more. But it was not enough to steal a few fish from Bear. They needed more to feed the rumbling bellies.

Rabbit placed her hands in sympathy on her stomach. The child next to her did the same. Oopsy, on the other side, whispered, "Umm, fish!"

Little Mother gave Oopsy a stern glance. He stopped, but not before catching the appreciative eye of Rabbit.

One man noticed how Bear caught the fish using his claws. He decided to try growing claws too, and for days he tried to shield his fingernails from harm. But they kept breaking, and though he stuck them back with sticky pine resin, they broke off again. He tried other things—choking down bits of bear dung, pasting tufts of bear fur around his fingers, gluing little chips of stone or bone onto his nails. But nothing worked. He was about to give up when his brother wandered by with a broken-off antler in his hand. The man wanted to try attaching it to his hand but the brother sneered; anyone could see it would break right off. Instead he should hold the antler in his hand and use it to stab. And so the very first knife was made, though they soon figured out that a single tine or blade was easier and could be sharpened.

This story always evoked pleased smiles from everyone. How fortunate they were that their ancestors developed that first simple tool! Every day they made use of knives and blades of one sort or another; without them they would go hungry. A worthy tool, borne of materials provided by the Great Mother, the idea itself blown by Father Sky in the wind from Bear to Deer's skull to the People so that they might prosper.

Ho.

Birdy touched her amulet as he concluded, letting her fingers linger. *Nicely done, Antler*, the gesture said. *Nice, round, and smooth.*

"Good story," Rein called out. "Well told!"

"Lovely," Cookie agreed, loud enough for everyone to hear.

"Good, good, good!" Dagoote approved. Though he understood only part of it, he was inclined to cheer at almost anything that could possibly be cheered at. At anything the men did, that was.

"Feesh caamp! Feesh caamp!" Unqileer waved enthusiastically, which got the children standing and cheering with him, kicking their arms and legs out with glee.

Antler ducked his head modestly.

"I told you he could do it," Bison hissed at Turtle. "You owe me one daart. Pay up!"

"Later," Turtle whispered furiously. "He did all right, I guess, but I've seen better. Falcon didn't hesitate; you never got the feeling he couldn't remember it."

"Give him a break, guurd breath. This was his first storytelling. Nobody does anything perfect the first time. Remember your first knife? The handle broke right off as soon as you tried to use it."

Turtle flushed. "Shut up. He's getting ready to tell another. We'll see how he does this time."

"Long ago, long ago, long ago," Antler began again. His voice seemed more confident, Birdy noticed, pleased for him.

Now he was telling the story of how they came to wear clothing. The long days of sun, wind, and work were beginning to show their effects on everyone around the circle.

The occasional pops and hissing from the hearth startled the sleepy listeners into momentary alertness. Some of the Walhunters grew restless, shifting around from time to time, though they kept polite smiles on their faces. For the children it was harder to stay still. They leaned against each other, slumping horizontally. Every once in a while one of them would jerk awake, and a leg or arm might flail. Sometimes one accidentally hit another with just such a random tic. Little Mother kept her arms ready to soothe them, or draw them apart.

The first time Birdy had to prompt him, all she did was move her jaw in a chewing motion which was subtle enough that no one but Antler saw. On the next occasion Birdy had to use her hands, one fist circling over her open palm reminding Antler to tell the part about washing the hides with stones in the river. That movement was more noticeable. Rabbit picked it up and imitated Birdy's gesture with enough enthusiasm that the other children were startled awake.

Oopsy, who knew the story well, began calling, "Wathy, wathy!" bouncing up and down in his place. It was something he said when Birdy told the same story on the trek. "Washy, washy!" for the washing movements, and earlier, when the grandfather tried chewing the hides to soften them, "Chewy, chewy!" which always made Birdy smile. Today, however, she whispered, "Hush, Oopsy! Be quiet for Antler!"

"But Birdy, you liked me to say it before," he protested. "You did!"

Little Mother reached over and hugged him against her. "Shush now. Let Antler tell the tale."

"It was all right before," he grumbled, but finally he subsided.

Antler was thrown off by the interruption and took a moment to resume. He picked up the story with a few words, then realized he'd already said them. Coughed, took a sip from the bowl someone passed over to him, passed it back down the circle and began again. But his momentum was broken, and the children were squirming. He finished the story without further prompting, but Birdy noticed his voice was less sure.

At the end Trapper took him aside and complimented him on a very good performance. Rein came forward. "Nice job," he encouraged. K'enemy clapped him on the shoulder, Two Stones nodded, and Cookie gave him a big hug.

"You're the one who owes me," Turtle argued with Bison as they left the circle. "I told you he couldn't do it right."

"All he needs is a drum," Bison insisted. "He'll be fine when he has that. The drum will keep the kids quiet. You saw him before all the commotion; he did great then. You owe me; I don't owe you."

"Wrong." Turtle poked him on the arm, and the two left still disputing the matter, their voices fading away.

"I could have done better," Antler confessed to Birdy.

"You will next time."

"If I can only think of how to keep the kids quiet. They're always going to be restless and it'll keep breaking my focus. I don't know what to do about it."

"What did Falcon do?"

"Nothing ever fazed him. Any commotion, he just beat the drum louder and ignored it."

"Then that's what you'll do when you have a drum. You'll see, it will be fine. But Antler." Birdy took a deep breath. "That gave me an idea. Why can't we have some stories, not the most sacred ones for sure. But the clothing one, there's lots of stories like that that could almost be family stories, they're not really about the spirits or anything." She glanced up at him, looking for reassurance. "Why can't we have someone like me tell that kind of story, and the kids can stand if they want and do some movements like I was doing to prompt you? You should have seen them. They really liked doing those washing motions and all that. It gave them something to do besides sitting still." She paused to catch her breath. "Kids get wiggly. When we have storytelling, why don't we start with something like that where they can move around and get all the wiggles out and tell the most sacred stories later while they drift off to sleep?"

"I don't know, Birdy. If they're standing and waving their arms around, it'll distract me. Like when a hunter aims his spear at a moose, if a bird comes flying out at him, it's going to throw his aim off. I don't think I could tell a story that way. Not even with a drum to keep the beat."

"Not you, Antler. Me. I could do it. I told Oopsy and Lynx lots of stories while we were traveling. It kept them from playing tag and tripping people all day. If I can tell stories while watching my feet so I don't trip and fall, I can tell stories watching the kids make gestures that go with them."

"You're saying you'd tell the stories?"

She looked at him, suddenly nervous. "Not the sacred ones."

"All our stories are sacred."

"Well . . . some are a lot more sacred than others, aren't they?"

He raised an eyebrow skeptically.

"Some of them don't say anything about the Spirits."

"You don't have to invoke one of the Names to be sacred, Birdy. Every time you take a mouthful of food, that's a sacred thing even if you're foolish enough to forget to appreciate it. That an animal is born and grows not deformed but whole, and offers itself to the spear? And the hunter is able to carry it back with his two good arms, on his two healthy legs, and we have the miracle of a fire to cook it? When your arms carry it to your mouth, and your jaws and teeth work well enough to chew, is this not all miraculous and sacred? You don't have to mention the Spirits to make it so. It simply is."

She sighed. "Of course you're right." She thought for a moment, then frowned. "But aren't family stories the same way? When Thunder saved Bear during the big waves, that was a sacred gift of life, but it's a family story too. Nobody cares if I tell it around the campfire. I think," she paused for a moment before plunging ahead, "if we did something that lets the kids wiggle around first, then everyone will be more relaxed. Wouldn't that be a good thing?"

There was a time when anyone could tell such stories. But the stories got muddled, with different versions told, and nobody knew which ones were true. It didn't make much difference if family stories were told every which way. Different tellers might disagree within a family; someone might have to stop them from arguing over it. But the tribal stories told them who they were. And if they got it wrong, they might begin to think they were some other kind of People. A sort of rot could set in and change them from what they should be, given their long and hard-won history.

The shaman long ago had a vision directing him to take over the tellings so they would always stay the same. Since then the stories were protected from the possibility of wild storms and winds blowing them around, of arguments and forgetfulness creeping in to change them. The shamans kept them true by testing, repeating and correcting so they stayed the same no matter who told the story, no matter who was listening. That was the way it had been for so long that no one but the shamans remembered it any other way.

And here she wanted to change it.

She had a point about the children; their restlessness distracted everyone. He didn't know what to do about that. Falcon might have known, but Antler did not. At least not without guidance. He really needed to have a vision time. He needed that solitary period of thought and meditation. Falcon always said that a shaman's visions made sense of what he had to do for the People. This winter he would have one, he decided. A vision retreat. He wouldn't wait until he got old enough to fast for three days; a one day fast would have to do. Actually he ought to do it soon. As soon as he could manage.

Usually such a thing was done in the summer. But he couldn't wait that long. He needed help with too many questions. When it got cold enough for everyone to move into the new shelters, he would keep one small shelter set up for occasional things. A place for healing. A place for meditation and prayer. He'd have his vision time there, apart from them all.

Afterward he would have a better sense of how to answer their questions. Being the Cushion was a serious responsibility. He had to take it seriously.

Even if he was still a kid himself. Even if there were times he'd rather set everything down and go climb a few trees with Bear.

"I will consider it carefully, Birdy," he conceded. "I will have to think and pray."

He turned abruptly and walked off.

Birdy's hand reached for the amulet and stroked it absentmindedly. Was he angry? Did she remember to tell him his storytelling was getting better than Falcon's ever was?

She wasn't sure, and it bothered her for the rest of the day.

Chapter 5: A sickly gray sky

Long before the sky began to lighten they were woken by terrible crashing sounds coming from the sea.

Steadily it was getting colder. The river froze. Ice grew in chunks along the seashore.

The previous day those chunks bumped together as the tides lifted them high, dropped and raised them up again. The clamor was unnerving, like giant bones rubbing and bashing each other. An edge sometimes slid on top, and the eerie squeals were hard to bear. The Walpeople paid little attention. They'd heard it before, but everyone else was uneasy.

Overnight the alleys between the blocks froze up. The remaining sheet of ice was lifted by each tide, only to come crashing down. Icy spumes of water shot out every time the sheet fell. Droplets froze in mid-air and came raining down like hail, bombarding the shore.

The noise was frightening, even behind the hill. "How long will this go on?" Rein shouted to Dagoote; it was the only way anyone could hear.

The man shrugged. "Maybe two day. Maybe many. 'Til it freeze all way out."

"Out where?"

"Past there," he pointed at the hook of land to the open sea.

The People looked at one another. How long could they stand that unbearable noise? The ground underneath trembled every time the ice lifted and dropped. It reminded them of the day the Earth trembled, when the cave toppled over and the sea tossed their loved ones away.

"Will the land break off?" Rein inquired, pointing at the ground beneath his feet.

Dagoote shook his head. "Is this way every year."

"Do we have to stay here, Papi?" Swan asked. "I bet it's quiet on the other side of those hills. Why don't we go hunting for a few days?"

Why not indeed?

Everyone was eager to escape and to leave camp once more before it got too cold. Surely that would be better than gritting their teeth and cowering inside. Everyone but Birdy wanted to go. Birdy was determined to finish the winter footwear she'd started and they needed someone to stay and make sure their hosts didn't come into the shelters and borrow anything, which they did sometimes, though they were willing to return a missing item. If you noticed it was gone, and you knew who to ask.

"Are you sure you won't be lonely?" River asked.

"I'll visit them if I am," she assured her. "Anyway, Great Uncle is staying too."

"You can still change your mind."

"No thanks. We'll probably go and eat with the others. I'll be polite, don't worry."

Bison passed, his spear and atalaatal hanging from one hand as he attempted to work his way into his Walpeople-style parka. One arm was in, though his head and other arm were struggling to follow. "Help me, Birdy," he asked, and she reached to take the weapons. "That's better," he said, shrugging things into place. "Now get me a bowl of tea before we leave. I should be over there already." He nodded to where Antler was leading prayers for good hunting.

Something about the tone of his voice bothered her. He sounded too much like the Walmen, she decided. They were mean to their women, and some Ogwehu were beginning to act like them. Ever since they came here, Staunch and Turtle, and now Bison were ordering the girls around in a way that none of them liked. As if they weren't already working hard enough. Did they have to do things without anyone even asking nicely? And without doing anything to thank them?

Anyway she already decided she was through being everyone's best helper. She was getting good at being strong, like Mami was. Oopsy was doing more for himself. And Bear helped her out one day after she refused to help him with his chores because she was so busy. That was an unexpected change.

But she felt bad refusing Antler. It hurt his feelings when she wouldn't practice stories with him. But then he gave her this beautiful amulet. She stroked it briefly, considering. Maybe she didn't have to do the stone-Mami thing all the time. At least not with Antler, who tried harder than any of the men to be nice.

Bringing Bison a bowl of tea meant she'd have to put down her sewing and dress for outside. Go to the creek, bring ice back to melt. Then he'd want her to steep it, using her own supply of pine needles for tea. Bring it humbly and sweetly to him, as if he was doing her a favor instead of the other way around.

"I'm busy," she announced in a frosty tone. "Get it yourself." She turned her back on him so she wouldn't relent, no matter what kind of face he made. Even if he did look handsome in his new winter clothing. Even if the twins and half the Walwomen didn't all have terrible crushes on him. Even if River said that he was not too much older, and the two of them might make a good couple some day. After all, who knew what matches would work out for the best?

Even so, he could do it himself.

★   ★   ★

Rein leaned against the trunk of a pine watching the herd of reindeer in the valley below.

He sighed with a deep sense of contentment. Soon he would call the men to plan their attack. But for this moment he was happy to simply stand there. No decisions needed from him; no more miles needed traveling. It was best to take such times when you found them and savor all that was good.

That morning he sent the boys climbing to look around for signs of reindeer or elk. A light layer of new-fallen snow made it easy to sight the nearest herd. Their tracks were distant but easily seen.

They were not the only ones tracking them. By the time they reached this overlook, most of the herd had raced ahead leaving a smaller group of deer surrounded by a pack of wolves. The wolves were circling, their gait measured, eyes probing for weakness. Pacing back and forth, snarling occasionally, the predators prepared to wait the herd out, letting fear wear down their resistance.

The deer aligned themselves into a defensive circle. The Does and the young inside seemed almost stunned with terror. In the outer ring the males were snorting and pointing their antlers, ready to impale anything that pounced. Their thick-furred sides were heaving. Breath came steaming out of their nostrils. Beneath these sounds Rein sensed a guarded stillness, for at the moment things were in a precarious balance, and any small movement could topple it.

Their camp dogs came hurtling down the slope, peeling off in all directions. The hunters pulled back behind the trees to watch while dogs and wolves both began to attack.

This seemed like a good time to bring out the atalaatals. The hunters were distant but they might make a shot.

Gagaatade made the first kill from the edge of the overlook. There was a "thunk," and a buck sank into the snow. Bison and Rein flung their darts at almost the exact same moment. One hit a doe and the other bounced off, and which one was which would be a topic for debate around the fire. K'enemy shot a dart, wounding a doe in the shoulder. She lurched forward, and he jammed another dart into the shaft. This time his aim was better, and it sank in, the blood spurting but soon coming to a stop.

By this time the herd was shifting in confusion. Does and fauns were milling about every which way. A dog nipped at the legs of a buck, who lowered his head and hooked him on the tips of his antlers. He flung the dog, who howled in pain, over the heads of the other dogs and wolves. The injured one landed, barked furiously a few times, and slunk away.

Another dog broke away and began licking his wounds. A third dog came to investigate, but she bumped one of the wolves, who turned away from the reindeer to snarl at her.

The threatened dog was River's companion, Stripes. Her son Guard broke from the pack to help her. Just then, from far back where the women and children were, Oopsy gave a cry of recognition and tore himself out of River's arms. He went running downhill, intent on pulling his favorite doggies out of danger. Bear grabbed him, but the boy sped by so fast that he missed him altogether. Staunch reached for the child but caught only the neck of his parka. Thrown off balance, Oopsy started sliding down the snowy hillside. In no time at all he was in the middle of what was becoming a dog-against-wolf fight.

Antler cried, "I'll get him," and began finding footfalls here and there, moving quickly but carefully down the slope. Several wolves sidled closer. Antler wielded his knife as a club with one hand and his spear with the other, lashing out on both sides. Bison started down the hillside, followed by Two Stones, Gaagatade and Turtle. Dagoote continued shooting and downed another deer.

Antler reached the child and scooped him up. But that left only one arm for defense. Bison arrived and beat back a wolf who was snapping at Antler's thigh or Oopsy's foot, whichever he could get. "Quick, up the hill!" Bison urged Antler. "We'll give you cover."

The reindeer were sprinting away, tails flickering in a flash of sunlight. Some of the dogs and wolves were taking advantage of the chaos to tear at the downed deer. But with more people arriving, the dogs rejoined their two-legged allies. Together they chased off the wolves, wounding one or two.

Yet restoring the peace was not without cost. Bison was gored in the belly by one of the departing bucks. He lay half-collapsed against a fallen log losing blood from a number of punctures. By the time Rein began directing people, Bison's eyes were glassy and could no longer hold a focus. No one was sure if he would live.

"We have to get him somewhere and lay him down," Falling Leaf worried. "This is terrible. He looks like he's already half the way Beyond."

So they set up a shelter in the clearing nearby. Rein sent some to gather firewood and others to find ice to melt. Willow and Falling Leaf prepared a fresh batch of pine resin wash to dab on Bison's wounds after they laid him out on a fur inside. Willow stitched several deep gouges and bites on his leg and poulticed them with honey. Falling Leaf peered inside the belly wound. It was hard to tell because of the bleeding, but it looked like that big purplish-brown slab inside was torn at one end. She considered cutting it off, but finally decided to push the edges together. If Mother Earth gave him strength and Father Sky looked with favor on him, it might possibly heal. Maybe. She once nursed a hunter whose insides were ripped apart. He died in pain in spite of all their prayers, in spite of all her careful work.

She and Willow stayed with Bison all night. Little Mouse and the twins vied to wipe the fever-sweat from his brow. Falling Leaf asked Little Mouse to hold her son's hand. "I don't know whether he can feel it or not," she said. "But if he does, he'll need you to hold on." She sent the twins to melt ice into water. They could make willow-bark tea for pain. Whatever was left would get drunk by someone, if only for the warmth.

The important thing, the medicine woman finally decided, was to bring him back home. There they had more soft skins for bandaging, a bigger supply of plants for salves and medicinal teas. It would be more comfortable there than in this temporary camp. Hopefully the Spirits would halt that terrifying din from the sea. So the next day the men rigged up a carrier, lashing a hide between two long branches. They rolled Bison onto it and took turns carrying him.

⋆   ⋆   ⋆

That goring—it should have been him, Turtle fretted, picking the bark off a branch and tossing it into the fire. It would have been him if Bison didn't see it coming before he saw it himself. Those deer were fleeing, heedless, when Turtle inadvertently stepped in their path.

Bison with his customary ease had sidestepped that buck. How did he do it? How did he always manage to look so handsome and graceful with every move? Turtle wanted to look that way, but he could not figure out how. He wanted the women to see him and feel about him like they all, always felt about Bison.

Turtle saw the buck out of the corner of his eye, but he was bashing away at a she-wolf and didn't see him soon enough. He was about to get gored, or trampled under foot, when Bison flung him out of the way. Bison was left dangerously close to the stampeding buck who, with a snort and a shaking of his head to the left and the right, managed to pierce his friend on two prongs. So much damage, and all in the merest eye blink.

That wound should have been his. Not that he wanted it, but it should have been his. He loved Bison like a brother, but did the guy have to always be so valiant? He was always doing stuff like that. Sharing the good things with Turtle and keeping him from getting hurt. Their families lived near each other and the boys grew up together regardless of two summers' difference in age. All his life Bison was there to play with, to practice throwing sticks and spears. But Turtle was tired of always being the younger kid. Now that they were both men, it was time to right the balance.

Bison was even sharing the women in this new place. They were willing, even eager, not like the girls of their clan who wouldn't let them do, you know, stuff, with them, not unless they were married or about to be. These Walrus girls let him touch them, push up against them and . . . he was stiff already just thinking about it.

Not only was Bison better at the weapons and hunting and all that, he was a lot better at getting the women to want him. Every night at least one of the women invited Bison to put his sleeping fur next to hers. Not that they did a lot of sleeping. Actually they kept other folks from getting any sleep also. Sometimes it was two women who invited him, and he spent the night in between!

As much as he loved Bison, as much as he owed his friend, sometimes he felt almost sick with envy.

Though Bison never seemed to notice. He completely ignored the occasional carping that slipped out of Turtle's mouth before he could bite it back. Ignored the sometimes bitter jokes he made that weren't really funny.

And if a third woman made eyes at Bison the same night, Bison, who didn't need a third woman, a guy only had two hands after all, had only one prick and nobody could split his attention that many ways, he aimed the extra woman at Turtle or Staunch instead. For that, Turtle was grateful. But it kept tipping the balance, and not in his favor.

There was one thing he was better at than Bison and that was figuring out how things worked, and how to make them better. Like the throwing sticks. Turtle was maybe ten summers in age when he realized that if he tapered it just so, it flew smoother through the air. This tapering meant he could hit his target more often. A few days ago when they were making their new weapons, Bison chose a bad stick for his handle. After watching the Walrus men use their atalaatals, Turtle was sure that the handle needed to be longer or his friend wouldn't get the dart to go much distance at all. So he found a better stick, a longer one, and, *guurd!*, now Bison was better with his weapon than Turtle was with his.

Well, now Bison was wounded or even dying, and Turtle was alive and well. If you wanted the truth, part of him was glad. Not glad that Bison got gored, of course not. But happy to be alive, healthy, and strong.

Maybe while Bison was healing, he could take advantage, couldn't he? Maybe Turtle would get more of that girly attention. The twins kept crowding around the shelter all sad-eyed and weepy. But maybe when they got back to camp, they'd notice him. And there were the other women, especially that really curvy Walrus woman with the big ... oh yeah, he liked her. A lot. For a time he let himself dwell on some very pleasing thoughts about her.

Turtle realized that they were stuck here at least until morning. He had nothing to do. Yes, he could hurry after his Papi and Bear, but he had a better idea. Antler was banging a couple of sticks together to go with the prayers because he still did not have a proper drum!—Which Antler *said* he would make before the winter solstice. Though as far as he could see, Antler hadn't started making a drum of any kind. Not even a small one.

They still couldn't listen to stories at night because Antler said he needed a drum first. That little phony had made one excuse after another. Probably he couldn't do the proper prayers for healing without it either. Bad enough they were bored in the evenings without any good music or dancing, all for the lack of a drum. Turtle decided he would do something about all that and make a drum. He would rather go off and risk getting frost-bitten than let his friend die for the lack of good prayers.

There weren't any trees around here with wide enough trunks even for a small drum. He needed something small, but not too small; it had to be big enough to make a decent sound. Where would he find something large enough to use? Didn't they pass a tree with all those bowl-shaped growths on the trunk? If he could pry off one of the big, round growths, that might do. They were wider than they were tall, so any drum he made should have a nice sound and still be small enough to carry later.

Remembering now where he saw that tree, he set off in that direction. He could probably pry it off with the blade of his spear. An axe would be useful but he didn't have one with him. He didn't have an adze either, for chopping out the excess wood, but he could use something else to hollow the thing out: A burning ember. Maybe he could get the skin from one of the fauns they dropped today for the head of the drum. If he was lucky, one of the women already cleaned and de-fleshed it. He could smoke it over the fire to tan the thing. The weather was too cold to prepare a skin by pounding and rinsing it in the river.

That gave him plenty to do while they were stuck here, and it would help right the balance between him and Bison. And, who knew, it might even make that curvy little Walrus girl admire him. Since it looked to him like, for some time to come, Bison wouldn't be visiting anyone at night in their sleeping furs.

⋆ ⋆ ⋆

Thunk.

The daart hit smack inside his practice target, a knothole where a branch had broken off. A satisfactory hit, Imaleen thought. Too bad he didn't do as well today when the deer were in front of them.

He picked up another daart and hooked it to his atalaatal. He aimed carefully, but it went wide, and he cursed himself for missing. The annoying presence of these Walking Disaster people threw off his aim. Not only did they press in and take over, not only would they litter the settlement afterwards with their left-over meat bones, driving the campdogs into frenzies, not only did they make too much noise every night with their stupid singing and such, but they were killing many of *their* walrus, and Dagoote made him, Unqileer and Gaagatade help hunt and butcher the creatures so they could have their precious shelters. He didn't know why they couldn't just crowd in with everyone else. But they insisted on having separate places. They probably thought they were too good to share with people like him. Not only were they noisy, rude, and demanding, but they wouldn't share what they had, which was wrong, after all his people shared with them.

He kicked at a frozen clod of dirt, annoyed with the thin sprinkling of snow. Bring on a heavy storm, he fretted. Bring on the chill blanket, cover the prissy grasses and flowering shrubs. He was tired of the easy warmth, the sun still bright in the sky instead of hidden in banks of frozen fog. Let frigid

air put a stop to the needless socializing between the shelters. Let death come
to fools too stupid to don an extra layer of fur before venturing out with the
true men of the ice.

Hunters always shared what they had; that was the way of it. To share was
to survive. Not to share was the way of certain death. Hunters were brothers.
They faced the Death-spirit together and wrestled it to the ground. If they
were hunting walrus and the ice floe cracked underneath so that someone slid
into the freezing sea, the others had to quickly reach in and haul him out or he
was dead. And if they didn't immediately pull off his wet furs and surround
him with their body warmth, he'd die anyway. If White Bear snuck up behind
one of them and the others didn't hear and chase him off, the Death-spirit
would take him. And none of his brothers would ever share another meal with
him, or a spear, or a woman.

Hunters were brothers. They had to be. There was no other way. If one
of them needed a daart, another hunter offered his. If someone needed food it
was willingly given. And if one of them needed a release, and all the not-mated
vedeelon were paired up for the night, a mated hunter would offer his vedeelon
of course, or risk all of their lives if his brother was too distracted when they
faced danger again.

But these new hunters did not share. Food, maybe. Weapons—when he
asked that Turtle-Disaster near him, he was rude enough to say, "Not that
one, that one's no good. Not that one either, I still need to sharpen it. I don't
have any to spare, sorry." The selfish *guurd*-foot. Imaleen had to walk all
the way over to Unqileer to get more daarts, and by that time he missed his
shot. Ingrates. He thought that Turtle-Disaster would be glad of the chance
to share back. He sure took plenty of turns with their vedeelon whenever he
could.

Though not so many as that Bison-Disaster. Imaleen was not at all sorry
the man suffered a painful chiding of the Great Spirit this day. That Staunch-
Disaster fellow also took more than his fair share with the vedeelon, and
shared not one thing back. He had a nice daughter he could offer, but did he?
No. He wouldn't let them anywhere near her.

Imaleen was beginning to hate the outlandish sound of their voices, grabbers
and takers that they were.

Especially at night. He'd be pleasantly tired and ready to lie down
somewhere, get himself a nice release and then fall asleep. He'd look around
to see which vedeelon was available, and it seemed that *none of them were!*

They were all smiles for the Disaster-men who stuck their heads in the shelter, but they totally ignored any signals he made. Dagoote sometimes took pity and offered his vedeelon for the night, but she was so old. Better than nothing he supposed, but not what he needed to blunt that hungry edge.

There were several vedeelon in the new shelters to choose from. But none of them paid any attention when he tried to signal them. When he ordered them to get ready for him, they pretended not to understand. Instead they offered him food or tea and made stupid, puzzled looks and ridiculous *tsking* sounds when he knocked those things out of their hands. And that one Disaster-vedeelon, the one who made all those unnecessary designs on her clothing, he tried to pull off her wrap once and got shoved, rudely, away. By a vedeelon, if you could imagine that! Insolent woman.

She was the worst of them. The worst of a bad bunch. She called attention to herself with those designs, teasing a man to notice her, each one screaming, "Look at me! Choose me!" Then when he did look and tried to choose her he got repulsed and humiliated in front of the other hunters. She was a vicious tease. It was an indignity he would never live down.

He couldn't possibly avoid her. And every time he saw her, her clothing called out, "See me! Here I am, the pretty one!" and he was reminded again of the pull of her. And how he was shamefully slapped away.

I hate her, he seethed. Stupid, insolent, outlandish vedeelon. I hate her. I hate her.

I want her, and they'll never let me have the use of her.

★   ★   ★

"You're carrying all his things." Left complained. "Let me take some of them."

It was so unfair. Her grabby sister got there before Left even had a chance to think about it. By the time she had reached Bison's little pile, Swan had already gathered everything together and hefted it onto her shoulders for the trudge back home. Left was stronger, and not careless like her sister; she should be carrying his things. At least she could hold his weapons. It wouldn't matter so much if Swan dropped his sleeping fur, and it got dirty, but if she dropped a spear or banged it against a tree, she might ruin the blade.

All Left wanted was to help, which she couldn't do earlier, because Falling Leaf only let her do a few boring chores like gathering firewood or carrying water. Frustrated, she reached over to take the spear and atalaatal hanging by a lashing off her twin's shoulder.

"Stop it, Left! I have his stuff! Let go," Swan fumed. "You'll make me trip and fall."

"Come on, let me carry something. I want to help Bison too."

"I already have it, and I don't need you getting in the way. Find something else to do if you're so eager. Go hold his mother's hand or something."

Left grimaced at her sister's back. She was still working on an appropriately savage response when Little Mouse came up from behind. Wordless, she pushed Left to one side and lifted Bison's gear off Swan's shoulder. Gave them both a withering look before marching fiercely forward.

"See?" Left poked her sister. "If you were only nice about it ..."

"Like this was my fault? I was just helping out when *you* started making a fuss. No wonder she glared at you."

"She glared at you too."

"No she didn't."

"Yes she did."

"Did not."

"Did too."

Shove.

Shove back.

Bear came up from behind and careened into them, inserting himself firmly in between. "Oh, sorry," he feigned. "I must have tripped or something."

Both girls turned to swat him.

Still Left brooded for the rest of the afternoon. Bison wouldn't even know what she tried to do. If he even ever woke up again, her sister would be sure to claim the credit. Or his mother. Or that scar-faced Walrus girl that invited him into her tent every evening. Left threw her hands up in disgust. Everyone was absolutely loony over Bison. Bison this, Bison that, they all had Bison-fever. Well, she decided, she had enough. Sure, she was impressed at how brave he was and sorry he got hurt, but that did not mean she had to get lost in the crowd goggling after him. All those blushers and stammerers, it was entirely too much. The very thought of Bison was beginning to make her feel like vomiting. She was sick of it all. She would find someone else to like.

But who? She cast an eye over the moving line. Turtle? She could never take him seriously. Not with those funny, sticking-out buck teeth. He'd be solemn, and she'd take one look at his teeth and start laughing. But who else was there, Staunch? He was so, well, old. Her eye flicked on Owl, young enough to play sometimes with Lynx and Oopsy. A quick snort. That was the end of the Walkers. Unless someone died. River, maybe; K'enemy was kind of cute. But she shouldn't think that—River dying, that was a rotten thing to think.

But. Walking ahead was Gaagatade, tallest of the Walpeople. Walstupies, she and Swan called them, but that was back when they didn't like them. Gaagatade was actually cute, in a Waldoodle kind of way. Much nicer than that nasty Imaleen, who was always skulking around. Gaagatade was funny and strong. He made her dance with him at Fish Camp. She smiled at the memory. He even tried to kiss her, but she laughed and ran away. Maybe she shouldn't have run.

Maybe she wouldn't if he tried again.

"Hey." She moved up the line to tap him on the shoulder.

"Hey you, Eider."

That was the other thing she liked. He actually bothered to use her new name. Not even her own family did that for her.

"I was just thinking about you. What does your name mean?"

He slowed so she could draw up next to him. "Gaagatade. Deer running." His grasp of their language was halting so his hands explained what his words could not—antlers on his head, then fingers, like legs, moving rapidly away. "Means, swift. Like deer running fast, for he life. See," his hand gracefully indicated the length of his legs. "Big by my People."

"Big for your People. Longest for your People," she corrected him.

"Long-gest," he enunciated. "Longest. Yes. So I fast, like deer."

"And sweet. Like a young deer's meat." She smiled at him sideways, her eyes daring him to smile back.

"Sweet." He repeated it, testing the word, not quite certain what it meant. Young deer's meat was lean, tender, and not very plentiful. A lot of possible meanings there, some good, others not. He didn't want to grab any of the kids to translate; that would surely break the interesting mood growing between them. "Also," he said tentatively, "there means Tade."

"What does Tade mean?"

"Crevasse." He looked down at his feet, not meeting her eyes.

"Crevasse. Like there, between those hills?" She pointed to where two knolls met abruptly in a steep canyon.

"No. Different kind hills." His hand moved to his own backside and slapped it twice, still not looking directly at her. "Different crevasse. Not for good name, just between the men."

She looked at him for a long moment. Realizing finally what he meant, she blushed furiously. "What a mean thing to call you!"

Gaagatade glanced at her curiously.

He was embarrassed, she realized. Probably nobody called him that awful thing except when they wanted to give him a hard time. It must be entirely a guy thing; she was sure the women never called him such a name. Swift, that's what she would call him. It had a nice sound. He was short, but not squinchy-short like some of his People. It was nice talking with a guy who was her own size.

She was tired of being towered over by Bison and skinny old Turtle. Tired of trying to get Bison's attention when every other girl and woman around was doing the same. Tired of Turtle making crude jokes and pretending it was an accident whenever he bumped up against her breasts or backside. Gaagatade was different. For one thing, he was nice. With him she'd have nothing to be ashamed of. He was a good hunter; he was the first to bring something down yesterday. He was quieter than the other Walrus men, who could be so exuberant it embarrassed her.

She would call him Swift among the clan. But she might call him Tade, or Taaaade, carrying the sound a little bit longer to make the point around the Waldoodlies. Just to see them give her a look. Make them wonder if she knew what she was saying.

★   ★   ★

Usually two hunters walked at the head of the line, but Little Mouse insisted on staying ahead for the journey. This way she could push aside any branches before they snapped in the faces of the men carrying her son. She could warn them of uneven ground, be the one to stumble over any frightened animal running from them. She carried her son's spear, using it as a walking stick. His atalaatal and darts, his fur and water bags, she slung across her back.

Antler walked beside her, alternating words of comfort with prayer.

They made their way carefully through the passes. Staunch and Willow went ahead to ready a shelter for nursing. Falling Leaf stayed by her patient all the way back.

Thus began the vigil that lasted for days. Little Mouse brushed away all offers of food, though she accepted a warm bowl of tea when Willow insisted. For the baby, she said. Afterwards the distraught mother fell to her knees, murmuring the prayers Antler taught her and adding variations of her own.

Sweet but distracting, Falling Leaf concluded. Her constant presence forced the medicine woman to maneuver around her. It was awkward, and it could make things worse for their patient. But Willow argued that her prayers, like Antler's, might actually help.

That evening Little Mouse's belly started contracting and nothing would make it stop. "It's too early," Falling Leaf worried. "Her baby cannot come now. It won't be big enough to live."

"Hush, Mami," Willow warned. "Don't say that. She's right here; she can hear you."

"She's too busy muttering prayers. The part of her that hears is up there," her eyes moved skyward, "begging to be taken in her son's place. Look at her, she doesn't notice anything. And a good thing too. She'd be in a lot of pain otherwise."

Her hand moved against Little Mouse's belly, massaging it to see if that would relax the cramping, but her efforts did not change a thing.

Now they had two patients to nurse. Willow laid some bedding for the mother across from where her son lay. The contractions came and went, and groans issued out of her mouth, but she hardly seemed to notice. Her prayers were all for Bison. She didn't bother with any for the baby or herself.

Bison grew hotter, and the stomach wound, stitched up, was now an angry red. They spooned tea and herbal broths into him whenever he would accept any. At night when Falling Leaf and Willow took turns napping, two of the Walrus women slept on either side of him. Which made it harder to get near with cool compresses or broth, but the women swore it would draw out any evil spirits.

"Is that so?" Willow asked Falling Leaf.

She shrugged her shoulders. "Who knows? The Walpeople have different medicine than we do."

Antler came and went, using the rough new drum Turtle made. Their campmates kept poking their heads in, hungry for news. The smaller scrapes and scratches were attended to by River and Fierce.

The oddest thing, Willow pointed out, was that when either Bison or his mother strengthened, the other grew weak. When the weak one's life force rose again, the stronger one would ebb.

The baby was born finally, but with no cooperation from her mother. Willow had to push down on the belly while Fierce supported the afflicted woman from behind. Falling Leaf pulled the child out. It was born dead, a tiny, misshapen baby girl, with a chord wrapped round her neck like a strangling vine.

And still the mother seemed unconscious of anything but the rise and fall of her son's breath. When his breathing grew labored, her beseechings became desperate. When he lay still and peaceful, they softened again.

The second night was the worst. Willow and Falling Leaf were clearing up the afterbirth. Bison's forehead was hot to the touch, so they wiped him down with rabbit skins soaked in a bowl of water. Falling Leaf removed the poultice around his stomach and noticed it oozing blood and pus. "No more iris root," she instructed Willow. She sent Trapper to see if any of his snares had a fresh rabbit to flay and apply raw to the wound. Well-wishers looking in were asked to retrieve more wood for the fire, more water, and more blankets.

Falling Leaf finally left to get some sleep. Willow got up periodically to check on her patients but found herself dozing off in between, slumped in an ungainly huddle, her head resting against one of the women sleeping beside him in the tent.

During the deepest part of that dark night when every other person was fast asleep, when the wind died down and even the frenzied ocean finally fell silent, Little Mouse bolted upright. She made a triumphant silhouette in the fetid air, though no one was awake to see. Her head tilted, baring her neck and cascading her hair loosely down her back. She called out to the heavens in a clear voice, "Yes! Me!" before sinking back into the bedding.

When Willow rallied enough to check on them, she saw an exalted look on the woman's face. And was not at all surprised when, the next morning, Bison opened his eyes and asked for something to drink, which his mother would never do again.

★ ★ ★

Bison blinked, closed his eyes for a long moment, then let them open. Sensing the change, Willow roused and moved to his side. She placed a hand on his forehead. Still damp but no longer fiery to the touch. "Can I get you some broth?" she murmured, keeping her voice soft.

A small nod in response. Even that modest movement seemed to drain him.

She picked up a ladle, dipped it in the skin bag hanging over the fire and poured a scant amount into a bowl. "Let's see if you can get some of this down. It has herbs and a few shreds of meat to build your strength." She balanced the bowl in her lap, and with practiced grace, slid her arm under his neck to support it upright.

"Enough," he motioned after only a few swallows. He sank back into the bedding. His eyes closed, and he seemed to drift back to sleep. Willow put the bowl on the ground and smoothed the fur covering him. His hand emerged from underneath, found hers and pulled in onto his chest. He kept his hand on top of hers. No strength at all, just the weight of it pressing down. He kept it there, eyes closed, his heartbeat faint but steady.

Finally he broke the silence. "Mother?"

"She's gone. I'm sorry, Bison."

He nodded briefly. Like he suspected it, but needed confirmation.

Finally his eyes opened and he stared dreamily at the smoke hole overhead. "Willow," he croaked.

"I'm here."

"Willow." His voice was a low, cracked whisper. "Willow grows by the water. River or lake. You live near Willow, and you never go thirsty." A long pause. "Makes the best wood for darts and traps. Gives shade on a hot afternoon. Willow." His eyes closed. His voice fell away, and he said nothing more until long after sunset.

She sat with him for hours quietly holding his hand. Several times tears came to her eyes. She had to use her other hand to wipe them away.

★ ★ ★

"She died to save me," Bison proclaimed. A single tear escaped, freezing on his cheek.

They'd waited until he was strong enough to walk before organizing her funeral. He was still weak though, and needed to hold onto a staff for support.

Where to leave her remains was a matter for debate. Their custom was to bury the dead in the earth during the warm months when a trench could be dug. Otherwise they left any new corpse high in a tree to freeze until they could dig in the spring.

But practicality forced them to do something different here. The trees were not tall or sturdy enough to hold her body safe from wolves or hungry dogs. Instead the Walpeople suggested consigning the body to the sea, as they did. Since the harbor was frozen, they had to walk out to the spit of land on the far side, where a small area of open sea remained.

"She raised me, clothed and fed me for 17 years," Bison continued. "She told stories of my grandfathers and nursed me at her breast. She taught me to be kind to children, to respect the elders, and to keep my friends close. She offered her life for me, and it was accepted in my stead. Now," he held up one arm, baring it to the cold. "I offer, with my blood, to do for others the same. Any that are hungry, let them come to me."

He took out his knife and made a quick slash at his arm. A gasp went through the crowd as the bright red drops fell on frozen ground. "To them I give my life's blood. As she cared for me and looked after me, I vow to do the same for others in my tribe. My tribe *and* my family to come." He paused, his voice still shaky. Every eye was on him. Every ear strained to hear over the sound of the shrieking ocean wind.

"She who heard my mother's last words, she who nursed her so that she could die in peace, I ask her today to be my wife, that we can make a life together that would make my mother proud."

Another gasp. Every head turned to look at Willow, who was as surprised as anyone else.

"Willow?" Rein asked. "You mean, Willow? She can't marry you; she's not a woman yet."

"She will be," Bison answered, and turned to look for her in the crowd. Willow caught his eye and held it. Then turned to her father with a question in her eyes. Staunch shrugged and lifted the palm of one hand upward. He wouldn't stop the match; it was up to her. She looked at her grandmother standing between Fierce and Cookie, huddled together. Falling Leaf nodded, beaming. It was an excellent match.

Willow reached into the bag dangling from her waist thong, removed a length of hide and approached him. She took his bloody wrist and bandaged it, which made the crowd laugh with surprise. She pulled his parka sleeve down over it, pulling his mitten back and using it to secure the bandage.

"Yes," she finally whispered, her answer meant for his ears only. "I will marry you as soon as I am woman-bled."

He looked at her for a long moment, then took her hands in his, the hands that just finished binding his wound. The hands that cleaned and dressed his mother's spent body, and a cheer went through the crowd.

Though several of the women and girls looked woeful.

The rest had turns speaking their final words to send Little Mouse on her way. How she cooked Owl's favorite foods. How she offered kindness and encouragement to this person or that along the journey. How she was scared but kept going and made one last, heroic gesture for her son, though he was already a man.

They offered her body into the care of the deep, where it would return life to feed life, as other lives had fed hers in turn. As the world cycles each day and year, the sun rising and falling in the sky, and the moon following a path of its own.

Ho.

Chapter 6: Bringing light into the dark

Everyone felt the excitement in the camp.

Solstice time was almost upon them. They kept asking Antler for the day-count, though they could almost tell by themselves. For the days shortened, and darkness stretched unbearably long at night. In this new place Father Sky held the Sun ever closer to the ground, reaching barely over the treetops before falling back under the rim of the Earth.

With the pinching of daylight came a great and bone-aching cold. A teeth-wrenching cold. A bundle-up-in-so-many-furs that people-shapes became bear-shapes.

"Something about this place makes the Sun weak," Two Stones complained. They discussed it endlessly around the fire circle. At their old home, Sun seemed stronger, leaping higher across the Sky. Did Sun weaken only in the winter here, or was He weak all year round? Was it even the same Sun or did another take His place? Maybe a woman Sun with less strength, someone suggested.

Always in their travels, Antler reminded them, going North meant going towards more cold. In some places there were great walls of ice, and their people had to turn away. Just as going up a mountain meant being greeted by snow and ice at the top. And when they traveled downhill, or turned back towards the South, Sun eventually grew strong again.

Though the Walpeople had their own explanations.

"One day Great Spirit make everything hot," Dagoote told them. "Then White Bear complain, no ice to walk on, how I hunt seal and walrus? Great Spirit feel bad for White Bear, so He make many ice here. Now everyone happy." He beamed, pleased to explain this simple thing and put an end to all those bothersome discussions the Walkers kept having.

★   ★   ★

"We're running low on wood for the fire," Cookie muttered under her breath. "Where did Bear go? He needs to build up the stack of firewood for our shelter."

"I'll go," offered River. "I've been sewing so long my eyes need a rest. Bear disappeared after breakfast. He's probably practicing that new weapon of his."

River was hardly outside when a deep queasiness hit her. She leaned against one of the support poles, gulping mouthfuls of air to soothe her stomach. "I will not throw up," she muttered. "I will not reject the food our Mother sends our way." It seemed especially wrong, heading into the coldest time of year when finding food was hard, and every morsel should be cherished.

Finally the feeling passed. She whispered a grateful prayer and headed off to the cache, still guarding her belly with both hands, which left neither one free to catch her balance when she bumped into Imaleen, barreling around the side of the shelter. She reached out and grabbed his arm in order to steady herself—that or fall. And realized immediately that such familiarity was something he would deeply resent.

Hurriedly she removed her hand and began apologizing, carefully keeping her eyes on the ground in proper Walwoman fashion. "So sorry, mister," she said with her limited knowledge of their language, wanting only to undo any offense. Practically every night Rein reminded them how important it was to get along with Dagoote's people. They were helping the Ogwehu get through the bitterest cold any of them remembered. And the winter was barely upon them.

"Mister, so sorry, I mistake," she repeated. Would that be enough? Looking at his face would be another offense, she reminded herself; it would only make things worse.

But he was already hissing, which could only be bad. She risked a quick peek, but it was apparently the wrong thing to do. He grabbed at her parka, and proceeded to slap her face on one side, then backhanded the other.

The raw pain seared her with a jolt that raced down from face to belly. "Sorry," she repeated miserably, tears forming in her eyes. Fortunately Dagoote and Rein came upon them. Dagoote pulled Imaleen away, chiding him in a burst of Walwords, while Rein pulled her inside the shelter.

"What happened, River?"

Shuddering with relief, she looked up at him. "It seemed like nothing. I was coming out of the tent to get firewood when he rammed into me. He wasn't looking where he was going."

"It was an accident, wasn't it? You didn't make him bump into you?"

"No," she reassured him. "You know I wouldn't do that. I tried to apologize but it just made him madder."

"You stay here." He patted her on the shoulder. "I'll smooth things out with them. But River, see if you can stay clear of Imaleen for a while. He already has a thing about you."

"What kind of thing?" she worried.

"A not very good thing. He seems to feel you're the worst of all our disrespectful ..." He paused, searching her face. "What he actually said was, insolent Disaster women."

Cookie put a protective arm around River. "How can he think River, of all people, is insolent! He should try running into Falling Leaf some time; then he'll see what insolent is."

"Yes, well, Falling Leaf has the good sense to stay clear of him, doesn't she? Anyway that's how he sees it; doesn't matter how wrong-headed he is. Even his own people think he's a little extreme. But we need to get along with them because it's much too late to find another winter camp. River, stay away from him so we don't make things worse between them and us. I shouldn't have to remind you, we don't want to spend the winter at each other's throats. It's best not give them any reason to drive us away. Or," he wiped a weary hand across his face, "to creep into our beds when we're asleep and slit our throats like animals."

"Rein!" Cookie's eyes were wide. "Do you really think it could get that bad?"

"I don't know, but I don't want to have to find out. Since I seem to be chief," here he grimaced briefly, "it's up to me to keep us safe, which means, finding a way to get us through the winter alive. Can I count on you to stay away from him, River? And when you can't avoid him, act submissive, at least until you get away?"

His sister nodded. "I'll do my best," she promised. "I wasn't trying to provoke him."

"Good." He sighed. Birdy was approaching with a bowl of warm tea for River. "You stay away from Imaleen too, Birdy girl," he warned. "He thinks you're almost as bad."

"What did I do?"

"Nothing, the way we view things. A lot, probably, the way they see it. I'll have to apologize for River. I can't ask K'enemy to do it. He wouldn't; he won't think she did anything that needs saying sorry. But they do, and it has to come from a man of our family." He looked around at the warm hearth, the bubbling stew he'd hoped to enjoy but now would have to postpone. "I guess I got some smoothing over to do. I will see you ladies later." He stretched his arms and neck as if preparing for a long and arduous journey.

The women looked uneasily at each other. A tense silence hovered, broken only when Cookie folded her arms. "We still don't have enough firewood for tonight," she fretted. "Where is Bear, anyway?"

"Don't worry, Mami," Left called from the far side of the shelter. "I'll fetch some for us."

Cookie looked up, surprised. The last thing she expected was to see her resentful daughter volunteer for more work. Though recently she was uncharacteristically cheery. She went out of her way to do extra, even when it brought her into contact with those unfathomable Walpeople. With her twin it was just the opposite. Ever since Bison declared himself to Willow, Swan had been moping.

"Thanks, sweet girl." Cookie patted Left on the shoulder. "That will do until your brother finds his way back. Starving to death, no doubt, and totally surprised that he still has chores."

Left snorted. "No doubt," she agreed.

Crossing the front section of the tent, the young woman pulled on her mittens and ducked through the flap without watching where she was going. It was one more careless moment like so many others she was prone to. "That girl will dash headlong to her own funeral," Falling Leaf commented. Sure enough, she banged heads with Gaagatade, bending to enter from outside.

"Owww!" Left complained, rubbing the sore spot while trying to smile. She did seem to see a lot of him these days. See him and brush up against him strategically, making it look almost as if by accident.

He clutched his forehead, mouth open in a mockery of great shock. "You got me good, giirlinga!" He looked handsome in his winter parka, Left thought, his cheeks ruddy with the cold.

She hit him playfully. "Why are you coming to our shelter, Swift?"

"I looking you. Come sit me to dinner?"

"Come sit *next* to me? Come sit *with* me at dinner?"

He grinned, mischief in his eyes. "Oh! I so glad you ask!"

This earned him another *thwap* on the arm. "You're the one asking me, silly."

"Oh." He pretended to be disappointed. "You say no, yes?"

"I'm saying yes, no? But first I have to bring firewood for momma."

"Oh, I help. We have best wood, right there!"

"Where?" she asked, indignant. "Are you hiding the best wood from us? Oh, there," she said as he led her to the woodpile inside his shelter.

"Come here, I show you better." He dodged behind a high stack and disappeared from sight. "Come heeeeere." His voice was soft and enticing.

"Why? What's back here?" All she could see were piles of branches and bark, much like any other woodpile. "What's so special about . . ."

A sudden grab of her arm, and she landed on his lap.

"This what special." He turned her head gently. With one finger he stroked her lips. Soft, very soft.

"This?"

"This." Whispering, he let his fingers drift, teasing.

Oh. He'd never touched her before. Certainly not like that. Her lips parted, and his fingers touched the pink tip of her tongue. "That?"

"This." One casual movement with his other hand brought her face towards his. "And this." His lips brushed hers. "Also this, very special," he murmured. His breath was fresh and sweet.

Giggling, she came up for air. "You were right. The wood here is entirely special!"

"Shhh. Don't want others knowing how special."

For quite some time lips explored lips, tongues explored mouths. She sat, squirming a bit in his lap. Nice, she thought. She felt warm all over. *Very* nice.

Then, "Whoops, what that?"

"What? I didn't hear anything." Left sat upright.

A quick inrush of breath. "A little mousie. You see him?"

"No, where?"

"There." His hand lifted. His fingers scampered up the length of her arm, then dove down the open neck of her parka. "Mousie!"

Left shrieked, then giggled, realizing it was only him. She squirmed, trying to extricate his hand without ripping the neck of her overshirt. "Swifty, take your hand out! You're not supposed to touch me there."

"Not?"

"Not."

"But feel so nice. Like this." His finger found the very tip of one nipple and touched it quickly. "Like this." His voice grew husky. He began moving a finger in lazy circles, brushing the tip again.

She shivered and moved against him, rubbing against his lap. Waves of some unfamiliar sensation washed over her. Her head leaned back, and a small groan escaped her swollen lips.

A footstep broke the mood. "Shhh," he warned.

Dagoote entered, walking through to the inner section. Dagoote, who already lectured him about treating Eider carefully, since she and her people were their honored guests. Treat her with the respect he'd give a man, he warned, not like he'd be towards a woman of his clan. He didn't want to have an incident between their two Peoples. Imaleen already almost provoked one and nobody wanted to repeat that.

Gaagatade had to be nice. But that was fine. He wanted to be nice. He *was* being nice, he told himself; he wasn't forcing anything on her.

They saw only the top of Dagoote's head. He didn't notice them, but the interruption was enough to bring Left to her senses. "Stop that, Gaage. Take your hand away. You can't do that!"

"But I can," he smiled at her dreamily. "I did doing that."

"Well you can't. You're not supposed to, unless we are married. Or planning to be married, or something."

"So, we planning to be marry, so?"

She looked at him. Decided he was teasing again. "Take your hand out. I mean it!"

Slowly he removed his hand. Gave her one last teasing flick as he pulled away.

"Mousie sad. Mousie like warm place, sad from leaving, all cold." He pouted, eyes drooping, lip thrust out.

"Oh you!" she laughed. She touched his mouth with her fingertips and let them linger for a moment. Stood up and straightened her clothing, then reached over to grab several good sized pieces of wood. "For that, I'm stealing all your best logs."

She marched off, sending him a last, saucy look. "And if anyone complains, tell them you owe it to me."

*   *   *

The women prepared vast amounts of food for the upcoming celebration. The men were carving masks and planning their reenactment that they did every year, usually of some hunt they took part in. The entire settlement was bubbling with activity but Antler, who'd been practicing stories with Birdy for the last two months, by now had had enough.

He had to separate himself from the hubbub. There were so many things to attend to, all pressing. Yet what seemed necessary instead was to settle himself after all the recent changes. To set aside a day for that retreat he'd been thinking about.

Rein wanted time to meditate as well. He had to figure out how to do a better job of leading, he told Antler. Every time he tried to think about such things, something interrupted. He needed time away from distractions, and these next few days would do nicely.

Trapper agreed to watch over them during the retreat. He would beat the drum to send them into trance, and peek in occasionally, make sure no bad spirit overcame them on the journey. He would keep the fire going and make sure they had water. There would be no eating, of course, during the fast. What they needed was to let go of the everyday Mother Earth concerns so that a Father Sky vision could expand within.

So that night after the evening meal, Antler and Rein began their fast, to be broken at dinner the following day. They slept that night in River's shelter, cleared of everything but their sleeping furs and the drum, two small bowls, a supply of firewood and a water skin of tea.

They spent the evening talking in the soft firelight. In the quiet between them Rein slowly began to relax. Gradually he let loose his hopes and fears for the first time in months. Once he could say anything to his wife or his lifelong friends, Two Stones and Staunch. But these days the tribe depended on him for vision and comfort, and whenever he expressed doubt, it made them worry. He had to hold it inside instead, and keep a cheery face for his People.

But here on this eve of fasting and prayer, he found himself expressing doubt with this dignified man-child. Not about the People's direction but about his own. Did he have the wisdom to make decisions? Even if they discussed things in council and argued their way to consensus, his word seemed to carry more weight than others. Yet what if his word was wrong?

Something else was needed, he felt. Because everybody made mistakes. Even the old chief was wrong sometimes, and he had years of being leader. They really should have something besides him that kept people moving on a good course, to fine hunting grounds, and to a sense of wholeness around the central hearth.

Antler felt much the same. Did he know enough to be their shaman? But instinctively he held back. Rein's need was pressing. It would be wrong to add his own misgivings; these would only confuse him, when what Rein needed was a space to rest in. That, and some idea of how to seek his vision trail the next day.

Instead Antler spoke of vision quests that Falcon had described. How this person relaxed within the steady beat of the drum, emptying his mind of all thoughts and fears, and gradually wisdom crept in. How that person watched his own breath going in and out, and found some helper spirit who led him to new understandings. In this indirect way he let Rein know how to proceed without presuming to instruct the older man.

Long before dawn they rose in silence. In silence they emptied themselves outside, and returned. They took enough tea to moisten their throats, a few swallows before setting it aside.

Trapper entered. Wordlessly he built up the fire, then took a few savory leaves and set them to smolder. He fanned smoke around each of them to sear off the influence of the Mother, letting the smoke rise skyward to invite influence from the Father. The remains he threw in the fire, then wiped his hands on his leggings and picked up the drum.

"*Hey, dai dai dai,*" His chant started softly. "May your journey be safe," he prayed. "May you find great visions on your way. May Father Sky keep you sheltered in the palm of His hand."

The drumming took on a simple, steady beat. *Dah, dah, dah, dah.* When the time felt right he added a twinning beat, *dah-dah, dah-dah.* Another complication was added: *Dah-dah, dit-da.* Soon the rhythms were moving fast and blurring together, until suddenly they disappeared from Antler's consciousness.

All sound and feeling fell away as his awareness was pulled within. With his dream-like inner eye he began to see a series of deeper, richer colors, and to hear and feel on a different scale than he ordinarily encountered. There was a kind of whooshing sound, like wind, and a pleasant weightlessness in his body.

He saw himself walking through rich meadows and deep into piney forest. Felt the soft, spongy earth beneath, smelled the tangy smell of needles shed by pine and cedar. Came upon an overlook where he peered down on a lake and into the sky, noticing the clouds spaced across the expanse. Eagle flew overhead, and Antler watched the flare of her wingtips, the beating of wings, the long breaths when he seemed to float on the breeze like a duck on a lake. After a long and glorious sky-dance, Eagle dove from on high and flew straight to him. Ever closer, until she was near enough to bend one wing towards the Earth, allowing him to climb on. "Let both arms hug my neck," she seemed to say, and without hesitation he did so.

Aloft they went. He looked down on their settlement below. His people seemed so small, seen from above! Two Stones was scowling, Turtle was strutting around, and Little Mother was chasing Lynx; it all looked so unimportant from up in the sky. He would have to remember the vision. Somehow he knew it would be important.

Now Eagle flew them over the paths they traveled, back to the fingerland with its mountains and volcanoes, back to their old home by the sea. They soared over the beach he'd been washed up on before finally turning back.

Ahead was the mountain of his childhood, where a circle of stones still marked the cooking hearth his mother attended every day. Beyond was where Bear lived, and down below, the meadow. Further, the ocean beach where he trained with the other apprentices. Each a world unto itself, but now he knew many worlds, every one of them small and yet so vast.

Down there, the shaman's hearth where he learned so much, and yet not nearly enough. But he learned the beginnings of how to learn, and perhaps that would be enough. Antler pointed down, and Eagle descended. He held tight as they skimmed the beach. There by the hearth he reached over, holding tight to her neck with his other arm. Let his fingers trail until they felt a small object, closing around it. As she lifted aloft, he marveled at the small piece of shell, delicate pink and yellow, pounded smooth by the sea. What was left was strong, and nothing he did with his fingers could break it.

"Like you," said Eagle, sensing his thought. "Keep it to remind you of who you are. From the water, into the air. The weak worn away and the rest made strong." Pleased, Antler tucked the fragment into his pouch.

They flew back, circling a long time over their encampment. There he could see two Peoples as if engaged in a dance. Sometimes they moved towards each other. At other times, apart. It was something like the dance of male and female together, also like the dance of young and old. The dances themselves the subject of many a story told at night around the campfires.

Eagle prompted him. "When I set you down I must say goodbye. So if you have a question, ask it now."

So many things he'd like to ask about. The wind on his face, the softness of feathers. The amazement of seeing from above the distance which, on foot, took so long to travel. The vision of two Peoples moving sometimes in harmony, sometimes not.

What came out surprised even him. "Can you teach me how people can fly in the skies?"

"You are speaking about stories?" she asked gently.

"Stories? I'm not sure ..."

"That's how most people fly from their nest to some far distant place."

"What can you teach me about stories then?"

But instead of a word-teaching, she let him see how Birdy sat with Oopsy and Lynx, the boys spellbound, the girl rapt in the telling. Then Antler saw himself speaking a story, the audience glazed but polite. And in that moment he knew it wasn't the storyteller, but the tale and the telling that were important. It wasn't the speaker, but the passing of story so that all could hear and let it brighten their nights, a light that might shine through their every day.

As long as the speaking was a true one.

He could let Birdy tell some of the tellings, and they would still have the favor of Father Sky. He could call the circle, he could beat the drum, he could instruct the People to respect the occasion, and she could tell the tales, whichever ones they agreed on. They would be a team, and the People would flourish.

She was the Birdsinger, and they were the birds she sang to. Her singing would help their People fly from the places they found themselves, to wherever they needed to go.

"Thank you, Eagle." And he reached into his pouch and pulled out a mouse, dangling it, straining to escape, by its tail so that she could easily snap it up. A fit reward for such a fine journey. She fed his spirit, and he fed the wings that flew him so far.

⋆　　⋆　　⋆

River was shredding lily roots and adding them to the stew simmering on the hearth. It would cook overnight and give them something to eat as they finished preparing for the solstice. The shelter was quiet; the tranquility was an unexpected pleasure. Rein and Antler were gone for their meditations. Oopsy was off playing with Lynx. K'enemy, Bear and Staunch were at the food cache. Birdy, Willow and Bison lolled around at the far end of the shelter, but their low chatter only added to her contented mood.

It was in the quiet moments like this that she noticed how happy she was. K'enemy was so dear—considerate, kind, protective. He helped her carry heavy loads even when the men teased him about being his wife's little scoldy-child. The other day when she stumbled, he was there with both hands to help regain her balance. Not every husband would do that. If she were married to Staunch, he might help her up but he would follow it with a joke at her expense. She'd almost rather not have the help. She was right to wait all those months for K'enemy. For a while it seemed risky, but look how well it had turned out.

She sniffed the air appreciatively. The last few months she barely ate anything, but now her desire for food was back. She often found herself eating more than ever. She already ate dinner and to be thinking about food already? It was almost embarrassing. Though K'enemy, endearingly, said he liked seeing her with such an appetite.

She added more to the stew, then bent to push a log closer to the center of the fire. She felt self-conscious moving around like that; fortunately nobody was nearby to see. Normally she would crouch modestly instead of bending over with her rear end sticking out. She knew it was the kind of thing that attracted lustful male eyes. She had no desire for such attention. But crouching was harder these days—she didn't know if other sheltering women felt this way, but for her, legs pressing up against the lower belly made it uncomfortable in that now-swollen place. As if the babe inside did not like being cramped.

She heard a footstep. Good, he was finally back. She missed him even if he were gone only a short while.

She heard a quick inrush of breath, felt him come up behind her and fit his body around the curve of hers, his hands grasping her hips and pulling her towards him. Her eyes closed. She gave an affectionate, wifely wiggle against him, enjoying the contact. For a moment she was still, feeling the touch of body against body. Odd. He seemed shorter than usual, his belly and groin touching hers a little lower down than she was used to. But the shelter floor was uneven. He must be standing in a bit of a dip, that's all.

No, something else was wrong. His smell was too strong. Too fishy. She turned her head and gave a frightened shriek.

It wasn't K'enemy pulling himself against her, Great Mother, no! It was Imaleen, his face all flushed and awry, with the same sick look that Oopsy had the other day. When she caught the child sneaking into Bear's sack and playing with his cousin's knives, though he was warned many times not to do just that.

★   ★   ★

Birdy sat with Willow, sewing in hand. Food bowls and spoons lay carelessly around. Bison leaned against Willow, his eyes half-closed. He was still weak from the goring, and often sat quietly with them instead of carousing with the men.

Across the shelter, some sort of commotion drew them in. "What is going on?" Willow asked nervously. They could feel tension in the air. Everyone felt the absence of Rein and Antler, gone until tomorrow. If trouble arose, there would be a long wait for guidance.

"I think I heard someone cry out," Bison mumbled, gingerly pulling himself up onto one elbow.

"That was River," Birdy worried. "Is that Imaleen bothering her again? Oh." She gave a quick sigh of relief. "Here comes K'enemy, he'll take care of the problem, whatever it is."

K'enemy came tearing through the shelter, looking around madly until he spotted River. Three long steps it took to reach her side. Several others entered the shelter behind him.

Birdy watched nervously. He grabbed River's arm and pulled her back so that Imaleen would have to face him instead. The Walhunters and the Ogwehu were sorting themselves out behind their kinsmen. Two groups of people were now lined up opposite each other. Tension mounted noticeably.

What was wrong with everyone today? Where were their usual antics? Surely this was a good time for Unqileer to do one of his ever-popular pretend-falls, or for Gaagatade to twirl around and mock-stumble into Imaleen. They'd both lose their balance. Everyone would laugh and things would return to normal. But their customary humor was missing tonight. For some reason everyone was on edge.

It reminded her of a story Bison told the evening she stood watch with him. Back at their old home, a party of Ogwehu went hunting on the far side of the mountain. After a lengthy trek they found themselves face to face with a herd of mammoth. There was a terrible moment of complete silence. Then someone led a charge. Bison did not remember which started it, Ogwehu or mammoth, but within moments bodies from both sides lay quiet, leaking blood on the ground.

Could it come to that here? Birdy suddenly knew it could. The sides were lined up like they might charge each other at any moment. And nobody was doing anything to stop it.

If Rein were here, he'd take Dagoote aside and confer; they'd each step in and pull the men apart. But instead of Rein there was only Two Stones who seemed bewildered, his mouth open, hands dangling useless at his sides. Across the way she saw a hard look on the faces of the Walhunters.

People kept entering the shelter, eyeing each other and sorting themselves out into sides. Birdy peered through the smoke looking for reassurance. "Imaleen is threatening K'enemy," she worried. His shoulders and elbows rose belligerently. K'enemy seemed to puff up, and both men swayed as if getting ready to lunge.

The two began circling each other, eyes locked together. Their pacing was identical: Shift one foot over, leg bent for crouching; move torso to follow. Pull other leg over, thrust head and shoulders out, fists resting on hips. Imaleen's sharp white teeth flashed in the firelight. K'enemy clenched his jaw fiercely. Occasionally one of them threw a jab—almost as if testing his opponent's alertness rather than intending to wound. And yet to Birdy that seemed more ominous, as if they were building up to something more serious than a quick brawl.

"Can't you stop them, Bison?" she implored her friend.

But he seemed surprisingly unconcerned. "Why would I try to do that?" he wondered.

"One of them's going to get hurt."

"So what if they do?"

Birdy paused. How could she convince him of the danger she felt pressing down? She only half understood it herself. Instead she sidetracked. "They respect you. Maybe they'll listen if you tell them to quit."

Bison snorted. "In the hunt they respect me, yeah. But outside of that ..." He gave her an exasperated look. "I can't tell them what to do, Birdy. They're my elders, you know."

"Couldn't you try? Someone has to stop them. You know how important it is for us to be respectful; Uncle Rein's always saying we have to be good guests while we're here."

"Birdy." He had to muster all his patience; it was hard to explain a man's thinking so a girl could understand. "Imaleen's not going to pay attention to me. And if K'enemy stops to listen, he'll lose respect just by hesitating. Imaleen will keep bothering River, and what's the good of that? Being respectful is one thing, but they have to respect us too."

"Respect won't matter so much when one of them's dead," she argued.

"Let it go, Birdy. Guys get punchy with each other all the time. It doesn't mean anything."

She glanced over at the hearth again. K'enemy's nose trailed blood. One of Imaleen's eyes looked bruised. Maybe it didn't mean anything yet, but it would start meaning something if they couldn't keep the fight from getting bigger and meaner than it already was. This was exactly what Rein had been warning against when he said that they had to work on getting along with their hosts. If Rein were here he would stop the fighting. Antler would try to do the same. Even Bear would understand and try something. Anything. Where was Bear, anyway?

Their survival through the winter depended on goodwill. If K'enemy whomped Imaleen, let alone killed him, their hosts would surely resent it. They'd blame all the People for what he did, and maybe make them leave. In the dead of winter! And if Imaleen killed K'enemy, how could the Ogwehu live in harmony with them, even for a few months until they left? Surely River would not be able to, nor would Birdy. She was sure the rest would find it impossible as well.

Two Stones should do something; he was there in Rein's place to prevent just this kind of thing. She had to prod him out of his stupor. But when she tugged on his arm, he frowned at her. "Those two got to work it out between themselves, Birdy," he demurred.

"But, Uncle, they're all going to hate us!"

He shook his head mournfully, returning his attention to the circling men.

"Uncle Rein would stop them if he were here," she protested.

He raised a skeptical eyebrow. "This is not girl's business, Birdy." A clear warning not to butt in.

Why could no one else see what was so clear to her? Of course none of the others grew up with the sudden, unpredictable violence that her mother excelled at, none except for Oopsy, and he was too young to count. Was this any different? Birdy had little experience with casual male fighting; she rarely encountered it, isolated at the hot springs cave. On the trek the tensions between men were mostly dissipated through casual jibes and banter, drained off through the rigor of travel or the intensity of the hunt. Now that the first exciting month of getting to know another People had passed, tensions that she was unfamiliar with were beginning to rise. Fighting, in order to release the fighters back into haodisah? It didn't make sense to her. Birdy could accept a beating if she had to. But it made her cringe, seeing pain casually inflicted on another.

She protected little Pout from beatings whenever she could. Sometimes by offering herself in her place, by diverting Mami's attention or sending her sister to a chore outside their mamma's line of vision. If only such a thing were possible here, she thought, desperate to stop them somehow.

And now it was getting worse. The dogs outside were growling and whining, wanting to come in. Birdy stood on her toes to get a better view. "He's got a stick," she said in dismay. "It's sharp at the end. Glowing, like it's been in the fire. He went around K'enemy and now he's pointing it at River! Willow, he's aiming it between her legs!"

Willow too was horrified. "Papi," she called to Staunch. "Can't we stop him?"

Staunch turned to Two Stones. "It's between K'enemy and Imaleen," he fretted. "I'm sure K'enemy will protect her. I don't like to see a woman threatened, but he's doing all right and I don't think we should interfere."

"But River might get hurt," Birdy protested. "Maybe even killed! Somebody has to stop that man!"

"Unqileer is over there," he pointed out. "He's Imaleen's elder. He's the one who should put a stop to it if anyone should." He glanced over at Staunch, who nodded in agreement.

"You're wrong! He's not going to stop," she insisted. "The Walmen hurt their women all the time. They don't think there's anything wrong with that. Anyways, it's our shelter," she fumed. "They're our guests. Doesn't that make you the elder here?"

Two Stones frowned. Maybe it did. Maybe if he were Rein and everyone thought of him as chief, he would feel more sure. Certainly if it were a fight between two of their own he could step in. But this was between one of the Others and one of their own. He wasn't sure how much authority he had. If only this happened yesterday when Rein was still with them.

Frustrated, Birdy turned away. "Bison, get up," she urged. "We can't sit around worrying about being polite. Someone has to grab Imaleen and shake some sense into him. There should be people helping K'enemy stop him."

Even as Bison stumbled to his feet, the situation worsened. One of the orphan boys started chanting, "Do it, do it, do it," in the language of the Walpeople, and others picked up the rhythm. Their eyes were glazed. They were beginning to enter into a kind of blood lust, an intense focus, which, once begun, was almost impossible to avert. A sneer formed on Imaleen's lips, and his eyes grew fierce.

"Do it. Do it."

Birdy leaned over to Willow. "Why doesn't she run?"

River's face was a mask of rigid terror, her eyes so wide there were white circles around the dark. "She looks like she's in shock," Willow whispered back. "Probably too scared to move."

K'enemy was angling to pounce from some direction that would keep him from landing on River as well, but Imaleen, slyly, kept shifting his stance, first one way and then another.

"Do it, do it, do it."

The poker, red hot at the tip, was only half an arm's length away. Imaleen crouched, staring at River, and edged it closer. K'enemy finally leapt upon him and was hanging onto Imaleen's back, but he didn't have enough of a grip to pull him off course.

"Do it, do it, do it."

Now the stave was weaving back and forth only a short span away. K'enemy managed to hook his arms through Imaleen's. He angled him sideways, but Birdy was afraid he would be too late. Another lunge and poor River might be skewered by the time he prevailed.

"Do it, do it, do it."

A massive shift of K'enemy's weight toppled both men onto the ground. There they squirmed, sweat gleaming on their bodies, K'enemy on top and punching, Imaleen trying to pull himself back. Blood was running in each of their eyes, K'enemy's from a split in the skin on his forehead. There was a crack of bone, Imaleen's nose bearing the worst of it, but K'enemy got scratched and gouged as well. Imaleen finally got a lock on K'enemy's arm and twisted it, using it as leverage to get back out from under him.

While K'enemy was pulling himself upright, Imaleen slipped away, picking up the stick again and moving toward his target. Sickened, Birdy could see the grim enjoyment on his blood-tracked face. River's face was white as ice. Her poor legs trembled but her feet were stuck to the floor. She was helpless, and for the moment no one came to her defense.

Then, suddenly, someone was. Fierce strode grimly into the inner circle and stuck her stocky body between Imaleen and River, arms spread, glaring directly at the crazed Walman, which gave Cookie the time she needed to pull River out. Dagoote, from the other side, quietly motioned his wife to edge around the circle. From there she led Cookie and River outside, where they could recover their breath.

This distracted Imaleen enough for K'enemy to lunge forward and knock the staff from his hand. It went flying, and Gaagatade caught it in the air before it could impale anyone. The taller Walman clutched it upright as a walking stick. The tension in the air diminished somewhat.

Imaleen reached toward Gaagatade, motioning for the stick. The younger man shook his head, almost imperceptibly. Imaleen frowned but returned his attention to K'enemy, who stood warily, knees bent to spring forward, arms still poised for attack. K'enemy was no longer at a disadvantage. With River safely gone he could focus on his adversary.

"It's back to just a couple of guys fighting," Two Stones reassured Birdy. "You don't have to worry about River anymore."

Better, yes. Yet she was not at ease. "You still should stop them," she insisted. "They're gonna hate us, no matter who wins. This isn't keeping the peace."

"We can't stop 'em," Bison shrugged. "It's too late. Their dignity's at stake. If someone steps in to pull them apart, it's like their mommies saying, come home little boy, before you get hurt."

The orphan boys chanted, "Fight, fight!" Birdy was vexed to see Staunch and Owl joining them, and then Unqileer across the way. She felt the energy shift again, the crowd-lust rising, egging them on.

She could not sit by and watch; it was too awful to bear. Their hunter's precious dignity? What was that to her when all their lives were at risk? No matter who won, the Walpeople could turn on them to avenge Imaleen's honor. Yet what could she possibly do? For a moment she was tempted with a quick vision of leaping across the fire and punching Imaleen's smug face. Of course it would never work because she wasn't strong enough to overcome him. K'enemy himself was having trouble doing the job. Anyway the Walpeople would never let a girl attack one of them without turning on her. And she'd never overcome them all. In fact there was only one strength she had, and it was not in her arms; it was in her stories.

Even the Walpeople liked stories. They responded even to stories they only half understood.

She could tell stories.

She could.

She shouldn't.

She had to. Their very survival was at stake. And most of the People seemed blind to it, or frozen, unable to move.

There were times when a person could do nothing, and there were other times when they could. Times when they had to withstand the injury looming ahead, and times when the right word or gesture could, wondrously, keep disaster from destroying them. Like when she diverted Mami's wrath from her little sister. She was proud of being able to do that. For the other kind of time, it was best not to think about it. Yet in spite of her determination not to, a terrible vision flitted past, of another man hulking over a limp female body, aiming to launch himself at the poor girl's legs. She heard a rushing river, heard the owl's *Prrrrek-prek*, smelled an acrid smell. She flushed with shame at the memory, and for a moment she could neither see nor hear anything but that.

She shook her head violently to clear it. Without another thought Birdy reached behind her to the small pile of wood for the evening's fire. She picked out two sticks of roughly similar size. Quickly she began banging them in the storyteller's opening cadence. *Dah dah dah, dit. Dah dah dah, dit.*

Heads turned from the far end of the tent.

Dah dah dah, dit.

Would it work? It had to work. Please, Great Mother, help me stop this disastrous fight.

A big grin appeared on Oopsy's face. "Come on," he said to Lynx and Owl, grabbing each by the hand. "'Thtories! Birdy's gonna tell 'thtories, let's get good seats by the fire!" The three of them bounded over to the hearth and sat down cross-legged, facing her.

Dah dah dah, dit.

Reluctant to be left out of anything, the orphan kids followed their lead.

Dah dah dah, dit. "Long ago ..." Birdy called loudly, in her best Antler imitation. Somber, and as authoritative as she could make her girlish voice sound.

It was like a sudden leak developed in one of the filled water skins. At first a fullness, then a gradual seeping away. In the line of the Ogwehu, Turtle shook himself and stretched his arms wide, as if breaking free of some spell. He looked up and caught Birdy's eye. Turtle, who loved stories himself. Turtle, who'd sometimes overheard bits and pieces of the tales Birdy told Oopsy and his brother along the journey. Turtle who, she heard it whispered, sometimes rivaled Imaleen at night under the bedcovers in the Walpeople's shelters.

Now Turtle broke from the crowd. He pulled Swan by one hand, and one of the Walwomen with the other. "We're having stories tonight," he announced loudly. "Come on, everybody! Birdy's going to tell some family stories." He left the women sitting at the hearth, returned to the milling crowd and began dragging others back to the circle. Still standing in the crowd, Left glanced at Birdy and, with a relieved look, pulled Gaagatade over. Others followed on their own.

Dah dah dah, dit. "...long ago ..." she continued.

Dagoote looked over at Birdy. He tapped Unqileer on the shoulder, and they too sat down.

No one remained but Imaleen and K'enemy, who were still circling round. Imaleen glared at Birdy, then back at his foe. His eye was blackening even as she watched. He was not ready to concede. A vicious look still darkened his face, but he stood alone, his supporters all gone, which made him look silly. His face twisted in fury while everyone else was happily waiting around the fire.

Imaleen turned to K'enemy and spat on the shelter floor. "Smeared with women's blood," he muttered, shooting him an icy stare. The insult was deliberate.

"From a woman like her, I consider that an honor," K'enemy said quietly, in a perfect Walpeople accent. He held his gaze long enough to ensure he made the point. Then he turned away, signaling that he considered Imaleen no more of a threat, turned on his heel and strode out.

"...long ago..." Birdy continued. Tearing her eyes away, she gazed with relief at the expectant crowd, whose eyes were locked on her.

She began with the Wedding Tale, since people always liked that one. "...there was a beautiful young girl, Neriagadwen, daughter of Hearth, daughter of White Rose. Now Neriagadwen was as beautiful as the sunrise, as sweet as the taste of honey on the tongue."

She scanned the circle, noting each face. They were with her; she knew it by the way they waited for every word. "Her father sang her praises when he went on the hunt. Her mother spoke pleasingly of her as she gathered kelp with others along the beach ..."

She felt a huge wash of relief through her body. She had never told a story to more than just a few people. Yet her instinct said to throw her entire being into the tale as it flowed through her, letting the rise and fall of her voice calm the listeners and enthrall them. Sometime during the telling, Bear crept in to join them, and River and K'enemy silently followed. They were all with her, and the story drew them together, teller and listeners, completely hao. Except for Imaleen, who was probably sulking somewhere by himself.

When it ended, there was an expectant hush. Turtle looked at Birdy, a pleased smile on his face. "How about another?"

Which inspired Oopsy to yell out, "More 'thtory, Birdy?"

The other children picked up the cry. "Story! Story!"

Birdy looked at Two Stones, who flushed, but nodded in approval. So she began to tell of a time back at their mountain home when the hearth fire in front of Rein's shelter would not stay lit no matter how Bear stacked the wood, no matter what kind of fuel they threw on the flames. The story had them hooting and snickering. Cookie laughed so hard that tears trickled down, and the entire gathering was at ease.

Then they asked for yet another. For a moment Birdy's mind went blank. Suddenly what filled the void was a tale of the Ogwehu's ancient journey from the mountains far to the West. She knew, somehow, she had to tell it. Even though it was one of the sacred tales. Even though Antler would tell it at the Solstice. Even though many were beginning to yawn, and the young were getting cranky from the lateness of the eve.

She'd already risked so much that night, based only on the feeling that she had to do this, had to restore haodisah between their Peoples in any way she could. Yet the same feeling, impelled by a force greater than her 11 summers' self, was pushing that story onto her lips and tongue. She shouldn't tell it, according to everything she once understood. She was a mere girl and to tell that tale was clearly a shaman's task. Even the shaman only told it on that one sacred day every year.

But every other story fled her brain, and this one only was volunteering its way forward.

She shouldn't.

She couldn't.

"One more?" Turtle asked again, and in spite of her resolution, the words began to emerge. "Long ago, long ago, long ago . . ." followed by the lengthy unfolding of that ancient journey their grandfathers and grandmothers took, so many birthings ago.

There was a gasp as first one person, then another realized she was telling a story normally reserved for the shaman. Staunch actually walked out of the shelter with a scowl on his face. But the others settled back to listen, though

Two Stones exchanged an uneasy glance with Fierce, and Great Uncle looked quizzically at her across the circle.

The story flowed smoothly, chronicling catastrophe and response. The fighting among the clan when the crowding became too much; the bewilderment of the survivors. They strove to figure out some better way than slaughter. For them and their children, who would someday need places to set up cooking fires in a homeland where their generations could run down like a river, from the upstream which was then, to their downstream hearth, for now in this frozen land. Tomorrow's current would carry them even further.

Finally the evening came to an end. Children were bundled into their bedding. Adults who had been listening with great pleasure, laughing at the joyous parts, wiping away tears at the sad ones, now looked around, bewildered. Hurriedly they said thanks, and "Good sleep," though some would not meet her eyes.

Even feeling a bit hurt by the uncertainty of their response, Birdy was exuberant. *She did it!* she told herself. She openly did the thing she longed to do ever since she first heard the stories as a young child. And the People thoroughly enjoyed them, even if they weren't sure they should.

Without a doubt it was a success. Like a hunt where the men came back with meat for the hearth, and no one was hurt. No matter what happened afterward, nothing could take that from her. She was giddy with the sense that, even if tomorrow brought shame for the family, even if she was set to some horrible task as atonement, for one night at least, the thing she wanted to do, and thing she knew she had to do, were surprisingly the same.

★   ★   ★

All the next day Birdy worked in silence. It was not that people shunned her, it was more that they didn't know what to say. She did something no girl had ever done. Nor any man not trained. And she did it beautifully, as if born to it. She was like Cookie at the stewpot, River with her sewing. Falling Leaf with her medicines, Bison at the hunt. Dagoote, for that matter, with his daarts.

Last night they were caught up in the magic of her storytelling. Today was altogether different. When she walked through camp bringing ice to melt for tea, people fell silent, only to begin whispering again after she passed. When she entered the shelter, conversations died and slowly resumed, though none would meet her eyes. No one knew if they should speak to her, nor would they know until their leaders conferred.

Willow squeezed her hand encouragingly but did not break the silence. River hugged her, but she too did not speak.

During the long morning her thoughts alternated between fear and a running stream of justifications. The People were in danger. She did what she could to save them. K'enemy looked like he was about to kill Imaleen, or they might kill each other, and how could their two Peoples live together after that? Someone had to do something, which no one but her seemed to understand.

Anyway, people shouldn't hurt other creatures if they didn't have to. Surely he wasn't planning to eat River, was he? Waste today means hunger tomorrow; the old saying taught that they all might go hungry if someone was hurt for no good reason. And certainly a woman's life was more important, wasn't it? Than some stupid old idea that only the shaman could tell the stories. Especially if the shaman didn't do a very good job of it.

Not that Antler wasn't trying his best, but really! The difference in their faces, entirely rapt as she told the first one, and the second one was even better! The third, well, some of them were falling asleep by then, and others wondered if she should be telling it, so that one didn't count. But the difference between how they looked, listening to her, and how they looked, listening to Antler back at Fish Camp, it was so clear to her. Why couldn't everyone see?

In the late morning, when the sun finally peeked out above the horizon, K'enemy sought her out. He stood directly before her until she looked up from her stitching. Her vehemence worn down, she had sunk into a kind of dull dread, though angry tears sprang occasionally to the corners of her eyes. K'enemy looked at her with gratitude and sympathy. She had saved him from doing something they would all regret. She risked great punishment in order to stop the fight, and now people were whispering about her and looking askance.

He too had once been the object of gossip and wariness. He too had lingered in a fog where no one knew what to think of him, nor if they should include him around a hearth. Now he waited patiently until she put her needle down. He watched while she hurriedly wiped her eyes before looking at him, and waited until her eyebrows lifted, questioning his presence.

Wordless, he bent his left arm, firelight reflecting off the tattoo of sacred symbols joining the Father, the Mother, and the circle of the People together. Such a beautiful image; would she be allowed to live and eventually wear it herself? K'enemy's fist moved quickly, decisively, cutting through her misery. He thumped it hard against his chest, right over his heart. Once, twice. He nodded solemnly at her, then hit his chest again, the rhythm sounding exactly like the words the hunters said to the boys who followed them into danger for the first time. "Be strong," the beats sounded like. "Be strong." He wouldn't leave until she acknowledged him with a grateful nod.

She was aware when Antler returned to camp that night. Noticed him stopping to speak with Rein, then with River, who took something from his hands and did some small bit of sewing for him. Finally Antler broke his fast. He ate quietly, solitary even as people came up to address him, some clapping him on a shoulder, bringing cushions to sit on, a blanket to place around him, though it was warm enough inside.

He rose, finally, and walked toward her. He was wearing an eagle's feather looped over his left ear and dangling down. River had wrapped the base with red-dyed sinew, a beautiful contrast with the handsome mottled brown. The shaman's feather, she suddenly recalled. From Eagle, the bird that soars highest and sees farther than any other creature they knew. Falcon used to wear one during ceremonies and storytelling. Antler had never worn such a thing until now.

"Birdy," he said, coming upon her. She could not read his face. "Come with me to the prayer shelter." He indicated River's tent across the way.

She followed, her thoughts in a whirl. Should she confide in him as a friend? Should she beg for his help as shaman? Would she have to do something hard to set things right? "Oh, Antler," she finally burst out, no longer able to contain the chaos inside. "Did they tell you? I had to do it; there wasn't any other way to save us."

He did not speak, but his hand moved across the divide. He was holding another feather like the one he wore.

"What's this, Antler?"

"For you." His voice was easy. "For you, if you decide to accept it, Birdsinger. You may want to think about it. There are many responsibilities that go with this feather, you know."

He wasn't chastising her. He was offering her the storyteller's feather.

She took a deep breath, realizing she'd been almost too scared to breathe.

He waited until she nodded, then gave a sign with his hand. A motion often used to welcome people inside a shelter. "Come with me, Birdy. We have much to discuss before the Solstice."

Her eyes brightened. She was hardly able to believe her vast good fortune. Thank you, Mother Spirit, she whispered fervently. Thank you, Father Sky. I will do my best to deserve this, to be faithful to the stories of the People. To be faithful to all that brings haodisah to the hearth. To be good in every way, and deserve Your trust in me.

Ho, she whispered.

Watching closely, Antler nodded, and his lips formed the same word. Ho.

Chapter 7: Lift high the sun

As the camp began settling in, as the quiet became a sound itself, broken only by the scuffling of dogs trying to push their way into the crowded shelters, Rein put his arm around his wife and pulled her near. "Are you still awake?" She groaned and drew deeper under the furs. "What's with Swan?" he murmured, moving his head closer.

"Ummm," she grumbled, but turned to face him. "She's still moping about her own bad fortune."

"I guess she really liked that boy," meaning Bison.

"Who wouldn't?" Cookie began sleepily ticking off her fingers. "Handsome, good hunter, and kind to children. Big enough to scare away intruders. Any woman would be happy to sleep beside him for the rest of her life."

He poked her, playfully stern. "Hey, keep your thoughts right here, woman. You already have the best guy around."

"Of course, dear." She gave him an affectionate squeeze. "So naturally she's moping. It's not like there's some exciting new man to turn her head another way. That's one thing you didn't think of when you led us north."

Rein peered at her face in the dim light of the embers. "Are you sorry?" Through every danger Cookie never made him think she regretted his choice.

A wistful sigh. "No; you did what felt was right. But that's something we didn't think of, and our children suffer for it."

"If more families had come, it would have been better. Safer. More hunters to face danger together."

"More men for our daughters to choose from."

He shook his head with regret. "I hoped Otter would come."

"And his two strong sons."

"Or Dolphin."

"He was a good-looking fellow."

Rein poked her again. "Hey! You keep forgetting me, the best guy around."

"Sorry," she chuckled. "Don't know what I was thinking."

They were silent for a time. "You can put your hand back there," he suggested hopefully.

Which she did.

But his mind was still not ready to settle for the night. "How about Left? What's going on with her?"

Another sigh. "She's spending a lot of time with that Walboy."

"Gaagatade."

"Yes. He seems like a good one. But ..."

"He's not ..."

"... one of us. I'm worried for her."

"Because ..."

"... the Walmen ..."

"... treat the ladies ..."

"Like they treat their dogs."

"That bad?"

"That bad. And I hate to think our daughter might have the same fate."

"They don't eat them. Their women, I mean."

"They might as well. It would be quicker. Kinder."

He snorted. "Did you try talking with her?"

"Only five or six times. Didn't do much good."

"What's she say?"

"That he's different. He *absolutely* loves her." She mimicked her daughter's distinctive tone, making Rein smile. "He would never treat her the way the other Walstupies treat their women. Of course I couldn't *possibly* understand."

"Because *obviously* you've never been in love, dear."

"That's right. She's the only one of Mother Earth's creatures who ever felt like this."

"She's special, our little Eider duck."

"Absolutely," Cookie agreed. "So, since I obviously cannot understand her, you should talk to her next time."

"Me."

"You."

"I have a hard enough time getting the men to listen to me. Daughters are tougher than men, don't you think?"

"You do admirably with the men, dear," she soothed him. "That's why I thought you might try with her."

"You could put your hand there again," he suggested, stalling while thinking it over. Finally, "You've probably said everything already."

"Yes, but maybe she'll listen to you. Just say what you've been saying. He's a good man, but if she stays, we'll never see her again. And we're afraid for her, because the life of a woman with his people seems unbearable. All she has to do is look around and she'll see how bad it is. And we want her to have better than that."

"She'd have to work hard. She'd hate that."

"Don't say *that* to her; you'll just make her mad. She'll insist she works hard all the time and nobody appreciates her. Just remind her you love her, and you don't want her to ruin her life."

This time it was Rein who sighed. "All right, I'll do it. Right after the celebrations. But you owe me. You owe me big."

"Mmmm," she suggested, generous now that she'd gotten her way. "What did you say about something big?" Her fingers teased him, touching.

"That's right. Something big. Getting bigger even as we speak. Mmmm. Right there."

"Very big," she agreed.

"Yes, and I think we already decided you owe me. Because of this outrageous request. And how very difficult it will be to satisfy you."

"I thought you'd see it that way."

He wiggled underneath her hand, sighing in contentment. "Of course, woman. Because that's pretty much the way it is."

"I know, dear. Should I take care of it right now? Unless," she inquired politely, "you'd rather wait until after you talk with her and get everything settled?"

"No, no, that's all right. Now would be just fine."

Thus the deal was struck and agreed on.

★   ★   ★

They woke to find fresh snow covering the land. A blanket just deep enough to mark their footsteps. A good omen, for the snow magnified the meager light outside. The early morning sky was dotted with scatterings of stars and an almost full Moon. The sun would not make its appearance for a while, but many were already dressed and completing their preparations. The men were taking down the partition of skins dividing the largest shelter so that they would have room to gather inside. Everything had to be moved except for the food, furs to sit on, and the drum and clapping sticks of both Peoples.

By the time the sun finally shot its first rays across the horizon, people were already gathering outdoors. The frigid air pinched their nostrils and chilled their eyes, but they were braced to withstand it. It was the shortest day of the year, so as long as the Sun lingered above the horizon they would celebrate the light. There would be a break for food, and if any had to go inside to warm up, they could.

A long drum sequence, and then Antler cried, "We greet the arrival of Sun."

"We greet the arrival of Sun!" they echoed.

He positioned the drum on a flat-topped boulder and began tapping out a steady beat.

"We gather on this day to add our strength to the Sun, that He may rise again and warm us all. We add our strength to the Circle of the People, that we may rise daily in the seasons to come. From the darkness to the light, from weakness into strength."

"Ho!"

"On this day, the shortest of the year, we put down our ordinary tasks to declare Your greatness, Father Sky. To celebrate Your many gifts, Mother Earth. To dance and tell the stories that mark us as a People. Worthy, we hope, of Your continued blessings."

"Ho!"

Trapper handed Antler a handful of smoldering leaves, and they walked in a circle around the gathering. Together they fanned the sacred smoke around each person, cleansing them of ill wishes and foul spirits on this weakest of the Sun's days so that all could begin the new cycle building strength.

The circle completed, Antler threw the remains on the fire. He picked up the stick and began another sequence of drumbeats. The beat was necessarily slow, his hands hampered as they were by mittens. This rhythm signaled the beginning of the women's dance which all were allowed to join, though the men rarely did. They stayed back and chanted, or stamped their feet in time to the drumming.

The central step of the dance involved a kind of pantomime, the women using their hands to pull up the Sun, rhythmically lifting Him higher in the sky. Thus with each step they added their strength so that Sun on subsequent days could rise higher and higher, until He had the power to bring warmth back to the land.

Finally Antler signaled the ending by speeding up the drum beats, then bringing them to a halt. Next came a children's dance that Little Mother taught the young. It celebrated the warmth they hoped would return, and the things children could do freely in the warmer months. They spun around, pretended to climb trees or splash in the water, all to the beat of the song and the drum. They shrieked every time snow filtered down their parkas.

Laughing, the women began corralling the wildest of them, and with Sun now as high as He would get, they ducked indoors to warm up and eat the first meal of the celebration.

Cookie was in charge of food. She and River doled out big ladles of stew into the bowls people kept thrusting at them. The line had not ended when people began returning for more. Willow and Sparrow took over so that Cookie and River could eat like everyone else. Having had a chance to warm up, many took their bowls outside again. In spite of the cold biting their cheeks and noses, it was a pleasure to enjoy whatever light they had on this darkest of days. The vast quantities of food were gone by the time the sun began sinking below the horizon.

"So soon?" someone complained, indicating the darkening sky.

"Too soon," everybody agreed.

"Anybody still wanting eat?" Dagoote asked, and motioned to Sparrow. She disappeared inside one of the Walshelters and came back with a tray of thinly sliced raw seal liver. She circulated among them, presenting this traditional Walpeople food. Some took and savored its dark, rich flavor. Others decided that perhaps they were full and politely declined.

More chatting. More lazy laughter. Men commented about the women, who were too busy commenting on the children to notice. Children chased dogs, who chased each other. The twilight deepened, and they were left with the faint illumination of starlight on snow, which meant it was too dark and cold to carry on a conversation. The children were shivering, their faces red with cold, fingers and toes starting to swell. People began moving indoors.

Antler picked up the drum and brought it inside. A new cadence signaled the singing was about to begin. Everyone joined as best they could, even the Walpeople—the men boisterous and the women shy.

Eventually some of the Ogwehu slunk away to get ready for the play. The singing quieted down. The young ones were lulled and drowsy, and the celebration took on a soft quality, a yearning, even a sadness.

"The last solstice festival," River whispered to Rein and Cookie. "Think how different it was." Cookie blinked away tears because, indeed, so much had changed. Even if the songs were the same. Even if the prayers repeated the ones said before.

But even as they mulled over the sad changes, a burst of energy stormed inside. Men and boys wearing costumes—and what costumes! There were two baby bears—Oopsy and Lynx, with bear-snout masks tied around their faces. Bison and Staunch, dressed to look like women, wearing hides tied in the style of the woman's wrap. Two animal bladders had been blown up and glued to each of their chests, a red mushroom cap stuck lasciviously in the middle. They sauntered in, hands on hips. They thrust their artificial breasts forward, shifting their bodies so the breastpieces shimmied and jiggled with every step they took.

"Whoo hoo!" Dagoote cheered, and others joined in.

Over the clamor Two Stones announced, "Most years we act out a hunt. This year we decided to act out our hunt to find this winter home. We present Our Travels, acted by me, as Rein." He bowed his head acknowledging the cheering crowd. "Cookie." Staunch wiggled his chest salaciously, to even greater applause. "K'enemy." Turtle beat his chest twice with his fist. "River." Bison rotated his hips, which brought forth much wolfish whistling. "Two Stones, or sometimes Dagoote." K'enemy gave a dignified nod. "Sometimes acting as Staunch, sometimes Right or Left." Bear pumped his fists skyward, to great acclaim. "And of course we have our fabulous baby bears!" This was the cue for Lynx and Oopsy, who made the most of it, prancing in circles until Oopsy toppled over Lynx' foot and fell down on his bottom, bringing more laughter and cheers.

Thus began the enactment, starting with a council in the meadow by the sea where the actors argued over which direction to travel, and a few wiggled their voluptuous, glued-on breasts. Rein, sitting in the audience, grinned as most of the play-actor Rein's arguments for heading northward seemed to point the same way. Strangely enough, they all had something to do with enjoying a nice meal of fresh-killed reindeer.

Oopsy and Lynx cavorted around the edges of every scene.

Bear hurriedly slapped on another set of fake breasts and screamed prettily, while Turtle, with stripes of charcoal on his face, pretended to make cuts all along Bear/Swan's shoulder. After slicing him enough to make him bleed to death had he actually pierced the skin, Turtle pretended to slip and punctured one of the breast-bladders on Bear's chest. It burst with a loud popping sound, deflating unattractively, making most of the women in the audience groan, though the men got a kick out of it.

Next, River and Cookie came running, shrieking, eyes wild as the hot lava, which was portrayed by Oopsy and Lynx in bear costume, chased them around the tent. The men in that scene—Rein, K'enemy and Two Stones—sauntered casually behind, making heroic postures all the way.

Then River, played by Bison, and K'enemy, played by Turtle, were married, and this time Two Stones took the shaman's part. Not that his role lasted long; the focus was on tying Bison and Turtle together for their night of bliss, and much bawdy wiggling and thrusting followed. Bison, as River, was taller than her new husband, which added to the hilarity.

They did not act out anything about the Strangers at all.

The next part, instead, showed Bear playing Left, dragging Two Stones as Rein to meet K'enemy as Dagoote in a comical first meeting of the two Peoples. They pretended to eat way too much and their bellies stuck out outrageously, illustrated by hands patting grossly extended paunches. A lot of jokes about fish breath were made, and the two leaders pretended to jab each other many times with their spears and daarts, sometimes breaking the routine by hitting each other over the head.

"Thank you for watching, everybody," Two Stones concluded amid tremendous clapping and cheering. Then Staunch and Bison tore off their breast pieces and tossed them into the crowd. Unquileer caught one and noisily pretended to suckle on it. More raucous play ensued until one of the breasts landed in the fire. The flimsy skin began to smolder. In the high excitement the rest were tossed in to burn as well. Though the prudent among them tried to save them, for bladderskins had other uses besides the one they were put to that night.

⋆   ⋆   ⋆

Antler picked up the stick and beat the opening sequence on the drum. Once he had everyone's attention he put the stick down again. "Thank you. I know many of you were wondering about the storytelling tonight. We will be telling all the traditional stories. Yes, I said 'we'. Most of you heard Birdsinger telling tales the other night. I know you were wondering about that too."

Rein caught his eye and nodded encouragingly.

"You all know that I was an apprentice for a few months only. We started this journey together and there was no one else who could be shaman. Trapper, himself, did not feel able."

Trapper nodded, his gaze unwavering.

"Nor did I feel fully capable since there was so much I did not learn. With Trapper's help I have been able to take up this duty for you. But Trapper did not know the stories. Some he never learned; some he knew but they faded from memory. We are lucky to have another who knows most of the stories of our People. Back at our old home Birdsinger took an interest and learned what she could at the solstices, and sometimes listened in when the apprentices were practicing."

He waited for questions, but no one had any. They were staring, blank-faced, waiting to be told how to feel about this revelation.

"I have had a vision from above. We are blessed to have her. All this might otherwise have been lost. Lost not only to us, but to our children's children forever. She was guided by a sacred impulse, and for that we must be glad."

Every face turned from Antler to Birdy. In the complete silence, her cheeks burned at the attention. It was coming out now; all the secrets. For a girl used to hiding in the shadows, it was somewhat unnerving.

"Tonight and tomorrow," Antler smoothly continued, "I will tell the first tale. Birdsinger will tell the second. We will take turns telling the rest, some told traditionally, some in her own way. Each way, I have learned, has a rightness to it." He scanned the circle, pausing until every pair of eyes met his glance. Finally he concluded, "Ho."

There was an awkward silence.

"Ho," Rein finally said, and, with a sigh of relief, the others followed his example.

It was as easy as that.

Antler picked up the stick and began beating the opening sequence again. "Long ago, long ago, long ago, Father Sky looked down and said, I will make a world."

And so it went, beginning with the most sacred of their tales. Birdy, still flush with nervous energy, held herself tight. She doubted he would need her help on this one. Yes, he paused here and there, and once she started to signal, reminding him of what came next. But he was only giving space in the narrative before starting the next section. Just as she sometimes paused, though hers were more dramatic.

Tonight the People were completely attentive. There were a few coughs, and some shuffling of legs, but they followed every word. Even the Walpeople were respectful; no joking or whispering was heard.

His voice faded with the ending beat. "Ho," people said. Fierce and Cookie were wiping tears away, for Antler's tale was beautifully told.

Now he passed the talking stick to Birdy, who placed it in front of her crossed legs. She touched the eagle feather dangling from her ear, rubbed the golden amulet around her neck for luck. She took in a deep breath, feeling slightly shaky. Looked around the circle, then at Antler.

"Long ago, long ago, long ago," she began. And there she paused, like a swimmer about to jump into a lake, not sure if the water was warm or cold. She was actually doing it, she thought to herself. The real thing, in front of them all. A great glee arose inside her, and she began to ride it like a wave buoying her up.

She took a great breath. Her mouth was already forming the next word, her hands poised in front, when she remembered to signal Antler. It was time to begin that background beat so she could tell the stories as they deserved to be told. For the first time ever, as far as she knew.

(thrum) "... when the People were settled *(thrum)* in their home by the sea, *(thrum)* there was a man named Raven who lived on the mountainside. *(thrum)* Now Raven had a family ..."

★   ★   ★

They liked it! They liked it!

People kept coming up to them. First was Bear, who bounded over as Antler finished the final cadence. He pressed him into an exuberant rendition of their favorite fist-pounding, hip-bump routine, after which Birdy got hauled up for more of the same.

The kids were pleading for more stories, which Birdy reassured them they'd have the next day, and for the rest of the winter as well. Little Mother led them away, all but Oopsy, who held his arms high to be picked up. Once he was at eye level he reached to pat Birdy on the head. Flashing a benevolent smile, he said "Good 'thtory!" in a voice that echoed the exact tone she used, encouraging him.

Laughing, she let his head rest on her shoulder as people kept coming up to thank her and Antler.

"I knew you could do it," Rein complimented them. "I knew it would go well."

"You make me proud to be your aunt," Cookie agreed, squeezing Oopsy between them while hugging her niece.

Great Uncle was speaking quietly to Antler. Finally he clapped the boy's shoulder and announced, "He is no longer the apprentice!" A cheer went up, and no one wondered any longer what Antler could do.

By this time Birdy's face was starting to hurt, she was smiling so hard. Others came to thank them, even including a few shy Walwomen. Willow and Bison were last, Willow squeezing her hand, Bison threatening to bring back enough dinner to feed a mammoth.

Laughing, Birdy dismissed them.

The sudden quiet was a relief, really. Finally she'd have a chance to talk with Antler.

"Everybody seemed to like it, Antler! Rein said so, Uncle Trapper said so, everybody came to say we were great ..." She stopped, realizing she was babbling nervously. Sure, people said nice things, but it was his judgment she worried about. If he thought the Spirits were angered, she would not risk doing it again. It wouldn't be right to bring punishment on all of them just for the pleasure of telling stories here and there.

If that was what Antler decided, she'd work with him until he could tell them perfectly himself. She would. But please, let Them approve what we did tonight! Look with favor on this girl who just wants to do right. Please, she prayed, pretty much the same prayers she'd been saying for days now.

Nervously she began fingering the feather dangling from her ear. "I'm sorry, Antler. What I mean is, how do you think it went?"

There was a moment when he did not respond. He was looking off in the distance and did not catch her eye. The moment seemed to stretch on forever. Finally he looked at her and grinned. His old, carefree smile, with that one crooked tooth seeming to wink at her. "I'd say, Birdsinger, your instincts were right. We made a very good team tonight."

She blinked. Gradually her hand stopped fiddling with the feather.

He looked at her. She looked right back. If they were dogs, their tails would have been wagging up a storm. If they were children, they'd be jumping up and down with glee, for their worst fears were demolished.

Because on this night the heavens opened up for them. The Moon seemed fuller and the Sun promised to strengthen with the dawn. If it were summer, the two of them might chase each other around the hillsides, or jump into the river and race for the other bank, seeing who got there first. If they were fully adult they might hug, or lapse into formal congratulations by now.

But they were neither kids, dogs, nor fully mature, and there were no well-traveled paths for these churning emotions. Glee, relief, ebullience. Joy. Camaraderie. Hope for the future. A sense that there was someone to help shoulder these great visions from the past.

It was all too much. So they stood there mute, grinning madly. Finally Antler raised his fist and pounded her lightly on the shoulder. "There's food waiting for us, Birdsilu. Aren't you starving?"

"For something," she agreed eagerly. "It's been a long time since I ate my fill."

*   *   *

The second day of the celebration started slowly.

After opening prayers and a quiet meal together, people sat cross-legged around the fire circle awaiting the long cycle of stories. But first, Antler told them, Rein had something to say.

Rein picked up the talking stick and toyed with it, running his fingers down the carvings along the side. "Some of you know that I went into the tent of healing the other day to think about things," he finally said. "I fasted with Antler, and we prayed for guidance from above.

"While I was there, I had a vision. And part of the vision was that I needed to share it with you." Around the circle they watched, each in their characteristic way. Two Stones cocked his head, ready to follow his leader. Cookie gave him an affectionate look. Staunch watched for the opportunity to make a laconic joke.

"In my vision, I saw that there are six directions, and each one has a teaching about how to live our lives. I want to share these instructions with you. You can share them with your children, and they can share them some day with theirs."

Bison inclined his head respectfully. Trapper nodded, a faint smile on his lips.

"The first direction," he pointed at the sky, "suggests the first teaching: You shall honor the Great Spirits who make all things. And when you feel the wind on your face, or the flesh of Their creatures on your tongue, remember to thank Them for sending these gifts to you. Honor these gifts, and never let them go to waste." He looked around, assuring himself that they paid close attention.

"The second direction," he pointed downwards. "This fire circle is what grounds us. We must decide all important matters by talking together in the circle of the People. Because no one among us carries all the wisdom inside."

Pointing east, he continued, "You shall honor your ancestors who came before you, for they fed you, and helped you walk the earth until you could walk on your own." East being the direction of the rising sun, the beginning of each new day, the direction to celebrate new beginnings and creation.

Pointing west he said, "Honor your children, and your children's children, who are the only part of you that will walk the earth when you no longer can." West for the setting sun, and the setting of every man's life at the end of his days.

Pointing to the south he continued, "Honor your family, friends and People, who remind you how to walk the earth whenever you need reminding." South where the warm Sun lived, the reminder of warmth from those who had it to give.

"Honor your own body, mind and spirit," he said, nodding northward, "for without these, no one could walk underneath the heavens."

There was a long silence, broken at last by Trapper, saying the thing that signaled both completion and acceptance. "Ho." Which the others echoed, agreeing with their lips and hearts.

Among the People there were yet no words like "rules" or "laws" or "commandments" to describe the kind of teachings these were. Those ideas came later, as they came to live with the wisdom of these directions. For now they called them, simply, Rein's Words. And everyone knew which words they spoke of when they used that special tone of voice. Certainly Rein was a man of many words, and he was often teased for just that. But his words were rarely foolish, and often they were as wise as words could be. So when the People referred to these particular ones, it was with respect instead of laughter.

Every once in a while someone suggested a new name for him, honoring this special wisdom. Word Maker. Elder, though he was reluctant to be thought of as old enough for such a name. Teacher of the People was proposed. But they stayed with Runs Like Reindeer. They had to, because no other name ever really took. It fit because, as his son said, he ran with his words, not just his legs, and the words were swift and many, lively and nourishing. Much like the herds for which he was named.

And his name was spoken with honor for many many summers, long after Rein went Beyond.

Book 5: The crossing

Chapter 1: Feet move forward again

They set out under a mild, cloudy sky two months after Solstice. The days were growing long enough to travel, while the ice was still firm under their feet. The People were joined by new companions: The vedeelon Cookie started calling Sparrow, who would come along as far as Seal Beach where she had family to take her in. The sisters they named Braids and Knick, one widowed, one never mated, who attached themselves to Staunch. Gaagatade, who was adopted amid much merriment as a son to Bison, who would be his family at the marriage to Eider.

Also the children, Rabbit and Auk. Rabbit, a girl of 7 summers, accepted when Little Mother urged them to take her in, for what kind of life would a girl with a malformed face have with the Walrus People? And Auk, Owl's age, who was nephew to Gaagatade.

Of the other children who clamored to come along, Rein felt compelled to say no.

This was the tally of the People going forward: 8 hunters, 9 women, 10 children.

⋆   ⋆   ⋆

Snowshoes in the Walstyle were crucial to their progress. Without them, people sank into drifts and every footstep was a hardship.

Sleds too were a welcome change. The Walrus People used these devices made with pairs of gently curving whalebone ribs attached on a snowshoe-like frame pulled by teams of dogs.

Cookie almost fell to her knees in gratitude when she saw the men piling supplies on the sleds. Anything hauled by dogsled was a burden the women would not have to carry. Not that their packs were empty, but at least they wouldn't lug every possession they owned on their backs.

Bear couldn't help but tease his new brother-in-law, who was harnessing teams of dogs together. "How many dogs you got there, Gaagatade?" he said, pointing at the sled Gaagatade was adjusting.

"Two, two," the man cheerfully replied. Two dogs were harnessed in the lead, followed by a pair immediately behind.

"I don't know." Bear shook his head sadly. "Looks like four dogs to me."

"Two, two," the man insisted, using his fingers to point out the obvious.

"That's four, silly. One, two, three, four. Four, not two."

"Shut up, Bear," his sister intervened. "Leave my Swifty alone."

"He can't count," the boy mock-protested. "I wonder what else he can't do right."

Eider rolled her eyes. "You will never know."

"I bet you could load more on each sled if six dogs were pulling," Turtle mused, off to the side.

"The Walrus People would never put six on a sled," Bear joked. "They can't count that high. That would be two, two, and two a third time. Too confusing for them."

"It wouldn't confuse us," Turtle insisted. "We can keep track of six easily."

"Give it a try tomorrow," Rein suggested. "Some of the dogs following us could be put to work if you can round up enough lashings to harness them."

They tried it the following day, and it worked. But it didn't make sense to add more than that. More dogs didn't mean more supplies would get hauled. Because if they piled the loads too high, things fell off, and the overloaded sleds veered sideways with every bump or curve.

"Maybe if the sleds were longer?" Turtle wondered.

But Rein insisted Turtle tinker some other time. Next fall, for example, if they were through with the trek. Or the one after that.

Anytime but now. Please.

*   *   *

Maneuvering the sleds took time to learn. Gaagatade ran in front, shooing the dogs onward with a series of whistles, rasps and growls. But each sled needed someone riding on top to correct its movement or slow it down. On downhill slopes, sleds might careen into the dogs, or overtake them and slew around facing backwards. Sometimes they went so fast that the sleds began jittering and the loads started shaking loose.

Mid-sized children were best for this. Bigger ones couldn't balance on top; smaller and they weren't strong enough to hold the braking stick through the bracings, pressing it into the ground. Owl and Auk were the perfect size. But there were four sleds, so Antler and Bear, Birdy, Little Mother and Rabbit took turns as well.

The worst misstep happened toward the end of the day. The wind cut into gaps between mittens and sleeves, fur scraps and faces, chilling their hands and tempting them to shut their eyes. Everyone was getting tired. They weren't used to moving after months of the lazier pace at winter camp. Chests hurt from breathing in the icy air. Noses, fingers and toes tingled. Too tired and too cold—it was a dangerous combination.

They stayed on the flatlands as far as possible, but there were times they couldn't avoid the hills. Fierce and Cookie trudged uphill together, trying to keep their spirits up. They kept reminding each other how happy they should be, carrying such light loads up the icy slope. "Can you imagine," Fierce nudged her friend, pointing at the sleds. "With that on our shoulders, we'd be slipping downhill every step of the way."

"We'd be in a heap at the bottom underneath our stuff," Cookie agreed. "Gaagatade would be waiting up ahead with the dogs, wondering where we were."

Fierce mimed a confused lookout peering every way but down. The two women shared a laugh—a last happy note that was cut short by a sudden scream. Cookie flung her arm out, stopping Fierce in her tracks. It was a child's thin voice they heard, and it grew fainter, the longer it went on.

"That's Birdy," Cookie guessed. "She's up there on one of the sleds."

K'enemy charged past them, heading to the top. Others followed, the men crowding together at the top to peer down the farther slope.

Each sled as it came over the rise was pulled to the side to let the dogs rest. All but Birdy's sled. Her dogs had been fussing at each other most of the afternoon. They were poorly matched, one more energetic than the rest so they never settled into a pace together. When they reached the crest, one dog surged impatiently ahead while his mates scrambled frantically to keep their footing on the ridge.

Birdy tried to halt the sled by stabbing the brake-stick into the ground, but her best efforts only provided a pivot point. The back end of the sled went swinging wildly, twisting the whole structure. After a breath-stopping moment hovering on the brink, the entire assemblage went sideways, skidding and bumping down the steep edge.

For the space of a breath everything was still. And then the cry began.

*   *   *

"We need ropes," Gaagatade warned as the men joined him. He pointed down the slope. A knot of dogs, furs and lashings lay entangled below. Birdy, unmoving, was pinned underneath.

Bear began uncoiling the tether round his waist. There were more, looped around the other sleds, and they could untie the loads to retrieve those lashings if necessary.

The men knotted long lengths, end to end. The lightest and nimblest, Bear and Turtle, would climb down. Rein wound a rope around Turtle's waist. Extra lengths were draped diagonally across their chests.

Turtle stared down the nearly vertical chute, calculating. If he and Bear descended that way, most of their weight would have to be supported by the men at the top. It would be worse on the way back, hauling dogs, goods, and the girl all up the hill. But to one side there was a ravine which wasn't so steep, though the path was less direct. They'd have to tack back and forth but at least they could support most of their weight themselves.

He indicated the ravine with a wordless nod. No need for explanations.

Down they went, back and forth, with each new zag a series of steps until some change in the steepness or a deep drift forced them to zig again.

The footing was patchy, with a granular layer of snow over ice. Turtle instinctively understood the need for speed. For the injured, a long wait in the cold would do no good. On the other hand caution was wise with any untested descent.

After a time, they came to a slippery spot and decided to trace their footsteps back and go around it. Safer that way. He moved down the newer path and took several more steps, then looked back to make sure Bear was following. He stood there considering shifting direction again when, unexpectedly, one foot broke through a shelf of ice into a nothingness with no support for his weight. The sudden drop unbalanced him. He stumbled, scraping his shin and swearing. The rope held, and he was stopped from tumbling downhill, but he dangled for several wild heartbeats, arms gripping the rope overhead.

A glance below showed a steep drop-off, and for a moment he felt queasy. Above and to the side, an overhang threatened to drop an unstable load of snow, the reason he tried to veer away. Any sudden movement and the load might topple on him. That or his poor footing could easily send him tumbling down.

He took several deep breaths to restore himself. He had to pull his feet onto firmer ground. The forward foot balanced on the icy rock, but it could easily slip if he wasn't careful.

"You need a hand?" Bear offered.

"Stay there," Turtle decided. "Let me try this first." If Bear came close, their combined weight might cause the brittle ice to crack, and both would go tumbling. It would do no good, the rescuers breaking their legs at the bottom of the mountain.

He inched his dangling foot upwards, constantly rebalancing his weight against the rope. Finally he could stand upright again. Still he kept tension on the line, slowly moving towards Bear.

Carefully he veered away from the snowy overhang. Another foot forward, then one more. Now they could begin a new trail towards Birdy and the dogs.

Up above, they heard a collective sigh of relief.

"Any injuries?" Rein called down.

"We're all right," Turtle shouted, and in the release of tension he forgot all his former caution. His arm flew up exuberantly, smashing into the side of the snowpack. There was a creaking sound, and a squeak, and then the entire pack slid away, picking up speed and flowing off the edge. It was so close that it almost carried him with it. Below, the snowpack smashed at the bottom and loosed a plume of powder flying up in the air.

Turtle looked at Bear. Bear looked back, his jaw agape. "That could have been you, brother," he warned. "Good thing it missed hitting Birdy and the dogs."

"I need a moment," Turtle told Bear. "Don't follow me yet." Shaking his arms and legs to restore warmth to fingers and toes, he muttered a quick prayer of thanks, though he was usually lax about such things. Then he stood and tugged on the rope, notifying Two Stones and Bison to prepare to anchor his weight again. "All right, Bear, let's go," Turtle called out.

Inside his furs, Turtle was sweating. It was getting late in the day. The sun was sinking below the high rim of the mountain, though light lingered in the sky. At least they were nearing now. He could see that the dogs were unhurt; they just needed a firm hand to release the harnesses and keep them from turning on each other. Birdy, he couldn't see yet.

He was closer to her than Bear was. "You work on them," he called, nodding toward the dogs. "I'll go help the Taleteller."

The sled had come apart, he noticed. The whalebone rib runners skewed outward, one of them lifting up in the air. The snowshoe-like frame had split, leaving ragged edges that might not fit back together. They could rig something up but it wouldn't be as strong.

Just then Birdy made a sound. Turtle pulled himself away from his calculations to see what she needed. She was underneath some of the sacks, but they didn't look heavy. Why didn't she get up? He veered around the broken sled to approach where she lay, motionless in the snow.

"Birdy, it's me." He crouched over her. "Are you hurt?"

She looked at him, but in a foggy kind of way. "Thunder?"

He frowned. "No, silly. It's me. Turtle. Thunder's dead, remember?"

"...thought you were Thunder," she murmured, and her head rolled to the side.

She didn't look good. Her lips were tinged blue, and her hands were as cold as the ice underneath. "Birdy, wake up," he urged. Getting no response, he pinched her arm, then reluctantly slapped her face. "Birdy, we have to get you to the top."

Still no response.

The sky was beginning to darken. If she couldn't walk, he would have to carry her. But could he carry her safely up that long, jagged path with no light to guide his steps? Even tethering her to him, it was risky.

They had to leave right away if he was going to try it. Now, while the sky still had a bit of light, for the moon would be only a thin sliver tonight.

He stood looking toward the top where the People were watching. "She's hurt," he called, but they couldn't hear, so he gestured, indicating a knock on the head.

Rein gave a wide shrug, questioning him.

Turtle looked around, assessing the possibilities. It would be dangerous for anyone to climb down slope in this fading light. It was risky even for Bear, who'd already returned safely to the top. He knew the path, but he'd be exhausted and his footing unsure.

It would be dangerous to spend the night here, but Turtle was sure there'd be food in the sacks scattered around. He could wrap them in what was left of the reindeer shelter, lying nearby in the snow. It was torn but not badly. The pieces were big enough to set up an underlayer for protection from the snow along with another layer, fur-side up for warmth. The rest would go overhead, wrapping them snugly together. *Hao*, that would suffice. As long as he and the girl stayed bundled together, they should survive the night. In the morning Bear could lead the others down and bring everything up the mountain.

He gave the signal for sleep, and farewell, and they echoed a farewell back. Antler was sending blessings their way, which Turtle appreciated, knowing they were needed. Sleeping without the others was always risky. Sleeping with an injured girl brought a new set of worries.

He was clumsy pulling her onto the furs. By that time he was deeply exhausted, muscles trembling with strain and cold. But at least he didn't hit her head on anything. *Great Father!* he could cry for a warm bowl of stew, some tea, anything to revive his aching arms and legs. He couldn't light a fire, of course; it would burn the fur over their heads. It would be too hard to start one anyway without embers to spark it.

In one sack he found strips of dried, pounded meat. He put them in his mouth to chew slowly. He was still cold, and so was she, even covered by the fur. He would have to warm them both up with the heat of his body. *Guurd*, that meant peeling off her clothing, and his too. He was so tired. He wasn't looking forward to more work.

But he couldn't waste all he'd done so far, to have her freeze in the night. She was worth the effort, anyway. Without her, who would tell the stories he loved to hear? Antler was not up to it. Antler was good for many things; Turtle was ready to concede that, but not so good with stories.

Sighing, he peeled one layer over her head and another down her legs, careful not to let her head drop, though he wasn't as careful with her feet. He left only the thin innermost layer on her, then peeled away most of his own clothing. And lay next to her, remembering to take her hands and blow his warm breath on them, holding them until the sharp iciness began to recede.

She stirred once and asked for water. Oops! He was thirsty too, though he'd been too busy to notice. His water skin lay by the broken sled. Away from his body heat, the water would be frozen solid. Instead he reached outside and scooped up a handful of snow. He watched it melt into a few precious drops of water, then, guiding with his fingers, let them trickle into her mouth.

"Thank you, Thunder," she croaked, opening her eyes briefly.

"Thunder, indeed," Turtle muttered. *Guurd*, she was a lot of trouble. And such a little thing. He looked at her child's body. Not that he saw much in the darkness. His fingers were doing most of the seeing for him.

He knew he shouldn't. Touch her, that is. If his mother knew, she'd scold him something fierce. But he saved the girl's life, didn't he? He felt entitled to something. Guiltily he let his hands run up the sides of her. Ahhh, he could see her now in his mind's eye. So different than Braids' lush curves. Though he could sense the shape beginning to form. She was no longer straight as a stick. She'd be a 12 summers' girl at the upcoming solstice. He'd be sixteen himself. Twelve wasn't full grown, but it was getting there. He'd seen his little sister naked plenty of times, and she had no hint of a woman's softness.

She was kind of pleasant to look at, he decided. In a few more years she'd be womanly, maybe even pretty by then. Something began to stir inside, an odd energy, some beginning of a possibility. He couldn't put a name to it, but he felt it nonetheless.

All this scrutiny had its effect. Birdy began to shiver and her teeth chattered together. His movements lifted the coverings and allowed a chill to wash across.

He drew her close, snuggling her against him for extra warmth. It had been a long day, and a dangerous one. He could have died! And this womanchild, Taleteller, Birdsinger might have died too if it weren't for his careful work and smart thinking. He was actually keeping her alive. It was pretty amazing now that he thought about it. He smiled, sleepy and content. He would keep her safe until he could carry her up the mountain. Tomorrow for sure, unless a blizzard blew up and kept them under these wraps for another few days.

All those months spent traveling, making a name as an adult for himself, all that time when he had to be on guard, and now in one day it all changed. Something was different—better, though he wasn't entirely sure what. He gave her a last affectionate glance before closing his eyes. Just for a moment, he reminded himself, yawning heavily. Tonight he was strangely at ease in a way he hadn't felt since the great tides swept most of their world away.

⋆   ⋆   ⋆

Brrrr. She was cold. Shivery cold. She couldn't feel her hands or her feet.

Her head hurt. Someone was cradling it. "Thunder, shouldn't you be ..." she mumbled. Getting wood for the fire that must have died down, it was so cold.

Not Thunder, he said. Then who? She couldn't seem to catch the wisps of sound that were his words. Turtle? Sea Turtle? Was it a person or a spirit helping her?

On and off she sensed things, but they kept vanishing. A feeling of warmth, then nothing. Fingers stroking her hair, and gone again. There, another moment of warmth, her toes held between a set of bony shins.

More dreams, frantic and miserable. Hot flashes of pain. Blinding lights. For an eternity she was beset by those terrible sensations she dreamed of sometimes, her head banging against the rock, her spine pressed hard with too much weight pushing against her. A nightmarish wash of fear ran through her. An aching in her chest, there and there, where that wicked man squeezed her, and soreness where he slapped her face.

She must have moaned, because again she rose out of the nightmare and into the world. It was quiet here, and the ground underneath was soft and furred. Much better, lying on fur instead of cold, hard stone. Someone was holding her close and whispering, "Shhh, shhh," in a comforting way. She could feel his body warmth. His heart beat with a steady, regular cadence, and she relaxed against it, holding herself completely still. She moved closer into his arms and drifted away again, feeling safer than she had in a long time.

⋆   ⋆   ⋆

K'enemy carried Birdy up the slope the next morning over Turtle's protests. Turtle did enough already, the older man insisted; her own kin should do the rest. Without bothering to wait for agreement he picked her up, nestling her head against his chest.

He was used to hauling heavy loads for the family. It was one of the things he liked to do, offer his uncomplaining strength; one of the ways he thanked them for making him feel welcome. He often carried Trapper's daypack or part of River's load. Birdy was like a daughter to him, though he wasn't sure she felt the same. It took her a long time to warm up to him but at least she was friendly these days. He didn't mind waiting. He was, after all, a patient man.

Yet when Birdy, drifting in and out of awareness, reached her hand up and let the back of it touch his face, and whispered "Papi," even though she was probably dreaming of the father she never knew, he couldn't help the dampness that kept appearing in one eye no matter how often he wiped it away.

It must be the wind, he told himself. That constant wind was irritating. Yes, that was probably it, the wind. A nasty little spirit which would blow itself away when it was good and ready, and they'd all be happier, soon.

⋆　　⋆　　⋆

Late one snowy morning fighting headwinds all the way, ice crystals beading their eyelashes and mouths, the People stumbled into Seal Beach.

High, excited barking brought the inhabitants outside. Soon everyone crowded into the biggest shelter for introductions and hot tea.

Gaagatade had family here. "You come meet cousins," he insisted, pulling Eider to the far end of the crowd. "Hey, my Papi," he signaled Bison. "You meeting family too!"

"This is my wife," Eider understood him to say in his native tongue. An uncle made a gruff sound, reluctant, perhaps, to acknowledge a mere woman. His aunt looked sideways, giving nothing away. A cousin raised his eyebrows and growled, a noise that was much a question as comment. At least that's how Gaagatade responded. He put his hands underneath her breasts, lifting them up as if to offer them over. "Look at these," he said. "And this." He placed his hands tenderly on her slightly enlarged belly. "Already, eh? Aren't I good?"

Embarrassed, Eider whispered, "Stop it, Gaagy!"

Her husband gave her a wounded look. "I just showing you off. Always nice, make him eat his own liver." The Walpeople term for envy.

The man muttered something rude about Gaagatade being smeared with her blood.

The next thing Eider knew, he was pushing her behind him. He growled, and his arms rose outward, his weight shifting forward onto the balls of his feet. His cousin mirrored the aggressive posture, and everyone grew quiet.

"What is it," Cookie whispered nervously to the aunt.

"Is all right. For wrestling," the woman assured her. But Bison and K'enemy were checking their waist thongs, making sure knives were in easy reach.

There was a hush. Then Gaagatade issued a verbal challenge. If the cousin won, Gaagatade would stay there at Seal Beach, to be told what to do every day of his life. If Gaagatade won, Eider would get to determine the cousin's fate.

Eider took in a quick breath. "Gaage, no!" she protested. "You promised my father you'd take care of me and our baby! You can't stay here."

But his eyes were locked on his cousin. His name was Qelquyym, he who accepted the terms by slapping Gaagatade's hands.

Hurriedly a space was cleared on the floor. Cooking pots were pushed to the far edge of the hearth. The combatants reached across the gap and linked fingers together. They leaned back, weight pulling against weight. Slowly their bodies descended, settling cross-legged on the ground.

The Walmen began chanting a song about Raven watching overhead and then something about honor. The chant grew louder, then came to a complete stop.

At that moment the wrestling began.

Their fingers locked, each man pulled and jerked to try yanking the other off balance. The first to make the other lose his seat would win.

Several Walmen were already betting on the outcome. The Walwomen seemed indifferent, though they watched the entire thing. The Ogwehu were uncertain how the game was played. Nervously they looked around for clues to determine what was going on.

Qelquyym leaned back, pulling Gaage towards him. But Gaage's arms were longer and they took up some of the slack. He allowed himself to be pulled, then used the stillness of the moment when his cousin came to the end of his reach to seize the advantage and jerk him back to the center. Pulling downward, he wrenched his cousin's fingers in a painful twist.

An indecipherable insult emerged from between his clenched teeth. Qelquyym pulled Gaage back towards him.

But again Gaage's greater size kept him in place.

A small smile crept across Gaage's face. He let his cousin fling his arms around for several moments, feeding the ruse with an occasional grunt. Firelight gleamed off their sweaty bodies. Qelquyym swelled with a rush of pride, anticipating the win. They grappled, the host pulling, the guest letting himself be pulled, monitoring his opponent who was beginning, perhaps, to flag. Finally Gaage made his move just as Qelquyym allowed himself to get a bit careless. As his grip loosened, Gaage pulled his arms above his head, then over his own shoulders with a fast downward jerk. There was a wrenching sound, then a howl of pain, and the cousin lost his seat.

"I think that boy dislocated his shoulder," Falling Leaf whispered to Cookie. "Should I offer to help?"

"They must have their own medicine person," Cookie frowned. "He probably wouldn't accept help from a woman anyway."

Through the haze of the seal oil lamps they saw several people rush to his aid. Gaagatade, in the meantime, was being buffeted by the jubilant Bear and Staunch. Rein stood, worriedly, to one side.

Eider flung herself into her husband's arms. "I was so scared, Gaage! You might have lost, and then where would we be?"

"No worry, Eiderduck," he said gleefully. "I could beating him with one leg missing! I could beating him with mouth full of dinner! I could beating him ..."

"All right," she laughed, "I get it. You're bigger and stronger, and he can go soak his head in the sea. But Gaage," she pouted, pulling his arm around her, "I was so scared!"

"Not be scared, Eiderduckling. I take good care, you and," he rubbed her belly tenderly, "little baby ducky. Is good?"

"Is great! It's the best! And now I get to decide his fate, isn't that what you said?"

Gaagatade nodded, a slow grin stretching across his face. "You having some good torture ideas, my little duck? We showing him, yes?"

"Well, there is my sister..." Eider took a moment to think. All those months when her twin flirted voraciously with Bison and Turtle, and Eider felt left out. Now Swan was the lonely one. That would be fun, wouldn't it, assigning her leftovers to Swan? So that she'd know what it felt like to be last?

Yet now that she thought about it, she wasn't angry at her sister anymore. That burning anger seemed to vanish, and she didn't even know where. For the last few moons she was happy, in love. It made her sad to watch Swan seek their mother's company every day because there was no one else. Eider was caught up in her new marriage, and the only other girl remotely their age was Willow. But cozying up with Willow while handsome old Bison hung off her shoulder just added more pain and humiliation, so of course Swan didn't even try.

For all the fleeting pleasure she got having things her twin didn't have—happiness, a husband, a baby in the sheltering—she didn't want her sister to go without having them too. What she really wanted was a lifetime of sisters sharing good things. They should have husbands together. Their children should run around with each other. They should grow old together, and if one had trouble threading a needle, the other would do it for her.

That cousin of Gaage's, Qelquyym, actually he was kind of cute. Not as cute as Gaage, of course. He had that nasty Walstupie sneer on his face when they first met him. Gaage didn't do that, though a lot of the Walmen did. But now that he was hurting, the man seemed less arrogant. And judging from Gaage, Walmen could make good mates, as long as you let them know they couldn't push you around. She couldn't force the two of them to marry; her sister would have to agree to it. But she could make sure they had a chance to get to know each other.

"That's it," she announced, and Gaagatade began to translate for their hosts. "While we're resting up here, every evening he has to carry my sister to her bed. And every morning he has to get her breakfast and feed her. She hasn't been feeling well." She paused to give Gaagatade time to catch up. "Oh, and he has to let her teach him at least 10, ummm." She stopped, remembering they would not understand the number. "I mean, a bunch of words in our language. Then we'll see who's smeared with woman's blood!"

And with that, every man but the injured one hooted. The women smiled, and some were bold enough to laugh. And though many children failed to understand the gibe, they took their cues from the others and hooted at the contest, if not at anything else.

*   *   *

Birdy rose early. She still wobbled, but she felt more confident moving around before everyone else rose and crowded in. She helped a wizened Walwoman build up the fire, then fetched enough snow to melt for tea.

By the time it was steeping at the hearth, others were stirring. Birdy filled two bowls and stepped between the bedding until she reached Great Uncle in his place. Setting them on the ground, she sat at his feet. He stretched, pulling himself up to sit cross-legged. Gratefully he accepted the steaming tea from her hands.

"That smells good, Birdsilu." He sniffed the pungent brew. "Remember how we used to do this every morning?"

"Back at the hot springs cave? That was the best part of the day!"

They sipped for a while in companionable silence.

"Things sure are different now," Birdy said.

He nodded, clearing his throat laboriously. "Birdy," he ventured, peering at her. "Birdsinger. I ask you now to do something for me."

Ah, he called her by her formal name. This meant something serious. "Of course I will, Great Uncle, I promise." She might be wary when others asked for favors, but she would never be wary of him.

He sighed once, reluctant to begin.

She prodded, knowing that their time might be cut short. Cookie might need her, or River, or Falling Leaf. "Great Uncle, what do you need?"

He blinked at her, then nodded. "I want you to listen to my story. Then you can tell it around the fire circle when I'm gone."

"Of course I'll do that. I would be honored. But you'll be ... won't you ... Great Uncle, it sounds like you expect to be gone soon. Beyond."

"At any moment any of us might go Beyond," he gently pointed out. "You, I pray, not for many a summer. But for me, I can feel it nearing. My moment will be soon, child."

He noted the woeful look on her face. Her brow furrowed, and she seemed about to deny that it could be so. Not that it couldn't happen; more likely she couldn't bear it to happen. He placed a hand on her shoulder. "Birdsilu, do not fret. The prospect does not frighten me. It shouldn't frighten you either."

"But Great Uncle, we need you." Her hands pleaded with him. "Antler needs you. I need you. Don't you want to meet River's baby when it's born? We can't have any more dying, there's been too much already."

He raised his hand to stroke her cheek. So soft, so tender. She always was his favorite. "Child, I have been a lucky man."

"Lucky?" she said, startled.

"Lucky, yes. I have had a life that often seemed empty. But here at the end I found a new son to raise to manhood and a new purpose helping my People. The Great Father has given me these final blessings. So that now, whenever He is ready to take me, my spirit is willing and ready to go."

"Oh, Great Uncle!" Tears sprang to her eyes.

"And the last gift I can give," he continued, politely ignoring her desolate face, "is whatever light my story might bring. So will you tell my tale when others feel sad and defeated, or when someone needs new vigor to keep walking their path?"

To Birdy it sounded almost like a sacred story. Sacred or family story, she would tell it whichever way made sense. Fiercely wiping away the tears, she agreed. "Go ahead, Uncle. I am ready to listen."

★   ★   ★

Long ago, long ago a son was born into the hot springs cave. Fifth child of the family, he was only the second one to live through childhood. Growing up, his sister assisted their mother in her duties as mistress of the cave. His own interests ran elsewhere. He and his friend Eyas spent their days stalking fox, deer, and ptarmigan. Not just for food, but for the sheer joy of it.

To follow the animals so quietly that they never fled was to begin to know them as they knew their own brothers and sisters. They came to understand how the animals moved and fed themselves, what they feared or favored. They learned their hearts and spirits, and from there to the shaman's hearth was an easy next step.

"Eyas," Great Uncle explained to Birdy, "I followed him wherever he went. I loved him as much as I loved the animals. And maybe more than the Spirits themselves. But that elusive boy," he gave a deep sigh, "he loved the Spirits more than me."

"How do you know that?" Already she was rapt in the story, her tears completely forgotten.

"Ah," he sighed, letting the memories collect themselves. "He was the chosen one, again and again. Not even once was I. And for a long time ... a long time ..." He shook his head to clear it. His jaw tightened until he consciously relaxed it again. "It's taken me all these years to accept that it was for the best. He grew to be a fine shaman. And I got to have the pleasure of you near me." He looked back, warming her with an affectionate smile.

He finally gave up waiting to be chosen. Instead he went to live high on the mountain, far from the shaman's circle at the beach. In time his uncle helped him choose a woman to pair with, one who was capable and quiet like him.

They were shy with each other. "The dance of male and female," Trapper commented wryly. "It was a pretty slow dance at first." But they got used to each other's ways, and he came to love her quiet humor and her uncomplaining attitude. By the time she started sheltering, they were one. And he joined again the gatherings led by those who once included him.

"It no longer hurt to see them," he commented. "By then I had my own place among the People."

But that winter his wife was consumed by a ravaging that swept through the tribe. Some evil spirit passed among them. Many succumbed, and the wailings were loud in the hills. The child died inside her and she expelled it from within. The effort wracked her weakened body. "Maybe her spirit followed the baby," Trapper mused. "It seemed like she disappeared after that, though she still rose and made food for me to eat."

"But none for herself?" Birdy wondered.

"She ate too little. And some of that, she could not keep down."

She was gone, he said, before the spring.

Thus began a long period of emptiness for him. Nothing filled him, not food, not family. Not joining the men in the hunt. Not sitting on the banks of rivers, fishing. Not a cleansing ceremony made for him by Eyas-become-Falcon; that only made Trapper feel his losses more. One day he gathered his belongings. Moved into his sister's space in the hot springs cave. There, even if he felt empty, he was at least not alone.

Many summers passed. Others grew up around him, or died, or came into their own. He stayed and endured, becoming a still center of the busy cave. For too long there seemed to be little point to his living. True, he was part of a family. He held his space around the hearth. But he raised no sons and taught no one to be a man. Raised no daughters with love in their hearts. Warmed no one under his blankets, carried nothing and brought it forward to some greater purpose.

Until the cave-in woke him up.

On that terrible day he was there to gather Oopsy and poor, broken Pout in his arms when the rumblings began. And though he could not save Pout, he did save her brother. There in the rubble, he who had only chaos in his heart found order and purpose again. He who had lived in a void, could fill a void for his People. He who had no son found Antler, who needed a father to train him.

And now this work was done. He had walked the young shaman as far as he could.

"Don't be sad when I'm gone, child. When the Father takes my spirit, when my body is laid to rest in the arms of the Mother, do not grieve for me."

"Of course I will grieve for you, Great Uncle." Furiously Birdy wiped her eyes, while Trapper pretended not to notice. "All of us will mourn."

"You may grieve, child, but do not be sad. I have led a full life." He stopped for a moment to cough. "I am tired. I have completed things, and soon it will be time to go. There are rough trails ahead of us still. And if my passage in some way lightens the load, or if my leaving helps to save another, do not sorrow, for the sacrifice will bring one last smile to my face. It will be a joyous way to bid farewell.

"Never let it be said that a life is a sad one, Birdy. Because you cannot tell until its end if a person made a good job of it. Making a life—it's like making anything else—a shirt, a blanket, a fire, a shelter for your family. It doesn't much matter if you're happy every minute while you're making it. What matters is, did you make it as best you can? Did you make it well, so that it shelters others and keeps them warm through a cold winter, or gives them light to see by? When it is done, can you look on it with pride and say, I have done what I can to help my family and my People? Am I at peace with the great universe around me? Nothing else matters but that, Birdy. Nothing else but that."

She gave him a puzzled look, trying to comprehend. Storyteller though she was, there were tales beyond her that she would understand better when she was grown. "And that's why you feel lucky, Great Uncle? Even though you lost so much?"

"I feel blessed indeed, child." He sat straight. His body seemed taller than before. "You have to find that purpose and grab hold of it. There is always something around that needs building or nurturing. Healing, or mending. Teaching. There's always someone or something you can take up and devote yourself to. Find that purpose, child, and grab onto it. The rest is ashes, to be blown away by the next wind."

Birdy thought about that for a while. "I already have a purpose," she said slowly. "Mine is about keeping the stories alive."

"That's an excellent purpose indeed," he nodded. "An excellent purpose indeed."

⋆　　　⋆　　　⋆

"Yeah, those, we see them," the village elder told Rein about the clan following the reindeer herds. "No this summer. No last summer. Few many summers."

"How few many?"

The man squinted, his eyes darting around the shelter. "Maybe when he born, that few many." He pointed at a child, three or four years old.

"You saw them the summer that child was born?" Rein asked.

The man looked over at the boy's mother, holding him on her lap. "Vedeelon," he commanded. Then a quick string of words, too fast for Rein to follow.

The woman nodded and replied, her words high and soft.

The elder turned back to Rein. "She still stained with the childbirth blood when your cousins pass through."

"And nobody's seen them since?"

"Not here. Maybe at Fog." One finger flicked northward. "Reindeer heading there."

There would be many more steps in their journey, Rein thought. Still he felt a sense of relief. They seemed to be catching up. And there'd be others to ask in the next village that maybe saw them since.

"How do we get to Fog?"

"He take you." The elder indicated Qelquyym, whose shoulder was functioning now that it was reset, but whose status seemed greatly diminished.

"Stupid boy." He spat on the ground. "All upset over silly woman. He show you Fog, maybe he toughen up coming back, then be good hunter again."

"Gaagatade," Rein called out. "Would you ask your cousin if he is willing to guide us on the way to Fog?"

A quick conference on the other side of the hearth. Some vigorous give-and-take, marked with emphatic nods on both sides. A fierce crossing of the arms across the chest.

"He say, Fog, yes. But no one step more."

Qelquyym turned to stare at Swan as Gaagatade translated for him. Swan did not return his glance. She looked instead at her fingers with a great deal of fascination.

Rein would have to ask Cookie later what *that* was all about.

Chapter 2: Inside walls of snow

The way from Seal Beach to Fog took them back through the mountains instead of traveling along the shore. Qelquyym was guiding them now, and what he decided held. "Shorter, better," he explained, and though the path looked more strenuous, no one knew enough to argue. Gaagatade had never been this way. Rein did not recognize it from his journey, years ago. Only Qelquyym had traveled these hills, so he was deemed chief of the walk.

By now the days were almost as long as the nights again. Earth had longer to warm up, but they continued to suffer from occasional blasts of ice and sleet. On a morning several days north of Seal Beach a light dusting of snow began to fall. By afternoon the stiff headwind brought a blizzard upon them.

Gaagatade pulled Qelquyym up short, and they decided to set up camp. They must do it while they still could see, since the storm would likely worsen. Pulling the shelters together was tough under the circumstances. Fingers were clumsy inside mittens, but quickly froze and became useless if mittens were shed. Desperation hurried them. Even so, they had little chance to rest. Fear of what would happen to the dogs who couldn't fit inside kept the able-bodied working, heaping snow in piles they molded into walls. These would provide some protection from the wind for the animals, and for their shelters as well.

At least there was hot tea and stew when they finally retreated indoors. Food, sympathy, and fingers to massage warmth back into hands and toes, cheeks and nose.

*   *   *

The first few days of the storm went slowly. The wind howled outside, setting their teeth on edge. On the third day the wind eased, and they began packing up.

But when Bison went outside to look around, he was blown back by a fresh blast. Another storm was moving in.

*   *   *

By the fifth day they began running short on food. The long winter had depleted their supplies. Back home, by this time in the cycle, lilies and iris and other plants would already be sprouting. They could pick the tender roots or stalks, and these kept them going. Ducks would be returning from the southlands; deer and rabbits would bear their young; birds laid eggs. But here where the Sun was weaker they sat trapped inside, the winds blowing hard enough to make them lose their footing when they ventured out. Here no animals offered themselves yet; no tiny tracks decorated the new-fallen snow, and it was dangerous to journey farther out than just far enough to relieve themselves.

Rein had them pool the supplies in each shelter, reminding them to ration what was left. A handful of grains in the morning, a few shreds of jerky for each at night. Nothing should be hoarded or wolfed down in between. Trapper claimed not to be hungry, so there was a bit more for the others. Falling Leaf eventually followed his example. Next, Braids and Knick, who ate little enough as it was. K'enemy took his full portion but, worried for River and the baby, insisted she eat half of his.

By the sixth day River's baby stopped moving, and she felt great pains shooting out from her belly. Willow did what she could to keep her comfortable. Teas to give a sense of fullness. Massage for her temples, belly and feet.

At some point, though she'd been stoic until then, River let out a whimper. "It hurts so bad, Willow. I don't know if I can carry this child any longer."

Willow looked up to K'enemy, whose eyes were closed in an effort to absorb her pain. She glanced at Antler, one brow lifting to silently ask a question. Antler motioned Owl over, and urged him to fetch Bear from the other shelter.

When he arrived, flicking snow away, Antler made him sit next to River "River's afraid she's going to lose her baby, Bear. Tell her. Please."

"Oh, River," Bear assured her, regretting he hadn't spoken out before. "You don't need to worry! I've seen you in a dream. You're walking your little girl, holding her hand. You're standing in a field full of flowers somewhere on the other side. She looks like she's about 3 summers old, and you're sheltering another in your belly."

"What do you mean, on the other side?" she urged, noticing only the worst possible part of his statement. "Where is that?"

"The other side," he wondered. "I don't actually know where. That's just what I sense in the dream."

"Bear. I have to know. The other side, like, Beyond? I might be walking my little girl in Father Sky country?"

"No, no. Her cheeks are plump and rosy. There are animals grazing, off in the distance. It's somewhere on the belly of Mother Earth. But it's not around here, it's on the other side. The other side of something, I don't know what."

Immediately people began speculating. The other side of some mountain? A big river? Huge fields of ice? Something significant, it sounded like. A barrier they had to walk past. But they would manage. He saw it in his dream. People began nudging Bear and asking, did he see them in his dream too? No? How about their daughter, son, wife, did he see them there?

Never before had anyone paid so much attention to Bear and his dreams. But today there was nothing to distract them. They had worn out each other's company and were worried about surviving. His other dreams had come true, they reminded one another. Remember that beast in the meadow; who would have thought a sea lion could get way up there? And he dreamed about Antler coming to walk with them, when everyone thought he was gone.

It gave them all something new to chew over. The revelation comforted River and K'enemy. Gave them a secret thrill to know they had a daughter on the way and another child beyond that.

Mostly Bear's dream gave them all hope.

★   ★   ★

The eighth day of the storm dawned calm enough to venture forth. On empty bellies they fled this bleak spot in the mountains and trudged ahead. Luck was with them. By midday they arrived at a sheet of ice stretching as far as they could see. It was a bog, frozen flat across its expanse. Easy walking, as long as they avoided the occasional rift in the ice.

There were times they were forced to backtrack, where there was no safe passage across the rifts. But the very existence of these gullies gave them easy access to food again. Fish, teeming just below the surface of the ice. Hand-sized codfish that milled around the opening like dogs at feeding time. It was easy to scoop up several at a time, and the more they caught, the more there seemed to be.

Qelquyym and Gaagatade showed them how to catch the fish by lowering nets or even their food bowls into the slushy spaces between. They reminded people to keep their footwear dry in spite of the slush, and to stay far enough from the edges to be safe.

Qelquyym took one for himself and gave another to Swan. "Like this," he suggested, "The eyes—best part. Nibble them, so!" He demonstrated with the fish in his hands.

Swan shuddered delicately, but watched nonetheless. Fish was never her favorite food, especially eaten raw.

"You no like?" Qelquyym gave her a quizzical look. "Hungry girl eat anything."

"You're right, I should. But I can't," she protested. "Those little eyes ..."

"Here." He reached over with his hand and gently shut her eyelids, using the back of his hand so she wouldn't get a shower of fish scales down her face. He bit off a piece of the fresh, moist belly flesh and placed it in her mouth. "Now you eating."

Surprised, she closed her mouth on it and chewed tentatively. Then swallowed, opening her eyes to receive his smile of approval.

"Eat, eat," he encouraged, biting off another chunk to slip between her lips.

Gratefully she nodded, closing her mouth around it.

Sure enough, it was better when she didn't look at the eyes.

★　　★　　★

They arrived at Fog, awkwardly, in the middle of a funeral. The dogs interrupted the ceremonies, barking with excitement. It couldn't be helped, but the chaos resulted in resentful frowns on their hosts' faces. Inside, the men of Fog were solemnly dancing in a circle around the body of their deceased elder. The dancing was a sacred rite and booked no interruptions. The children outside were the ones greeting them, but their complete lack of status meant they could not even invite the newcomers in.

A boy was shooed within to ask a hunter, any hunter, to come and speak for the men. One of them finally emerged, pulling his paarka over his head. The man was scowling with the impertinence of it—sacred rites should never be interrupted, and certainly not the funeral rites of their chief—but his face softened when he saw the mass of people and sleds strung out in a line. Visitors, after all, were rare.

"*Aiyiyiyiy!*" he cried, slapping Qelquyym on the mittens. "Who we here?" They conferred, naming each of their ancestors for many generations back. Finally Qelquyym introduced Rein with all the traditional greetings.

"Visitors, visitors," the man called, leading them indoors. The drumming ceased, and people surrounded the newcomers. There was no room for them all, so after an abbreviated welcome, everyone except for Rein, Gaagatade and Quelquyym were led to another shelter and given food while they waited for the ceremony to conclude.

The women told them that the body of the chief would be taken by sled to the Edge of the World and deposited in the sea. Three hunters would accompany the sled, and would not return until the sea gave them something of equal weight or merit to bring home. Two of the hunters had already been chosen. The third one had not yet been decided upon.

And if the Walkers wanted to leave at the same time, travel would be easier, following their trail.

"You!" their new chief shouted, once the ceremonies concluded and the evening meal commenced. He was pointing his finger at Qelquyym. "You from Fog! Your mother, cousin to old chief! You be third hunter, go with sled to Edge and come back with blessing from Great Spirit!" His eyes gleamed fiercely. His gravelly voice allowed no argument.

"Me?" Qelquyym looked around, bewildered. "I'm not from here. I live in Seal Beach. You have me confused with someone else."

One of the bypassed hunters was emphatically nodding. "Ah, very good. He definitely best choice."

"Absolutely," agreed another man, relieved to be staying home. "Look, he has big muscles, strong!"

"Qelquyym, Qelquyym!" the Walmen cheered. He was taken aside, protesting, stripped of his clothing, ritually combed of body lice, painted with circles and other symbols on his chest, genitals, and face, and otherwise made ready for the pilgrimage.

Which made Swan break out in giggles for the rest of the day.

★   ★   ★

"The Edge of what?" Rein asked Gaagatade, later. "I don't understand what he said. Do you know anything about this?"

"Means, Edge of Everything. Edge of the World. I not sure meaning. You, Qelquyym?" He poked his cousin in the side, switching languages. "You know this Edge of Everything place?"

"I have no idea where they're taking me," he complained. "Maybe they'll dump me off a cliff into the ocean. I told you I didn't want to go one step further than Fog."

"He no know," Gaagatade translated. "I ask Foggers for you."

Later the new Chief of Fog came to visit Rein, chief to chief. "You know of the Narrows?" He spoke exclusively in his own language once they were done politely discussing their recent travels, and giving greetings from cousins in the settlements to the south.

"Narrows?" Rein tested the word on his tongue.

"You know the land turns east from here, and gets narrow with ocean on each side? If you go far enough, it is a land of white bear and walrus. No People live there. There is a place with hot pools of water and islands of ice. Occasionally a herd of reindeer run over the whole thing and disappear from sight."

"We're looking for a herd of reindeer, actually. I wanted to ask you about that."

"Reindeer? None here now," the man warned. "But sometimes we see."

"We're looking for a herd that might have gone by. There's a tribe of our cousins following them." He pulled open the neck of his parka to display his shoulder tattoo. "They'd have this on their arms, like me. You ever see anything like that?"

The chief stared for a long time at the marking. When he looked back, he was frowning. He slapped his arms in front of him. A deep growl escaped. "You leave tomorrow," he abruptly announced.

"Tomorrow? Actually we were hoping to rest up for a few days."

"Be gone by first light." And he turned away, ignoring them for the rest of their time at Fog.

"You better do some asking around, Gaagatade," Rein worried. "All of a sudden their chief hates us, and I don't know why." He shook his head, puzzled. "We have to know more about that herd and where they've gone. Doesn't make sense to leave until we figure out which direction they went."

"I finding for you," Gaagatade promised. "Me and Qelquyym, we ask."

★   ★   ★

Just as he and Cookie were getting ready to sleep, Gaagatade approached. "Is too late? I go now, you asking."

"No, no," Rein reassured him. "I'm glad you came. Did you find out anything?" They were whispering, both of them.

He nodded. "Daughter Stealers, the chief call your cousins."

The fire sparked up, and a popping sound broke the silence. "*Our* cousins, Gaagatade," Rein reminded him. "You're one of us now."

"Our cousins," he agreed. "These reindeer-followers, he call them Daughter Stealers. Cousin people come through, few many years past. When leave, he daughter missing. Where she go? Hunters follow trail. Catching up, look in shelter. She inside! Like Eiderduck, she find handsome man like me and grabbing him."

"Handsome, you say?" Rein raised one eyebrow, amused. "All right, go on."

Gaagatade grinned back. "Handsome man, beautiful girl want him. Papi mad, say come back home. Girl say she wanting reindeer life, no like walrus meat life no more."

"Bless her bold little heart," Cookie interjected. "I'd make the same choice."

"She no come. Papi all grumpy. Now nobody talking her to his face. When he away, young men talk."

"Daughter stealers, that's what he calls us? He shouldn't hate us. We didn't do anything, it was our cousins. Of course, maybe to him it's all the same." Rein frowned.

"Mmmmph," Gaagatade commented neutrally.

"That's probably why he wants us to leave right away, before we steal anybody else. But this End of Everything, what's with that?"

"Qelquyym ask hunters, where you taking me? They say, Ice not real settlement, Ice just hunting camp. Many days north and east from Ice is Edge. More land but sometimes waves cover it, sometimes not covering. Edge of Everything, for sure; beyond that, the Narrows and sometimes they disappearing."

"Waves, eh? How deep do you think it gets there?"

He shrugged. "Who know? Sometimes maybe water to here," he pointed mid-thigh. "Sometimes here," indicating his ankle. "To here sometimes." His hand hovered above his head.

"That doesn't say much. Except maybe if you time it carefully, and Father Sky gives you enough days without a storm, you can walk across. But, here's the thing, across to what?"

Gaagatade shrugged. "He say, foggy there, no see much. But that's last place they see reindeer cousins. One dry day reindeer running across, cousin people follow."

Rein thought for a long time. "I think we'll have to have a council about this. But I'd like to take a look." And he sent Bear and Gaage to remind everyone to be ready to leave at first light.

*   *   *

They rose early and hurriedly left, following the tracks of the Walhunters. It was a clear morning, the sky so blue it hurt to look up. Sunlight sparkled off the ice underfoot. Birdy squinted frequently, and whenever they stopped, she closed her eyes for relief.

The Walhunters moved faster and ranged further ahead. Once, climbing an ice-ridge, Bear saw Qelquyym off in the distance looking back. Bear waved, using big arm movements to catch his attention. Qelquyym tentatively returned the gesture.

Bear reported to his sister, teasing. "He waved at me. I don't think he noticed you at all."

"If he was looking this way, I doubt it was you he was looking for," Swan said haughtily.

"Oh, it was me all right. I could tell by the way he grinned." Bear pretended to consider the notion. "You know what? I think he likes me better than you."

She sniffed.

"But I could probably convince him to turn his attentions on you. If you're nice to me, of course. Yup. I could have two Walbrothers if I don't watch out. Gaagatade and Qelquyym." He rubbed his face, brushing away the accumulated ice-dust. "Boy, I'm a lucky guy. Some people go all their lives without a single Walbrother, but I think I'm gonna have two of them."

"Lucky!" Turtle called out, joining the fun. "Sure wish I had one myself."

"You just have to work harder, Turtle. For some, these things take time. But if you ever get to be smart and handsome like me, maybe you'll get a Walbrother for yourself someday."

Turtle batted his eyelashes and preened. "Like this? Would that do it, you think?"

"Oh, shut up, you guys," Swan said crossly, pushing past them to walk ahead.

⋆   ⋆   ⋆

In the way that council circles went, this one was relatively easy.

Rein spoke first, once they finished the evening meal. "I know you're all tired, and you probably don't want to sit around talking all night. Some of you know why we had to leave Fog so soon. They call us Daughter Stealers there, because the daughter of their chief ran off with one of our cousins and he blames us for it. Maybe all he could see were these eyes and noses like our cousins', or our height. Maybe he figures we stole Braids and Knick; I don't know. But either way we were not invited to stay. We had to leave without deciding where we're going next."

An uneasy murmur went around the circle.

Rein raised the talking stick, reminding them he had more to say. "At least we found out a few things. Gaagatade, you want to tell everyone what you learned?" He handed off the stick.

"Our cousins," the newest member said, pausing until Rein nodded his approval. "From Fog to Ice, many days walking across ice bay. Then many days across hills from Ice to End of World. Walrus hunters see them run after reindeer, down the cliffs to sometimes-under-water land, falling into sea. Hunters not seeing them again."

Two Stones asked for the stick. "Did you say, falling into the sea? Is the land falling into the sea, or did the people fall into the sea? Do they think our cousins are still alive?" Gaagatade shrugged. "Not knowing."

"Could we ask those two out there if they know anything more?"

"They not seeing; other hunters seeing these things."

Fierce took the stick from her husband. "If the land actually falls into the sea, our cousins would have turned back before it was too late. Would the Walhunters see them if they did?"

"They go for hunting, not watching after cousin people like little childrens."

Rein lifted his hand, and the stick was passed back. "There's no way to tell if they actually crossed this passage and survived, or if they turned around and came back. Reindeer are smart. They would turn if they came to some impassible place. So most likely our cousins are alive somewhere. But where? That's why I wanted to have a council, to decide what to do. I don't want to blindly keep going when there's a chance it's the wrong way."

K'enemy reached across, asking for the stick. "Let's go ahead. I believe in Bear's dream," he announced, and River, recalling the vision of her child in a field of wildflowers, nodded unblinkingly beside him.

"You believe me?" Bear said, wondering. Up until recently everyone ignored him whenever he mentioned his dreams, except for his friends.

Two Stones picked up the stick. "I believe in Bear's dream too," he agreed.

"Are you sure?" Rein's eyes darted around, seeking confirmation.

Staunch signaled, and the stick passed to him. "I think someone would have seen the cousins if they came back this way. Seen them hunting, or come to trade with them. But no one has, not for three or four summers. Have faith in your son, Rein," he encouraged him. "He had a Father Sky vision. You should trust it like the rest of us do. Isn't that right, Antler?"

"Father Sky has blessed him," Antler agreed.

"We will follow Rein," Staunch announced stoutly to the entire circle. "We follow Rein to the other side."

"Then we go tomorrow," Rein decided, since no one else asked for the stick. "At least we'll go and look it over. We can't tell much of anything without taking a look."

"We go to the other side," Two Stones agreed stoutly. "Whatever that might possibly be."

"To the other side," Bison cheered, and gleefully punched Turtle in the shoulder.

"To other side we going," Gaagatade agreed. And he gave Qelquyym a pleased glance, which his cousin seemed reluctant to meet.

★   ★   ★

Several days of hard travel took them the rest of the way to Ice. There they camped out, resting for a time, mending harnesses and lashings, catching crab and fish and smoking the excess over the fire. Gaagatade and the Walhunters speared a seal and they feasted that night, stuffing themselves silly on the fresh meat.

Then they began another long trek through more rolling hills. Their path wound around, first more northerly than they wished, then more easterly, but the Walhunters assured them they were heading the right way. Yet there was one location in particular that they seemed eager to avoid. When Antler and Rein heard about it, they asked why. "Many hot, stinky water," Qelquyym warned them, his voice full of foreboding.

"Could slipping in, make drowned," Gaagatade added.

"Many bad spirit live there," Qelquyym complained, and made a series of gestures to ward off misfortune.

"A lake? A hot spring?" Antler tried to clarify. "Warm water to bathe in?"

"I'd love to bathe again," Cookie said. "We've been filthy so long, the lice think I'm their central fire circle."

In spite of their misgivings, Rein convinced the hunters to lead the People to the mysterious waters. Antler would do special prayers to keep the bad spirits away. Bison was still weak and he needed to soak in the bubbling waters. The springs would be good medicine for Qelquyym if his shoulder went out again.

Clouds of steam obscured the valley as they approached from the hills above. A thick layer of snow covered the gently rolling slopes. The dogs went charging ahead and the children steering the sleds had trouble keeping them under control.

As they neared, the valley floor flattened out. There, snow covered every inch to an abrupt drop-off into the bubbling springs. There was no bank to sit on, though there were islands in the middle. People would be able to linger there, cooling off from the heated waters, but to get there they would have to swim or wade across.

As they descended towards the valley floor, some began running. Men and women shed their loads, shucking off parkas, leggings, and footwear in their eagerness to scrub themselves clean.

Oopsy wanted to be first, but Birdy held him back. "Wait until I make sure it's safe," she told him. And though Turtle beat her into the water and was daring her to join him, she carefully put one foot in, then her lower leg.

It was shallow in places. Men and women bobbed up and down, splashing each other, scrubbing at stubborn patches of dirt on faces, hands and necks. The steam made them sweat even as the freezing air around them chilled the tops of their damp heads.

Children shrieked excitedly, making snowballs and pitching them onto the islands to melt. Lynx and Oopsy jumped in and out of the water, laughing at the impressions they left in the snow. Their new friend Auk was reluctant to join at first, but he put his feet in, then hopped back and forth, making footprints in patterns that paralleled the stream.

The only ones who refused to join the joyous hubbub were the Walhunters, restlessly pacing nearby. They muttered, eyes darting around, wondering at the wisdom of the Walkers and whether they would survive. For most of the afternoon they huddled together, and approached only if they needed to speak to someone in the springs.

Eider tried to entice Gaagatade in, but he fended her off with jokes and excuses. Swan managed to get Qelquyym to remove his footwear and put a toe in, but he jerked back, surprised at the sting of the heat. He watched fearfully, not trusting that she would emerge unscathed. Eventually she got him to submerge both feet up to the knees, and he actually left them there for a while.

Everyone else was bubbling, exuberant in the carefree pleasure of this extraordinary place. From a deep state of contentment in the middle of the stream, with his naked wife bumping up behind him, squeezing and rubbing his tired muscles, Rein surveyed all that surrounded him and declared they would stay and rest for a day. No, he decided, two days.

Actually, he concluded, let's make that three.

He knew he'd never get his people out of there until they had their fill.

Chapter 3: Watching the tides

Step after laborious step brought them through the snowy hills to the last height overlooking the ocean.

This close, the wind was a constant murmuring in their ears. Over that, the sounds of gulls crying in triumph, the exaltation of whales breeching the surface of the water, the cries of seals and walrus readying to give birth. As they descended, the constant pulse of water against rock became like a heartbeat, and brine coated their lips.

There was little beach to gather on. Sand was scarce and the thin shifting shelf was too narrow to hold them all. So they set up camp in the black cliffs instead. From there they would watch for storms.

Peering down, Rein saw a shallow drop-off under the surface of the water. Later the tide would recede and they would see how far they could walk, but for now it was water-washed.

"Didn't our Dehsda brothers know the pattern of the rise and fall?" Antler asked.

"Yes. But we here are mountain people," Rein reminded him. "Sagye had little need to understand the tides."

"Might be useful to figure out how high the water gets," Turtle mused. "I could put a stick in the sand when the water comes up the beach. Then we could see if it gets higher or lower tomorrow. We could put a stick in the highest place every day."

"And we'll see when it gets to be highest and lowest in the cycle of the moon," Antler added, excited. "Falcon used to do that."

"So if we choose a walking-across-the-waters path, we can start off on the lowest tide," Turtle agreed.

"Good idea, guys," Rein affirmed. "Very smart. Go ahead, Turtle, you're the chief of that."

Turtle took off, scrambling down the cliff.

"We may only be mountain people," Rein said to Antler, "and not as fine and fancy as our Sagueo cousins ..."

"...who have mostly passed Beyond," Antler reminded him.

He nodded. "But we can still learn and do what they did, even if we never did it before."

Yes they could, Antler thought. Teaching sometimes happened even when the teachers were no longer there. All that was needed was a telling about it, and someone patient enough to cull through its wisdom.

"Ho." He looked up at his chief.

Rein glanced at him, startled. Somewhere inside him things seemed to settle, and his face slowly cleared. They were learning; they were maybe even prospering, and his People did not regret the places he led them. He nodded at Antler gratefully. "Ho," he agreed, "indeed."

★   ★   ★

The Walmen were in no hurry to return to Fog. They held the final funeral rites the day they reached the Edge, calling loudly to the Great Spirit. They festooned their leader's bound body with kelp and feathers, and carried it down to the beach, letting the tides tug at it until it drifted out to sea. But then they lingered with no apparent purpose. They were not actively looking for the thing of equal weight or merit to bring back to Fog, most likely a cache of whale meat or walrus. They were simply sharpening their weapons and looking off in the distance as if waiting patiently. But for what, Rein wondered; for what?

The two from Fog spoke none of their language, though Qelquyym could understand simple conversations by now. The Walhunters took turns edging near enough to observe everything the Ogwehu did. To listen to the rise and fall of their voices, and perhaps intuit any change in their plans.

Though Qelquyym seemed more often to edge toward Swan, who was only occasionally near the Ogwehu hunters. And she went out of her way to walk along the periphery of camp whenever she saw him nearby.

"Maybe they were asked to keep an eye on us," Two Stones said to Rein.

"Their chief didn't trust us," Rein agreed. "He may have told them to make sure we leave like we said we would."

"We could hold a really long council and invite them," Staunch suggested, an amused gleam lighting his eye. "They won't understand a thing we say. It'll bore them silly, and make us seem real considerate at the same time."

"What a devious idea, Staunch," Rein commented dryly. "You may be developing a knack for leadership."

"I guess I better watch out then," Staunch drawled. "Some day, if I'm not too lucky, you guys might ask me to put it to good use."

Two Stones rolled his eyes. "May Father Sky keep the Sun from rising on that day," he muttered. "May I be off on some long expedition, far from camp."

Yet Staunch's plan was exactly what they ended up doing.

★   ★   ★

They would leave in a handful of days, they decided around the circle. Go just as the tides were dying down, assuming they had clear skies and no storms blew in. They'd seen the path, and they knew they could walk far out into Ocean. And if the reindeer could cross over, so could they, who carried provisions with them.

They would carry extra water, for they could not drink from the sea, and who knew how far it would be to the next river or pond.

They would stop once a day to make a warm meal, but could nibble from their daypacks anytime.

"Meanwhile we can fish and hunt," Bison suggested. "Gather more provisions for the journey."

"And sort through our things," Cookie added. "We should lighten the load so we can go faster."

"Won't the dogs carry most of it?" Falling Leaf asked.

"Do you see any snow beyond the Edge?" Two Stones pointed out. "The tide melts the snow away. The dogs can't pull a sled if there's no snow to pull over."

"It's getting warmer," Rein reminded them. "We can leave a lot of our furs behind. We'll have to trust Mother Earth to provide these things when we need them, next winter. Wherever we are, on the other side."

"We need to have faith," Staunch agreed.

"That's always a good idea," Antler commended him.

By now the Fogmen were growing restless. "When you go," one of them thrust into the silence.

"We leave when we leave," Fierce said crossly, refusing to speak their tongue. "What do you care how long we stay?"

Of course they ignored her, being a mere woman.

Rein, diplomatically, responded in words they could understand. "On the next low tide with good weather. And you, when do you leave for home?"

"Soon," the man replied enigmatically.

Rein stroked his chin. The Walhunters were not helpful, but perhaps he could squeeze something useful out. "Have you ever seen anyone come through here?" he asked. "Gaagatade said neither of you were at the Edge when our cousins came through, but have you ever seen anyone else go this way?"

Surprisingly one of them nodded.

"Well," Rein coaxed him. "You know this land, and we are strangers. We would like to hear more."

The second man whispered furiously at the first, who used the back of his hand to wave off his advice. A heated conversation ensued, ending with the second man crossing his arms and staring up at the smoke hole, wanting nothing to do with the first.

"A man come through." Gaagatade leapt in to translate, since the story came out faster than the Ogwehu could follow. "He all by hisself. Not cousin to you; some other kind of man. I hunting with father and uncle there," the man pointed down the beach. "See him, but he don't seeing us. He stumble off rock, fall into icy crevasse." Gaagatade glanced over at Eider, who sent him an encouraging smile.

"We pull him out. Shake him. Try talking him but he no know our words. He shivering. We peel off clothes and pee on him to warm him up, set him next to fire. Cover with furs, give him hot to drink. We say, who you? Where coming from? Live at bottom of sea? He just shaking head."

The Fogman paused, giving Gaagatade a chance to catch his breath. "We bring back to Fog. One day he say few words, draw with stick in sand, then we hearing story."

At the first mention of story, Oopsy brightened and poked Lynx in the side. Birdy, who was braiding cordage, let it drop so that she could listen closely.

"He say his people hear, good hunting grounds on other side of Edge. Some Peoples go there, few coming back with reindeer, saying very nice. They wanting to see. They get ready to go when sky quiet. But part-way across, big storm come up, sudden. High ground here and there but no time to go back. Big wind, big rain, big, big waves flooding sand. Everybody look for rock to hide behind, some no finding. Wave hit, pulling little ones from mamma's arms. Babies screaming, then quiet. One man try to get baby, wave washing him away too.

"Some tie to rock with ropes, but big, big wave come and smash rock against rope, all break apart. Waves so big, loops of rope float off and carried away by ocean. Finally sea calm down. This man untie self and look for others, but only see bodies floating in the waves.

"He think, throw he self in water with them. What good, living with no People? But then he think, no, warn others. So he come back. We find and bring him to Fog."

"What happened," Little Mother asked. "Does he still live with you?"

"He leave one day, no say goodbye. We don't know where he go. Now my brother here," he pointed to the other man, "he say chief say no tell you. But I say, ocean-man say warn others, Great Spirit let him live to telling us so we warn Peoples, we should do this warning thing."

Rein looked worriedly at Two Stones, who turned to Bison, who looked at Antler.

"Ropes," Bear immediately suggested. "We should tie all of us together."

At the same moment Turtle called out, "Ropes! We better bring all our ropes!"

The two of them looked at each other and laughed at the coincidence, which was maybe not a coincidence. Both knew from experience, after all, how a secure line could keep people safe.

A rope for each person, lashing them to a rock—clearly that would not forestall the anger of a violent sea. But if each of them were tied together in a long line of the People? And if the line of the People, in the event of storms, was tied to the rocks, or to any trees they found? So that they all were each other's rock, and beyond that they found whatever additional anchoring they could?

It might just work.

Something had to. Because, after all, Bear's dream let them know there was reason to have faith.

Chapter 4: Water washes our feet

They rose that morning aware they were beginning something momentous. Everything was prepared the day before. Anything that could be discarded was left. The Walhunters would take whatever they could use, leaving the rest for any who wandered by.

Every waterskin was filled. Each person carried a supply of food, easily at hand. Ropes were readied—one very long lashing looped around each person binding them loosely in line, shorter ropes draped over shoulders for use in time of need.

Antler smudged them, praying for safety, endurance, and strength.

Two Stones held a position of honor at the front, with Bison immediately behind. Mindful of the responsibility, he picked his way down the hillside, going slow enough that even Oopsy found his footing, though Poor Thing would be carried the entire way.

They wound their way down to the sea, this line of brave ones, with their leader staying at the end so he could watch over them.

"You may be the first among us, Chief," Bison teased him. "But here, on the rope, you are last."

"Leadership," Rein responded mildly, "often comes from behind."

*   *   *

The way forward cut across a stony, beach-like terrain. During high tide, the swath narrowed because so much was submerged. The land remaining was cut by streams or lagoons, higher and broader where there were hills, sunken elsewhere and obscured by tidepools or eddies. But on this day, with the tide low and promising to stay that way for days, the footing was solid, though soggy.

"It tickles," Birdy said to Willow, walking on sand that sank under her weight.

"I know what you mean," her friend agreed. Already dampness entered through a worn seam in her footwear. "It feels like the water is washing my feet. At least we have sunshine today. It's not so cold as it was."

She was right, Birdy realized. The days were growing longer and were often sunny. They still shivered without their parkas, but the snow disappeared, and ice was melting everywhere.

They had only been walking a short way when they heard a shout from behind. Birdy looked back, checking first on Oopsy and Lynx.

That young Walhunter Qelquyym was running towards them from the mainland. He carried his atalaatl and a spear pointed down for safety. A small carrying pack bumped against him as he ran.

He caught up, running past the rear where he could have stopped to speak with Rein. He passed his cousin Gaagatade and the Walchildren who were now part of the People. Ran until he reached Swan, taking her by the arm and swinging her around to look at him.

This action made the entire line came to a halt. They were not yet accustomed to walking, hooked together, and people bumped into each other all morning long. Stopping someone in their tracks as Qelquyym did, was awkward; it puddled them all together and they couldn't help but watch.

"Swan-girl," Qelquyym greeted her tenderly. He blushed, seeing the eyes on him, and began whispering fervently in her ear.

She whispered back, frowning at the curious faces around them. Edging close, turning her back, she continued, her finger entwining itself in the neck of his parka.

By this time Rein reached them, dragging the line with him. "What's this," he asked gruffly. "Qelquyym, why did you stop us? Do you bring news?"

Qelquyym hurriedly unfurled himself from Swan. Clearing his throat, squaring his shoulders, he squeaked out a heartfelt request. "Sir, I go you?" His hands pointed to himself, then circled, including all the People.

Rein stood there scowling. Maybe he should have expected it after watching them together, but he didn't. They'd spent a long time making plans. Who would lead, who would follow; how much rope was enough, and how many torches. The food was packed; the line was set, and now they were supposed to add someone new? Why didn't the young fool ask when they were still figuring everything out?

"Papi," Swan implored, seeing his frown. "We can always use another hunter, right? He won't be a burden; he's strong and capable. Please, can he come with us?"

His mouth set in a frustrated grimace. He hated being surprised like this. Another hunter would of course be welcome. He could help feed the others, and it wouldn't be hard to insert him somewhere along the line. In fact he could squeeze in right there in between Swan and Cookie. Bear could move back just a bit, and things would even out, pretty much.

But what about the men from Fog? Would they care if Qelquyym left their People? They already regarded the Ogwehu as Daughter Stealers. Now this son would be lost to them too. Would they chase after their kinsman, and an ugly fight break out?

He called Gaagatade over for his opinion. "They too scared," the young man guessed. "They no like water-walking, just like they no like water-washing. They no like Edge place, only come special time, too much water all around. They leave when see us going."

It seemed likely. At the hot springs, most of the Walmen refused to bathe, though Auk was coaxed in, and Qelquyym himself survived a footbath.

"You don't much like the water either," Rein reminded him.

"But I have reason to follow you." He pointed to Eider, then nodded towards his cousin. "He have reason too."

Qelquyym waited with a pleading look in his eyes, arms tucked behind his back. Gaagatade questioned him in their language, and he responded briefly.

"No worry, chief. He conk on head," Gaagatade reported. "Use his long spearblade and go *whomp!*" he mimed using the flat of the blade, "*One! Two!* each one, then running here. They no wake up, long time."

Rein nodded gravely. It might lack subtlety, but it sounded pretty effective. He might actually come to like this fellow, Qelquyym. Cookie seemed to approve, judging by the grin on her face. Swan frowned at his hesitation. Nobody else protested. "All right," he tentatively concluded, "I don't see why not."

Qelquyym nodded gratefully. He turned back to Swan and asked the same thing he asked her father. "I go you?" The identical question, but his tone shifted subtly.

"You mean, you and me?" Swan's hand circled between them. "You and me, together?"

He nodded briefly.

Gaagatade broke in. For his cousin to join their journey was one thing, but this looked like something else altogether. He himself had to get adopted in, with all kinds of preparations before he could even think to ask her father formally about Eider. Flushing with embarrassment, he spoke to his cousin in a frantic mixture of languages. "You asking to marry her? You cannot doing like that! You have to be part of these Ogwehu, you have to asking her Papi. It's a complicated bargaining, you doing all wrong!"

Eider placed a restraining hand on his arm.

Gaagatade looked at her and hurriedly reined himself in. "All right," he mumbled, and then brightened as a new thought entered his head. "Actually I could probably adopting you myself. I now big man of the People; I can do these things. Then you, Qelquyym, be my son, sort of. And you be," here he chortled, unable to hold back a surge of laughter, "grandson to Bison. Bison, a granddaddy! Hoo! Wait till I tell him the good news, who's going to be grandpa! Bison, you hearing all these things?"

Eider gave him a quelling glare. "Don't embarrass him," she whispered fiercely. "Don't you mess this up for my sister."

Qelquyym looked at Swan beseechingly, his question still hovering between them.

Swan looked at her mother, who flashed a contented smile. She looked at her father, who was assiduously studying the clouds on the horizon, careful to give no hint of his feelings. Because he was beginning to admire the young buck, but he didn't want to make it easy for him. Joining them on the journey, hao, that was one thing, but not his daughter, not yet. Surely they understood it would take more effort. Letting Swan catch his eye right then would make everyone think he approved of the match. The young man should make up his mind to come with them or not without knowing for sure about marrying her. It might be a long journey ahead of them yet, and if the fellow was weak-willed, better to leave him back.

As for his daughter, well, he had a tough time saying no to her, but it wouldn't be the easiest pairing, she and this Walhunter. Harder even than Eider and Gaagatade, who seemed to fit right in. Qelquyym was prickly with that Walhunter pride and stubbornness, and who knew if he could treat a woman with respect? Swan would have to push to make it happen. At least as much as her sister did, a few months before.

Staring at her father, she finally dragged her eyes back to Qelquyym. Silently she nodded. But then added in an undertone meant only for him, "You're still going to have to ask my father, Qelcu. Hey, don't look like that; at least he didn't say no."

The young man grinned, relief plastered all over his face.

She smiled back. The two of them stood there, grinning manically, holding hands.

"Hooey, I'm gonna have a son," Gaagatade cheered, and Bear gave him a congratulatory punch on the arm.

"All right, folks, we have to keep moving," Rein urged them. "Let's put some distance between us and the shore. We don't want those Walhunters coming after us in spite of being scared of the water."

The line opened up to include the newcomer.

"Hey, Bison," Gaagatade called out. "You grandpapi, and you not even married yet."

Bison strutted, just a bit. "I'm so virile," he bragged playfully. "I'm a granddad already!"

"But we see who has little babies first," Gaagatade hastened to add. "You or big man, me."

"Maybe me," Qelquyym said, attempting to join the easy flow of banter in spite of his tentative grasp of the language.

"You? Having children with who?" Turtle asked, just now joining them, having been completely absorbed adjusting the lashings up and down the line while everyone else listened avidly.

Bison rolled his eyes. "Who do you think?" He nodded at Swan, who pretended to ignore them.

Turtle followed his glance. "Oh," he said. Realizing finally why Swan stopped flirting with him and why she got up the other day when he sat beside her to sit next to that short Walfellow. Why she smiled so much these days, even when there was no good news. "Ohhhh," he concluded. "So that's it."

All this excitement kept them moving a long distance that day.

⋆ ⋆ ⋆

Gradually the land rose high enough that the ground under their feet was dry. Here they saw snow again, and ice remained in the crevices. Wind whipped their faces and roared in their ears, and everyone's cheeks were raw.

From high ground they could see the sea pressing down from the north. Blocks of ice smashed up against the shore with every pulsing of the tides. To the south there was ocean again, but it was less ice-strewn, with seals and walrus congregating on the sands.

Now a whisper passed down from the front of the line. "Listen, flowing water ahead!"

There was a trickling sound, so welcome as their supply was running low. There, where the land began to lower downhill, it bubbled out of the earth. A small spring, but when K'enemy, in front, reached down to capture a taste in the palm of his hand, he found it clean and sweet

They crowded around, bending heads to drink, flicking the traces laughingly at each other. A fresh supply just when they were beginning to worry. Just as they began to speak about rationing the remaining provisions among them, or turning around and heading back. "Thank the Mother," Staunch nodded to Antler. "She's taking care of us, just like you said."

The spring cascaded down and into the river below. Or so it looked—a river separating the land as it ran across. It was a wide and rock-strewn waterway, cutting a deep swath as it rushed fiercely past them. Turtle, Bison, and Willow clambered down the hillside. They'd unhitched themselves from the line when they filled their waterskins at the springs. It was such a pleasure to move at any pace they liked; move without pushing or bumping into anyone.

Turtle reached the water first. "More to drink!" he exulted, and leaned his head down for a taste. Immediately he spat it out. "Pahh! This isn't river water; it's Ocean!"

Ocean, cutting its way through this shelf of land. Not river, though it looked like one, finding its way to the sea. Ocean cut a pathway from north to south, completely cutting off this land that they stood on from the land they saw across the way.

The flow was rough and wide, rushing across boulders, pouring down the waterway. They would have to ford it somehow. Someone had to explore a safe crossing.

Turtle backed away and began pulling off his boots. Placing them carefully on a dry outcrop, he picked his way barefoot over the rocks until he stood in the water. The others watched him attempt to cross, bobbing higher when he stepped onto a tall underwater boulder, lower when he could not find footing. Then he sank precipitously, flailing his arms for balance. He struggled to keep from being swept along.

Bison picked up one of the loose ropes. He wrapped it around his waist, sprinted several paces ahead and flung it in the water. It floated just beyond Turtle's grasp, but he kicked in that direction and grabbed on. Let his feet float free before reaching arm over arm to pull himself back on land.

"Thanks, brother," Turtle panted. He shivered underneath his wet parka. His teeth chattered and his lips turned an interesting shade of blue. Fierce draped furs around him, and wrung water out of his streaming hair.

"No problem," Bison said carelessly. "I thought about letting you go downstream by yourself, but then I thought, why should you have all the fun? Next time you go for a swim, invite me."

"Yeah." Turtle tilted his head, hitting his ear repeatedly to clear the water out. "Next time I probably will."

★   ★   ★

They had to find a way to cross; otherwise they would have to turn back. Because there was no direct path around this area where the sea had somehow eaten up the land.

They tethered Bison with a rope looped around Two Stones, Staunch and Gaagatade. Turtle and Bear began chanting, "Go Bison, Go Bison," but Rein quashed that.

"Don't distract him, boys," he scolded. "Just watch. He's doing a difficult task; don't make it harder for him."

In the water Bison made slow progress using his walking stick to test the bottom. Occasionally a particularly strong pulse of the tide forced him to hunker down and wait, though the current was mostly steady, this far from the open sea.

Now he dropped and almost lost his footing, but he regained it and turned to grin at them. He moved higher, climbing onto a shelf of rock. Lower again, then veering at an angle. Straightening until he reached the other side.

He emerged from the water, twisted around and raised his walking stick high in triumph.

But that was not the end of it. He marked the landing with stones, then reentered the water, retesting each step until he came back to them, marking the path in his mind so he'd be able to lead them safely across.

Though not yet. In fact, maybe not until tomorrow. He was soaked through. His skin was frigid, and a deep shivering set in. The men were keenly punching him on the shoulders but the women pushed them aside to tend to him. Fierce and Falling Leaf pulled off his sodden clothing. Birdy and Willow fetched fresh water to rinse the salt residue away. Braids and Knick surrounded him, one on either side, keeping the chill off his nakedness while River and Eider found a dry parka and leggings to wear.

Turtle, Bear and Antler placed rocks on the sand leading to the inlet, neatly lining up the first stone with the spot Bison entered the water. The next was positioned across from where he found a stone shelf to stand on, midway across the passage. The third indicated the landing where he had to angle in another direction. The last was lined up with the place he climbed onshore. These marked the way so that they would not lose themselves when they all crossed.

Over breakfast the following morning the men confirmed their plans. They would station the strongest men like boulders on either side of the water, and in the middle: Two Stones at the starting point, Gaagatade on the rock shelf. Staunch, halfway between the rock shelf and the far side, making a mid-point to secure the longest part of the passage. Bison on the far shore. The rope holding them together would be a handhold for everyone else. The rest would be roped in their usual line and would move carefully across. The littlest ones—Poor Thing, Oopsy and Lynx—would ride on people's shoulders or backs, for they were too small to keep their footing.

The first ones to enter the water gasped at the chill. But they moved forward nonetheless, stoic as was their way. They would build a fire ahead, they knew, or walk quickly to warm up afterwards.

Swan stumbled on the way to the rock shelf. K'enemy caught her elbow and kept her upright, the rope holding taut while she struggled to balance on the uneven floor of the sea.

By now the head of the line reached the other side, though Rein, in the rear, was just putting his feet in the channel.

Turtle, carrying Lynx, was almost to the shore. Behind them were Auk and Owl, followed by Bear carrying Oopsy on his back. Oopsy was thrilled with the luxury of being carried, something they rarely did otherwise. The child kept pointing out things he was interested in—a hawk soaring in the sky, the way Auk's head bobbed in the water—which left him dangling too loose for comfort. "Hold tight, Oopsy," Bear reminded him several times, but the reminders only helped for a few moments at a time.

From atop Turtle's shoulders Lynx called to Oopsy, "Look at me. I'm almost there!"

"Come on, Bear, go faster," Oopsy urged. He was bouncing on his cousin's back, rocking his body and only loosely holding on.

Behind them, Falling Leaf suddenly tripped and lost her footing. Her feet were pulled from under her by the current. Her head and shoulders rammed into Bear, hitting him just below his waist.

"Sorry." She managed to set her legs back underneath her. Bear regained his balance quickly, but Oopsy tumbled off and was twisting in the surf, tied only by a single rope wound around Bear's waist. The rope was tight when they started out, but Oopsy had apparently kicked it loose.

The end unwound even as Bear grabbed for it, and Oopsy was carried away by the current.

"I didn't mean to!" Oopsy cried before his head was pulled under the surface.

Qelquyym, already onshore, saw the danger first. Like all Walmen, the water made him nervous. But surprisingly, he managed to live through his first soaking in the hot spring. And he'd survived crossing this stretch of ocean water so far. Now sweet Swan's little cousin was in danger. Maybe this was his chance to prove himself to his new People.

Hurriedly he slipped out of his rope fastenings, bounded across the rocky shore and into the water. He plowed through the surf, awkward but fast. The waters, gray and merciless, pulled harder here. Oopsy's arm was visible for a moment, and then only the back of his head. He choked on a mouthful of air, shouting before disappearing under the surface again.

Qelquyym was closing in. He reached in the water to grab him but came up empty-handed. He ran in an arc around the boy, turning to catch him as the tide surged. A wave lifted the child right into his arms, looking like a gift from the sea. He hauled him up on the bank where Bear joined them.

"Oopsy, what were you doing? I told you to hang on. You could have died there!" Bear scolded, fierce with the knowledge of what might have happened.

"I sowwy!" Oopsy sputtered. "I didn't mean to!" and so on until Birdy came over and took him in her arms.

"Stop it, Bear!" Birdy was indignant. "Don't yell; he just had the scare of his life."

"If he hadn't kicked the rope off my waist, he would have been fine even falling in the water." Bear was equally indignant. "If he hadn't kicked the rope off my waist, he would have been fine, even falling in the water," he fumed. It wasn't easy.

It wasn't easy carrying a squirming child across that treacherous divide. They would probably blame him for almost losing Oopsy. Or at least for being careless, for tying the rope too loose.

"Next time tie a second knot on top of the first," Rein suggested, putting a comforting arm around him. "It's better to take more time and make sure he's safe. You just can't trust the whims of a child."

No one else berated Bear. They were too busy complimenting the newest member of the tribe.

"I thought you didn't like the water," Swan murmured, standing at his side.

"Didn't," he agreed. "Not like. Water make people gone."

"Then you were especially brave," she said, her eyes shining with pride. She hugged one of his arms tightly against her.

He beamed. Though he didn't have the words to say so, Qelquyym knew that his actions this day made him one of them. Even loose of the rope he felt tied to them in some new and deeper way. And apparently they were beginning to feel the same towards him.

★   ★   ★

Birdy was sick of walking behind Swan and Qelquyym. Her cousin kept rubbing up against him, murmuring things that made him blush. He deserved it, of course, for saving Oopsy's life. Not everybody would dive in like that, seeing the danger, and deciding immediately what to do about it.

It reminded her of Turtle, she admitted reluctantly. She knew she should do something to thank him for saving her on the mountain. But she couldn't imagine falling all over him like that. It would be completely embarrassing, she thought with a tinge of disgust.

"Too gushy," she chided her cousin after yet another sappy compliment.

Swan turned around, aiming an acidic glare at her. "He saved your brother's life! Of course I'm grateful, and so should you be!"

"Do you have to be so drippy about it?"

"Pffft," she said dismissively and clutched his arm against her.

Maybe Swan was right, Birdy thought disconsolately. Maybe that's exactly what a girl should do if a person saved somebody's life. Turtle saved her, and what did she do to thank him? True, she was dizzy for days afterward, not back to her usual strength even yet. Still she should have done something. Because things, she suddenly realized, were out of balance. She had to do something special. But what?

She understood the idea of haodisah; she'd heard it all her life. But she had little experience feeling the balance or doing what was needed to shift things back into harmony. She'd lived most of her life, after all, in a family that lived distinctly askew. Mami had her own sense of balance, Birdy figured. She kept a careful equilibrium with the rest of the tribe, making sure that people paid well for her services—a fresh caught rabbit, for example, thanking her for an afternoon soaking in the hot springs—but within the family things were completely akilter. Or Birdy would have spent a lot more time pursuing the pleasures other girls were allowed at least occasionally to enjoy. So she understood the idea of the balance between things; she just didn't have much experience living with it.

That evening she asked Great Uncle to teach her about haodisah. He told a long story about the beginnings of the world, how there were lightning storms and volcanoes, and no good balance between Sky and Earth until the very plants and animals began to complain. How Mother Earth and Father Sky gradually learned to respect one another and live in greater harmony, and how each who lived between them had to learn the same.

"So if something happens," she asked at the end, "like if a man saves a girl's life maybe, and the girl who was saved forgets to do something nice back, then it's like not respecting him?"

"Well, it's not respecting the great deed, or his courage, whatever he did that was out of the ordinary," he said thoughtfully. "If what he did was easy, then things are not very far out of balance. The girl should do something, but it doesn't have to be much. But if it was extraordinary, then I'd say the girl owes him something big, don't you? Something that has about the same effort behind it, or the same importance. It's like the Walmen who give their chief's body to the sea, and have to return to the community with something of equal merit or weight."

"I guess," she mumbled, feeling worse than ever.

"But it doesn't have to be done right away," he comforted her. "These things can work themselves out eventually. There may come a time when the girl's help is needed and she'll be glad to give it. Your grandmother took me into the cave when I needed a new hearth, and I repaid her by helping your mother over many a year."

But Birdy didn't feel right letting the indebtedness linger. She didn't want to restore the balance by being nice to Turtle's children; she wanted to do something now. The sense of imbalance weighed too heavily.

Cookie, overhearing, proposed making a special feast. "You're talking about Turtle, right? He likes his food, he does. You can make him some flapcakes, or some of those ptarmigan cooked inside the leaves, he loves them."

"But Aunt Cookie, that kind of food isn't available here," Birdy protested. "We have plenty of kelp and dried walrus meat with us, but that isn't very festive."

"You can tell him what you want to do once we settle down somewhere. Go tell him now, Birdsilu. You'll feel better, I promise."

But that didn't seem quite right either.

The next day she and Antler were walking near the back of the line. They had just finished practicing a story. He had the cadence nice and smooth, and there was nothing more to go over.

So she veered onto the question that concerned her, without a thought that he might misunderstand. He was, after all, their shaman, not just her friend. If anyone could help her figure it out, it was him. "I need to ask you something, Antler."

He felt a quick rush of affection. "Ask whatever you want, Birdy. You know I'd do anything for you."

"It's, well, what do you do when someone has done something wonderful, like saving your life? How do you thank them? Because I have to make things hao again with this person, but I don't know how."

Something wonderful, he thought, for someone who saved her life. Was she trying to thank him, Antler? In a way he saved her life. Finally being able to tell stories was wonderful; she told him almost every day. That alone will make her life extraordinary, he thought with satisfaction.

Without him she would someday die, worn out in the usual ways of childbearing, hunger and disease. But because of him she would live forever, her words passed down as long as there were tongues willing to repeat them. And now she wanted to show how grateful she was. What a sweet nature she had. Every month she grew dearer than before.

"Oh, Birdy," he said modestly, "you don't really need to ..." There he stopped, feeling suddenly self-conscious. The look on her face was not what he expected. It was not the look of his young friend, Bear's girl cousin. It was the look of a woman staring boldly into the eyes of a man. It made him aware of things he never considered before. It was a grown-up look, and grown-ups had responsibilities, and measured each other by how they carried them out. Grown-ups had to choose for life, and the wise ones chose their companions based on things like that. She always liked him, he reminded himself. She'd shored up his weakness, and never let him down.

Perhaps they were young to make this choice. But they were not too young to feel a connection that might hold them together across a lifetime. "Oh, Birdy, you don't have to do anything," he murmured, looking down at the ground. "It's not necessary. You know it was the right thing for everybody. No special thanks are needed."

She gave him a confused look. "But if somebody pretty much saves your life, don't you think you owe them something? Because you wouldn't have a life without what that person did for you. And if you don't do something, doesn't that show disrespect, and break haodisah, because things are out of balance?"

"Well, yes," he conceded, secretly pleased she felt that way. To expect a present for what he did, that was too much. But he was human, and a child yet himself. Presents did not often come his way. And for her to recognize the imbalance when it seemed so slight, because she paid him back every time she helped him practice his own storytelling, so for her to go out of her way to do something special . . . He could hardly wait to see what kind of present she would give him. Something precious, no doubt, like the golden amulet he gave her. "What I like to do," he added cautiously, "is to pray for the right thing to come to me. The right idea, maybe, or the object itself. I keep a lookout for something perfect for the person I'm thinking about. Like that," he indicated, nodding at her pendant.

Birdy fingered it thoughtfully. "And the right thing just comes to you?"

"It always does," he assured her, a gracious smile on his lips.

"Thanks." She was silent for a long while, though her step was lighter than before.

*   *   *

Birdy slept that night between Oopsy and River. She was restless, her mind churning as it mulled the possibilities. When the sky began to lighten, she slipped out and started rummaging through her belongings, taking everything out of her sack.

"What are you looking for, Birdsilu," River mumbled sleepily.

"Antler said I'd know it when I saw it," she replied. It wasn't anything obvious, like giving him one of her furs. And it had nothing to do with that leaf-wrapped object that still made her shudder when she touched it accidentally, with its faintly acrid smell even this long after K'enemy put it in her hands. Instinctively she flinched away, her lip curling in disgust. The package was important. She had no intention of throwing it away, or casually leaving it behind. Someday she would open it up and remember what she had to, and do a cleansing ceremony or something. But not now. It felt too raw and she wasn't ready to pick at that scab. She thrust the thing back inside and moved her hand away.

Finally she felt it at the very bottom of the sack. The little package Mindawen gave her. She held its small weight in her hand for a moment, closing her eyes and breathing the fragrance of home. She didn't know what was inside, but it was time to find out. The image of Mindawen was comforting. She was probably living in some warm place now, where the trees were green already and the fruits starting to ripen. She raised her finger and pointed toward the south. And knew, somehow, that Mindawen was thinking about her across the distance with the same love and longing.

She let her fingers pick apart the leaves rolled around it. Oh, look. There were two little figurines carved of a fine grained wood. One was shaped like a bird, for herself. The other, the fish Mindawen was named for.

Birdy held the precious carvings, remembering the times they spent together. Sitting side by side at a full moon ceremony. Swimming in the creek. Picking whortleberries, each of them sneaking enough to make themselves sick.

She would keep the Mindawen carving, she decided, but give the Birdy figure to Turtle. It wasn't much, but the carving meant a lot to her. It came from their old home, and the things were few and precious that remained from there. He could keep it as a token. He'd saved her life, after all, so if anyone should have it, it was him.

Later, when Turtle came down the line securing the rope around everyone, Birdy stopped his hand. "I want to thank you, Turtle. I need to thank you for saving my life."

"Oh, of course." He said it lightly, but he paused, preening at her words.

"Please, take this." She tucked the figurine in his hand. "To mark the memory of it."

Antler, positioned just ahead, turned around in time to see Turtle hold the carving up to the weak light of this overcast day. He stared for a moment at the figurine, then looked at Birdy, whose attention was entirely focused on the other young man. His eyes moved to Turtle, who did not notice his hurt and puzzled look. Turtle was absorbed, inspecting the workmanship, turning it around in his hand.

He seemed uncertain for a moment why Birdy would give him such a thing. A tiny little bird, Turtle thought at first; a kind of doll, not really something for a grown man. But the carving was nice, he supposed. Suddenly he felt Antler's eyes on him.

He looked up, taking in the wounded look on the younger fellow's face. Antler wanted Birdy to give the carving to him, he realized. Now why would the shaman want such a thing? Would it be useful in some ceremony or another? Did he admire the skill? Or, hmmm, was it that it was a gift from Birdy, and he wanted it for himself?

"Thank you, Birdsinger," Turtle said, seeming to realize its value at last. He looked back, a triumphant gleam on his face. "A token of you. I will put it somewhere special. Yes," he agreed. "I certainly will treasure this."

She restored hao, Birdy thought to herself, watching Turtle insert himself back in the line. That was a good thing, right? She glanced ahead at Antler, puzzled now at the look of raw hurt he wore. That *was* a good thing, right? Suddenly she wasn't so sure.

Things seemed so much simpler, at the hot springs cave. Not that she wanted to be back there. But at least that old life was easier to understand.

*   *   *

A storm was coming; they saw it in the darkening of clouds over the next several days. They smelled it on the breeze and felt it in the rude gusts of wind blowing through the openings of their furs.

Rein was looking for a place to weather the storm: A cave or an outcrop big enough to keep them dry, or at least some flat ground. Unfortunately they were walking along a mass of cliffs rising from the sea, and the slope was so steep and sheer that few trees or shrubs flourished. They kept moving, their steps precarious, hoping the terrain would improve. They asked for help from the Great Mother, but nowhere found shelter to keep them dry.

By the time the rain began pouring down in cold, heavy sheets, they could delay no longer. They had to secure themselves to keep from being washed down to the sea.

They wouldn't be able to get to the top of the mountain; they tried, and found the climb too treacherous. Instead Rein chose a narrow ledge about a third of the way down that offered some shelter from the wind. It was far enough from Ocean that even the tallest waves would leave them untouched. There were cracks in the rockface, and crevices here and there, but that could not be helped.

Turtle and Two Stones went up and down the line making the rope knots secure. Bison and Gaagatade tied additional cords around people, anchoring them on outcrops and stable boulders wherever possible, rubbing each other's cheeks and bellies for luck.

As the crack of the first thunderbolt reached their ears, the men fastened themselves within the line. They passed blessings down from Antler and Trapper, with words of encouragement for all. Some reached for their amulets and stroked them for whatever reassurance they gave.

Birdy sat with Antler on one side, Bear on the other when Turtle wedged himself in. "Here," he said to Birdy, "do you want to sit under my arm?" He held it up so she could take cover under the cape he wore.

"Oh," she hesitated. "No, that's ... thanks but no," she said shyly. "You'll get wet yourself." She could see that, by letting her share the garment, his belly would be exposed to the rain.

"I don't mind," he insisted.

She thought for a moment. "Maybe if it gets cold, later?"

Later. That was good, Turtle thought. The longer the rains went on, the more she'd need him to warm her up.

Antler frowned his way, but he was too busy protecting the coal to argue, Turtle happily noted.

People shouted to one another when the wind grew quiet or the rain let up. Mostly they were silent, huddling under their furs, yet comforted, remembering they'd withstood worse.

Turtle offered shelter and Birdy refused it again, but when he raised his arm once more she changed her mind. Gratefully she pulled herself inside the nest his body made. She fell asleep for a time, huddling in his warmth.

A loud cracking sound made them both startle. "What was that?" she asked, and he looked around but saw nothing.

Bear pointed up the mountain where a lone tree rooted in the bedrock of the slope. Rainwater worked its way down the trunk. Now the rockface was cracking where the tree rooted, and threatened to split apart.

Was the tree endangering them, looming overhead? Nobody was directly underneath, but it might not tumble straight downhill. Rein shouted to Bison, and he and K'enemy unknotted themselves, crab-walking uphill to investigate. Turtle watched, hastening to explain what he could to Birdy. The men came back. Evidently they decided no one would get crushed if it fell. Rein was the nearest, but it looked like it would miss him.

Rain fell in relentless torrents broken by bouts of nerve-shattering thunder. Below, the water whipped into a furious froth.

Birdy settled back in the crook of his arm. She was so young, Turtle reminded himself. He found himself thinking of her often. The smell of her hair. The feel of her body pressed into his side. Would she share food with him, would she smile if he did this thing or that for her? The sound of her voice telling stories over the night fire. The teasing memory of her shape in the darkness the first time he held her close.

They were both half asleep when another loud cracking sounded.

It was hard to see anything clearly. Shapes loomed—the pitch black of the mountain, a faint outline of its cone-shape against the sky. The rare star shining through a temporary hole in the clouds overhead. Turtle looked down to see if she was all right. He touched his finger to her face, then pointed up the mountain. "The tree, remember? I think it's cracking apart."

"We're not in danger, are we?"

"Shhh. Nobody is underneath. I think we're safe."

But another tremendous crack followed. They felt a deep rumble, followed by lightning that lit the entire mountain, blinding them for a moment.

The fierce power of Sky drew them together for the sheer animal comfort of another warm body, knowing they were at the mercy of forces completely beyond their control. Pulling her hand in, which she'd left outside earlier, to play with the raindrops, Birdy now placed it, trembling with cold, against Turtle's bare chest. He allowed it, though he grimaced at the first shock of contact.

"You're freezing," he said.

"I would be if it weren't for you," she admitted. "You saved me again."

He nodded, wordless. He wanted to say something to impress her, but anything he thought of sounded stupid. But he was happy. It could have been worse, he thought. Things could definitely be worse.

Another lightning bolt struck, followed by a deep series of cracks and rumblings. They felt the mountain itself tremble underneath them. Turtle looked at Birdy, who frowned. The entire mountain shook beneath them, and a series of terrifying sounds—rumbles, cracks, vibrations, and thuds—ensued.

They looked up towards the damaged tree just in time to see it jerk forward. It tumbled down the hillside, carried along on a massive chunk of rock, slipping and falling towards the sea.

"Uncle Rein!" Birdy called out. "Great Uncle!" for he too was near the end of the line.

The rope uniting them suddenly strained downward. Next to them, Antler disappeared, and beyond him they could not see. They heard screaming, then felt another jerk. Now there was no more tension on the rope, and the sounds ceased altogether. Which was more frightening, even, than the screams before.

⋆   ⋆   ⋆

Qelquyym was dozing when he felt a sharp tug on his waist. Swan and everyone beyond her were being dragged away, and the rope around his middle was digging in so hard that it cut off his very breath. He was getting pulled downhill with them, but the lashing snagged on an uneven outcrop of rock, and now he couldn't see Swan at all, though she was probably still attached.

In the panic of the moment he could hardly think. All he knew was that he couldn't catch his breath. He had to breathe, but he couldn't seem to, not with that rope binding him so hard it felt like he was splitting in two. He opened his mouth but couldn't get any air in. His knife, he had to get his knife. His hand moved by long habit to the waist thong. Where was it? Hurry!

He was gagging for breath, and his vision starting doing funny things. He grabbed the blade with one hand, groping for the rope with the other. Applying knife to lashing, he began sawing away, putting pressure on the *guurdish* thing. There, it's fraying apart. Wheezing, he could get a bit of breath now. Keep sawing away, good, there's another strand gone. One more to go. There it goes!

A deep rasp inward. Breathing never felt so precious to him before.

He began to notice things again, especially a slithering sound of something dragging down the rockface. Followed by the most horrible noise he'd ever heard—Swan screaming his name, her voice sounding far away.

The rope. In order to breathe, he cut the rope. The rope that held them all together. Oh Great Spirit! what did he do?

★ ★ ★

For a few moments after he stopped falling, Rein knew nothing. Felt nothing, heard and saw nothing but emptiness around him. Then his eyes opened with the urgent need to figure out where he was. Even in a state of shock he knew people depended on him. Even if he couldn't remember who he was or what happened, he knew he had to figure it out soon.

Things came back in focus, one at a time. He was lying on top of a rock pile; he could feel the sharp, unyielding edges pressing into his buttocks and back. He was surrounded by stone, partially buried, and more weighed down his legs.

He tried lifting his head, but dizziness prevented it. He let eyes and ears explore instead, still painful but not as bad. There, yes, the sounds of Ocean, he could make out the crash of waves breaking against the rocks.

His face was clear, at least. He could breathe. He could see, too. At first he thought he couldn't see, but his eyes were open; there simply wasn't much light. It was either just after sunset or just before sunrise.

Rock pile. Rockslide, that's it; that's what brought him down. It made an island of boulders, separated from the black mountain by a small span of ocean running fiercely around him in tremendous, stormy waves. A constant rain spattered his face. Wind gusted about, whipping up the water. It muffled any voices he might otherwise hear.

Rein, that's who he was. Runs like Reindeer, son of Thunder in the Sky. Leader of those who were left of the Sagye Ogwehu, he recalled. His People whom they now called, simply, the Ogwehu, since the few Dehsda survivors chose to go South. He wondered who led them now, and if they were somewhere safe.

Safer than he was at this moment, probably. Lucky them.

The rest of his people, where were they? He looked around, noting the pain and deciding to ignore the sore back of his head, the throbbing ache in his thigh. That old man over there seemed familiar. Right, that's Trapper, testing himself for damage. There he went, over the edge of the rockpile towards the channel of ocean.

Trapper was extending his hand toward a woman, who? Something Leaf. Falling Leaf? He's helping her out of the water, and just beyond, Swan was scrambling up on her own. Good. His mind was working again, that was a blessing.

"Papi," his daughter cried. "Are you hurt?"

"Of course he's hurt," Falling Leaf said dismissively. "Look at him, lying under all that stone!"

Trapper began pulling rocks off, and Swan tossed them in the water, all but the heaviest, which they pushed to the side. Trapper moved carefully as if he was wounded. Falling Leaf had scrapes and swellings, and Swan had a long, bloody cut down one of her legs. But they were alive, that was lucky. They could have been killed, tumbling down the mountain.

Falling Leaf began prodding him as more was uncovered. "You may have a break here, Rein," she warned, probing his thigh. She pulled at the leg, maneuvering it right and left. Rein gritted his teeth, letting her concentrate without distraction. "Not quite a break," she concluded. "That's good. But we should wrap it for support. Fortunately some of my bundles followed me." Rein smiled faintly; his was torn off in the slide. Neither Trapper nor Swan's had theirs either.

"Give me some help, Swan girl," she ordered, and Swan helped lift the soggy pack off her shoulders. Falling Leaf rummaged inside and pulled out a baby seal skin, the fur scraped thin, as well as several lengths of cordage. She wrapped the hide around Rein's thigh, signaling Swan to hold it tightly while she looped the lashings, securing it in place. "This won't make it all better, Rein. You should stay off the leg for several days. Half a moon would be better. But I know you," she said, holding up her hand to stop him from protesting. "You're going to want to get us off this ugly black mountain. So if you have to, you can move, but let the men support you. We should rest and let it heal as soon as we can find a good campsite."

He looked at her weather-lined face. She was a survivor, with her gritty tongue and her wide trove of healing lore. She had nursed many a wounded hunter, and, though few of them relished being in her care, most of them endured, and lived to tell the tale. If he wanted to survive, if he wanted them all to survive, he should try to heed her advice. "Tide's coming in," Trapper warned them.

A new worry. This little rockpile was barely above the waterline. If the rise came fast, they would soon be adrift.

And even if the rising tide came slowly, every battering of the waves shifted the new-fallen boulders. They should leave, even if it risked his leg. They ought to leave right away. Before another shifting dumped them into the frigid sea.

They needed to cross the narrow channel, and climb up the sheer face. If they could wait long enough, help would come in the form of strong rope and muscles. But he didn't want to risk the wait.

Immediately ahead was a big obstacle. How could they get out of the water and onto the mountain? They might find footing through the tides, but there was no easy slope to climb anywhere within reach. Too steep, too sheer, as far as he could see. Hmmm. They could climb onto the mountain if they could get just a bit higher, he decided. There was a ledge about a man's height above the waterline, just beyond, and the slope was slightly more forgiving above it. But they'd need a firm place to stand on in order to reach it. If the footing wasn't there, how would they pull themselves up?

There was no telling, from the look of it, if there was a chasm or a seafloor below the water's surface. Yet looking in either direction, there was no other obvious place to mount. They couldn't withstand being submerged in the freezing water long enough to pick their way across to a better landing spot. Falling Leaf and Trapper were the oldest members of the tribe. And him with his hurt leg? The frigid water might numb the pain, but the cold would sap his strength, and he would need every bit of strength to move toward safety.

Argggh, the pain. It was intense, but he had to ignore it. He couldn't give in. Giving in might mean death, not for him alone, but also for the others with him.

"Grandfather," he said to Trapper, calling him by the title of greatest respect. "We need to cross right there," nodding to the spot under the ledge, "but I don't see how we can do it."

Trapper thought for a long moment. "Let me test the footing. It looks deep, but maybe there's something to stand on." Though when he tried picking his way across, there was little to support him.

"Can the three of you shift some of these rocks there, and make a platform for us to climb?"

Trapper looked at the women, who both nodded. "Let's get to it, fast," he urged. The tide was rising, threatening Rein. Another wave rolled in and the rock-island shifted again. Rein dropped lower with a sickening lurch, the waves now lapping him. The sky was lightening. They could see far enough now to notice several of the men making their way down the mountain toward them. But would they arrive there in time to help?

"Go, go," Rein urged. So Swan picked up a large stone, lugged it towards the ledge-place, and dropped it in. It disappeared without a trace into some crevasse under the water.

Trapper and Falling Leaf began tossing rocks in as well. But when Trapper put his foot in, he was no closer than before.

"Should we wait for the men?" Swan worried.

"Can't," Falling Leaf said. "There's no time."

"I could lift him," Trapper suggested, a doubtful look on his face.

"You?" Falling Leaf snorted. "He's twice your size. He'll have to support at least some of his weight himself."

Another surge washed one of Rein's supports away. He flailed, trying to stay above it, but the water tugged at him, and the current pulled him off balance. He yelled out, and succeeded in getting their attention. He was holding onto a boulder with his head and shoulders above the water, but the rest of him was floating sideways, at the mercy of the cold, grim sea.

The three rushed back to rescue him. Swan got there first and hoisted an arm over her shoulder. Falling Leaf did the same on the other side. They got him upright, with only one muffled gasp of pain. The going was awkward, and the women stumbled trying to keep their balance.

Each of them was shivering. Swan could no longer feel her feet. They had no more time for debate or experiment. "I will wedge myself in the water," Trapper shouted as they neared him. He pointed to the place they had pitched the rocks. A few had fallen against each other under the surface, catching them in place; if he shoved his feet between them, it might be enough to hold him steady. Risky, but what else could they do? "Swan goes first. She can stand on my shoulders and haul herself onto the ledge. Rein goes next. Falling Leaf can boost him from below while Swan pulls him up. Falling Leaf will climb up last. From there you can wait until the men reach us, and you can rejoin the People."

"What about you?" Rein asked. "We can't pull you up without some kind of boost."

"That's right."

"You'll be washed away on the tides," his nephew warned.

"Do you have a better plan?" Trapper asked mildly.

Rein closed his mouth with a sudden, helpless thud. Even after praying for the help of the Mother, he could not think of anything better. Not without chancing all their lives. And they couldn't stay in the water; there they all risked death.

"Sometimes, my son, you have to make the hard choice," Trapper quietly reminded him. "Sometimes a sparrow must die in order to save the nest. Sometimes the old sacrifice themselves so the young ones can fly onward."

"I'd rather find a way to save all the sparrows."

"You cannot always save everyone."

Rein shook his head, trying to think. He did not want to leave Trapper, the last of his generation, behind.

But the very next washing of water made their footing shift again. Swan stumbled, which made Rein lurch forward, taking on a mouthful of water before Falling Leaf grabbed him and helped him up.

"This sparrow is ready," Trapper said firmly. "There is no time. We go now, while we can." And he moved boldly towards the cliff, crossing the few steps to wedge himself in place.

Swan, following, shifted gingerly along the rocks, her arms lifting to keep in balance. "You have him?" she asked Falling Leaf, nodding at her father. As soon as the woman gritted her teeth and nodded, adjusting herself under his weight, Swan went ahead. She mounted Trapper's shoulders, his arms helping steady her. As she moved, she leaned to touch her rain-pinked cheek against his. "Thank you, Grandfather," she said solemnly. "I wasn't always the best to you, but I thank you and honor you."

"Go forward in good health," he said. "Be strong. Raise your children wisely and well."

With Swan secure above them, Rein hesitated, but finally he sighed and did as planned. Tears in his eyes, he clapped him on the shoulder. "We will not forget you, Grandfather."

Trapper, legs immersed in the cold, was grinding his teeth to keep from shivering so hard that he'd shake him off his shoulders. So he merely nodded, though he watched Rein with affection and dignity.

Falling Leaf boosted him up, one hand under Rein's uninjured thigh, the other supporting his bottom. Rein was sweating with the pain, but he made it. She waited until Swan got him settled as far back as the ledge would allow. Then she clambered onto Trapper's shoulders. His shivering worsened but she kept her balance. She took a moment to thank him. He unclenched his teeth long enough to say, almost ceremonially, "It is an honor."

Swan tried to reach her hand down, but the gap was too wide. The men above were getting closer, but were still too far away to help. Trapper's lips were turning blue. An incoming wave smashed against him, cresting to his chest. He almost lost his balance. Clearly he was close to the end of his strength. He did not even bother lifting an arm to try meeting hers. Instead he called out one last request. "Remind Birdy of her promise," he shouted, though his voice was weak and the words could barely be heard over the sound of the rising waves.

"What's that?"

"To tell my story when I am gone."

"Hold on, Great Uncle!" Swan called out, looking over her shoulder. "Qelquyym is coming! He can help us pull you up!"

"Tell Birdy," he said firmly.

A young falcon circled overhead, watching from on high. An oddity, for they had seen no falcons for months. Trapper lifted his head to catch a view of it. Watching him, Rein saw his shoulders relax. His features eased, and an almost joyous look settled onto his face. A wave smashed against the cliff, pulling his feet from their footing, and he was washed by the current sideways along the channel. Trapper's parka snagged on a sharp spit of rock, and for a few moments he was adrift in a narrow gap not too far away. "Tell Birdy," he repeated, his voice echoing faintly back to them.

Qelquyym was coming hard and fast down the mountain, followed more cautiously by K'enemy and Bear. Seeing Trapper in the water, Qelquyym slid down the final section and landed on his feet, thigh-high in the waves.

"Wait, Qelquyym! Let's tie this tether around you," Bear called out, and K'enemy was already flinging a rope, but the young hunter would not pause for his own safety, not even for a moment. He did not hold back in spite of his distrust of the water.

"I get him," he yelled over his shoulder. He had, after all, saved Oopsy just a few days before.

But the tide was crueler here, and the edge of open ocean stretched out endlessly before them. A fresh, stiff wind blew in, and the wave rolling toward them hit the rock where Great Uncle was snagged. The force of the tide rolled him under, then lifted up and smashed him against the black cliff. Qelquyym was caught too, and dragged under the surface. The next pulse tossed him sideways, hurling him with great force against the mountain. His body folded oddly and sank under the water. As long as they looked, they saw no sign of either one again.

A high keening came from somewhere. Falling Leaf reached over and placed her arms around Swan, folding the girl into her breast. She blocked her from seeing anything further, though the small glimpse she'd had was more than enough. It would likely stay burned in her memory forever.

"Two gone," Rein whispered, looking in horror from the ledge. "Two," he hesitated, and then gave them the highest accolade he knew. "Two great hearts, gone. May the Great Father bless their pathways Beyond."

⋆   ⋆   ⋆

They continued forward over the next half moon, stopping long and often to let the healing settle in. Yet the mood was severe and many faces were blank with the effort to hold something back.

Until they stopped for the first time, setting foot on a new land. At the time, it looked much like every other place they stopped to rest, after crossing yet another inlet of ocean cutting between soggy, eroding places on the sands. But it turned out to be the last such crossing. Later, all such streams were sweet water rushings, not salt or brine. And the land gradually rose and dried, becoming more solid and welcoming, with plants and creatures that could sustain them.

And on a day that started out no different than the sad one before, Bison scouted a single track, and then more, the four-footed creatures whose sign they sought. K'enemy discovered several two-footed tracks amid the four-legged ones. And Rein gladly set them to follow this new direction rather than the way they were heading before.

Though they did not reach this long-awaited herd of cousins and creatures for several months, there was new hope that evening around the campfire.

Oopsy, Lynx and Turtle called for stories. And so Birdsinger began a telling, a new one she was devising.

"Long ago, long ago," she began, and they settled in with the sound of her voice. "Long ago our People lived on a Southeast-facing shore.

"There was a mountain at their backs, and they hunted through its meadows and streams, or fished and gathered from the sea below. And in the middle, between ocean and mountain, was a cave with a hot springs to bathe in, and a beautiful woman lived there, tending the cave.

"Now this beautiful woman lived in the cave with her elders, her sister, and her children. There was food enough for all, and the People were happy.

"And yet the Earth, Great Mother to us all, was not content, for She wanted Her children to come together, the ones who lived by the sea, and the ones who left many seasons before, to follow the reindeer in their tracks ..."

The story wove its way among them, binding them together and holding them with the comfort of a healing embrace. The People had endured much in coming this far. But as she looked around, she knew, as most of them did, that there would be other treks, other hunts and celebrations. Children would be born, and people would grow old and die in their time, here on this other side of something, just as Bear had dreamed.

One day, she knew, she would look back and remember this first storytelling on their new shore. She would be sad for the many who would never share a tale with them again, and glad for the many who could. There would be new stories for her to tell the children and the children's children, who would someday pick up this rope binding the People together and carry it further along.

Hao, she thought to herself, even as her tongue and lips continued to form the words of the telling.

Haodisah.

Hao.

Author's afterword

The cavekeeper's daughter tells of a tribe of people more than 10,000 years ago who traveled through Siberia, crossed the Bering Strait, and came to North America. We might consider them ancestral Native Americans; they might have considered themselves more simply as The People.

Although we know little about their actual lives, there is much we can guess at, using our knowledge of anthropology and the peculiarities of the routes they might have taken. These findings and speculations continue to be controversial, but they were sufficient enough to inspire my imagination. These, along with a lovely poem-saga called *The walking people*, which may possibly be an oral history of such a trek.

Writing about a world so different from our own is almost like writing a work of science fiction. The setting, the culture, the language, and the degree of technology available at that time need to be researched or inferred, and then used consistently through the book. The underlying assumptions of this novel are explained below; readers may judge for themselves the results.

Ethnic origins of the people: Fossil evidence sets most of early human evolution in Africa, but at some point our species began to split in many directions. Where today's Native Americans fit on the evolutionary tree is still a matter of debate. Anthropologists working with ancient teeth tentatively point to the peoples of Northern China as their closest cousins. Genetic studies of mitochondrial DNA point instead to Eurasian or Mongolian ancestry, not Asian, as was long assumed. Several recent studies have looked at markers in the blood and concluded that those who came to the Americas ten or more thousand years ago are related to the traditional people living around the Altai Mountains (southwest of Lake Baikal, Siberia), eastern Kazakstan, and western Mongolia. Their closest cousins may be the Turkic-speaking peoples in these regions; next closest may be the indigenous Ainu of northern Japan. Some genetic mixing with other tribes no doubt occurred as well, as people took partners coming from other branches of the evolutionary tree.

A small minority of researchers speculate on European origins via migrations across the Atlantic in prehistoric times. However the genetic evidence indicates that any such in-mixtures play a minor role, if any, in the ancestry of today's Native Americans.

Nomadic tribes would have migrated many times in the past, settling down for a week, a year or for many generations in one place or another.

Relocating might have been as simple as packing up the tent poles and carrying everything away, yet any such event would have been risky. Hunter-gatherers moving to a new area needed to find clean water, favorite plant foods, and a well-drained site to set up their shelters; they also had to study the patterns of local predators and prey. They had to figure out what new food resources would nourish and what might poison them, as well as seek out supplies of firewood, tool-making stone and medicinal plants. They needed to stay clear of unfriendly tribes and avoid crowding out the friendlier ones. They likely moved only as circumstance forced them, whether due to resource depletion, the migration of favorite food sources, famine, or other natural disasters. The catastrophic combination earthquake/tsunami that forced the People in this book to flee their homeland is only one such precipitating event.

Methods of travel: Although it is possible that they came to the Americas by boat, or a combination of boat and foot, it seems more likely the migrants walked across eastern Siberia and over the connecting land bridge to Alaska and beyond. To date archaeologists have discovered traces of only very simple watercraft among the peoples living in Northeastern Asia ten or more thousand years ago. Experiments with replicas indicate these could not endure the harsh conditions of an ocean crossing over the North Pacific. In the warmer South Pacific, hunter-gatherers crossed from Southeast Asia to Australia and the various island chains at a significantly earlier date, but these involved crossing calm waters with survivable temperatures. Longer crossings over large stretches of frigid seas where somebody falling in would die in minutes from hypothermia—this seems an uninviting though not entirely impossible prospect.

Thousands of years ago Northeastern Siberia and Western Alaska were connected across a sandy, boggy, and occasionally mountainous lowland. This gradually disappeared as the world warmed and the sea levels began to flood its shallow shores; around ten to twelve thousand years ago the global warming of that era resulted in the seas rising high enough to cover significant segments of this land, and they continued to erode more land away over the next few thousand years. What was once a land bridge is now a sea floor with a few islands poking through. The bottom is fairly shallow. Come the next Ice Age, the waters may retreat and the beaches gradually reemerge until our descendants can once again walk between Siberia and Alaska.

For many millennia, people and animals could have migrated back and forth, completely unaware they were crossing what we now think of as a bridge from one continent to another. The span may have been only 50 or 100 miles wide. They would not have seen it as a bridge between two different regions. Plants and animals spread easily along the passageway, and the ecosystems on both sides were more alike than not.

It is unlikely that many people made this migration. Far Northeast Siberia and Far Western Alaska are harsh and challenging environments, and their human populations would have been sparse. Traces do exist of humans living in Siberia more than 15,000 years ago, and perhaps as early as 45,000 years ago. There was at least one settlement in the Kamchatka peninsula as far back as 13,000 years ago. Thus this novel, set around 11,000 years ago, represents a movement of people that was entirely possible based on what we know from geology, archaeology, and anthropology. In fact there may have been several such movements over the millennia. It is unlikely, however, that there was an outpouring of people across the divide.

Geographical considerations: The Kamchatka Peninsula of far Eastern Siberia, where I have located the beginning of this novel, is a region of volcanic mountains, forests, beaches, and geysers; it is a wild and romantic area even today. The climate in Kamchatka is more temperate than most of Siberia, with its relatively southern location and the mitigating presence of the ocean. Kamchatka is part of the Pacific Ring of Fire, the horseshoe-shaped zone of frequent earthquakes, volcanoes, and tsunamis, which themselves play a role in this book. The real Kamchatka is so active a zone that, though some of its volcanoes are extinct, others erupt regularly. During the voyage of Captain Cook, crew members reported a volcano near Petro-Pavlovsk that erupted every day they were anchored there.

Tsunamis, by the way, are caused by earthquake activity offshore; thus earthquakes and tsunamis along a tectonic plate may easily occur from the same geologic shift, as happens in the book.

Beyond Kamchatka, including the land to the northeast where the later part of the novel takes place, temperatures would have been more severe. It is a testament to human endurance and resourcefulness that people can and did live there, even many thousand years ago, foraging for a living in this region of ferocious cold. Actual temperatures at the time are not easy to determine. Some scientists speculate that the coastal regions may have been more moderate until the land bridge disappeared, warmed by the currents circulating northward from Japan. These warm currents today are overwhelmed by a cold current coming from the Arctic through the Bering

Strait, but if the Bering Strait was blocked by a land bridge, those frigid
waters would not have come further south.

Some archaeologists speculate that the cross-Bering migrants came from
Central Siberia following the Lena River northward and then abruptly turned
east to take a straight shot roughly along the 70°N latitude line, following
reindeer herds across the land bridge to North America. There is some evidence
of early human habitations along the Lena River that lends credibility to this
theory. However the Central Siberian migration route travels through some of
the coldest places known on the planet, with winter temperatures between
−50 and −90°F for months at a time. Thus I have opted for a route with less
archaeological evidence to support it, so far, but which common sense votes
for—the coastal regions of far Eastern Siberia, where the winters are mild in
comparison. Perhaps archaeologists will some day prove me right.

Siberia has a surprising lushness in spite of the extreme temperatures.
Many plant and animal species have adapted themselves for the intense cold.
Food may not have been as much of a challenge as the temperatures, which
can get to −20°F or below, even along the more moderate coastal regions
where the People traveled. Western Alaska may have been slightly warmer
but its food resources more sparse; it is more arid, with less precipitation to
nourish plant life. Arriving on the Alaskan side, travelers would have had to
scramble to sustain themselves. They would have done better to move quickly
south and southeast, finding easier pickings in those directions. The scientific
community continues to speculate whether it was possible to travel along the
milder seacoasts of Alaska and Western Canada 12,000 years ago, or whether
these were entirely blocked by glaciers at the time, restricting migrants to a
narrow ice-free corridor further inland.

Some of the migrants would have been following their prey, especially the
herds of reindeer, which would have been safer to live near than herds of more
dangerous animals such as mammoth or bison. Reindeer herds migrate twice
a year, traveling up to 800 miles at a stretch, often traveling the same paths
along fairly predictable routes. The bands of humans following them had to
hustle to keep up, but the rewards—a certain supply of food and furs for
clothing and shelter—would be substantial. Other tribes may have hunted
and gathered their way across, making use of a wider variety of food sources,
spreading out over the centuries, settling eventually in the more hospitable
areas and creating tribal homelands across the Americas.

Childhood's end: Modern children mature younger than has usually been true in the past. Better nutrition and medical care have made a huge difference compared to times of periodic hunger and disease. If today the average girl begins menstruation somewhere around 12 years in age, in less prosperous times it may have occurred at 14, 16, or later. Similarly, boys would have reached puberty at older ages. However emotional maturity and family responsibilities may have come at younger ages under circumstances which did not allow much time for creative play or learning for its own sake as is common today.

On the further end of the age spectrum, people living in prehistoric times rarely lived beyond their 40s due to the dangers of hunting and childbirth, the lack of preventive medicine and the vagaries of nutrition for people with no modern refrigeration or access to remote sources of food. People would have "worn out" earlier in life after enduring lost teeth, badly set broken bones, more frequent illness, and other such miseries. Most tribes would have little surplus to support those with chronic conditions or handicaps. Every age group would have suffered higher mortality rates: Young children died of childhood diseases, women faced childbirth with its many dangers, men were wounded in hunting accidents and people of all ages were exposed to illness and danger, food spoilage and infection.

General intelligence: The people of the late Pleistocene age enjoyed the same range of basic skills and intelligence that we have today. Their daily lives focused more on survival, however; their world had less technology and a smaller body of abstract thought than we have now. Yet their brains had the same capacity as ours, and they would have been just as able to follow the reasoning of any well-explained argument. Had these same people been born and raised in our world, they would have little trouble fitting in. Instead, with less use for abstractions, they probably made greater use of instinct and intuition. They would have turned their curiosity and attention toward the life around them, including the people sitting across the central fire. In their time they had to be resourceful and capable, skillful in working together or they would not survive.

Language: This book was written in 21st century American English. Modern language may sometimes sound wrong in a Stone Age setting. If you find yourself occasionally saying, "They wouldn't have talked like that," try thinking of this book as a translator's best effort to make their words and their world comprehensible to us today.

Acknowledgements

Many thanks to the following people:

Orson Scott Card, Lois McMaster Bujold, John Irving, Seth Castleman, Philip Gomez, Shonda Rhimes, and Molly Giles for teaching me much about writing and storytelling.

Dan Gorlin for reading, insight, support and humor along the way. When I came to a lull in the writing, Dan, my first reader, would tweak my weary brain for comic relief. For example, there was the night early on where he made an impassioned argument for titling the book, *Daycare for Oopsy.*

Jane Schofer for insight and friendship. My second reader, she gave me confidence when we met over tea and sat gossiping for hours about my characters as if they were actual people.

My friends Sara Tolchin, Joel and Joanne Levitt, and my sister Karen Finesilver for encouragement, editing help, and suggestions along the way. Richard Crandall, for use of the MacBook, and for providing the retreat that kickstarted my rewrite of the novel. Reb Josh Waxman for wise counsel in tough times. Tom Gorlin, for great music in many forms. Barbie Henig for the hugs and hikes. Maggie Wollman for New York Times Book Reviews and their on-going guides to worthwhile reading.

Paula Underwood for starting the whole thing off by letting me read her writing while it was still in manuscript form, and for entertaining the idea that I write a prose version of her family's stories, then encouraging me not to worry about sticking too closely to her rendition of the exodus. "When you're the storyteller, you get to tell the story your way," she said. Her book, *The walking people*[1] is a wonderful 700 page poem/saga, understood by Underwood to be a true oral history of her ancestral people's journey to North America, from which I drew heavily for ideas and inspiration. If you enjoyed this book, you might also enjoy reading hers.

My parents and Alva Dworkin for liking my writing even when there wasn't yet a lot to like.

Janet Feliciano for helping me establish a certain amount of economic security, giving me time to write this book.

---

[1]P. Underwood, *The Walking People: A Native American Oral History*, Learning Way Co; Story tellers' ed edition (June 1994).

Tom Brown, Jr, Tim Corcoran and Scott Gorlin for teaching me much about living in the wilderness. Bob at Marin AIDS Project for the extensive insights on the life of an abused child.

Professor Lucian Frary of Rider University for providing references to Kamchatka ecology.

Note regarding this 2010 edition: *The cavekeeper's daughter* was first published in 2008. Since then, some readers have requested more information about the geology, anthropology, climatology, etc. which underlies this story. PSIpress has graciously agreed to publish this new edition, including this afterword including some of the scientific basis behind it. I thank PSIpress, whose great efforts have brought about this more inclusive publication.